By Raymond Burke

The Starguards – Of Humans, Heroes, and Demigods

The Magna Aura Genesis
The Axalan Revelation
The Terra Chronicles

The Terra Chronicles

BOOK THREE OF

THE STARGUARDS
Of Humans, Heroes, and Demigods

Raymond Burke

THE STARGUARDS

Raymond Burke is a British-born author - The Terra Chronicles the third in The Starguards series. His background includes an early life in Canada and the US, employment in the British Army as an aircraft technician, an MSc degree in Archaeology from University College London, and short-article writing. He is also a member of The Mars Society. Raymond cunningly lives without a fridge, satellite TV, iPods, and he also can't drive. He's a self-confessed 21st century caveman . . . and loves it! Through all, he has been a keen and aspiring writer. He currently lives in London.

To

Aunt Vern

Acknowledgements

My continued grateful thanks to my family and many supporters and friends: John MacMillan, Nigel Livingstone, Mark Emsley, Chris Bellay, Mark Veal, Dave Basely, Chad Dixon, Neena Katwa, Lori Buttermark, Anke Marsh, KJ Waters, Jody Smyers, Leigh Mack, Carl Bialik and Lydia Serota. To my fellow writers Nick Cirkovic, David P Perlmutter, Jon-Jon Jones, Stephen Marriot, Anne John-Ligali, Soulla Christodoulou, Benjamin Smith, and Nilam A McGrath. And to the members of the LOTNA sci-fi group – you guys rock!

Many thanks to StressFreePrint.

Cover design by Janet Dado. Formatting by Ivy Port.

Any leftover errors are mine alone to claim.

I can spell; I just like to make words up!

BOOK THREE

THE TERRA CHRONICLES
Of Lore and Viruses

Prologue

The Mesa Flats Café, Arizona. Present time

She should have been dead.

She probably was. But for now she was here, on Earth, and had been for over a year.

Maybe this is the afterlife, she thought.

She had made herself a new name, changed her looks and wormed her way into society, keeping out of the limelight by working as a waitress - *In a cheap, godforsaken roadside café*, she sighed to herself wondering why she had chosen to. But she needed time to sort out a new course of action. She could be stuck here forever, though she didn't believe that. In truth, she didn't really want to leave: she was having too much fun living in the real world, neither part of the ancient past nor the future, and away from universal wars. She was in the heyday of human civilisation—just out of primitiveness; just on the cusp of greatness. These were times to really live.

The reflections of those moments in time and life faded away and she saw her own sad, blue eyes staring back at her in the glass she held. Back in reality and the job at hand, she picked up the rest of the empty plates and cups from table four, setting them on her tray before wiping the surface clean.

Behind her, the large flatscreen TV blared away from above the diner's serving counter, the lunchtime news or something droning on. It was quite loud, which bothered her, but she kept working.

She started clearing another table with only a couple of empty plates to collect, which she squeezed onto her tray balanced in her left hand. Successfully gathered, she turned to go into the kitchen, when she noticed that the TV had become noticeably louder. Looking around she realised it wasn't so much that the TV was louder, it was the fact that the usually busy conversation levels had fallen considerably. A sudden hush had fallen upon the diner. Even outside seemed quieter than normal; the dusty summer day devoid of afternoon rush-hour traffic and diners. Flicking dyed-blonde hair out of her eyes to see what the fuss was all about she saw everyone staring open-mouthed at the TV. She looked too.

The tray's contents of plates and glasses came tumbling out of her hands and crashed upon the floor, though no one noticed nor paid attention. She couldn't believe her eyes. The TV couldn't be right. She watched in disbelief with the others as four costumed figures made their entrance to a press conference, teeming with reporters and dignitaries. But that wasn't what she couldn't believe. What she couldn't believe was that she, alone, recognised them. She had seen them before, a lifetime ago. Distant memories come to life. She couldn't believe it. This wasn't the afterlife. This was real. They were Starguards.

They were here, on Earth.

And suddenly, Zane knew where her life was heading.

CHAPTER ONE

South France, AD 1197

"All I know, Decion, is that someone, somewhere, sometime is going to pay for this. I swear it!" Alpha Rion cursed again.

This was a wretched world. Cold, wet, muddy and getting dark; not that it affected him or Decion, but he wondered how anyone could live here. Wherever here was.

A few days ago, according to this world's rising and setting sun, Alpha Rion, Decion, and Astara had stood victorious on Alphatron City-State. The Lore were gone. Azure had saved them. Now they listened in alarm as comms reported that Starguards were disappearing.

And just as suddenly, Decion had started to disappear. Alpha Rion had instinctively reacted quicker than his sister, reaching out to stop Decion, but promptly disappearing with him. Now they were both stuck somewhere, where people resembled them, but were not of superior breeding. The brothers could only suspect the Astrals for this despicable act of cosmic interference.

In fact, he and Decion hadn't believed that anywhere else in their new universe (if this was the same universe as Magna Aura) had been inhabited by others like themselves. The people here may have looked like Celestians, but they weren't. They were inferior Fifths: primitive in being, barbaric in nature. Emphasising this, the region was at war, or at least a form of it, for armies in worn metal armour marched or rode around on magnificent beasts that Decion would have given his lancesword to ride. The metal-clad warriors fought with metal swords, long pointed staffs, and shorter sharp projectile weapons which bloodied the fields indiscriminately. It made them both yearn for battle. But so far, the two warrior sons of the Celestian Knights Alphatronius and the Goddess Elysius, had kept a low profile. They were alone, away from the other Starguards.

Alpha Rion felt incomplete without Astara and wondered how his twin sister was faring—no better than him, he suspected. He cursed again. Who knew for how long they were going to be here.

One thing which had kept the brothers fascinated with this world was the forest they were in. It was greener and larger than anything on Halcyon or Placia, though not as magnificent as the treefields of the forest continent of Anturia on Galatia they had played in as younglings. They had revelled in the new environment at first, but now it was wearing thin quickly.

"Hold your tongue, brother," Decion cautioned in his usual growl through his thick black beard, from across the cooking fire they had started. "We will make those Astrals atone for their actions. We may be the only ones left alive, so we need to conserve our thoughts and energy." He swatted at a small flying insect that had a whine like a twin-engine skimmer.

He tossed over a piece of roasted meat he had carved from the hide that lay spit-roasting over the fire. Alpha Rion caught it in midair.

His beardless face was framed by his long black hair and chiselled cheeks, blues eyes accentuating his handsomeness. His demeanour and looks far less rougher and wilder than his older brother's.

"Are you . . . sure . . . it . . . was . . . the Astrals?" he asked between mouthfuls.

They had watched other people eat this animal while they had patrolled nocturnally; a large grazing beast not built for battle. It was new food for them, not exactly as intoxicating as Alphatron's food, but at least it was cooked, tasty, and filling.

Alpha Rion thought about Decion's words and though he wasn't an ardent admirer of his older brother, he had to grudgingly admit that he was right. Anything could happen at any moment so they needed to be ready. He was still thinking and chewing when both he and Decion heard the distinctive thundering foot-falls of multiple riding-beasts approaching.

They rose together and headed for their lookout point. They had camped at the edge of the forest, just enough to hide from prying eyes, yet still able to spy on the outside world with their enhanced vision or through their visor imagers. In the coming twilight, Decion saw twenty warriors riding purposefully toward their position. He turned to Alpha Rion, who kept on chewing on meaty morsels, while turning to douse the fire, which hissed out of existence.

"No sense in letting the meal burn," he whispered at Decion, who rolled his eyes.

Decion donned his helmet and cape and was now his usual huge giant of a warrior in red and black armour. They had no set defences, they didn't need any, save for themselves and their weapons.

The score of riders grew closer, Alpha Rion observing with interest that one of them wore no bulky metal armour. The stranger's blond curly hair flowed freely in the brisk wind away from a handsome angular face. His loose-fitting purple garb was of a thin, shiny fabric, but Alpha Rion knew he was no less of a warrior than the rest of them, even though he seemed to be unarmed. He could see it in the blond one's eyes, sense it. This one was dangerous.

The riders slowed as if they knew danger awaited them. Decion let them approach. He and Alpha Rion had left their formidable weapons stowed in their other-dimensional sheaths. The riders stopped at the edge of the tree line and dismounted, the big animals nervously grunting and stamping. Alpha Rion could smell the riding-beasts now noting how powerful they were.

Beautiful, he thought.

Alpha Rion and Decion watched as the mysterious warriors dismounted and approached cautiously, but purposefully, staring at him and Decion as if they were the strange beasts. They may have appeared strange to each other, but Alpha Rion knew they were all no strangers to battle and that they were about to renew their friendship with blood and death.

The blond leader signalled and his warriors marched forth wordlessly and purposefully through the brush and trees to form an ominous semi-circle around the two brothers who stood still. Not a word was said, not a sound was to be heard in the forest, save for the sigh of impending death.

Without warning, half the warriors charged Decion. Alpha Rion didn't move and didn't have to look to see that Decion's left hand had shifted toward his right hip to activate the dimensional sheath. Before the warriors had gone five steps, Decion had forcibly drawn his lancesword which stretched out and in one back-handed swoop ten heads had fallen to the mossy ground. Decion continued the cutting arc in a figure-of-eight motion, until the end of the lancesword rested in his right hand, holding the weapon out in front of him before turning it ninety degrees and planting its tip into the now bloodied ground.

Alpha Rion hadn't even waited for the lancesword's tip to reach the ground before he launched himself at the other terrified warriors who had started to run away. Releasing his two energy swords from their sheaths, within half a dozen lethal swipes he had felled the rest of them. His last strikes had landed him on the opposite side of the blond leader across from Decion. The last warrior was trapped.

But the blond warrior still wore his arrogant smile and remained unmoved. He regarded them, almost in kinship.

"Well done, Decion. I expected no less of you and I must say that I'm quite, quite impressed. I must admit, however, I only expected you to be here," he said (translated to the Starguards through their crystalators).

He turned his head to look behind him at Alpha Rion, who remained silent, swords still blazing at his side. The stranger remained unperturbed.

"No matter," he dismissed the younger Starguard's presence. "I've never seen weapons quite like yours before. May I touch it?" He stepped forth toward Decion.

Decion hefted the sword two-handed upon his own shoulder. His demeanour needed no explanation.

The stranger halted and retreated a step, hands up in supplication. He laughed at their mutual predicament.

"I'm sorry," he apologised, before Decion grew angry at being laughed at. "My name is Marquis Edgar de La Valtare and I am your host here on Earth." He bowed to the brothers.

"Earth?" Decion harrumphed. "A fitting name for a mud ball of a place. And what is to stop us from killing you Marquis Edgar de La Valtare?" Decion mocked, his hands resting on the crystal pommel of his lancesword.

"Please, call me Valtare," he grinned. "And, well if you kill me, I guess you'll never know why my master wanted you here," Valtare answered back, confidently.

There was silence as Decion and Alpha Rion traded glances.

"Your master? You mean the Astrals?" Alpha Rion was suspicious, Decion's hand twitching on the pommel.

"The Astrals?" Valtare spat, "I know them, but as for one of them being my master, no, I detest them as much as you do. My master is no friend of the Astrals as you shall see. I take it that this means my life is to be spared?" Valtare inquired, seeing Decion and Alpha Rion visibly relax. He was clearly having fun at being in charge.

"For now," barked Decion.

They both knew they had no choice really.

"Good!" Valtare said, without a care that his life was in danger. "Good. Then follow me."

With a rueful glance and tut at his dead men, he turned and walked back toward his horse at the edge of the forest. He mounted and slowly trotted in the direction from which he had arrived. The brothers looked at each other, sheathed their weapons in a flash of dimensional energy, and started towards the horses who reared and galloped away, much to Valtare's amusement. They followed on foot, Alpha Rion resisting the temptation to curse again. He had a feeling he would be using them later.

The green-brown tufty grass around the forest gave way to a muddy trail trampled by transiting armies. The Starguards' manoeuvre suits tried to self-clean the boots with little success. Along the way, Valtare patiently explained to them where and when they were.

"This world is called Earth. We people are called humans. Currently, you are in a country called France ruled over by different Kings. The year is 1197, after the birth of an alleged divine man called Jesus Christ, a so-called son of God, which is one of the reasons for the conflict. The country is afflicted by the Crusades, of which this is the fourth such war, affecting most of the northern landmass called Europe and a part of Asia," he pointed eastward.

"Although this is supposedly a religious affair, it is mostly political, greed-ridden, expensive, barbaric and unnecessary, all in all the usual human contradictory ingredients of war," he shook his head in pity.

Decion and Alpha Rion had already suspected this world was the very same as mentioned in Olesseus' *Tales of Adantus*. It explained the humans' war-like Fifth nature. And Decion's curiosity was also sated:

"The riding-beasts are called horses."

They talked more as the sun went down.

Presently, the muddy trail widened into a more solid, but well-worn rutted road, so that two carts could pass each other comfortably. It led to a small settlement, similar to one where Decion and Alpha Rion had previously watched the drab folk prepare their meal of cow meat called beef. They also realised that one of the other animals they had hunted and eaten was nominally a domesticated pet called a dog. Celestians didn't have such pets; animals were for labour or for food or remained wild.

"This Earth really is strange," Alpha Rion quipped quietly to his brother who eyed the squabbling chickens by a hut, wondering if they were pets, too.

Riding through the village, the Starguards expected to be stared at in their red and black manoeuvre suits, but Valtare had turned to them.

"Don't worry, we won't be bothered."

And to the brother's surprise, nobody had even seemed to take notice of them. As the two loitered around, Valtare had watered his horse at a trough and collected some bagged supplies from a local merchant, which he slung across his horse's back. Then they were on their way again.

But as they travelled, Alpha Rion became even more suspicious of Valtare. He didn't talk much about himself and was evasive in manner to the many questions about him. From the sideways looks Decion gave him, Alpha Rion could see he was thinking the same thing.

It was night when the three had arrived at Valtare's castle, on a rise above the village. Though called a castle, it was more of a built-up and fortified large manor house. Alpha Rion's crystalator-enhanced visor scanned the dark, solid-stone structure; men walking along the battlements between watch towers. There was nothing there that could harm them, he decided. A sturdy drawbridge lowered across a half-swampy moat, which they trotted across entering a large courtyard protected by the gatehouse and a low guardhouse to the right. A dozen men-at-arms talked and laughed with each other, milling around before their duties. As Valtare rode in they quietly dispersed to their posts. Various buildings of stone or wood cluttered together around the central keep, a chapel attached to the left side of the structure.

Squires and servants rushed over to attend to Valtare as he dismounted, taking away their master's horse to the stables to be groomed. They barely acknowledged the two Starguards.

Valtare led the brothers through the courtyard. Before entering into the main building, Valtare turned with an amused look on his face.

"Forgive my ill manners, Decion, but who is your companion?"

Decion patted Alpha Rion on the shoulder, "This is my brother, Alpha Rion," he said, as if it was the most obvious thing.

Valtare nodded. "Of course, I should have seen the resemblance," he noted, the joke lost on the two black-haired, red and black-clad warriors.

Upon entering the great hall, a stone-floored, hearth-warmed room with squat windows set high in the wall, there were two men waiting. Valtare introduced them.

"Sir Decion and Alpha Rion, this is Duke Fabien L'Coyle," Valtare spoke warmly, clapping the man on the shoulder.

The young, brown-haired man nodded a grim greeting. His predatory looks reminded Alpha Rion of Valtare. He was no doubt his protégé. And Valtare seemed fond of him, Alpha Rion noted.

"And this is Guillaume de Roth," Valtare said of the young-looking man with a shock of white hair. Guillaume also nodded hello, but his blue eyes flickered friendship.

"I wish my wife were here to greet you," Valtare indicated a large painted portrait of a beautiful auburn-haired woman on the wall above the large fireplace at the end of the hall, "but the Lady Van Tager, is unavoidably away due to family matters. For now, L'Coyle and De Roth will be your guides and will tell you everything you want to know about our customs. I have a meal prepared for you . . ."

"We are not hungry," Decion answered for them both. "We ate in the forest."

"Well then. Your bed chambers are ready and in the morning we shall talk of things of interest to you."

"We are ready to talk of such things now," Decion rumbled as politely as he could.

But Valtare declined, "The morning would be better. We need time to rest, for tomorrow will be a long day, believe me. Now, if you'll excuse me, I'll leave you in the capable hands of my two best knights."

He bowed to the two Starguards before turning and disappearing up winding stone stairs, leaving the four men alone.

L'Coyle spoke first. "You have travelled far, then?"

"Far enough," Decion replied with in humorous growl.

"We had hoped to meet some of our . . . other warriors here," said Alpha Rion, trying to drop a hint. L'Coyle nodded, as if he understood, but Alpha Rion knew that he didn't. So he asked, "Do you know why we're here?"

"Do any of us really know why we're here?" Guillaume replied, looking up above them.

Decion also looked up only seeing a rough-hewn ceiling of thick wooden beams. Spying nothing untoward, he scowled.

Guillaume rephrased his answer, more cautiously. "I mean, we're here for the same reason that you are, which will be explained to you tomorrow. We cannot tell you," he said, "Because we do not know either." He looked pointedly at Alpha Rion.

Alpha Rion, for his part, sensed that this was a man to be trusted. But there was something not right here. And if he and Decion didn't get their answers tomorrow, then they would go on their own crusade.

He wasn't going to get any answers now, so Alpha Rion made his excuses. "I think I will retire for the night."

Decion looked displeased, but followed suit.

"This way, if you please, sirs," L'Coyle led them up the narrow stone stairs and showed them to their bed chambers.

Somewhere else

Waiting. In another place, a solitary figure watched. He had sacrificed lives, interfered here, manipulated there and now all his plans were coming together; the pieces in his grand scheme coming alive: Valtare, the Starguards, his army. The end of the universe was fast approaching.

Valtare's castle

Alpha Rion's chamber was a drafty stone tower room, opposite Decion's room and across the castle from their host's quarters. The room was decent enough, Alpha Rion thought, but basic in decor with a sturdy wooden bed with too many heavy blankets on the feather mattress covered with soft furnishings and cushions. Faded tapestries of past battles and hunting scenes attempted miserably to block some of the damp smell and draughts through the walls. Still, it beat sleeping in the forest. He sighed as he thought of Astara and what had become of his twin.

Where was she? Was she still on Magna Aura? He hoped Valtare would have answers for them in the morning.

"Armour off," he commanded, his black and red manoeuvre suit disappearing in a sigh of air into the same other-worldly realm as his sheathed swords.

Naked, he slid into bed covered with three thick blankets and a large brown fur covering, letting himself drift off into sleep.

He thought of Astara and her image came into his mind, a feminine mirror to himself, his constant battle companion. He saw her laughing, as only she did in his company, her jet-black hair waving in the breeze as they sailed across the ocean of Halcyon, her eyes as blue as the ocean, her sword poised against his as they duelled together, her dark, lithe features blending into the shadows cast by the sentry fires as she approached the castle unseen, a glowing bow ready for action . . .

Alpha Rion stopped dreaming. Or was he still dreaming? There was a different woman in his thoughts. One he hadn't met before. But he could see her features as clear as if he was awake: an extraordinarily beautiful woman with brown skin, short black curly hair, and inquisitive dark eyes. She reminded him of his sister, for she was a warrior, too. That he knew. He felt as if he was standing right in front of her, she as curious about him, as he was in her. He was about to ask her name, when her smiling eyes sent him drifting to sleep. He didn't dream again that night.

Alpha Rion had been awoken by a young fair-haired youth who laid out clothing over a dividing screen and a maid who brought in a bowl and jug of fresh water.

Alpha Rion rolled out of bed to pour himself some water from the pitcher into a mug. The maid had blushed deeply as Alpha Rion, still naked, strolled around the room to inspect the clothing.

Eyes down, she announced, "My lord, breakfast is ready." Scurrying from the room, her saucer-wide eyes snatched a last furtive glance at the warrior's dark hair and well-muscled body her mind racing with juicy gossip to spread in the kitchen.

Alpha Rion paid her no attention. He had a lot on his mind.

"Armour," he instructed, his protective dress flashing into existence over his body.

Alpha Rion's black armour was dominated by a red, broken-cross motif over his torso, which led down to a red belt, adorned with the cross of Alpharion, an emblem to denote universal energy. He kept his visor off. He also disdained the chain mail and leather and cotton garmets laid out for him. He knew Valtare had meant for him and Decion to blend in, but Alpha Rion had no such desire to hide his nature.

Alpha Rion exited his chambers at the same time Decion left his.

"Brother," Decion greeted curtly.

Alpha Rion acknowledged him with a grim smile.

He wasn't surprised Decion had also eschewed his disguise. Decion's large frame was comfortably hugged within his red and black armour, his great helm tucked under his arm. Sheathed were his lancesword and four-armed shield. Alpha Rion led the way. Decion's bulky bifurcated cape flowed behind him scraping the sides of the wall as they descended the stone stairs. They strode along an adjoining corridor and through the large open wooden doors into the great hall.

It was empty. Their host was late.

Decion noisily grunted his dissatisfaction at this.

They chose one of the two long tables to sit at. Several maids served various dishes in front of them, the Starguards leaving it untouched. They sat silently, facing each other at one end of the heavy wooden table which could have sat a dozen men, the brothers growing impatient by the minute.

Finally—

"*Bonjour.* Pleasant dreams, I hope," Valtare greeted as he swept into the great hall. Again, he was dressed in silken purple robes tied with a simple gold-coloured sash. He wore no sword. He occupied his accustomed chair at the head of the table away from the brothers.

Valtare looked expectantly at Alpha Rion, who nodded back, though he couldn't remember if he had dreamed or not. Decion, for his part, wasn't interested.

"What do you have to tell us, Valtare?" he boomed, leaning forward over the table and his untouched food.

Valtare seemed bemused, smiling without actually smiling; hawk-like eyes unfocused, yet intent.

"Ah, straight to the point as always, Decion," he lamented.

He uncorked a bottle of wine and poured a liberal amount out for himself, the red liquid sitting like an offering of blood between the three of them. Valtare took up his glass, holding it up to the brothers showing them that this was the customary thing to do, indicating the bottle at their end of the table.

"To your health," he saluted them with an upraised glass. He sipped a mouthful, swilling it around with his tongue, then swallowed, breathing in heavily to engorge the whole aroma.

Alpha Rion watched Valtare intently, whose eyes were now closed as if the wine had sent him into a deep sleep. He was totally immersed. Alpha Rion turned to Decion whose dark features threatened to explode with rage. But before they did, Valtare eyes suddenly opened to their full blueness to gaze unswervingly at the two brothers.

"I have an offer of battle," Valtare stated, bluntly, "One which will determine the fate of this world and the future of our kind."

He smiled; a deliberate pause to see their reaction, which was muted, but tinged with interest.

"I see that I have your attention, then!" Valtare said, delighted.

"Is this what your master wants? Why we're here?" Decion demanded, palms pressed on the table which creaked. "What battle can you offer us, the sons of Celestian Knights?" he sneered. "We, who have fought against the greatest enemy known to the universe. Who is your enemy, Valtare? Where do they hide? Who do we fight beside? I see no army, no plans, no nothing. And yet you offer us battle?" he growled. He sat back down, arms folded, scowling.

Valtare regarded Decion calmly, their eyes locked. Alpha Rion sat and watched Valtare's hawk eyes. There was something about his glare, something hidden behind his unlined face and wavy blond hair that Alpha Rion thought could twist the minds of men. It worried Alpha Rion, but whatever it was it didn't seem to faze Decion. His brother could out-stare a supernova. Alpha Rion watched as Valtare's face slowly melted into his never-far disarming smile, though his eyes remained a cold blue glare.

"My, but you're impatient, Decion. Why can't you be more like Alpha Rion? Look at how he sits calmly."

He indicated Alpha Rion who had elected to eat some freshly-baked bread and was apparently taking the whole situation in his stride. Though he had done so out of boredom.

Decion thumped the table with his fist, sending the wine bottle at Valtare's end of the table teetering on the edge before Valtare caught it.

"Do not mock me! I have no time for youngling larks, Valtare. I only have so much patience!"

His hand moved slowly, but deliberately to his side.

Valtare's smile almost wavered, to Alpha Rion's satisfaction. But the human caught himself. He knew Decion wouldn't draw his lancesword without finding out what he wanted to know.

So he told them.

There was a very long silence.

Alpha Rion turned to Decion in astonishment at what Valtare had said only to see that Decion's face had turned uncharacteristically pale beneath his bushy beard.

"That's impossible!" Decion replied in a hushed tone, recovering some semblance of nobility.

Confidence returning, Valtare continued, "I assure you both it's true and I can prove it to you, tonight." He casually grabbed a handful of bread and meat, chewing heartily.

Decion offered thoughtful silence.

Alpha Rion was confused. "I require enlightening, Valtare. This thing you talk about is only a myth, a youngling's story from the time of my forebears. How did you come by this information?"

This gained a stern look from Decion. "I used to think so as well. But I've read the scrolls and our forebears were no myth tellers. I believe Valtare is right. This is the battle we warriors have craved for!"

"So how did you come by this knowledge, Valtare?" Alpha Rion repeated, trying to show dispassion.

"My master knows of such things. And it is no myth! I have seen the evidence myself!"

Decion's eyes gleamed; the kind of gleam Alpha Rion knew was the battle-cry calling to his soul. But it didn't call to him. Something, whatever it was, was not right and until he found out what it was he would not be a part of it.

I swear it! his dark thoughts rebelled.

Almost precisely at that moment, Valtare suddenly shot a sharp look over to Alpha Rion. His keen eyes seemed to search the Starguard and Alpha Rion had the distinct feeling that somehow Valtare knew what he had just thought.

"Are you okay, Alpha Rion?" Valtare asked, with his charming smile. "You seem a bit . . . quiet."

"I'm fine, just thinking," Alpha Rion answered as cordially as he could. Something clicked in his mind, but he couldn't think clearly past the jumbled haze of his thoughts.

All Alpha Rion could ask himself was: Who are you really, Valtare? And what do you really want?

As if in answer, Valtare said, "*Bon*, as you suspect, I am no ordinary human and while I have an army of five hundred, I need you to train them. But besides the main reason you are here, there are also my enemies to defeat first, who even as we speak are drawing closer. They and the Astrals did my kind a great injustice centuries ago and continue to do so. They must be defeated if we are to survive."

Decion and Alpha Rion exchanged looks, mulling over Valtare's plan.

"We shall think it over," Decion spoke for both of them.

Valtare seemed to expect this as he stood up, wiping his mouth with the back of his hand.

"Well, gentlemen," he said, "I have laid my offer on the table, so to speak, and I await your answer by sunset."

He excused himself with a bow to them and then left the hall, closing the big wooden doors behind him. Breakfast was over.

The two brothers stared at the closed doors, still digesting the news Valtare had given them. The hall was eerily quiet now even with servants shuffling about clearing the table.

"I want no part in this, Decion," confessed Alpha Rion. "Something is not right here. I still suspect that the Astrals are behind this."

But Decion scoffed at the thought. "No, not all the Astrals, I'm sure. But you are right; nothing is right. Nothing can ever be right again. Not until the battle is over."

Alpha Rion was baffled by his brother. Decion had never been more fervent in his life.

"You actually believe him, don't you?" surprise in Alpha Rion's voice.

Decion's voice took on a tone of reverence as he answered.

"This is the answer to it all. The Tomes of History, written by the first Spheron himself, told of this. How could you not believe it, brother?" Decion stared off into the distance, his eyes agleam in glory.

"I believe in the Tomes of History, Decion," Alpha Rion iterated with a knowing tone. "But these aren't strictly. . .official texts are they? They are the beliefs from the Knight Destina's Tomes of War!" he challenged his brother.

His voice was harsh as he spoke the name of the heretical sect of the Celestian Knights who disappeared millennia ago. They believed the Storm of Stars were their creators and thus the Celestian Knights were divine and destined to rule the Universe. This, against the prevailing view that the Great Father and Holy Mother were the true creators and rulers of destiny. The Knights Destina had also prophesied the return of the Storm of Stars and the Antiqchronals—the first Four Peoples of Energy, Matter, Psyche and Time. And at this historic juncture in time a great war would rebirth the universe and its chosen rulers would be the Knights Destina. But now that there were no more Knights Destina this reasoning, and the Knights Destina themselves, had become forgotten.

Until now.

"We may have been brought up on such myths by our father, but why would this revelation be passed to Valtare by his master?"

For a moment, Decion snapped out of his revelry.

"That, I do not know. The Universe has its ways." He nodded to himself as if coming to a decision. "But if Valtare is lying, then I will deal with him." He smiled grimly, Alpha Rion echoing his sinister thoughts.

He sincerely hoped Valtare was lying.

"In the meantime, I will prepare myself," Decion added. "Just in case," he winked at Alpha Rion, who already had a mental image of Decion honing his sword play and of Valtare's dangling head.

"I have some tasks of my own, too," Alpha Rion replied, leaving the table. "I'll see you later, at sundown."

They retired from the great hall, Decion pounding up the stairs. Alpha Rion headed for the courtyard. Just as he was about to exit the hall, he almost bumped into Guillaume, coming the other way. They eyed each other warily, before a vein of trust opened up.

"Just the person," Guillaume said with joviality, which was just as well, for Alpha Rion had wanted to see him, too, for answers.

Sensing Alpha Rion's mood, Guillaume stared around in caution.

Alpha Rion realised immediately with certainty that Guillaume must have been waiting for him. They were like two conspirators lurking in the dimly-lit gate entrance.

"What did you want me for, Guillaume?" Alpha Rion tried to make their conversation normal enough, as the white-haired man causally started walking to the stable.

"As one warrior to another, I wanted to invite you for a little hunting. Sharpen up both our skills, yes?" Guillaume replied in such a tone which Alpha Rion understood they'd be doing anything but hunting.

With a curt nod of his head, he answered, "I accept." He followed Guillaume.

Arriving at the stables, Guillaume dismissed the hands wanting to saddle the horses himself.

Alpha Rion just stared at the horses, more than a score of the magnificent beasts of black or brown, with powerful muscles and flowing manes. So transfixed was Alpha Rion that Guillaume stopped working and looked back.

"Impressive, yes?"

Seeing Alpha Rion's tack still on the floor and his hesitancy around his mount, Guillaume guessed the issue, almost with amusement.

"You have ridden a horse before, yes, Alpha Rion?"

Stirred from his admiration of the horses, Alpha Rion glanced at Guillaume, not sure what he should answer. He wished he could scan his visor's crystalator database for any such equivalent but he was sure Celestians had never had anything other than machine power for burdensome work.

He made a noise through his nose.

"No, Guillaume, I have never ridden such a creature before. . ." He felt the strange sensation of his cheeks turning red.

The expression on Guillaume's face was unreadable, but Alpha Rion knew his admission had settled something in the human's mind.

Words weren't needed, but Alpha Rion knew he was in Guillaume's trust. What would he do with that information? But there was no judgement on Guillaume's angular face, just acceptance that a warrior Alpha Rion's standing had never ridden a horse.

Alpha Rion tried to gauge the measure of Guillaume. Despite his mane of white hair, Guillaume was a young strong noble warrior. His chain mail with hood down was dyed blue and was covered with wide leather straps on his torso, thighs, and long boots fitted with knives and other assorted tools. His belt was adorned with a stylised 'H' for the buckle, a long sword attached on his left hip. Even Alpha Rion knew Guillaume was an unconventional knight, but then again, wasn't that what Valtare was seeking.

"Very well," Guillaume seemed more amused and a little impressed. He motioned to Alpha Rion to join him.

Once Alpha Rion was beside him, there followed a quick lesson in horsemanship. Guillaume was even more impressed with Alpha Rion's ability to pick things up quickly. Gordell had chosen a black stallion, named Fortune with a white fluffy cloud-shaped mark on its forehead. Alpha Rion's mount was a chestnut mare with a black mane. Soon they were saddled up and riding through the settlement and out toward the forest.

It had started to rain as they set out, their horses splashily galloping through the wet undergrowth which swelled up before the forest. Despite never having ridden a horse before, Alpha Rion's natural balance and skills allowed him to master riding easily.

Alpha Rion found that he enjoyed it, too.

If I ever return to Magna Aura, I hope I can take a few back with me, he mused.

Alpha Rion and Guillaume rode mostly in silence, broken only by Guillaume's explanations on this bird, animal, or of settlements and local history. Alpha Rion appreciated the man's knowledge and candour, which at times seemed well beyond his years.

Guillaume was also enjoying himself on the ride. "I am a great teacher, yes?" he had jested along the way.

They rode on through winding trials for a while until they came upon a thick knot of fallen trees. A flock of dark birds exploded in alarm from the canopy. Unperturbed, Guillaume stopped, dismounted and tied his mount to one of the trees, Alpha Rion following suit. Guillaume then unstrapped a bow and full quiver from his saddle, his sword hanging at his hip.

He looked at Alpha Rion for his weapon, who shrugged back. No sense in drawing his energy swords. Guillaume sportingly offered him a knife, which Alpha Rion refused, to which it was Guillaume's turn to shrug.

"Follow me," he said in a low voice. "There's some good game through this section of the forest."

The Starguard nodded and followed, not sure what to expect.

The ground was moist and almost covered the noise of their footfalls. Droplets of rain sporadically escaped from the heights of the forest targeting Alpha Rion's head.

He sighed at the nuisance. He thought back to the forest continent of Anturia. The trees there would have covered Europe twice over with a variety of trees four times as wide and ten times as high as the tallest on this world, with their intricately woven branches and horizontal trunks supporting each other. He wondered if anywhere on Earth had such wonders.

Guillaume broke into Alpha Rion's reverie.

"You see these deer tracks?" Guillaume pointed out a pattern of distinctive divots in the matted ground.

Alpha Rion nodded remembering the tracks Guillaume had shown to him on their travels. Guillaume pointed along the tracks, which led off into dense vegetation.

"Let's go," Guillaume whispered, his bow drawn.

Alpha Rion followed, his hand poised at his side. They entered a darker area of the forest where the broad trees overhung so much that the sun was blocked out in places.

More than once, Alpha Rion had stopped them with a hushed breath or raised hand. There was something about the forest that concerned him, as if they were being watched. But he could see nothing.

Laughter in his eyes, Guillaume said, "You are just spooked by the forest's enchantments. Happens to the best of us sometimes!"

Alpha Rion scowled. He was not one to be afraid of shadows and cobwebs.

They stalked on crunching twigs and leafy undergrowth. So intent on the tracks was Alpha Rion that he didn't notice Guillaume disappear through overhanging vines, until he himself was at the threshold.

"Grrr!" he snarled as he was hauled in rather sharply by Guillaume.

Alpha Rion drew an energy sword so swiftly from its other-dimensional sheath that Guillaume didn't even see it until its energised point almost rested squarely upon his neck.

Guillaume's eyes widened more in fascination than fear. He smiled, as much as he dared, Alpha Rion pinning his back high against a cave wall.

"Relax, friend. Trust me," he said nervously. "That's some trick you have! What kind of sword is that?"

Alpha Rion stared darkly into Guillaume's eyes. There was no ill-intent there. He withdrew his blade, re-sheathing it into its invisible abode.

"Don't ever touch me again!" he warned, angrily. He released Guillaume who slid down the rough wall.

"Fair enough," replied Guillaume, brushing himself off and clearly impressed by a disappearing sword. "But I have a lot to tell you."

His breath was visible in the cold air of the cave and it was only then that Alpha Rion noticed the interior.

The short passageway, hidden from the outside by bushes and vines, led into a cavern, big enough to hold a dozen people, but it was the actual structure of the walls and ceiling that caught the Starguard's attention. Embedded in the walls were a myriad of crystals, almost like the ones used in Celestian crystalators.

Alpha Rion circled the cavern in confusion. The floor had been smoothed out, rough pebbles littering the ground, but the walls of the roughly circular cavern and the sunken rocky ceiling around four meters above them were studded with around twenty small crystals of every colour.

Guillaume smiled again. "Yes, Alpha Rion, these crystals are what you think they are."

Seeing more confusion, he said. "Let me start from the beginning. I have been living a pretense, Alpha Rion. I am not Guillaume de Roth. He died of. . . let's say, unnatural causes and I took his place. I am Gordell. And I am an Exmoor."

If the name was meant to mean anything, it did not register with Alpha Rion. He shook his head, "An Exmoor?"

"Yes," Gordell said. "My people are the descendents of the ancient crews of the star warrior called Adantus!"

"Adantus!" Alpha Rion's voice rose in shock. "But how? His journeys are myths to my people!" He remembered all the tales of Adantus' Antiqchronal Quest.

Gordell smiled triumphantly. "So you are of Adantus' world! I knew it! This is. . . " he grasped for words, ". . . *C'est magnifique*!"

His grin beamed from his face as if he had just discovered the secret to life.

"It is no myth. Adantus fought a terrible war here many thousands of years ago. Some crew were left behind and interbred with humans. We Exmoors are one strand of humanity from such unions. We safeguard the world from the Lore and their worshippers."

Alpha Rion was even more bewildered. "Worshippers? I don't understand. The Lore, are they here?" He couldn't think of all the questions to ask at once.

Gordell held his hands up to slow the Starguard down.

"I know you have a lot of questions," Gordell continued. "But I hope to answer the one big question on your mind: Why are you here? Long ago, the Astrals trained us Exmoors as agents to safeguard Earth . . ."

Gordell watched as Alpha Rion's eyes opened in anger, but the Starguard bit his tongue, as Gordell continued.

"We are allies and I suspect that they are somehow kin to you, yes?" Gordell asked Alpha Rion, who blew heavily through his nose.

"Not by choice," he muttered.

"Well," Gordell went on, oblivious to Alpha Rion's contempt for the Astrals. "We have not heard from the Astrals in a long time. We thought maybe they had died in a war with the Lore. Then strange things started to happen here, and my brethren sent me to investigate. We suspected our other enemies, the Devouts, but then Valtare appeared.

"He is something different, someone who shouldn't be alive. His so-called master is planning on starting a monstrous war far bigger and horrific than anything I have ever heard of. He talks of other worlds and a higher power who is his lord.

"Then you and Decion appeared. I thought you were Valtare's masters, but upon talking to you last night I knew that you were as much in the dark as the rest of us. I assumed that the Astrals became aware of Valtare's plans and must have sent you to help me. It is too much of a coincidence to think not, yes?"

Alpha Rion sighed. "No, Gordell, we do not know who brought us here. But I suspect it was the Astrals," he snorted in derision. "But Valtare does want us to kill his enemies, which I surmise is you and your people." He raised his eyebrows emphasising his point.

Gordell's face dropped.

"Oh, I see. Well, we both have a choice," Gordell said phlegmatically. "Something is happening here and I need your help. We must kill Valtare, tonight, before it is too late! Then surely the Astrals will reward you and take you home." Gordell was looking askance, almost pleadingly with Alpha Rion.

Alpha Rion opened his mouth to answer, when a blur in the corner of his eye caught his attention. He whirled towards the cave's entrance, but saw nothing, even though his instincts told him that something or someone was there, just like in the forest.

"What's the matter?" Gordell was instantly alert, his hand calmly gripping his sword.

Alpha Rion hesitated before answering. "I thought someone was in here with us."

"Impossible," Gordell scoffed, relaxing. "It's probably the crystals affecting you. They're Exmoor heirlooms of my family, leftover artefacts from the warships of Adantus. They are thinking crystals I carry with me and lay out in protected places like this wherever I go. They allow me to appear to speak and understand other languages and protect my thoughts from the enemies of the Exmoors who would pry into my mind for secrets. Valtare is such a man, as you probably suspect, who gained his ability through a union with an alien being. But these crystals repel his ability to read our minds here. Maybe they are trying to talk to you," Gordell jested. "But I assure you, we are quite alone."

But Alpha Rion had heard none of Gordell's words. He had been concentrating, bringing his mind into absolute focus to see what his eyes couldn't see, but that his instincts told him was there, until . . .

"So who is she?"

Alpha Rion pointed at the woman who had suddenly materialised at the cavern's entrance, a glowing blue bow aimed unerringly at them.

CHAPTER TWO

During the 1960s, or so their public records stated, a little-known and privately-owned facility located in Upstate New York had been founded to explore the highest degrees of technological and biological advances. Since then, Special Weapons and Ordinance, Research and Development Industries—SWORD—had made some spectacular breakthroughs. But only recently had their new inventions and advances attracted the undivided attention not only of governments, corporations, and other world figures of renown and repute, but also the general public. And now, the world's eyes were avidly focused on their newest unveiling: superhumans.

New York. Present time

"This is Martin Patchak, reporting live from the New York City HQ of Sword Industries . . ."

". . . Reports lead us to believe that these so-called superhumans are the latest brainchild of the secretive company, whose . . ."

". . . And the BBC has learned that we are expecting some form of official announcement . . ."

"CNN hopes to bring you live comments from the White House on developments . . ."

". . . This reporter has been reliably informed that the United Nations will be fully briefed as soon as . . ."

". . . We do not know who the individuals are and what they can and will do . . ."

". . . So there is the situation as it stands: an unspecified number of alleged superhumans, the breakthrough creation of Sword Industries that they predicted would safeguard . . ."

". . . Will keep our viewers informed, but now, this commercial break!"

Sword Industries Upstate New York facility. One year ago

The six men stood as their visitor appeared like some kind of angel: long blonde hair, piercing grey eyes and a caped-uniform of red and gold.

"Gentlemen," she politely nodded to each of the de facto board of Sword Industries in turn, "We Astrals believe that Earth could be in danger from the Lore. But Earth's safety is at hand. We have cousins-in-arms who have just defeated the Lore on their own world and will be delivered here shortly."

There was a mixture of feelings within the boardroom. They called it the boardroom, but it was located half a kilometer under the building, in a network of tunnels and secret labs, protected by armed guards. Uniform crests, sigils on equipment, and wall plaques were adorned by a stylised silver hawk with crossed swords for a heart—The Hawk of the World—a symbol of protection. The 'upstairs' boardroom had windows. This room was surrounded with large screens covering almost every part of the world and even a couple with real time views of the moon disc and of Mars. Their celestial visitor paid no attention to these. She was just delivering the message.

"You mean the Astrals will not defend us themselves?" A tall, suited and bearded man spoke up.

A younger man joined in. "Surely only you Astrals can protect us!"

Sighing lightly, Lightstream looked at him unperturbed and answered.

"Simon," she said to the youngest of the group, "You know that the Lore will be attracted to Earth even more if they sensed a great Astral presence. Even I, with my time-dampening abilities cannot stay for long. Our cousins are just as powerful even without possessing temporal powers, and will protect Earth as their own home. You Exmoors have provided a valuable service to the Astrals through the millennia and we will never forget that."

Simon was exasperated. He looked at the floor in disappointment.

The bearded man reached across and patted him paternally on the shoulder.

"My son is still a bit young and impetuous for an Exmoor. Give him a few more centuries, Lightstream," he grinned, "and he'll make a great leader."

Lightstream smiled. Simon Exmoor was like her cousin Aristedes, brash with youth, but she could see the growing wisdom in both men.

"When should this all happen, Lightstream?" asked Bastian, Simon's father, "And how many are coming?"

"Tomorrow, Bastian, and there will be four of them, the rest staying to guard their own world."

"Only four!" Qane harrumphed from his chair. He was the only one who had re-seated himself at the table after Lightstream's arrival. He represented the Asian Exmoor faction who favoured a more direct Exmoor intervention in human affairs. "How can that be enough?" his whispery voice still held authority.

"They are the most powerful," Lightstream countered aloud.

And the most human-friendly, she mused to herself. "They will do. I assure you. So prepare for them, welcome them, and work with them. I must go now."

The six men bowed. Even old Qane honoured her by standing briefly.

Lightstream blinked out of existence.

Simon swore he heard a 'good luck' echo out from the timestream.

"Well," Bastian said heartily to his companions, "You heard Lightstream. Alert New York City. Let's get to work!"

Arizona. Present time

Zane continued to stare in disbelief as the Starguards spoke, hounded by reporters' questions, cameras in a constant barrage of flashes. Zane felt left out. She needed to find out what was going on and join the action.

She shifted hurriedly between tables over to the counter, placing the broken crockery along its glass-top. She turned quickly to view the screen again and almost bumped into her boss' girlfriend, Irene, who with her constant sneer had just finished watching the TV and now scrutinised Zane like she was gum on a shoe.

"This ain't your break, honey. You got no time to watch TV," she drawled as she sauntered behind the counter to pour herself a free double cup of coffee, pushing aside Polly who was serving the till.

Zane smiled as politely as she could, having had to put up with Irene's constant verbal battering day in, day out. But no more.

This is going to be fun, thought Zane.

She'd seen this on the streets often enough. She leaned across the counter, raised her right hand and formed a fist, from which she unfurled her middle finger.

"I quit!" she said, with no small amount of satisfaction.

Irene's mouth flew open in indignation (Polly's in delightful surprise giving Zane a surreptitious thumbs up), her wide eyes following Zane as she threw off her apron and happily marched out of the café door for the last time.

"Hello, Zane," the Astral said to herself, once in the parking lot, "Welcome back to the land of the living. Now, how the hell do I get to New York?" The sun was still on its early rise. "So, that's east," Zane gauged. "So . . . never eat sugar wheaties," she recounted, pointing out the cardinal directions. New York was roughly northeast, she figured.

And off she ran.

A blustering Irene came bursting out of the café, followed by her boyfriend, Lou, who was still carrying a soapy frying pan he had been scrubbing. They were met by a dirty cloud of dust, leaving them sputtering through dusty lips and eyes. Lou waved his pan about, cursing the wind, which messed up Irene's twenty-dollar beehive haircut. When the dust settled, she looked around for Zane, but she was nowhere to be found among the parked rigs and pickups.

"Now where the hell did she go?"

The White House. Present time

The Oval office was a hub of activity. The President had been at a Camp David meeting with the Elders Council and hadn't been pleased at being interrupted by news of a press conference by some obscure biotech company. But when he had heard the details, he immediately announced that he would return to the White House. Marine One could now be heard chopping the air towards the White House lawn.

The Vice President looked out the White House window and was joined by the Defense Secretary. They were alone, away from the others.

"I know someone else who won't be pleased by this."

"Who?" the curious Vice President whispered back.

SecDef turned to him and gave a knowing smile.

"Don't worry. I have things in hand," he winked.

Lower Manhattan. Present time

Big business brought competition; competition brought bigger business and within those bigger businesses corruption was bred, corruption which spread its fingers, feeling for more and more.

Those fingers had been quite successful for one Penthor Thane, founder of Thane Universal, a business empire that stretched all over the world, an empire which hid his crimes and ill-gotten wealth.

But recently his prying fingers had been badly scorched by a company that would not sell out to him nor reveal its secrets: Sword Industries. Thane desperately wanted to expand his biotechnology empire and Sword Industries would have been perfect, but so far they had firmly resisted his advances and all his attempts to infiltrate the company, with his many spies and devices, had failed. He had reviewed the company's dossier many a time, knew it to be an independent and private company, but there was something about it which rankled him, like who was the real power behind Sword Industries?

This was compounded by the fact that the company had just

reportedly made another unbelievable technological breakthrough; one which strongly aroused his suspicions, because of his own similar special projects.

How had Sword Industries created these superhumans before him? the question burned in his mind.

This meant great power and wealth to whomever owned Sword Industries and Thane's lustful fingers were itching for the opportunity. He made an oath to himself that whatever the cost he would have Sword Industries.

To the outside world, Thane was hailed as a successful, black business man with a keen mind, large frame, and an even bigger chequebook. He had many friends in high places and contributed to several charities and political campaigns. But he had his own world and his own government puppets to rule his world, with agents to carry out his policies with the diplomacy or ruthlessness that was required.

His most trusted agents-cum-assistants were Mr. Spree and Ms. Charm. Spree had been with Thane the longest and was almost a friend; trustworthy with a cold calculating nature and vicious sense of humour. He was rumoured to have been a Cuban mercenary, training and fighting with many armies and secret organisations during his thirty-odd years. Now he was in the valued employ of Thane and very loyal to him.

While Spree was dark and swarthy, Ms. Charm's blonde, bubbly exterior appearance masked a more sadistic streak than Spree's. She had once worked for the U.S. government, but her fluid allegiances and questionable tactics had led to her inevitable dismissal. Bitter, she had been recruited by Thane, obstinately to get revenge, but she soon found that Thane's policies suited her style and she had found a new home for herself.

The only similarity between the two lay in their black-upon-black attire and dark shades, plus their total dedication to their profession and to Thane. Both were highly trained in weapons and martial arts, displaying a rather robust competitiveness between them. Romance was out of the question, but they deeply respected each other. They were each others eyes and ears. Nothing would harm Mr. Thane while in their protective keeping and they would get him anything he desired. And right now, he wanted Sword Industries.

The three of them sat glued to the plasma screen in Thane's boardroom and watched the Sword Industries conference with avid interest.

The Oval Office

"What the hell was all that about?" President Wes Langley almost yelled, to no one in particular. "Just what the hell is going on? Did no one see this coming?"

The room was silent as the President, Vice President Bibby Busby, Secretary of Defense General Abraham Westonheimer, Chief of Staff Kay Slaydon, Homeland Security Czar Hal Richardson, and two scientists sat glumly squeezed on two couches, having watched the Starguard Conference, as it was now being called by the media.

"Sir, Mr. President," said Westonheimer; a Korean, Vietnam and Gulf War veteran, whom even the most friendly insiders thought was well-past retirement, but who just seemed to march on like an old war horse, "these people are clearly not on our agenda, so much so as to be completely un-American and as alien to us as the Reds were, not so long ago. Their version of justice and means of justification are on a scale way beyond our scope of expertise and cannot be allowed to continue!"

"And if that is true, what do you propose, Abe?" asked an President Langley, wearily pinching the bridge of his nose.

He sat up straight behind his desk trying to flex his back after the helicopter journey. He hated air travel. He'd rather be sailing now, but the world was seemingly falling apart.

China was re-threatening the Far East, terrorists were still preying on Westerners around the world and now he had to deal with upstart superheroes.

"Can we deal with this?" Langley said pointing to the screen set ahead of him at the far end of the room. "Shall we rap them on the wrists or nuke them? Hell we can't even talk to them," he finished, exasperated.

"Sir, this Sword Industries totally kept us in the dark about this. Surely they would let Homeland in on this, even for legal and security purposes. Who's to say they aren't planning some sort of super-powered coup," added Richardson. "The public would love that," he said more sarcastically.

His thick black moustache seemed to twitch at the impertinence of such an action. One of three brothers in politics, the African-American Richardson family was often dubbed the Black Kennedys, an affiliation not entirely brushed off even as Republicans.

"Thanks, Ritchie," Langley offered, making him feel even more paranoid. It wasn't like his ratings were bad enough in his first years.

"Mr. President, sir, if I may," interrupted Dr. Sagerhawk with a distinctive South African lilt, one of the scientist guests, "myself, and my associate," Sagerhawk indicated the slim, neatly-dressed woman seated beside him on the couch with Westonheimer, "have been involved in research that may deal with the Starguards and many other situations. And with your permission, I would like to point them out." He looked anxious, his narrow eyes flitting around the room.

The President shifted his gaze between Sagerhawk and Westonheimer who nodded his head. They had been invited by him.

"Very well, Dr. Sagerhawk," he sighed, "you may so indulge yourself. And it'd better be good!" he added, rather irritably.

Sagerhawk coughed politely to hide his nervousness. His wiry frame stood up and the President couldn't hide his amusement at the scientist's rather abraded brown checked suit he wore. And even more so when Sagerhawk unpacked his worn briefcase to reveal several files, a laptop, and a memory stick. He realised then that this had already been planned. He gave Westonheimer a 'why-do-I-bother' look. Westonheimer winked back.

Combing a thin hand through his fading black hair, Sagerhawk indicated he was ready, holding up the flashdrive like he was in a school show-and-tell waiting for the start signal. At the President's casual wave of his hand to continue, he plugged in the stick. After some proprietary messages, a strident musical theme blared into existence, Sagerhawk apologising as he turned the sound down a little. Presently, the music died down and the picture resolved to show a computer-animation of a group of people in what the President took to be costumes, followed by scores of soldiers, scientists and support personnel.

"Sir," began Sagerhawk, clearing his throat "May I present the E-Corps!" he announced proudly.

"The what?" asked the President, almost choking from shock.

"The E-Corps—'E' for Elite," intoned Westonheimer, stressing the 'E' as if teaching a kindergarten child the alphabet. "The E-Corps will be the most technologically up-to-date U.S. military machine of its kind," he finished grandly, his grey eyes twinkling below frosty-grey brows. Langley could see that he was clearly excited and if it excited 'old man' Abe Westonheimer, then it had to be damned good.

Sagerhawk, unperturbed by the interruption, continued. "Yes, sir, it is the work of myself and my colleagues where we have managed to develop a most fascinating program to alter DNA combined with technology to produce what you might call superhumans!" Now it was his turn to beam with pleasure, practically teetered on his toes.

"Gene tampering? Superhumans?" gasped Vice President Busby, "You can't tell me that you've got freaks in costumes working for the United States government!" he drawled in his northern-affected, fading southern accent. "Geez, you guys might as well have hired Mighty Mouse or G.I. Joe. They would've been much cheaper!"

Several people, including the President laughed. The VP was not only known for his staunch religious views and for running a tight ship, but also for his cutting remarks.

"I agree. It's bad enough with these Starguards. Now we're escalating and accumulating our own powers?" Richardson's voice rose in pitch.

"Gentlemen, please?" pleaded Sagerhawk. "Allow me to continue."

But Busby continued, leaning forward in his chair like an interrogator. "How'd this get through Congress, Doctor? How did this get past me and the Boss, Abe? Who authorised this? Please tell me there's not a single Pentagon asset in this?" he asked in rapid succession, deadly serious.

Sagerhawk looked stymied, actually petrified. Then he glanced slowly toward Westonheimer.

All eyes upon him, SecDef sat up in his seat. "Sir . . ." Westonheimer paused, as one did before charging into verbal battle. He continued in a quiet voice, like a teacher explaining to a particularly difficult child a particularly difficult problem. "I was approached by, shall we say, a very influential constituent who was concerned that such a day would arise when beings, such as the Starguards, outside of U.S. sovereignty and/or control, would cause an intentional or accidental imbalance in the world order. He was further concerned that conventional means would not be adequate enough to prevent such an event and that something was needed, something beyond all current technologies in order to combat this event. This is such an event, sir, and we cannot afford to lose this advantage and technology. To that end, the E-Corps project was initiated to offer maximum protection against such events and to investigate and nullify possible future occurrences."

Westonheimer, usually confident, seemed on edge, his brow moist with perspiration. This was his job, hell, his life on the line. Make or break time. And if he lost, well he was past retirement age already.

"Jesus, Abe!" the President whistled, incredulously. "You should have come to me with this one first!" He wrung his hands, his mind pounding with a headache from a thousand questions he couldn't put into words.

Busby recovered first. "Abe," he said, his voice a mixture of panic and anger, "where's the funding coming from? It can't be public money. If the Press catches a whiff of a government funded, superhero program, they'll rip us to tiny shreds and then some. Did you think about that before you went behind our backs to create your own fancy-costumed freak show?" he barked at Westonheimer, his temper rising.

Westonheimer actually smiled. It almost relieved the tension in the room.

"I don't think I explained everything," he said, as he slipped into teacher-mode again. "We, the government haven't funded anything. It's all private, the research, the hardware, and the human assets. All I am is a possible liaison in the future. However, once in motion, and if necessary, the team could be placed under the auspices of the U.N., but should the need arise, we then have the option of resolving out our agents to serve America."

"Wait, wait, wait a moment there, General," Busby snapped, waving his hands frustratedly, "Why the U.N.? This E-Corps, aren't they all at least U.S. assets?"

"No," Westonheimer answered, steepling his fingers before his face, as if in prayer. This part was going to be hard. "In order to get his funding together and cooperation approved, the aforementioned concerned citizen had to pool his global resources throughout fifteen countries, though the superhuman assets come from the U.S., Britain, Japan and Russia, to create a truly multinational force. As a matter of fact, my counterparts in those various countries are now briefing their heads of state."

The room was silent.

Busby, shaken, wiped his forehead with the back of his hand.

The President was in a rare state of disbelief, but managed to ask, "All right, Abe, who is this loaded, concerned bastard son of a bitch, whose going save the world?"

Westonheimer almost seem to flinch, as if he was about to be hit by flak.

"Penthor Thane, founder, CEO and the heart of Thane Universal." He slumped back in his chair, as if his energy for fighting had drained out of him.

Busby realised his mouth must have been as agape as the President's when Langley had looked at his VP, his mirrored expression causing him to shut his mouth sharply. The shock was palpable and permeated the room in an almost touchable silence. Richardson leaned back in his chair, a low whistle escaping his lips.

The President rubbed his face. *How could this have happened?*

Penthor Thane, to him, was a mysterious man who had suddenly come from nowhere to create one of the world's most successful international technological-based corporations. It had been claimed he had built his empire upon the back of illegal deals and operations, but nothing had ever been proved. His background and lifestyle were also closely guarded secrets. All that was known about him was that he was extremely generous, especially to African-American issues and causes and was one of the richest men in the world. President Langley also knew the FBI and CIA kept files on Thane and his associates.

That played on his mind now, but Busby, the ever-sharp-minded-and-tongued politician that he was—that's why Langley had 'rescued' him from senatorhood—spoke his mind for all of them.

"He wants a deal: get off his back or he'll set his freak show on us!" He got up from his chair, pacing to stretch his cramped legs. "Oh yeah, a kindly donated force, my ass! This smacks of bribery, blackmail, strong-arming, you name it. He's out to destroy the government one way or another!"

A clamour broke out with everyone trying to present their own view, but it was the sharp voice of the Chief of Staff, which cut through the arguments, commanding the attention of all present.

Kay Slaydon was the daughter of the former chairman of the Joint Chiefs of Staff Admiral Pete Slaydon and was generally suspected for having—anonymously—implicated her father in a scandal involving false Navy procurements, leading to his forced retirement. She was the ice queen of Capitol Hill, rumours not abounding, and not to be taken lightly.

The room fell silent as she spoke, her pale blue eyes demanding attention. She combed her thin fingers through inch-perfect blonde fringe along her forehead before beginning.

"After listening to all your arguments, I think I have a few questions and suggestions. If I may," she turned to the President, only a hint of a smile crossing her lips when the President agreed.

"Mr. President, Bibby, Hal, do you, after today's revelations, still trust the General?"

"Of course," said the President, unhesitatingly.

Busby gave a non-committal shrug and a nod of his head while Richardson added a silent nod.

Slaydon continued, "General, do you trust Penthor Thane's intentions and motivations, given, excuse me Dr. Sagerhawk, Thane's alleged less than savoury enterprises and background?"

"Well . . . yes, I have seen the start-up operations and know enough that there are aspects that cannot be changed, so yes, I trust him insofar that I believe him to be sincere in his mission for the world to be protected against outside threats," Westonheimer stated firmly.

"Yes, but why superheroes?" protested Busby. "They look . . . well, silly!"

Sagerhawk answered that. "Ah, but Mr. Vice President, throughout history people have always respected and responded to heroes and even now, people still love the concept of the superhero. It's the post-TV age, these heroes will guarantee worldwide coverage and publicity for all their heroic deeds, and of course the praise will go to the government that sponsored them." He smiled warmly at his own vision.

"Or the shit will fall on us from great heights when they screw up!" Richardson snapped.

Busby agreed. "So great, we have some super-rich guy with his super-freaks. What's next?"

"If I may?" Slaydon asked. The room went quiet again for her. "Thank you. Okay then. Here's the situation. We have a generous offer from a citizen of our country who wishes to serve not only his country, but the world as well. With me so far?" She narrowed her eyes in her version of a warm smile. "He has the money, the know-how and the resources to create not one, but . . . " She looked over at Westonheimer for a figure.

"At least ten," he confirmed. "Two groups of five, with scores of non-superpowered ops units and support."

"Ten more superhumans, added to these four Starguards." Slaydon nodded to acknowledge Westonheimer's information. "I don't think the question should be if we trust Thane or Sword Industries, another ghostly organisation, but whether we can trust their creations, whoever owns them. Frankenstein's monsters notwithstanding, we may one day have to un-create them."

She carefully looked around the room to see if they were following her logic. She turned to the scientists.

"So, I ask you Dr. Sagerhawk, can we simply. . . nullify these superhumans if they go out of control? Is there a kill switch? Can we destroy the superhuman-making infrastructure and plans if we had to?" She directed a frosty glare at the diminutive scientist, who seemed hesitant to speak. "Well!" she demanded, eyes hard beneath her fringe. "Is there such a contingency plan or capability to destroy these superhumans?"

The room was uncomfortably silent for a few tense heartbeats.

"Yes," came the answer.

But it was Sagerhawk's associate who had spoken for the first time, that one word electrifying the air, not least because her voice was one of pure exoticism.

The men stared at her until they felt disturbingly lecherous. Even Slaydon seemed affected, transfixed by the female scientist's sultry presence and fine-boned beauty under lustrous long auburn hair.

"I'm . . . sorry, I didn't quite hear that," Slaydon said, slightly breathless. She rubbed her neck. The room seemed hotter than before.

Dr. Sagerhawk spoke first, staring around the room, bemused.

"She said 'yes'." He glanced back at his colleague, as if confused.

She continued in her exotic accent, deep brown eyes flirting around the room as she spoke.

"In fact it was Mr. Thane's idea that there should be such a failsafe should something go wrong." Her captivating eyes held their attention.

Everyone was taken aback by the news, hanging on her every word.

Sagerhawk shifted discontentedly in his seat, as she continued in her exotic accent.

"While Dr. Sagerhawk is the chief scientist for the project, I am also a project manager and Mr. Thane's liaison to the government. Dr. Sagerhawk and myself are also the only ones who know the secret identities of our proposed superhumans, their full capabilities, and their weaknesses. We cannot divulge that information to you, but the means to destroy them are available as an option to you should the need arise. I assure you, I can speak for Mr. Thane." Her smile was a shade paler than Slaydon's.

Westonheimer let out a breath of air, "Well . . ." he breathed, wiping his brow, resisting the urge to lick his lips, "there it is then."

"I still think this whole thing is a little shifty and we're putting our jobs on the line for this!" Busby iterated, though less irritably.

"I've put my neck on the line for this country for more uglier causes than you can imagine," Westonheimer retorted. "But I believe in this cause." He leaned forward confidently, smiling at the scientists in support.

Silence hung in the room again, less tense, more of expectancy.

All eyes turned to the President. He in turn looked at his Vice President and Chief of Staff.

"Bib? Kay?"

Busby was first, "Only if we can have complete assurances from Thane that he won't interfere with our policies, if we accept. This is no *quid pro quo*!"

"Same, and I want to see and handle any publicity arrangements before they go out," replied Slaydon, seeking out Sagerhawk's eye.

Sagerhawk, sweaty palms clasped together, looked nervously at his colleague, who nodded confirmation at both statements.

"How soon can Thane have his superhumans ready?" Westonheimer asked.

"The first five within the year," Sagerhawk eagerly answered. "Sooner now I think!"

They all looked in anticipation at the president again. He chewed his lip for a second, stopping as if remembering who he was. He looked all of them in turn in the eye.

"Then it's a go," he said. "And may God have mercy on us all."

Westonheimer stood up, clearly relieved. He went over to Sagerhawk and thanked him shaking his hand, turning to the woman next. He looked her in the eye.

"Thank you, er . . . you know I never did catch your name, sorry, Ma'am."

She laughed, a pleasant musical sound.

"No problem, I'm Dr. Van Tager. Elisabeth Van Tager."

An hour later, with a hastily written speech by Halydon and Westonheimer, the President had made a statement in response to the Starguard Conference, and how pleased he was that a superhuman group could bring about world peace and better understanding.

Dr. Sagerhawk and Van Tager were in the back of a Thane Universal limousine on their way to the airport and a private jet back to New York.

"I knew nothing of these contingency plans!" a clearly worried Sagerhawk protested, wringing his hands in agony.

"That's because there aren't any," Van Tager laughed heartily, as Sagerhawk's weasel-like face showed signs of breaking into tears. "Oh, but don't worry, baby, we do have plans, both for the E-corps and the Starguards!" She laid her head back onto the headrest. "Boy, do we have plans!"

CHAPTER THREE

Sword Industries, Midtown Manhattan

After the stunning world-spanning conference and a rather mundane session of answering inane questions such as 'What is your favourite food?', 'What are your costumes made of", 'How do you go to bathroom with those uniforms?', and 'who is your favourite superhero?' the Starguards were led from the stuffy press room by Sword Industries media staff, ignoring all other probing questions from the hankering press.

It was all bewildering to the Starguards even though the hysteria on Halcyon had been much more so during Novan's speech, before he had departed Magna Aura in search of his mother, the Goddess Elysius, the last Celestian Knight lost somewhere in the midst of space. But here, they were out of their element, alone on another world, full of Fifths, as Altair had called them.

And for once, Aerl agreed. He remembered how they had arrived a year ago.

After their victory over the Lore at his home aboard the wrecked space-borne Millennius City-State, a jubilant Aerl the Sceptre had been flying toward Halcyon. The planet was still under attack by the Traitor Synther. However, his transit had been interrupted by Lightstream who had intercepted and trapped him within a forcefield. That was when the brightest and biggest of blue explosions had surged through the system. Lightstream had told him it was over, but not elsewhere, then there had been a blinding flash of light.

Once he could see again, he had found himself in a large stone chamber. The room was dark and bare, surrounded on all sides by a meter-wide strip of reflective glass along the centre of the walls. And he wasn't alone.

Beside him still prone on the floor, but now awakening was his brother-cousin Altair. Both were the sons of the Celestian Knight Iria, but while Aerl's father was Sola Venga, Altair was the son of Auron, Sola Venga's brother. It was a source of friction between them.

Beyond Altair was their blue-haired cousin Urana the Protectress of State on Placia, and in the corner lay the newest and youngest Starguard, Deb, or rather Azure, to give her Starguard name—the former Sky Warrior and the Loremaiden daughter of their greatest enemy, the Traitor Synther.

It had been Azure who had used her hitherto-unknown Lore energy to defeat and destroy the Lore and her father. Now they were here.

Azure woke up last. "Where am I?" she croaked, sitting up, blue sparks still subsiding from her sight. Hazy figures moved toward her.

Azure held up her hands to defend herself.

"It's only us, Deb," Urana said, soothingly, stroking Deb's arm, until she was more steady on her feet.

The daughter of Hyphon and Ultra Ari, Urana's manoeuvre suit bore sun-like rays arranged in a spiked diagonal arc across her body painting half her armour golden and the other side white with a narrow red sash running across the opposite way.

"Where are we?" she asked, blue hair swishing around as she surveyed the room.

Altair was scowling. His blue eyes burned with anger, though he tried to let his loose long-blond hair hide his face. His blue-with-gold-trim armour still bore a few burn marks from the Lore, but it had already started to self-repair.

"Pah, it's those Astrals," he growled, lighting up his hands, the room glowing red. "They took us!"

"We don't know. . ." Urana began, wrinkling her nose in doubt.

"Yes, we do!" Altair cut her off sharply. "We have been captured by them! Look at this prison. Pah! Where are you?" he shouted out loud.

Sceptre spoke to Urana. "Altair's right. It was Lightstream. She was the one who took me!"

"And me!" Deb was able to speak better. "Something about. . . saving another world," she remembered. She looked down at her two-toned blue manoeuvre suit, her Sky Warrior uniform. It was undamaged, but she could have sworn she had almost ripped herself apart when her nascent Lore energy had exploded from within her.

"At least Synther is dead!" she grinned wildly at them, her dark blues eyes gleaming proudly from beneath her black fringe.

She only wished her best friend Classia had been able to witness her great triumph, but she was off with Novan on his mission. She hoped they were both alive after they lost contact with their swordships shortly before the Lore had attacked.

"Thanks to you, all Magna Aura is safe," Aerl stated. "I saw the blue pulse of light, we should talk . . ."

Just then, a scrabbling noise was heard on the wall ahead of them, like a locking mechanism being released.

"Remain calm," Sceptre whispered to Altair, who glared at him with a cousin-look, but while he kept his hands lit, he took a breath and stepped back. "I will talk," Sceptre added.

Internally, he pooled some of his energy into his blue chest-plated gold-coloured armour, making himself almost glow. His golden visor enhanced his sight and crystalators started recording at his silent command.

The door opened and a man walked in. He was no Astral. And certainly not a Celestian.

He was tall, bearded, with short black hair. Seasoned brown eyes scruntinised them. His clothing was unfamiliar to the Starguards. Rich dark-cloth material sporting thin vertical white stripes on his long-sleeved, buttoned-up and collared garment were coordinated with matching leg wear, ending in hard shining black footwear. A thin strip of red material hung smartly around his neck over a white lighter-material vesture, beneath the over-garment. He entered slowly, smiling confidently, hands up in a non-threatening position in front of him.

"Who are you? Where are we? And why are we here?" Sceptre demanded authoritatively, his hands burning to discharge energy. He was still very aware Altair had his hands lit up.

The man in the suit continued smiling and replied.

"You already know how you got here. As for me, I am Bastian Exmoor. Welcome to Earth!"

"That's not good enough," Altair glared Bastian down. "We want answers!"

"Sure," Bastian's smile never wavered. "Let me tell you our history."

And his answers had been extraordinary.

The Exmoors liked to think of themselves as ex-mortals. They had descended from Celestian stock after Adantus and his crews had voyaged far beyond any other and died while fighting the Lore. The surviving crew had then been marooned on Earth, intermarrying with the native humans.

The male descendants had then developed a longevity gene, able to live for centuries or more. The male-only society recruited females for missions and for procreation, though they could only produce male offspring. Around 1200 BC, the Exmoors had become allies to the Astrals who had entrusted them with Earth's safety. As Man had expanded over the oceans and become more aware of their world, the Exmoors had disappeared into the shadows, content to be Earth's secret safeguards, watching Man develop.

In contrast, the Exmoors' enemies, the Devouts, were an all-female sisterhood also descended from Celestian stock. But while their life spans were slightly longer than a normal human's, they had developed varying superhuman abilities. The Devouts had witnessed how decisively the Exmoors and Astrals had treated other powerful humans, especially the Chryrian-merged humans, so they in turn had countered and undermined the Exmoors where they could. The Exmoor-Devout wars would be immortalised by Man in myths from Babylon, Egypt and Greece. But Exmoors spies had long ago found the secret of the Devouts' power: a Lore stone.

As the Exmoors understood, the Lore were an exotic form of sentient energy able to travel time and change form. But they were not alone. Their temporalmorphic nature and their travels had taken them to the furthest reaches of the universe and beyond. It had often resulted in some Lore being 'infected' with other energy-like viruses. This mutated energy-lifeform would attach itself to the Lore and feed from it. The Lore would either die eaten from within or flit through time or dimensional space, using the continuum distortions like a large extra-dimensional filter to eradicate the virus.

A peculiar effect from being dis-absorbed or ejected from the Lore found the virus devoid of energy and transformed into a solid. Resembling a lump of cold, blue, translucent stone it was a very rare find. Indeed, if exposed to certain other types of energy, the virus could be reactivated, releasing untold energy. That energy could either kill normal humans or transform the DNA of those humans with latent Celestian genes endowing them with powers, like that of the Devouts.

"So," Bastian explained, "The last attempt to retrieve the stone was in France in the year 1197, but the Devouts' leader had already disappeared with it. And here lies our problem," Bastian looked gravely at them, "after thousands of years of warring secretly, we have intelligence that the Devouts are now threatening to revive the Lore stone, create more Devouts from Earth's female population, and conquer the world. But if the Lore stone is activated to such an infinite degree, it will surely attract the Lore."

Bastian continued amid looks of incredulity on the Starguards' faces. "We had to ask the Astrals to intervene. To keep our society and longevity a secret, we Exmoors employ many intermediaries, disguises, and doubles to take our places. We mainly stay out of the limelight to avoid exposure to the Devouts, but all of the Exmoor brethren together could not defeat the Devouts. However, the Astrals cannot operate freely on Earth as their temporal energy would only attract the Lore through something they called temporal warming. So they brought you! We are after all distant kin in a way. The Astrals want the Starguards to protect and guide Earth and bring all our peoples together."

Aerl had listened politely to Bastian's answers, but had not liked all he had heard. "So what exactly do you want us to do?" He looked around at the other Starguards seeing if they had misgivings.

"We need your help and protection," Bastian repeated. "That's all."

Altair swore. "You Fifths are just brutes and ignorants! Why should we protect you?"

Bastian was momentarily taken aback, trying not to flounder.

47

"Because we are all kin and maybe one day we may be able to help you!"

He sounds sincere, if not a little naive, Aerl thought. But he had to ask: "But why only us four? Where are the others?"

"Lightstream told us that some remained on your worlds to protect them. And that you're the wisest of them?"

The Starguards looked at Altair in amusement.

"What?" he snapped. At least he had de-energised and lowered his hands.

Aerl sighed inwardly. He looked at the others, their faces telling him they had no choice, but to accept their abduction with some grace.

"Fine," Aerl accepted on the Starguards' behalf. "We'll help you defend this world. The more we cooperate, the faster we can return home." He presented the others to Bastian.

"I am Aerl, also called Sceptre. This . . ." he turned to his right, "is Altair, my brother . . ."

"Cousin," Altair half-corrected. "Mostly!" His sarcasm was noted by Bastian.

Aerl shook his head. *Couldn't Altair just behave, even on a new world?* But he knew Altair would be seeking a reckoning with the Astrals.

"Beside Altair is our *cousin*, Urana," Aerl dared Altair to say anything, but he didn't.

"Hallo," Urana greeted Bastian.

"And last, but not least, is our newest Starguard, Azure."

She was on Aerl's left. Nervously, she combed her jet-black hair away from her eyes.

"Hallo, you can also call me Deb," she said, almost shyly.

"Thank you, and it is an absolute pleasure to meet you all," Bastian acknowledged them and bowed graciously, glad that part was over. "You have a lot to learn about Earth," Bastian said. "So to aid you, I have arranged for three primary contacts: myself, my younger son, Simon, and Qane."

The door opened again and two other men stepped in. Bastian looked back at them to introduce the newcomers.

"This is Qane, from China, which you will learn more about."

The wizened man with snow white close-cropped hair and long

moustache tilted his head in greeting. He looked like he wanted to sit down, but leaned on his cane for support. He wore a black tunic suit with a mandarin collar buttoned to the top.

Bastian smiled. "Don't let his frail-looking six-hundred-year old body fool you, he's our weapons expert and can still pull off sprightly endeavours."

Qane's eyes crinkled in a mischievous smile. "Welcome, we are honoured to have you here. I look forward to joining you on our interventions to keep the Devouts in check," his whispery voice said.

Aerl studied him. Indeed Qane's physicality seemed lacking, but Aerl knew force wasn't everything and Qane had the looks of being a very shrewd adversary.

"This is my son, Simon," Bastian gripped him on the shoulder. "Despite his youthfulness being forty, he is being shown the ropes to prepare him for the future leadership of the Exmoors. My older son, Delius, is with the Avalon sect in England the main supplier of Exmoor warriors called The Hunters' Association. I hope you get to meet them in due course."

Simon grinned at the Starguards, bowing his head. He didn't look like his father, having short dark brown hair, was clean shaven, and his eyes were kinder. His suit was navy blue and he wore no tie leaving his collar open.

"Usually, my cousin Korsten is here, but he is working on a secret project." His face told the Starguards he wasn't going to tell them more about that.

"As for myself," Bastian said, "I am the leader of the North American Exmoor Sect and a member of the Exmoor Council, which rotates leadership every ten years. I'm almost five-hundred-years old but I'm still a Renaissance man at heart," he smiled at some personal joke. "I also run this business, Sword Industries, which I will instruct you in and we will shortly be journeying to our city HQ where you will learn about this world."

Bastian finished his talk and looked at the Starguards as they stared blankly at him.

Aerl caught on and explained.

"Sorry, Bastian, we have been listening, but also our crystalators," he indicated the crystal padd on his forearm, "have been absorbing information and collating for us. We've learned thirty different languages, virtually travelled the world, and previewed thousands of years of your history. It is a remarkable world you live in."

"Thank you," replied Bastian, surprised and honoured at the same time. He glanced at Aerl's crystalator in admiration. "We have a few original crystals left ourselves, but we cannot decipher all the information without corrupting or deleting it, so we have just kept using them for data storage. But by extrapolating the crystal's systems and with our technology we have been able to build the world's first quantum computers decades before human scientists even thought of it. But I'm sure they can't compare to yours. I hope you will be able to help us with the original crystals." He was genuinely excited.

And so were the Starguards. To see original texts and images from Adantus' time fourteen thousand years ago would be one of the most momentous occasions of the Celestian civilisation.

"We would be very pleased to help where we can," answered Sceptre, manfully trying to contain his own exhilaration. He wished both his mentor Spheron and younger cousin Cirrius, Urana's brother, were here. This would have been their domain—the former a master of exegesis and Cirrius in technology.

But they weren't and it was up to them now to help Earth.

"Are you hungry?" Bastian's sudden question broke up Sceptre's thoughts. "You've just fought the battle of your lives and here I am babbling on for ages! My apologies, what kind of host am I?"

Azure laughed. Her infectious spirit caught on and even Altair managed a grin.

"I'll take that as a yes, then!" Bastian wasn't too sure what he had said, but he was glad the Starguards were in a good mood. "Let me introduce you to some of Earth's finest cuisine."

He led them from the basement chamber, deciding to forgo the tour of the facility, and up through ten stories to the upstairs boardroom where a large oval wooden table awaited them. By the time they arrived, there were a multitude of dishes laden with all types of food. The view outside wasn't much, mostly forested land, but they had privacy.

Bastian thought better than to ask about any Celestian food taboos or allergies, but he described each dish as it was served. He could see the Starguards' crystalators on their forearms discreetly scanning the foods and saving data. They ate mostly in silence, small talk giving way to savouring the culinary fare.

"Delicious food," Urana announced contentedly after the meal, echoed by the others. "Almost as good as home." Her tone was appreciative, Bastian taking it as a compliment.

They were off to a good start. And after dinner they were shown to their own private quarters in a connecting compound at the rear of the facility.

"Tomorrow we begin," Bastian pronounced amiably.

And so it had. During that year, the Starguards had secretly travelled around Earth, learning its history and cultures, both known and unknown to humans. They had trained in secret, using their powers in various Sword Industries facilities all over the world.

Simon was their so-called cultural liaison getting the Starguards used to 'civilian' life by wearing normal human clothes instead of their manoeuvre suits; shopping, travelling by public transport, eating out in restaurants, just being around normal people and seeing how to blend in, without using their powers.

"It's like being a school teacher," Simon had complained not-too-seriously to his father about his task.

Aerl loved being 'normal' and so did Deb, who had to be warned several times about talking too much to other people, until she had a proper story to tell. To avoid confusion, it had been agreed that Sceptre and Azure would be called so while in uniform but Aerl and Deb in their 'private' lives.

Deb also desperately missed the ocean of Halcyon. Luckily, she had permission to have night flights over the Atlantic sometimes joined by Urana. But more importantly, when she wasn't flying, they had to ween the young Starguard off the TV soaps she was using for her cultural homework.

Altair avidly delved into military history, especially the World War years and like Deb, was hooked on the TV, in his case sci-fi shows. He thought they were comedies, laughing at the technologies portrayed.

He often disparaged all the current nations' space efforts boasting he could build a better spacecraft from the junk floating in space while harbouring an ambition to visit the ISS. However, NASA, Roscosmos, and ESA were just as desperate to keep Altair away from the station. When he wasn't too busy being his usual surly self, he was training hard in the virtual reality training rooms.

Aerl absorbed politics and history. There were aspects to Earth's history Aerl couldn't reconcile and wondered how much the Exmoors and Devouts had steered the world for their own purposes. These two factions were kin to the Celestians yet instead of uniting to raise humanity persisted in an eternal war which could tear the world apart.

Whose side are we really on? he thought. He committed himself to keeping his eyes open and his mind free for an objective view on the world and their mission.

The Starguards all fell for sports, especially the tactics of American Football. While younglings on Celestia played group games there were no such global sports or contested leagues. Competition for Celestians was about art and aesthetics, sounds, vision and sensory games. The closest they had were war games, but there was no overt separation between the six races of Galatians, Elerae, Trinari, Xarians, Meccuns, and Neb. It took a while for the Starguards to understand the human fanaticism with sports.

While Urana reflected on World art and music, there was a genuine concern for her. Unusually for a Starguard, she had taken ill. The Exmoor doctor couldn't find any reason for it. But while Urana eventually got better, she wasn't the same. Aerl suspected some form of lingering psychological stress from the Astral's removal of her as the Protectress of State for Placia, but no one knew for sure.

But there was no stopping their mission, as Bastian explained.

"I do not know when this will happen," he said. "But the Devouts are planning something. Headquarters in New York have caught increased chatter on their comms. The Hunters' Association will initially deal with this, so if you run into them, they are on our side. The next step is to present you to the world as superheroes . . ."

He stopped as he drew blank glances from the Starguards.

"Ah . . . people with extraordinary powers who save people and protect the world and that sort of thing. What you normally do on your own world. Don't worry, we'll watch some films on the subject so you can get a better idea," he laughed, at the thought of them learning superheroing from Hollywood. "You can't do this in secret without using your powers, so this way people will accept you more when you use your powers to fight the Devouts."

"Now we're talking!" Altair grinned, ready for action.

Aerl shook his head, dubious at Altair's enthusiasm.

"Now it's time to meet the world," Bastian announced happily.

Aerl smiled to himself. For that long year they had trained, travelled, and waited; now they could go out into the public, use their powers and protect the Earth. With the conference over, they retired to their living quarters, a whole converted floor of protected penthouse suites within Sword Industries.

In his spacious room he looked out the window sixty stories down onto Lexington Avenue, to where Sword Industries security guards patrolled the outside of the building, making sure the media, fans, curious geeks, and stalking autograph hunters were kept at bay. They were also on the lookout for anything unusual, a sign that the Devouts would make an early move. They were playing with forces they knew nothing about, yet risked the entire safety of this world. If the Lore attacked Earth, Aerl preferred not to think about the devastation and death the Lore would cause.

Beneath the penthouse suites, the Exmoors kept their own apartments, and below them, their control ops and briefing rooms.

Bastian was in Ops engaged in a strategy meeting with Qane.

"Yes, yes, this group calling themselves the Hostile are becoming more of a security concern than first thought. Upgrade their threat level. . ."

There was a knock on the door.

"Come in," said Bastian, perturbed at being disturbed.

Altair walked in.

Bastian sighed with resignation and admiration. The former due to Altair's presumptive attitude of superiority, which was undoubtedly true, but Altair wore it as brashly as his manoeuvre suit which he constantly wore when in Sword HQ.

However, Bastian couldn't ignore the beauty of the technology behind it. He was assured by Aerl that the tight-fitting soft-armour suits manufactured from vortexite and which bonded to their owner, were as comfortable as normal clothes, protected the wearer with forcefields and provided continuous communications with others. It was a part of them, a second skin, which also harnessed their powers. The suits were 'controlled' by imbedded micro-sized crystals. When the Starguards needed to change into civvies, they simply instructed the suit to change its outer appearance. It also allowed for Urana to change her hair colour, replacing the vibrant blue with a colour of her choice. Hence, they were always in their armour. If they did have to physically take the suits off, then they wore a few crystals upon their person for protection and communication.

Bastian could only marvel at the Starguards' technology. Sword Industries may have been one of the best technology companies in the world, but that was because of Astral help. The Starguards' civilization had done it all from scratch.

He thought about this as Altair had waltzed in. He should have felt proud to be working with the Starguards, but Altair always contrived to bring out the uglier side of life.

"Altair, hello, did you need anything?" Bastian asked, bracing himself for the unexpected from Altair.

"No," replied Altair. "I'm here to plan our next move."

Qane looked over at Bastian, a surprised expression creasing his already crinkled face into one of bemusement, as he noticed Bastian's calm exterior slip for a slight second.

Altair continued, "On Alphatron City-State, I ruled, I protected, led warrior forces, planned defences and strategies, and built whole towers the size of your skyscrapers. I was in control of a city in space, almost as big as Manhattan. If I am to be here on Earth to protect it, I should have a say in how it is protected." He stood in the room, a defiant chin tilted slightly in the air.

Bastian regarded Altair. The Starguard was a proud warrior, who had too much power and not enough temperament to control his emotions. Bastian had the sense Aerl merely put up with Altair, but didn't really curb his wilder tendencies. One day, that would lead to trouble. And Bastian didn't want to be there when it happened.

So, welcoming hand or cold shoulder, Bastian thought.

He was about to answer when all the lights suddenly went off. The three of them looked up in surprise and then around the room as the computers, CCTV, and other systems powered down sighing into silence.

Bastian waited, apprehension held at bay. The back-up generators should have cut in almost instantaneously, but they didn't. No accident would account for that, it had to be on purpose.

"We're under attack!" he shouted.

He pressed a button on the wall to set off the alarms, but nothing happened.

"Dammit!" Bastian was angry, angry at having been caught off guard so easily. He grabbed his mobile, altered by Exmoor engineers, and made an all-call to Sword personnel.

"We're under attack! This is not a drill. All units assemble at your duty stations and carry out your orders. With me!" he called to Altair and Qane. The three of them rushed out of the room, Qane corralling a squad of four security officers.

They ran into Sceptre, Urana, and Azure. Bastian briefed them quickly. "We have to search every floor for intruders and damage!"

Qane and his guards headed to the roof to check the solar arrays, while Bastian and Altair headed toward the sub-basement generators. Sceptre, Urana, and Azure split up on different floors aiding security.

Bastian looked over at Altair running beside him as they entered the stairway, the elevators being out of service. The look on the

Starguard's face was one of pleasure, pleasure of doing his job, using his powers, hurtling into danger.

Maybe I should set Altair loose on the Devouts' asses, he laughed to himself, *then Earth could go back to normal again.* I could grow to like Altair yet, he grinned as they rushed down the stairs.

The two reached the basement, searching the corridors containing plant rooms. They unexpectedly came across a few unconscious security officers and engineers sprawled along the corridor to the central computer systems room, from where smoke drifted out.

Without waiting for Bastian, Altair rushed into the room, his hands already glowing red with energy, ready to unleash deadly hell.

Bastian ran after him, ready to . . .

He pulled up short on entering, "What . . . the . . . hell?"

CHAPTER FOUR

"Do as I say, daughter!" The voice was full of venom.

"I cannot leave without Edgar," Elisabeth pleaded.

"You must!" her mother insisted, auburn hair bouncing with the force of her words. "He is not the way. You must protect the Lore stone at all cost. This is the only way!"

Elisabeth twisted her head, staring defiantly at her mother. It struck her that her mother had hardly aged. They could have been sisters.

But to reiterate her superior position, her mother added, "I command it! Your lord commands it! Or I will kill your husband if you do not obey me!" Her dark eyes shone with anger.

Elisabeth Van Tager straightened up. Her and Edgar's bed chamber high up in one of the towers within the castle should have been her sanctuary, but her mother had invaded with a mission and an ultimatum. And she hated how her mother could never bring herself to say Edgar's name.

It was a windy night, the horses' skittish neighs could be heard from the stables and duty knights huddled against the battlements for shelter. The cold dark winds matched Elisabeth's mood.

"I hate you mother!"

Surprisingly her mother's mood softened. "I know. We've been together for too long," she smiled. "But I'm leaving now. And you have one more night with your husband." She reached out to caress Elisabeth's cheek, but she moved away.

"Good bye, mother."

"Good bye, my daughter. I will see you again."

Even as Elisabeth tried to discern if that was a promise or a threat, her mother turned sharply, ran to the open window, and jumped out. Elisabeth knew better than to check if her mother had survived a fifty-foot drop to the ground, but wished she had fallen to her death. However, she knew her mother also had her own destiny and duty to fulfill. And so it seemed did Elisabeth Van Tager.

Tonight would be her last night in 1197.

Elisabeth and Edgar were kindred spirits. The Devouts had endured terrible losses through the centuries at the hands of the murderous Exmoors. Such losses had drawn them to each other, first as allies, then as lovers, and finally husband and wife, much to the initial dismay of the Devouts, but always to her mother. But as Valtare's power and influence had grown, so the apathy toward him had lessened. Their power base in southern France had proved fruitful, though to Van Tager less so, losing three children during difficult pregnancies. She and Valtare seemed to be incompatible, much to the delight of her mother, who gloated that it was the will of the Lore.

The Devouts may have descended from Celestians, but they recognised that their ancestors' enemies were endowing females with far more power than the males. It was a gift from the Gods and to keep their power, the Devouts had established cults around the Lore stone. Van Tager's mother, the Archwitch, had been a leader of the cult, Elisabeth inheriting that role upon her mother's alleged death at the hands of the Exmoors.

It had been her mother who had been contacted by their master, a mysterious figure who stayed in the shadows. They knew not his name or face. And while he did not rule them or was their master, they supported him as their lord as he protected them; a male supporting them against the Exmoors—an irony not lost upon the Devouts. Their master had revealed to them events to come and prepared them for the future war. To that end, Van Tager needed an army, but the technology would only come eight hundred years hence and Van Tager needed to be there. The Devouts of that time were in disarray and leaderless. In the meantime, the master also had a role for Valtare. The master promised that they would be reunited in their time of triumph.

But now, in the future, Elisabeth Van Tager was a lonely woman. She and Edgar had such plans, but between her mother and their lord, they had contrived to see them split apart to achieve their goals. She wondered if Edgar had succeeded in his part of the grand plan. Van Tager's part was only really now beginning, but she had a big, unexpected problem: The Starguards.

They had not been foretold. Who were they and where did they come from? She could only surmise that the Exmoors had initiated their own programme. But to Van Tager, it had happened far too fast and without warning. She had no spies in the Exmoor network, such was their tight-knit security, so she had no answers; only that one day there were no Starguards and the next there they were. Van Tager knew that something else was at work here. Edgar had often told her of the Exmoors and the Astrals who had slain so many of his people centuries ago. Maybe those same Astrals had found a way to help their half-breed humans. But it was no matter. As long as she held the Lore stone, the Exmoors would be powerless.

It had been Elisabeth's idea to use the Lore stone to create superhumans once she discovered how to use it in that way. For the Devouts it was easy, it was in their blood—in their DNA. The Lore stone amplified their powers, but only for women. It did not work on men; hence the Exmoors did not possess powers other than longevity. However, she had realised that while ordinary human men could not be harnessed, some men descended from Devouts could be, but finding them was next to impossible.

That's where Dr Sagerhawk had come in with his genetic algorithm research. And with twenty-first century technology and the capability to so, the Devouts would flourish. But now she dreaded that the Exmoors had their own Lore stone and had figured out how to successfully empower human men as well.

The plan had seem so easy a few centuries ago.

Van Tager mournfully descended the tower stairs to see Valtare impatiently pacing in the main hall. The fireplace flickered with lackluster flames enhancing the gloom.

"Well?" he asked, too sharply.

Elisabeth had told Valtare of the plans their master had for them.

"This will be our last night together," she confirmed, regretfully.

Valtare accepted the news with a heavy heart.

Without a word they led each other back upstairs to their chamber. That night Valtare and Van Tager had lain together. They were soul mates, their eyes mirroring the depths of their love for each other. Their love and energy burned bright, their bodies writhing as one, their hearts aching from impending loss. Valtare's mind exploded in psionic orgasm as Van Tager synergic energies erupted in ecstasy. The whole village below the castle was overtaken during that night with unremitting passion as alien energies diffused through the villagers with wanton abandon. Unsurprisingly, a baby boom had ensued nine months later. And when Valtare had awakened in the morning, his wife was gone.

It had happened so quickly for Elisabeth after she had stole out of bed leaving behind a sleeping Valtare waiting apprehensively in the Great Hall with a few belongings and the Lore stone wrapped in a velvet casing. With a sudden shift in her perception accompanied by a flash of light, her lord had transported her to the future.

Van Tager had found herself on the same estate, but centuries in the future. The land was now part of a large farm with some of the castle ruins still standing in the eastern border of the estate. After walking through the fields a farmer had seen her and brought into a town worried about her health, considering she was wearing a strange old-fashioned dress and her French was garbled. Elisabeth hadn't resisted. She needed to find out more about this time. The local doctor had examined her, but found nothing wrong with her, except that her French (and clothing) was a little strange. She had then been taken to a local psychiatric centre. And it was there where she had met Claire Mouhetta.

Claire, a fellow patient aged ten, had been having terrible dreams. Her parents, who had immigrated to France from Algeria, worked on the farm to help with their daughter's fees in search for a cure. But Van Tager had seen her for what she was: a Devout.

For years Claire, a powerful psychic had been tormented by

visions about strange times and warriors and a mysterious traveller—and here she was. The young girl took instantly to Van Tager who used her own powers to soothe Claire's dreams, the two becoming fast friends, Claire able to relate to Van Tager. Elisabeth showed Claire her mind and all that happened and why she was here.

"Sooner or later, the Exmoors will come for you and kill you just for being different," warned Elisabeth. "But we will protect each other from now on."

That night, she and Claire had left the town, Claire taking on the Devout name of Clair Voyant. Claire was the strongest psychic the Devouts had ever produced. Her senses were acute to others of her kind, Devout in nature.

Van Tager's mission was to unite the disparate Devout sisterhood, which would see them travelling the world. That had been ten long years ago. But Clair Voyant's abilities had discovered more than they had expected.

"Do you trust this Penthor Thane?" Van Tager had asked Clair Voyant.

"Not by a long shot" Clair had laughed. "But we need him."

Clair Voyant was not sure what had led her to Penthor Thane. By male standards he was an extraordinary man with an even more extraordinary life. Everyone knew his history; how he had been orphaned in the 1960's and grown up on the mean streets of New York, only to be given a chance at education by a local priest's school, which sponsored him through college and after which he earned scholarships for his engineering and technology degrees at MIT. Now Thane had his own company and was living a normal life as much as a billionaire could, rumours of his criminal activities not withstanding.

Upon meeting Van Tager, set up through Clair Voyant, Thane had been his usual gregarious self and decided to enter into a business alliance with Van Tager. Thane wanted total domination for his biotechnology outlets. Van Tager needed funding for her biotech inventions. And the E-Corps was to be both their crowning glories.

Van Tager had never revealed the Devouts secret or the Lore stone to Thane.

"But I do think he suspects I have some other power source, which no doubt he would try to have for himself," she confided to Clair.

But now after years of experimentation, the E-Corps was ready for action against all enemies, including the Exmoors and the Starguards.

Van Tager's labs were located in the basement of Thane's Manhattan skyscraper. That was where all the wet work had been undertaken, the physical tests and specimen experiments, with further secret human testing and training carried out as far away as they could in the deserts of Africa or on the high international seas, away from watching eyes, human or otherwise. Thane saw to that. But the underground labs were Van Tager's so-called 'public' area, for show, for the likes of Sagerhawk and other human scientists on the project.

Van Tager also occupied a whole private floor high up on the sixty-sixth floor. Bomb- and psi-proofed, it was impregnable to all but the Devouts. Even Thane did not dare enter. Several Devouts, in assumed identities, worked directly for Van Tager accessing the floor with coded passes and a DNA scan. It was on this floor Van Tager kept the Lore stone; the twenty-kilogram brain-sized block of stone locked in a strong box in a vault, which only Van Tager could open.

In her own private quarters, one would think they had walked back in time. Antiques and reproductions of furniture, rugs, tapestries, art and literature from twelfth century France adorned her room, a little taste of home to remind her of what she was fighting for. As she walked past her desk she caringly spun the wood and bronze globe which stood on a tripod beside her large desk. She loved the smell of the room with mixtures of perfumes, incense, polished wood and spices for her wines. Behind her desk was a drinks cabinet from which she pulled out and opened a bottle of old French red wine inhaling the vapour for her health. Having a generous sip, Elisabeth cracked open her small cameo of her husband on a necklace around her neck, a reduced copy of the original painting which hung above their fireplace, next to her portrait, in France.

So handsome, she thought. She wondered if she would ever see him again. Van Tager knew that even if she saw him today he would still be young looking with crisp blue eyes and wavy blond hair. She, however, would have died long ago if not for their master's help.

"May we find each other again, my love, in this life or the next!" She sighed and put the necklace away.

It was time to gather her thoughts and end her mission. Her own boardroom adjoined her private quarters and she took the short walk through, past the concealed vault, into the room.

Elisabeth Van Tager, Archwitch of the Devouts, caster of synergic spell-fire and manipulator of Lore energy smiled as she entered the boardroom with her lieutenants sitting patiently around the large oval table.

"It is done!" she announced. "We celebrate today the culmination of the E-Corps project. The White House has agreed to our objectives," she announced to raucous cheers from leaders of various Devout factions. "After centuries of waiting and experimenting, the Lore stone has enabled us to succeeded in creating males with abilities. We Devouts will be able to procreate and have more children, natural children; a true bloodline of males. No more will we need normal undeserving males to mate with us to produce a female line, when we can have full-blood males from Devout descent to carry on the line. It means we now have the strength and capability to take on the Exmoors and their Starguards. And I want those Starguards, their secrets, how they were made, where they come from; whatever they may be." She smiled again, with a burst of exuberance thinking of all the power she would have.

Around the table, her principal Devout leaders cheered.

Clair Voyant sat to her right hand side as normal. Obitumary, a forty-year-old Floridian whose touch of bad luck usually ended in death, sat on her left. Kinecity, a brash British speed junkie who produced electricity when she moved and Cin—short for Cinder—a

Chinese firestarter who was quickly abandoned by her family as her powers had threatened to turn a once shy girl into a crime-spree waiting to happen, sat together near the end. Peril, a South African pensioner with super strength lounged in her chair beside Clair. And Sylphia, a self-proclaimed weather witch from Norway sat further up on the right. Van Tager had lamented sending away Were-witch, the previous week to England on a mission. She hadn't returned.

"How are we to draw the Exmoors out?" asked Sylphia, in her quiet voice.

Of all the Devout faction leaders, Van Tager wondered how such a timid and wall flower of a Devout could have led her sisterhood. Her limp blonde hair, pale skin with ruddy cheeks, and a wide pouty mouth made her look perpetually like a little girl. She exuded nervousness with ease. Even now she looked afraid as Van Tager replied.

"Oh, I'm sure they'll have a weak link. That Altair looks like a hothead. We bait him then put a word in the ear of the Defence Secretary and he'll take care of the rest. We'll just wind them up and push them into a fight and our teams will be ready. The Devouts will be ready! Vengeance and victory!" she shouted, punching the air.

"Vengeance and victory," came the chorused reply.

"What about Thane?" Obitumary asked. The others looked at her quizzically. The scientist of the group was looked up to by the rest as the former leader of the largest Devout group worldwide before Van Tager had appeared. Her sharp features, intensified by her neat corn-rowed hair and deep blue eyes mirrored her steel-trap mind.

Van Tager smiled. Obitumary was smarter than she looked. "What about him?" she teased, looking down the board table.

"He's different. I've noticed him struggle with it, but he doesn't seem to realise. You must have seen it?" Obitumary shrugged, not wanting to seem more cognisant of the situation than her boss.

But Van Tager allayed any fears of that. "Yes, 'Mary, I've known about Thane for some time. Why do you think we're here with Sagerhawk and this whole set up? This was all in my plan, approaching Thane, the Government, making Sagerhawk believe he was creating superheroes, and getting them all on board. We will destroy the Exmoors with Thane's help. And I'm sure he'll join us when the time comes. If not, he can die with the others. The only thing that matters is the Devouts and our continued success. And then the Lore will return and bless us all!"

The deadly sorority looked around at each other excited at the prospect that the chosen ones of the Lore would live forever in their paradise. Vengeance and victory were on the way.

"Hong Kong never ceases to amaze me," Ms Charm said to her partner. "It's the smell. I love it!" She tried to inhale the street aromas but the rain dowsed them out.

Mr. Spree and Ms. Charm followed Thanes' orders, scouring the world in search of Sword Industries secrets. During their travels, Mr. Spree never failed to fascinate Ms. Charm. They were colleagues, he more her mentor figure and a friend. They had met over ten years ago while on opposite sides of the criminal fence, though she would be forced to leap over to his side following her dismissal from the CIA for inappropriate conduct.

Since the Starguards had come to town, they were working overtime in trying to convince various sources to reveal anything about them and the Exmoors; find their weaknesses, secrets, and breaking points. But no one was willing to talk.

Armandes Graff had fled the Cuban communist dream state, which had failed him some years earlier with the death of his parents. He had one brother and one sister he hadn't seen in years and presumed them dead. With all his stories and battle-worn scars he claimed he was in his forties though Charm always teased it was closer to one-forty since he had so much to tell and had experienced so much in one lifetime. The first thing he had ever said to her was:

"Don't get working together mixed up with friendship and trust."

But while Spree had warmed a little to Charm, he was still ever-celibate claiming that relationships with women blunted his senses and skills. Charm, quite the bed-hopper in her day, suspected that his sexual preference was killing. Spree was now more circumspect about Charm's dalliances, though he could tell when she relapsed into one-night stands. He didn't approve, nor did he disapprove, as long as she got the job done.

His 'rules of war' or 'Spreeisms' as Charm called them were revelatory and brutal. Spree never really talked about his younger years, except when he once reminisced about a dream:

"I had met a man, a young man who had prying eyes—foul and intent, a killer's eyes. The violence behind them was overwhelming. Then I woke up and saw myself in the mirror. They were my eyes. And that's when my life was decided." He enjoyed telling Ms Charm, "Violence is an art form with the ability to create any picture you want. I know I'm stronger, faster, smarter, and meaner than anyone else out there and I prove it all the time. I'm a survivor. I kill just for the pleasure of hunting people down. And I fight well for my life, for I'll never get the chance to die again." Spree's philosophy ruled his life.

Charm always listened to Spree's rules, listening out for hints to Spree's inner self, as she did now on the streets of Hong Kong investigating Sword' Industries' East Asian hi-tech division in the Katana South Building.

". . . So I said to him 'Yeah, the name's Spree, first name Killin'. And he didn't get it, so how could I kill the guy if he didn't understand the punch line?" Spree looked deadly earnest at his admission, not bothered by the heaving rain pelting down upon them.

Charm's hair was soaked and it sprayed droplets as she spun her head in surprise. "No, you're kidding? But you killed him right?" Charm laughed, avoiding a splash on the pavement from a car as it hit a water-logged pothole in the road.

"Like two years later, when I saw him in Manilla, and he laughed saying how he had finally got the funny joke I had told him, so I 'accidentally' pushed him in front of a bus. That was funny!"

"You made that up!"Charm could never be sure about Spree's

sense of humour.

"No way, it happened. . . ."

They both stopped as they reached their destination; fifty stories of high-tech innovation. Hacking into the building's security had proved impossible so physical eyes on the site was their main method of assessing security, access points and vulnerabilities, employees, and site activities. After a few hours Spree and Charm had looked at each other with the same thought.

The trip to Hong Kong had proved fruitless. Even post-work kidnappings of employees under torture did not work. Either Sword had an iron grip on loyalty or their workers really didn't know what was going on.

"Curiouser and curiouser," Charm muttered, knowing Spree was just as suspicious. "The Exmoors are creating things their employees would give their lives for. That's almost frightening," she added.

"They're changing the rules of the game." And Spree hated when they changed.

Five months later, Spree and Charm found themselves in Paris.

"Anyway, I was in Thaitown and these guys, teenagers really, came up to me acting all tough, wanting a foreigner's money and all. I told them to beat it. They refused. So I gave my little spiel: 'Okay, here's the rules: come at me with a weapon and I'll break your arm; kick me and I'll break your leg; sneak up on me and I'll break your back; shout in pain and I'll break your neck. Simple—any questions? No? Let's fight . . .'"

"And you beat them of course."

"Hey, I do what I say on the tin."

Spree was proud of his rules, they were his lifeblood.

After another fruitless investigation into SeineTech (they knew enough to avoid London's subsidiaries as it was riddled with Exmoor loyalists), the two headed back across the Atlantic. On their return, they had informed Thane of their failure to gain any information on the Exmoors. Thane laughed.

"Then your trips have been quite successful. It tells me the Exmoors are very adept at keeping secrets and attaining loyalty I could only aspire to, excepting you two, of course. But more importantly it tells me they have all their eggs in one New York basket. They have something to hide, something they would rather take to their graves than be exposed. That is the key to taking them over. And I have that covered."

He was sure Van Tager was itching to unleash the E-Corps, but they would need the opportunity.

"In the meantime, I am tasking you to now keep tabs on the Starguards, themselves; a dossier on their movements and abilities. They can be highly elusive. For superheroes they shun the limelight almost as much as I do."

But he had his reasons for that. He wondered if the Starguards shared the same motives.

"Yes, sir," both Spree and Charm answered.

Thane walked off in thought.

Over the next few nights between assignments, Spree and Charm trained in Thane's private shooting gallery in the sub-basement above the labs. As they fired, Spree chatted away as usual about his downtime activities.

". . . He was, like, eighty years old, but I had my job to do, so I shot him in the heart as he lay in the bath," Spree stated in a matter-of-fact tone, almost scoring a perfect series on the downrange target.

"That's cold!"

"The water was by the time they found him," he quipped deadpan.

"Cold as ice, man."

"Cold is where the heart is."

"Absolutely solid," Charm mused, succeeding in a perfect score.

"So what did you get up to last night?" he asked.

They had finished their shooting session and started cleaning their weapons.

"I was in the Bronx, doing my charity work," Charm stated without irony, "for a lady who was going to be evicted for not paying the exorbitant rent for her flea-bitten flat by her greedy landlady." Charm still sometimes moonlighted as an urban mercenary.

Charm recalled, "So after getting my client a good six months refund, I said to the dragon landlady, if I ever see you again, I will hurt you. I'll kill your family and friends, anything and everyone associated with you. I'll wipe you from the face of existence."

"Not bad," assessed Spree. "How about something like 'I'll hurt you beyond your wildest dreams your unborn grandchildren will cry in pain."

"Ha-ha, maybe next time."

"I'm going to be the last thing you ever see," Spree carried on with epitaphs.

"Cliche, but I get the idea," Charm smiled at their targets. "But you can't hide the fact that I'm a better shot than you, see?" She indicated the targets at the end of the range. "So quit trying to distract me. Best of seven in falls?"

Spree gave her a resigned look. "Go on then."

They moved into hand-to-hand combat in the adjoining gym. Spree walked around the matted floor like an instructor teaching his class tricks of the trade, which indeed was his occupation in many Latin American revolutionary causes in the 1980s.

"Underestimation of your enemy is the sure fire way to get yourself killed. You must know your enemies' strengths and weaknesses. But more importantly, know your own. And guard them well. If you're asking yourself 'what can go wrong?' the answer is everything, but in asking that question, there must be that element of doubt, and that is the seed of self-destruction you must destroy."

Spree feinted to the right, luring Charm into attacking recklessly, before grabbing her arm. He flipped Charm over his back and she fell awkwardly on her back.

"C'mon Steph, what's a little pain between friends?"

"Oh, so I'm your friend now?"

He hesitated, a fraction of a second too long in thought. Charm swung around on her hip, the pain lancing through her back, but her left leg caught the back of Spree's knee, which buckled and he fell.

"Well done," he said.

"I guess women do dull your skills." She jumped to her feet and helped him up, a rue smile on his face.

"Told you so."

There was mutual admiration between them, but they were getting a little agitated about their lack of success in helping Thane. They were getting edgy, which meant Spree needed to kill something and Charm needed sex.

Stephanie Mikovitch's family was full of well-off lawyers in Chicago. Her father was an international trouble-shooter and took his spoiled daughter with him everywhere. She had learned six different languages fluently by the time she was eleven years old, learned to comport herself as a lady to kings, presidents, and dignitaries, and whether innocently or deliberately kept diaries of everything she experienced and witnessed. But the neglected Stephanie also grew up mentally and physically tough. And she chose to use that physicality in bed, usually with opponents of her father's law firm, though the seventeen-year-old's escapades didn't always win daddy's cases or affections.

Though she was far more capable, Steph barely scraped her way through college, but she developed a fascination with espionage; investigative and intuitive skills inherited from her father. There was something about her self-determination and street-wise ways which earned her a place within the ranks of the CIA, not to mention her diaries full of secrets ready to use as leverage. But Steph was careless, impatient, and prone to violence first over reason to solve her issues. The final straw arose from her entanglement with a double-crossing, Middle Eastern agent and lover. His wife and kids had been killed in reprisal and the agent was exposed. Steph had found herself disavowed and out of a job. But there were others who coveted her skills and Steph had travelled the world like her father, an international trouble-shooter, except her cases involved shooting the trouble.

One of her clients had been one Mr. Penthor Thane. After her impressive performance against a couple of stubborn business competitors, Thane had offered her a permanent position on his security retinue, which she had accepted. For a while, Steph had found it strange that both Thane and Spree had resisted her charms, but then she realised they weren't like other men. They were survivors. And for Steph, now Ms. Charm, she was all about surviving.

And that night, after training with Spree, she heartily engaged her survival skills in the apartment of a young business exec she had met in a club, their naked bodies sliding over each other to her urgent need. Needless to say, he couldn't keep up, and Charm left him even as he tried to regain his breath and panted for more.

Her fix attended to, Charm was ready to re-focus on work in the morning. She found Spree in the same rejuvenated mood. He'd catered for his needs, too, by the looks of it.

For the rest of the year they had tailed the Starguards over every continent, observed them on live TV shows and at events, discreetly photographing them for any secrets they could gain, any source of their power, any hints at their weakness.

In Rio, Charm had watched as Urana had posed for a sports calendar. Even Charm was envious at the Starguard's full-figured body, though she was amused that Urana didn't really seem to know what the bikini was for. She wore it like it was some alien contraption.

"The woman has no idea! Does she even need a bra with those!" Charm tried not to focus on Urana's assets. But Urana seemed a genuine and graceful person.

Almost too perfect, Charm thought, hating perfect people.

Charm began to wonder if she had powers, what would she want? She settled for invisibility. Of course she had applied for the E-Corps programme, but had not been selected, Charm believing that Thane had scuppered her chances, preferring her to remain 'normal'. He had practically told her this over dinner, as she relayed to Spree:

"Dinner with Thane wasn't a romantic affair or anything. We talk and it's like he can see me for who I really am, like he's looking for something or someone. I think he's lonely."

"Of course he's lonely. He has us for friends," Spree had quipped.

At the Paris air show, she and Spree had watched as Azure had out-flown an old F-14 Tomcat in an aerial display.

"Boring," yawned Charm. "Too young and eager to please. Talks too much!"

"But not stupid. She's always surrounded, confident, yet suspicious. We wouldn't get past her guard," Spree calculated.

In India, they almost admired how Sceptre carried himself on the world stage, discussing alternative energy sources, world security, India's space programme and more. He was a hero to be saluted. Even Spree suspected Sceptre had his own rules.

But it was Altair they liked the best. He was their kind; his surly appearances in front of audiences, his impatience at being in one place for too long, and tendency toward violence when confronting criminals intrigued them.

"He's their weakest link," Spree said.

"Agreed, I think we've finally hit pay dirt."

They reported to Thane, their boss nodding thoughtfully. For months, he and Van Tager had been deliberating over plans to accelerate the E-Corps programme. Now in theory they had a way to rid the world of the Starguards and replace them with the E-Corps.

But it would be up to Van Tager to play her pieces in the great superhero game. Their time would come almost one year later on the streets of New York.

CHAPTER FIVE

Gordell stared open-mouthed, stunned, at the woman with the shining bow.

"A Devout!" he shouted and charged with wrath, before Alpha Rion could stop him.

Alpha Rion had also been taken aback, not by her sheer presence: slender, black-skinned and beautiful, but because he suddenly remembered his dream. She was that woman.

"You!" he whispered.

The woman's eyes smiled at Alpha Rion even as Gordell bore down on her, sword raised to strike.

Alpha Rion had never felt so much emotion for anyone before. But he felt it would be over before it began as Gordell swung his sword down. . .

. . .and was flung half way back across the cavern skidding along the rough ground as if an invisible force had repelled him.

He grunted as he hit the ground hard. He growled in pain and anger and was about to strike again, but an upraised arm from Alpha stopped him.

"Who are you and how long have you been following us?" Alpha Rion commanded.

After the shock of her discovery and attack, the woman stood before them quite calmly. She lowered her bright bow, which shimmered out of existence

"Forgive my intrusion, gentlemen," she said in a soft and accented voice, "but your tête-à-tête intrigued me. I couldn't help but to listen in."

Her smile had both Alpha Rion and Gordell captivated.

"I asked who you were," Alpha Rion repeated, staring intently into her dark eyes.

With a slight hesitation, weighing up the situation, she answered.

"My name is Tera ZaVoir. I have been aware of you two for some time, but I was only following you from today. I was in the forest,

73

too!"

Alpha Rion almost asked about his dream, but thought better of it. *No need to embarrass myself,* he thought.

Tera looked and smiled knowingly at him, Alpha Rion feeling his cheeks grow hot.

"Tera ZaVoir?" repeated Gordell in surprise, recovering from his ungraceful landing. His eyes widened in awe at her. "Mon Dieu, forgive my attack upon you. My brethren have spoken of you: The Archeress. They praise you highly—for a woman," he ended.

Tera took no offense at his slight, but Alpha Rion did.

"Gordell, you dishonour this woman with your remarks . . ."

But Tera defended him. "Gordell means no offense, Alpha Rion, for those Earthly enemies of the Exmoors, the Devouts, are women who worship the Lore!"

Alpha Rion's mouth opened in disbelief. "How could that be? How can anyone worship the Lore?"

"It's a long story," confirmed Gordell. "And we don't have time to tell it now. But I am honoured to meet you for myself, Tera ZaVoir." He bowed slightly, grimacing while trying in a dignified manner to disguise some pain or another from his fall. "But why are you here?"

"The same thing that brought you two here: Valtare! He is not just your enemy, but an enemy to this world. He is one who will bring destruction for his own satisfaction. And he is mine to deal with, alone," Tera said, darkly.

Alpha Rion and Gordell glanced at each other. They both wanted to ask the same question, but Tera answered it for them.

"Valtare is of my people."

"Of course he is!" remarked Gordell as is this was the most natural thing.

"And they are?" asked a perplexed Alpha Rion, wondering how someone like Tera could be like Valtare.

Tera smiled. "That's difficult to answer. I am human by birth, but my people were visited millennia ago by an otherworldly race called the Chryrians. They were creatures of the mind, but were dying after an exhaustive war with the ones called the Lore."

Alpha Rion digested this information. The Lore had caused no end of misery and destruction to countless worlds.

Tera continued, "Many Chryrians escaped, eventually discovering Earth, and in time bonded with many humans, including my people in order to survive. This endowed us with their psi abilities. I left my people to explore the world, leaving behind my two brothers. I should not have." Her last words sounded sad.

"When I returned, I found that my village had been destroyed and everyone was dead, but I could not find my brothers. I believe that they are still alive and that they will know who was responsible for the destruction!"

Tera looked at Gordell in accusation, but he shook his head.

"We Exmoors had no part in that, Tera. The Purges came much later."

Tera's eyes tightened at Gordell, but accepted his response.

Alpha Rion wanted to know more, but Gordell explained.

"Some of the human-Chryrians were dangerous. We Exmoors, along with the Astrals dealt with it." Gordell left it at that feeling the hot glare of Tera upon him.

Tera carried on with her story. "So, I have been searching for my brothers over the centuries without any luck. Then I sensed another like me, a human-Chryrian. I thought that I had found a brother. But I found evil. Valtare must have bonded with a Chryrian at some point in time. He is very dangerous and must be confronted by one of his own. His psi powers are quite strong!" Her face was one of determination.

"No, Tera, we have a common enemy that we can defeat together," Gordell pledged.

Alpha Rion agreed, "Gordell's right. And with my brother, Decion, who is at Valtare's castle, the four of us can surely defeat Valtare."

He found Tera regarding him closely.

"You remind me of my brother, Aranu," she said. "So forthright, yet compassionate." Alpha Rion felt his heart quicken. "I must confess

Alpha Rion, that in your sleep, I heard you call for your sister. You must miss her as much as I miss my brothers."

She was quiet for a while, scrutinising the two men in front of her.

"Okay, you may accompany me on my mission, if only so that you can return to your sister," she grinned at Alpha Rion. "And Gordell, it will be a pleasure to work with the Exmoors again."

"*Bon*, so the three of us then," Gordell stated.

"Four, with my brother," Alpha Rion said. "But first we have to get Tera a weapon."

Tera and Gordell laughed.

"What's so funny?" asked Alpha Rion.

"You!" Tera grinned.

"Wasn't you bow just a holograph?"

"No, my weapons are up here." She tapped her head. "The psi bow is just as effective as any material weapon. And so is my psi shield, hence. . ."

She looked at Gordell, who still nursed a bruised ego. And wanted to forget about it quickly.

"Ah." Alpha Rion understood.

Tera asked, "Your name, does it not mean 'first among hunters'?"

Alpha Rion nodded, astonished at her knowledge.

"So where is your weapon?" she asked.

Alpha Rion held up his hands. "Right here," he smirked in reply.

Tera laughed again, a beautiful sound, thought Alpha Rion. He found himself staring at her and her at him.

Gordell broke the spell, scrabbling up walls retrieving all his crystals and placing them in a belt pouch.

"*Bon,* mes amis, what's the plan?"

"We take the castle!" Tera and Alpha Rion intoned together.

Gordell rolled his eyes. This was going to be some adventure.

The Marquis Edgar de la Valtare was of the French aristocracy, or so everyone believed. As far as anyone knew, he had been born in his father's manor and after his father's untimely death, had grown up to become an even wealthier landowner rebuilding the manor's fortifications and commander of his own private army of mercenary knights.

However, what no one knew was that Valtare was also one of the last humans during the early Bronze Age Europe to have merged with a Chryrian. Now he possessed formidable mental powers.

He had never forgotten his life as a a nomadic hunter in the northern lands, long ago, when malevolent spirits had swept across his territory. He had tried to run amid the fir trees and across the frozen lake, but even as the ice had cracked and he had sunk to the bottom of the lake. One of the spirits had possessed him. Saved him. He had been resurrected, a new man. The ordeal had almost sent Valtare to the brink of insanity, killing several tribes in his efforts to excise the demon within him. But over several decades, he learned to live with it or it had become dormant. He lived as a farmer, a metallurgist, an Iron Age warrior, and a learned man, utilising his powers to travel across the known Old World and elevate himself in society.

But foremost he had dabbled in the black arts, if only to quell his demons; to take the lives of those who would not follow him or those who wanted his power. Valtare believed himself to be God on Earth, though he had never been a religious man.

His journeys had brought him into contact with a secret sisterhood, the Devouts. Oft he would avoid them for they seemed hostile to men, but on a particular visit to France he had met and fallen in love with Elisabeth Van Tager, the daughter of the leader of the Devouts. She had shown him how to govern his rage and powers, to focus his ambitions. He had listened to their histories and showed his own. His now wife had then revealed to him the secret of the sisterhood. They were in possession of a mysterious blue stone, half the size of a human head. The Devouts claimed the nearly-translucent stone helped to nurture their powers.

The Devouts inhabited an entire village of their own—all women, where men were slaves. Valtare had no compunction against lesser men being enslaved.

The Devouts claimed to be in contact with a god from another world. Naturally, Valtare had scoffed at this. So they had showed him. He attended several Devout ceremonies where he was promised enlightenment. But nothing happened. However, on the fifth night their dark lord had unceremoniously yanked Valtare from one dimension into a mysterious realm. Though always in the shadows and unseen by Valtare, this lord of the stars had told Valtare things; the history of the Earth, her peoples, the universe, and of things to come. It had changed Valtare's life. He was no God on Earth. The Devout's lord was far more powerful. And he gave Valtare a purpose. From then on Valtare had pledged his life to the lord and the lord had promised him that salvation would soon be at hand.

And it was upon the arrival of Decion and Alpha Rion that Valtare thought events would materialise as the lord had promised, but they had not. Alpha Rion was not with them. He couldn't decipher Decion's and Alpha Rion's thoughts properly, probably because of their nature, but he could sense Alpha Rion's antipathy toward him. He was also suspicious of Guillaume de Roth. He had a very complex mind for a simple human knight, which was why Guillaume had been chosen for his retinue in the first place. But now Valtare was having doubts. There were things about Guillaume which did not add up. And he intended to find out why that was.

But even now, as he kept his enemies close to him, he felt something else; someone lurking on the edge of his mind. He felt he was being hunted. And Valtare couldn't have that. Not now.

"Time for a change in plan," he muttered to himself.

He concentrated, sending out a telepathic message, knowing his master would receive it.

He was on the eve of his greatest hour. Standing in the great hall, he toasted his wife's portrait with a goblet of dark wine.

"My dear Elisabeth, where are you now?" He drained the glass and threw it into the flames of the fire place. "L'Coyle!" he shouted for his knight.

The unflappable knight appeared moments later, wiping sweat from his face, training in the courtyard.

"Yes, my lord." His tone noted he knew something was wrong.

Without turning from his wife's portrait, Valtare said, "Round up the villagers. It's time!"

Tera chose to ride with Alpha Rion. The two were becoming close friends, a deep bond already developing between them.

"So where are you from?" Tera asked Alpha Rion, her arms clasped tightly around his waist.

A wistful sigh escaped Alpha Rion's lips.

"Another world," he confessed. "I don't know where it is in relation to Earth, but one day I hope to return home." He related the tales from Magna Aura leading up to when he and Decion had been stolen from Alphatron City-State after the Lore war. He cursed the Astrals again.

Gordell had suddenly stopped the horses at that point. The track was still muddy, but the smell of the trees and calls of the birds was pleasant enough. But Gordell looked annoyed.

"Not all Astrals are so callous, Alpha Rion," he said brusquely. "They must have had a reason for this. I am sorry you were treated this way."

Alpha Rion nodded understanding. "Well at least the three of us are united, whatever happens!" he tried to lighten the mood.

Gordell grunted in agreement, having tried his best to exonerate the Astrals. Spurring his horse on he rode on somewhat sulkily.

As they neared the castle, the conversation vanished as Tera had to concentrate on concealing her presence from Valtare whom she suspected was somewhat aware of her presence. They had to be careful.

The plan, formulated along the way, was for Alpha Rion and Gordell to distract Valtare long enough for Tera to attack. Alpha Rion would deal with Decion, whether he was with them or not. Alpha Rion had remembered his training sessions with his brother. It was tough enough when he had Astara by his side, but alone. . .

Please be with us, Decion, he beseeched silently.

They were still some miles out, when Alpha Rion, through his donned visor, spotted something in the distance.

"Look," he called out in alarm, pointing toward the scene.

Thick, black smoke was rising from the direction of Valtare's castle.

The three looked at each other in shock.

Could someone have beaten us to the attack? Alpha Rion thought.

"Hah!" Gordell urged his stallion into a gallop followed by Alpha Rion and Tera.

Their pace became more urgent, the situation more tense as they rode on, all attempts at concealment over.

"Do you think Decion became wary of Valtare and attacked?" Gordell shouted across to them over the noise of the horses.

"I don't know," Tera responded. "I can't sense anything. Either way, this will surely undermine Valtare's security; maybe enough to give us an advantage."

They galloped up the hill that led to the flat, grassy plain, which held the castle and surrounding village. The castle looked destroyed. The village certainly was with fires still burning. Homes and market stalls were broken and ransacked. And deserted, too. They found no one at all.

"What could have happened?" Gordell struggled to control his horse, which was jittery, stamping and rearing up. Gordell stroked the top of its head and the horse calmed somewhat, but it didn't want to stay in the village.

Tera shook her head. "I do not sense anyone. They're all gone!"

"Or dead," Alpha Rion said ominously.

"Let's go," Gordell recommended.

They rode on with a cautious, but quickening pace up the muddy road to the castle.

Gordell and Alpha Rion drew the horses to a halt before the half-destroyed drawbridge and dismounted. They balanced their way over the remaining rickety drawbridge planks and into the courtyard, followed by Tera. There they found only more devastation and ruin.

They were beginning to think there was nothing left.

Then Gordell had seen something.

He suddenly drew his sword and with a battle-cry rushed toward the burnt-out chapel where he had seen a bright flash of light.

Alpha Rion and Tera reacted, but too late. Before they could stop him, Gordell had disappeared into the light. And vanished. The light flickered out of existence.

Stunned, they ran to the spot where Gordell had disappeared, a portal.

Alpha Rion could only vent his anger: "What in the name of the Universe is going on?" he screamed up into the darkening sky, which was visible through the chapel's collapsed roof. He felt as if the eyes of the gods were closed leaving mortals to fend for themselves.

Where was everyone? Valtare? Decion?

"It makes no sense!" he uttered, angrily.

He ran around the ruined castle searching in vain for anyone, but they had all gone; Decion, Valtare, the knights, the horses, the villagers, everyone. He returned to the courtyard where Tera had remained.

She confirmed his view.

"There was a reason I could not sense anyone," she said, sadly. "They're all gone. . ."

She pointed to the chapel's interior, where among the blackened fallen roof timbers were the unmistakeable forms of many charred bodies.

Alpha Rion looked away in disgust. They had failed in their mission.

"Now what do we do?" Alpha Rion wanted to know.

Tera looked up at the sky. "It'll be dark soon, but I'm determined to find out what had happened. I'll stay the night just in case anyone, especially Gordell, returns."

Alpha Rion had no choice but to stay, not that he had anywhere else to go, but they both knew no one would return.

Tera continued, "Let's stay until morning. If nothing changes we will seek out the rest of the Exmoors, tell them what happened here, and decide a new course of action."

Feeling somewhat helpless, Alpha Rion could only agree.

Heading back across the broken drawbridge, they retrieved their saddles and packs unloading what food and supplies they had for the night. Alpha Rion had caught a rabbit while Tera had collected what unburnt food there was in the kitchens and from around assorted overturned tables. They supped quickly and quietly as the moon rose over a crumbled stone wall.

Meal over they set up rough grass beds in the corner of a half-intact smithy's forge, Tera could see Alpha Rion was still unsettled. She put a hand on his shoulder.

"We are like grains of sand in a storm-swept desert. Bigger things are in motion around us. I wish I could see it." She sounded sad, her voice lost in memories centuries old.

Alpha Rion could only sympathise with her. She'd been alone for so long.

"Thank you!" he said.

He hugged her, Tera's arms wrapping around his shoulders, their bodies pressed together. They felt their hearts beat as one, the world and their troubles melting away. They belonged to and with each other. And when they kissed, their souls ignited in passion, which carried them away in complete ecstasy. And the moon and stars watched as Alpha Rion knew love for the first time.

It was only at first light that they realised they weren't alone.

Alpha Rion shot awake, surprised by the intruder sitting on a stool outside the stables across from them. Even though he didn't recognise the newcomer's red and gold uniform, he knew who she was.

He roared in anger, hands dug into two shining portals as he rushed the intruder with two unsheathed swords, even though he was fully naked. But he was forcibly knocked to the ground, repelled by the temporal force-shield that blocked his path.

"You! Astral!" he snarled from the ground, as the pain wore off. "What have you done to us? Where are they?"

Lightstream regarded him. It had taken her an age to find Alpha

Rion. She thought he would be grateful, but she hadn't expected accusations and attack. Her gray eyes tried not to look down. The woman behind him—dark, as naked, alert, and ready for action, was also quite beautiful.

Two warriors in love, thought Lightstream. *Great! But I have a job to do.*

She inhaled and breathed out slowly. "I am Lightstream," she introduced herself, still averting her eyes, trying not to feel embarrassed or frightened. "You and Decion were taken from Magna Aura and brought here by forces unknown, though we suspect errant Astrals are at fault. They are not working with us. Earth in the future is in danger. We needed the Starguards to protect Earth, while the Astrals protected the rest of the uni . . ."

"You have no right!" Alpha Rion interrupted. He was slowly getting to his feet.

Lightstream blushed as he did, letting the wind blow her blonde hair across her face to hide it. Following her father's urgent wishes, she had continued looking for Alpha Rion and Decion. It seemed hopeless for a while, but on a hunch she had explored possible destinations and happily detected a temporal signature in Earth's past, which didn't belong there. She had tracked it down in order to rescue the two missing Starguards, only to find one of them post-coital and threatening her. Not an ideal rescue situation. She tried another tact.

"You're right. We do not, but we had no other choice. The universe rules our ways, but the forces of chaos are changing the order. And I'm sorry, Alpha Rion, but we cannot stand by and not fight. We cannot die sleeping in bliss while darkness roams at will!"

That seemed to have caught their attention, especially Alpha Rion, who just stood there, still naked; the words starting to sink in.

"What has happened here?" Lightstream asked, trying to bring some semblance of order.

Alpha Rion explained his and Decion's adventures over the past few weeks since arriving on Earth.

"So this Valtare wants to start a war or at least his master does, a war to remake the universe?"

"Yes," Tera confirmed.

"Now he has my brother and our friend. I need to find and help them," Alpha Rion said.

With a slow shake of her head, the Astral replied, "I'm sorry, Alpha Rion. I truly am. We Astrals can feel the war ahead, but I do not know where Decion is. That's why we will now need you. I am here to take you to the others in Earth's future!"

"What? Why Earth's future?" an astounded Alpha Rion shouted. "Why not back to Magna Aura? Take me home!"

Lightstream shook her head again. "I cannot take you home. Cirrius seems to have erected a temporal shield around Magna Aura. Even I cannot penetrate it." Which from the pain look on her face really did bother her. "Until such time, I cannot return you home."

She did not mention the battle with Netherlord which cost Zane's life, the fact she had seen unknown spaceships on the outskirts of the Magna Aura system, or more importantly that the supposedly dead Synther and the Lore had attacked and almost destroyed the Chronopolis, saved at the cost of Spheron's life.

No sense in confusing the situation, she sighed to herself.

"Okay, okay, so when do we leave," a resigned Alpha Rion waled over to Tera.

Lightstream cocked her head, as if listening to something.

"Ah, now actually. In fact, I'm receiving a signal from the future."

"From when?" Tera asked.

"The twenty-first century. . ." She hesitated and craned her head in the other direction. "Oh, strange, and an urgent signal from the Chronopolis! We have to hurry!" she said to Alpha Rion.

Alpha Rion started to protest, but Tera stopped him.

"Maybe it was fate that brought us here together," she tried to reassure her.

"I'm not sure I want to go," he replied, half turning to look at Tera.

"You must, Alpha Rion," pleaded Lightstream. "Earth's future is in grave danger. The others need you."

84

"And my sister, Astara?"

"She's . . . waiting for you," Lightstream lied. In truth she didn't know the fate of anyone else from Magna Aura.

Alpha Rion looked dubious. "But . . ." he began, looking at Tera.

Tera walked over to him, putting a finger on his lips, "You must go," she said, agreeing with Lightstream.

"Then come with me," he urged, looking over to Lightstream for acceptance.

But the Astral shook her head. Alpha Rion's temper rose, but it was Tera who responded.

"I cannot come, though I want to, Alpha Rion. I have my own quest; for my brothers and my people. I cannot let them down or I shall fail within myself. Go! And I will see you again in the future. I promise. Just remember me," she whispered the last words.

Alpha Rion grasped Tera by the shoulders ready to protest again, but one look into Tera's deep brown eyes convinced him otherwise. He kissed her, the passion flaring again. Then he let go.

"Armour on."

His manoeuvre suit enveloped him, Tera caressing the alien material in curiosity. He reluctantly walked over to Lightstream, giving her a hard glare that would have made even Decion proud.

"Take me to them," he ordered.

Lightstream nodded and bid farewell to Tera.

Tera glared back at Lightstream.

"Take care of him, Astral!"

Lightstream nodded. "I will!"

And even as Alpha Rion's and Tera's eyes met in goodbye, the two disappeared in a flash of light.

Tera was all alone, again. But now she had more to look forward to. Valtare was gone. And now she could concentrate on finding her brothers and reuniting with her love, Alpha Rion, in the future.

Tera got dressed and left the courtyard. She tip-toed her way across the drawbridge, and mounted the horse she and Alpha Rion had shared. As Tera trotted through the village, she stopped.

Out of hearing range, but within her mind's eye, Tera could sense riders approaching. They were coming for her.

"Oh, now what?" she sighed.

CHAPTER SIX

"Sorry!" gasped a flustered Zane.

She had her back to the ruined computers, sparks flying from the racked servers and screens joined by the overhead lights rapidly flashing on and off. They all contrived to cast flickering eerie shadows across the darkened room.

Altair stood about ten feet away, confused whether to blow apart a girl in a dusty pink waitress uniform. His hands still glowed red, adding to the weirdness of the light.

An awkward tension spread between them.

"Who are you?" Bastian shouted.

Zane hesitated, "Okay, umm, my name is Zane, er. . . Aristedes. Zane Aristedes and I want to join the Starguards," she smiled at them, trying on her charm.

"You have powers, girl? How did you come by them?" Bastian asked, hand ready on his pistol grip, suspicion punching his senses. *How could she get in here?* he asked himself.

"Born with them," Zane answered, eyes widening at the rising hostility from the two men in front of her. She tried to remain non-threatening.

"So you're a Devout," Bastian was glad she had admitted it, he had no doubt now, "Sent to spy on us. Deal with her, Altair!"

Obeying, Altair raised his hands, red energy already pouring forth.

"No!" yelled Zane desperately, not wanting to die again, feeling a surge of power within her.

Altair's energy hit Zane in the chest.

"Ahh!" she reacted, eyes squeezed shut, anticipating pain. . .

But the energy dissipated off her as if absorbed by some forcefield.

Zane looked herself over, not sure what had happened. Were her powers really manifesting themselves?

Altair and Bastian glanced bewildered at each other, wondering what to do next. Altair wanted another go, his hands already glowing with deadly energy.

But Zane had had enough. She'd been blasted with energy one too many times already and she didn't want her life ruined again. She came clean.

"Enough Altair, I think we've both proved our point. And as for you," she addressed Bastian, who she thought looked a bit like one of the old Hollywood stars Heston or Douglas, "I'm not sure which Exmoor you are and you probably won't recognise me, not like this," she pointed to her waitress uniform, "but I'm Zane, the daughter of Xathanius, Lord Aeon of the Astrals!"

"Pah!" Altair snorted derisively, "Another whelp of the cowards who stole us away. Prove who you say you are!" He clenched his fists, ready for a fight.

"I think I already have," Zane said, looking pensively around the room. "Which was an accident, by the way," she said, hands up, apologising to Bastian. "I seem to have problems around computers. I send them into overdrive or something." She smiled, hoping it would ease the situation.

"That still doesn't tell us why you're here," Bastian said, still suspicious. We were not told you were arriving."

"Or that we believe you," Altair added.

There was a commotion outside as the rest of the Starguards and some security officers arrived, Aerl's energy providing enough of a glow from his hands.

"So, again, what are you doing here?" Bastian raised his voice. "And if you are an Astral, then why can't the other Astrals come here?"

They all turned to look at Zane, who blushed deeply under the intense scrutiny.

"You can look me up in the files. I know the Astrals gave you Exmoors files on us to help identify us, our allies and enemies!" she said hopefully.

Bastian smiled. "That they did and they are being checked now."

He hoped.

"There's no need," Aerl stated, "My suit's crystalator recorded all of your files. I've compared her features and though there are slight differences, it is her, Zane the Astral."

Zane sighed in relief, and the room also lightened up in mood as the others relaxed, even Altair.

"Look," Zane said, "Sorry for all the mess and confusion, but I came here to download info onto my crystalator," she held it up, "and to find out what was happening before I revealed myself to you. My energy blew your systems and then your security guys attacked me, I defended myself, non-lethally, I might add, and now we're here."

Exasperation in his voice, Bastian repeated, "But you still haven't answered why you are here?" His impatience was at breaking point.

Zane took a deep breath. She wasn't sure how much she could tell, so she started at the end of her life.

"Okay, here it is in a nutshell. After the battle at Magna Aura, my father went missing, so my brother, Aristedes, and I went searching for him." She skirted around the twenty-third century Earth-Axalan war issue. "Then we found out that my father's evil cousin Netherlord was on a planet-killing rampage and we fought him. He attacked me, I expected to die, but I ended up here on Earth, way in the past. Been here for just over a year. First, I ended up for some reason in Oregon and then Arizona . . ."

"Oregon?" repeated Bastian.

Zane nodded confirmation.

Bastian let out a gruff sigh, looking at the others.

"We monitor the Earth for usual energy signatures, Astral, Devout, or otherwise and there was a temporal spike around that area about that time. We investigated, but found nothing."

He looked hard into Zane's eyes, his own narrowed in thought.

"Well, that was probably me," Zane confirmed. "Like I said, I don't know how it happened. I was placed in a psychiatric hospital for two months, which I had to escape from and then I found myself in

Arizona. Got a job as a waitress and called myself Zane Aristedes. I don't know how I ended up on Earth, but I don't think it's a coincidence . . ."

And just then, another coincidence walked in.

"Oh my God, Simon," Zane laughed with relief; glad to see a familiar face.

Everyone turned to Simon, whose face was a picture of innocence.

"Um, do I know you?" the confused Exmoor asked.

But Zane persisted, "It was years ago or rather years from now, I was a few years younger, had black hair," she ruffled her hair to shake his memory.

"Years ago?" snapped Altair. "You Astrals just took us away from Magna Aura, mere moments after our victory. And that was a year ago!" He glared down at her, though his hands had stopped glowing.

"Oh!" Zane was confused. Time travelling was confusing, especially when it was against your will. She didn't know what to say.

"Who are you? What's going on?" Simon asked; growing more than a little disconcerted that a random waitress knew him.

"It's me, Zane!" And then she realised, really realised, where and when she was. "Ohmygod, oh god! This isn't good!"

"What's wrong?" Bastian asked. "And how do you know my son?"

"Your son?" Zane's eyes widened in shock. "Oh god, I really shouldn't be here!" She started to panic, pacing up and down the room.

Altair stomped forth and grabbed her. "What are you doing, Astral? Is this some sort of trick?" He shook her, his temper rising.

Bastian and Aerl rushed over, pulling Altair away, while Azure ran over to Zane to comfort her.

"Okay, everyone listen up," Bastian ordered. "We're all going back upstairs to Ops. Deb, take Zane to med and get her checked out."

"I'm okay. Just a little time-shocked," Zane interjected, though she sounded tired.

"Okay, then. Come with us," Bastian said against his better judgement, but they needed answers. "Michael," he addressed the leading armed security officer, "get the engineers in and start fixing things. I want full power ASAP."

The officer nodded and trotted off to find a conscious engineer.

It was a long trudge upstairs for some, those who couldn't fly, but once upstairs, they convene in the boardroom.

"You expect us to believe that this is a coincidence?" Qane started the inquest, when he had been introduced to Zane. "That both you and the Starguards showed up on Earth around a year ago? And why you, when the other Astrals couldn't stay, because their powers would alert the Lore?" he added.

Zane sat at one end of the long boardroom table, while the Exmoors and Starguards sat on either side, with Bastian at the head.

"Like I said," Zane defended herself again. "I don't know how I got here. I should be dead; I couldn't have escaped Netherlord's blast, which is exactly the same reason why I won't attract the Lore. I have no real Astral powers, except when I'm defending myself, like with Altair's attack."

Zane looked at Altair for some support, but he turned his head away, though more out of embarrassment for not having dealt with a young girl. She let that fact hang in the air for a while. There were glances around the table.

She continued, "Isn't that in the file, Bastian?" Zane asked Bastian.

He sat stroking his beard and looking through a leather-bound book, a copy of an original gift from Xathanius, an abridged History of the Celestians and an appended file on the Astrals. He looked up at her, a twinkle in his eye of acknowledgement.

"There, I cannot travel through time, at least not in the typical sense. I can travel laterally through time, really quick, run faster than anything, run through time; yes, but not between time. So my powers won't attract the Lore."

That part settled, Qane was quelled for the moment. His chin rested upon his hands which cradled his cane's top.

Bastian then asked, "Zane, you know my son, Simon. How?"

All eyes were on Zane again.

Zane hesitated. She already felt unfairly persecuted, having to jump through hoops to prove herself. But what could she say? All she could remember was what Aristedes had said, that the universe has its own way of sifting and balancing time. But maybe she was here to change that. This couldn't be a coincidence. Someone, an Astral, maybe Lightstream, must have rescued her from Netherlord and sent her to Earth to save the Starguards. But why?

"Zane?" Bastian softly prompted again.

"This is just so confusing," Zane said, looking up at the ceiling, wishing Aristedes could come and rescue her. She missed him so much, and the others from her adventures in the twenty-third century Lynn Kellis, Aaron the ancient telepath, Starshina the winter goddess, the strange alien Solitude, and Lieutenant Paolo. *Poor Paolo.* She had never told him the truth or given him his answer to his proposal. But now she had to give other answers:

"I think someone, probably one of my people must have sent me here, but I don't know. As to why . . ." she hesitated again.

She looked at Simon, sitting beside his father and made a decision.

"But what the hay! Simon, I met you in the twenty-third century, during the war . . ."

There was a commotion, which she silenced quickly.

"That much I will say, but I'm not here because of that . . ."

She pursed her lips, not wanting to say anything else, but it was too late now and it could save lives. "I think I'm here because sometime in the near future . . ." she paused and closed her eyes, before saying, "the Starguards are going to die!"

You could have heard a pin drop.

Eleven months ago

Zane woke up—suddenly, like a bolt of energy had struck her into being. From what and from where she didn't know.

Peering around, she found herself in a stark white room, strapped to a bed with tubes in her nose and arms. Initially she thought she was on Home, her last memory, but the simple technology made her think again. Then in hazy flashes, her life had caught up to her and she remembered what had happened. Kind of . . .

The blast from Netherlord had hit her, enveloping her in anti-chroniton energy; Netherlord's energy de-temporalised objects, disintegrating them from time and space or reforming to his will. Zane had expected to die. But here she didn't know if she was living in hell or otherwise. And why was she strapped to a bed?

She had tried to call out, but her throat was so dry, the penetrating tubes uncomfortable. She tried moving around, but the straps cut into her and she panicked as she wriggled around trying to get loose. Zane cried out in pain, her pleas dampened by the padded white walls of the small room. She thrashed around more, trying to raise one shoulder and then the next, but she was too tired. She slumped down, Zane feeling betrayed by her body, already an Astral cripple, now as useless as a dead girl.

Just as Zane was beginning to think that this was to be her afterlife; one long death strapped to a bed, definite hell for an Astral, she heard a noise. Her head shot over to the door, a small window set high in the centre. A face appeared; human, female.

Thank god, Zane thought.

She heard a key being turned in the lock and a male and female entered, their white clothing indicating they were medical staff. They stood back and stared at Zane who stared back at them, wide-eyed not knowing what to expect.

She smiled. "Hello," she said rather hoarsely as much as she could with the tube up her nose, "I'm Zane. What am I doing here?"

There was a moment's hesitation as her visitors seem to rigorously assess her, following by a palpable sense of relief.

"Hello Zane, you had us worried for a while," the man spoke in a soft voice as with a child. "I'm Doctor Faziz and this is nurse Howlett. How are you feeling?" Faziz's slight Indian accent, carried a genuine sympathetic tone.

Zane produced a wan smile, "Fine, except being strapped to the bed." She wriggled her fingers for effect.

The doctor and nurse exchanged glances, Howlett seemingly more than a bit nervous. It was only then that Zane noticed the bandage on the nurse's arm. Howlett stared at her, hard accusation and acute fear in her eyes.

"Did I do that?" Zane was horrified that she would have hurt someone like that.

Howlett nodded, "You came in fighting, punching hard, shouting things, like weird stuff, you know. You took out a few others, much worse than me." She tried to look brave, but her skin was pale and her voice a bit shaky.

Zane could only shake her head in sorrow. "I'm so sorry," she said, wondering what she could have done to end up like this. "What happened to me? What did I do?" was all she could ask.

"We were hoping you could tell us," Faziz said, fussing over a chart by Zane's bed.

Zane pulled a blank face, looking at the bland white ceiling. "I have no idea how I got here or what happened," she fudged the last part. "Um, this might seem a silly question, but what year is this?"

Faziz gave her a strange look, "Year?"

"Yes, please," Zane said, calmly, trying to raise her head and smile, "Things are a bit fuzzy."

"Well, you're in the same year that you were admitted two months ago, two thousand fifteen."

"Twenty fifteen?"

Oh, my god, over two hundred years! Zane fought down the panic within her. *What was happening to her?*

"Okay, thanks." What else could she say? "Um, could I have these taken off me?" She raised her restricted hands as much she could, giving them her winning smile.

Howlett looked at Faziz, who nodded.

"Sam?" Howlett yelled through the door.

Zane's eyes widened until they hurt as the biggest man she had ever seen walked in. Built like a wrestler, muscles bulged from muscles beneath his white uniform, with a sharp crew-cut upon a square head. Sam was a physical monster. But what caught Zane's attention was the splint upon his nose and the menacing glare from his beady eyes, one of which was blackened.

"Did I do that, too?" Zane asked meekly.

Sam grunted. No hint of a 'no-big-deal-smile'.

"You were really, really, fighting, so strong!" reiterated Howlett.

"I'm very, very sorry, I won't do that again, promise," Zane really did promise.

Sam just looked at her and then at his superiors. Reluctantly he came over with the keys to unlock her cuffs. He stared straight into her eyes, daring her to make a move again, but Zane lay as quiet and as still as possible, staring only at the ceiling. She wasn't going to give anyone an excuse to try something. Or they'd be the ones to get hurt.

One by one the cuffs came off, straps were unfastened, and Sam backed away, all the while keeping an eye on Zane. He stood behind Faziz and Howlett, a massive back stop should she try to escape.

Then Howlett had come over and detached the tubes from her arms and nose. Zane rubbed her wrists and then tried to sit up, her head feeling woozy.

"Whoa," she cried, holding her head.

"Take it easy Zane, you're still full of drugs. For some reason your body just rejected them all so we had to put some pretty strong stuff into you," Howlett said. "You're one tough cookie for a little gal. We didn't think you would make it."

You don't know the half of it, Zane thought. *Gosh, what did they put into me?* She knew though that her Astral system would flush it out or burn it up.

"You said I was here for two months already? How'd I end up here?" she asked.

Doctor Faziz answered before Howlett, dragging a chair over to Zane's bedside.

"You were found out in the deep woods by a couple of hunters. You're in Oregon by the way, the Blue Mountain Psychiatric Centre, and you were half-dead from exposure after an attack or something, wearing a purple costume and ready to fight the world. It was lucky you were found at all, the hunters reported some kind of bright light in your vicinity and it was the police who air-lifted you in, since you were obviously in an agitated state. You have no idea how you got there?" he tried not to sound suspicious.

Zane shook her head, "None," said in her most innocent voice.

"Do you take drugs or was anything given to you? Were you attacked?"

Zane shook her head.

"Well you've healed physically," Faziz confirmed. "Do you have a last name? Any family in the area? We cannot find you on social security or any DNA and ID databases, none. The police still want to talk to you, too."

"Oh, I, er, Zane . . . Kellis, that's my name," she cringed at using Lynn's name. "And no, no family at all that I know of." She could only tell what she knew.

"And no recollection of what happened immediately before you were in the woods?" Faziz was concerned, still probing for memories.

"None," Zane said as she tried to purge all thoughts of the twenty-third century in a bid to seem more believable.

Faziz's brow furrowed. "Okay, I'll have to recommend a psychiatric course of treatment. See if we can get those stubborn memories back." He gave a doctor's smile of reassurance, which didn't reassure Zane. She needed to get out of wherever she was before they started poking around in her head.

But for now she just smiled and nodded her head, "Okay."

Faziz stood up, saying, "Zane, we're going to leave you in here for a while, while we sort you out a new room, more pleasant and roomy.

Are you hungry?" he asked.

Zane nodded. She was starving.

"Okay, hold tight. Anything in particular?"

Zane wasn't sure what people ate normally in this time, so she shook her head.

Faziz smiled and looked at Howlett.

"No worries, I'll get you something nice." Howlett left the room.

"Just as a precaution, Zane, Sam will be waiting just outside, in case you need anything."

Sam gave her what Zane could only describe as a downright dirty sneer.

As if, Zane thought.

"That's fine. I'm not going anywhere," she answered, demurely.

A wicked thought passed through her mind as she thought about racing out of the room at Astral speed. She could be anywhere around the world in minutes. If only she could see the looks on their faces. She lay back down on the bed, exasperated at the ordeal she was going through.

"Good to have you fit and healthy, physically, now let's get your mind up to scratch," Faziz said on his way out.

Sam just grunted, jutting his chin upwards at her. Although he shut the door, it wasn't locked, though Zane knew Sam would be outside, his massive arms folded like the Himalayas ready to unleash the force of an earthquake should she decided to leave. So Zane just laid back and got some rest. The war was over for her.

Zane ran.

She had no other option after three months of being cooped up. The police had interviewed her multiple times and taken her back to the scene of her 'discovery' on the chance of memory flashes. There was nothing unusual at the overgrown scene. Surrounded by thousands of giant fir and pine trees Zane sensed nothing. She had no recollection of anything (or arriving) and police reports and medical procedures had seemed to back her up.

As if such crude instruments would have worked on me, Zane thought.

Luckily, Zane had asked for and got back her 'costume' from the police, checking to see if the imbedded crystalators were still intact before detaching them from her Multiforce manoeuvre suit and keeping them on her person. Falling into the hands of twentieth-century humans, the crystalators' knowledge would have been catastrophic, not that they could have decoded the crystalator's encryptions. But Zane wasn't taking any chances.

She'd been trusted enough to leave her room and mix with other patients, all of whom shrunk away from her in the common room.

"Your reputation precedes you," Sam humourlessly remarked in a surprisingly high-pitched voice as he had escorted her through the corridors to the common room.

Zane scrunched her face together, "Not good," she whispered to herself. She walked past various characters, all mad to some degree.

God, I am in the depths of hell here.

Then she saw the windows and had to have a look at her surroundings. She was disappointed to see that the centre was located in a fenced enclosure encircled by snow-capped mountains and thick woods. A single paved road snaked out through the trees.

Within the common room were posters of scenes from around America. One which stuck out to Zane was Arizona, home of the Grand Canyon, as she was told by an old woman who had once lived in that state and who often told Zane about her former life in a little town called Mesa Flats. That simple life sounded good to Zane, especially after Doctor Faziz had told her that they were keeping her in for more tests. Zane had had enough and that night she planned her escape.

Although Zane could not truly travel time, her power allowed her to move at great speed, though not in the normal sense. Aristedes had called it temporal-popping, where Zane could teleport short distances at velocity, which allowed Zane to 'run' through objects.

It was easy enough to escape her erstwhile medicated incarceration. And she wasted no time in finding Mesa Flats, making a new life for herself as Zane Aristedes, until the Starguards had arrived six months later.

And now she was telling them they were going to die . . .

"Die? The Astrals brought us here to die?" Altair rose abruptly from the table, looking for something to hit.

"No," shouted Zane. "It's something written in the history books. There was a big explosion in New York, the Thane building, and you were all in it, except no bodies were found. . . well, Starguard bodies at least! But that was one possible past," she tried to convince them, "and now that I'm here, maybe I'm here to change that," she hoped.

Silence answered her.

But Bastian was intrigued. "The Thane building, you say, Zane? Tell us more."

Zane could only shrug. "That's it. I wasn't a big reader of history, I know, silly for a time traveller!" she made a face, "Though this time began the end of the so-called Age of the Superhero, which barely lasted ten years, in fact superhumans were outlawed soon after. There are some awful times ahead after the Starguards disappeared."

Zane was also fearful of revealing that one of them had survived.

I'm not going to stir that pot! she kept quiet.

"The only other thing was the discovery of Thanium, a new energy source discovered after the explosion, a blue element Thane was supposedly developing. They called it his legacy to humanity."

"Blue element?" Qane half whispered to himself. "I wonder . . ." his white brow knitted in concern.

But Bastian confirmed his thoughts, "The Lore stone, Qane. Yes, I believe you are right. Somehow Thane or someone he is working with has their hands on the Lore stone. He must be allied to the Devouts.

We must retrieve it at all costs. All costs."

He made sure Aerl and Altair understood his words.

"So we are the sacrificial blood in all of this, after all," Altair threw his arms up in frustration.

"What is this Lore stone, anyway?" Zane asked.

Bastian explained the viral aspect of the Lore Stone, emphasising its ability to transform human DNA to enable powers.

"But even worse," he continued, "is that the Devouts believe that the Lore are their Gods and that when there are enough humans with abilities, they will call down the gods, and only their kin will survive. This world will become a Lore infested hive and then they will seek out more worlds!"

"Including a re-invasion of the Magna Aura system, I'm sure," Sceptre stressed. He looked at Azure, wishing they had more Loremaidens.

Bastian had similar thoughts.

"Azure, your powers may work on Lore, but may they not work on the Lore stone derived superhumans?"

Azure wasn't sure, shaking her head in doubt. "I haven't tested that part of my powers."

"Can you detect the Lore stone?" he asked, hopeful.

Again, Azure shook her head. "I don't know, not having seen or sensed one before. At the moment, I'm not sensing anything Lore related."

"What are you getting, Bastian?" Sceptre asked.

Bastian's face was grave. "I'm thinking that the Starguards will have to destroy Thane and the Devouts, here and now, before it is too late."

"Even if we die?"

"We don't know that you do, but yes, even if you die," Bastian answer was unequivocal.

The shocked Starguards looked at each other, silently deliberating their next course of action.

"No!" Sceptre stated plainly, calmly. "That was not in the bargain.

We were brought here together and we will return home together."

Even Altair was happy at that. "That was a brother of a decision," he lauded Aerl, the other Starguards smiling at their private joke.

But Bastian was none too happy, "So now what?" He looked to Qane and Simon for ideas.

Just then, the lights flooded back on, lifting the semi-darkness of gloomy moodiness.

Simon regarded Zane in the returned light, looking at someone who knew him well, but he had no idea who she was.

"Zane, when did this explosion happen, the date?" he asked.

Zane started as Simon talked to her. It was like seeing someone for the first time, which technically she was, but knowing their older brother. She smiled at her memory of the older Simon, catching the younger's attention.

"What so funny?" Simon asked.

"Nothing, you're different from your future, that's all. Less serious. Less an ass," she added with a curled lip, remembering the way he used to treat Kellis.

Qane laughed out loud, "So, Simon will grow some balls after all? Well done, Simon, only two hundred years to go."

There was quiet laughter as Simon looked embarrassed, Zane giving him an apologetic look, deciding to rescue him.

"To answer your question, I don't know the exact date, but within the next couple of years. And I checked, but my crystalators are shot. Netherlord's energy corrupted them, no doubt. It's almost forgotten history on Earth. But there were no Lore, at least in the history books . . ." she let the thought hang in the air, as they all thought about what could have destroyed the Thane building.

"So we have no definite time frame. Father, do our contacts in the government have anything?" queried Simon.

Bastian shook his head. "Nothing concrete, though there rumours of some private biotech programme being pushed through, but they've had to retain their cover. I will chase it up though."

101

"Chase it up all you want," Altair scoffed, his face one big scowl. "I say we just call down that Astral Lightstream like we did before on Halcyon and get her to sort things out."

Sceptre and Urana also recalled when Sceptre, at the Starguards gathering on Cirrius' island home the night before Novan's voyage, had requested the presence of an Astral to explain what was going on. Lightstream had duly appeared. The Astrals had only recently revealed themselves to the Starguards after reversing time, saving them from death at the hands of the Lore. At the time, a vociferous Altair had accused the Astrals of using the Starguards as bait in their war. And here they were again, pawns in another war.

"Call them!" Altair urged to no one in particular.

But Zane disagreed. "No, Altair, if Lightstream found me here, alive, it could change the future for the worse . . ."

A loud harrumph silenced the incipient arguments, "Altair's right, Qane pitched in, surprising everyone. "We need to know what is happening and you little girl," he pointed at Zane, "do not order us around, Astral or not!"

Suitably chastised, Zane sunk glumly into her chair though she couldn't resist the last word, "Okay, but don't say I didn't warn you." She folded her arms, part of her wishing Lightstream would whisk her away back home to Zero Star or even the Chronopolis.

Bastian took out a mobile phone from his belt.

Zane almost laughed at the fact he could just call up Lightstream as if ordering a pizza.

Bastian saw her reaction.

"I'm not actually calling her. I'm sending a temporal text, a one-way signal which only she can hear in the time stream." He tapped in a message.

"How long does it usually take?" Azure asked, itching to actually meet the Astral.

"I guess it depends on if she's busy or if it's safe enough to travel without attracting the Lore," he answered.

"Or if she deigns to appear," Altair noted sarcastically.

"Then maybe we should have lunch or something. I'm starving," said Zane. She had discovered in the Blue Mountain facility that her very fast metabolism sometimes made her crave food in tense situations. It was a wonder she hadn't eaten her way out of the walls.

"You can make us some lunch if you want, seeing as that was your vocation," a sneering Altair unhelpfully suggested, not that all Earth food appealed to him.

Zane stuck her tongue out at him, a gesture which confused Altair.

Simon sighed, "Fine, I'll call down and we'll get something to eat in the mess. . . hey!" he threw his hands up over over his eyes.

"Universe!" exclaimed Urana.

Several 'Aaahs' rang out in the room.

A flash of bright light caught them off guard and a figure had appeared behind Bastian.

The afterglow disappeared.

"Alpha Rion!" exclaimed Urana, gliding over the table to hug him.

The Starguards flocked forth around the surprised warrior like a long lost brother.

Zane could only listen to various pieces of quick-fire conversation.

"Where have you been, Alpha Rion? How did you get here?"

"When have I been more like? Where's Astara?"

"Astara didn't come with us . . ."

". . . So Decion deceived us all . . ."

". . . and Valtare wanted us to destroy the Exmoors in the past."

Alpha Rion filled in the rest in the room with his adventures in the past, meeting Tera ZaVoir and Gordell, and the disappearance of the latter, Decion and Valtare, though he was a bit angry he'd been brought to the future a year after the others had arrived.

"I thought the Astrals were supreme time travellers, yet here I am arriving late to the fight. And Lightstream left with me!" he complained.

Bastian looked puzzled at that. "Where is Lightstream? We had signalled to her! Why didn't she come?"

"Because she's a stinking Astral," Altair smirked. "They're all alike." He returned Zane's gesture of a stuck out tongue.

Alpha Rion replied, "Oh, that was you was it?" remembering Lightstream's mention of messages in the timestream. Because of that he had spent less time with Tera.

Explaining, he said, "She had a simultaneous call from the Chronopolis. She could only drop me off and then return home. Seemed like an emergency! Sorry," he added, sensing some gloom in the air.

Everyone seemed a little disappointment, none more so than Altair. He had wanted more answers. Azure hadn't got to meet Lightstream. And Zane couldn't decide whether she was glad or not she wasn't discovered alive and well.

But Sceptre approached Alpha Rion and patted him on the shoulder.

"Well, it's just good to have you here. Decion will pay for his treachery. And we will find him."

"But there's more," Alpha Rion said, cryptically, "Apparently Cirrius has erected a temporal field around Magna Aura, with the help of other Astrals; the ones who took Decion and myself," Alpha Rion said.

"He did what?" Urana screamed across the table, horror on her face.

"Well good for him," grinned Altair. "Serve the Astrals right for poking their noses where they don't belong!" he chortled, pleased he had used a human phrase correctly.

"No, you don't understand Altair," said Urana, "It means he's up to something. He could try to stop us from returning!"

"He wouldn't dare?" Altair's voice turned grim.

"You obviously don't know my brother like I do. He's always got plans and if he's conspiring with some Astrals and keeping other Astrals away from Magna Aura, he's got a reason for it!" She sat silently fuming.

"This just keeps getting better," Altair shook his head. "But welcome to Earth!" he clapped Alpha Rion on the back. "Looks like we'll be here for a while." Now his mood had turned glum.

Sceptre addressed them all. "Be that as it may all we can do is focus on our present. Let's worry about Cirrius and temporal fields later."

Bastian approached and shook Alpha Rion's hand heartily.

"It is a great honour to meet you, finally. I had heard much about you from Tera over the centuries and we wondered if you were really real or not," he smiled happily.

Alpha Rion's eyes lit up at the mention of Tera.

"Tera, is she here?" He looked around for her.

"No, but I know where she is and she has been waiting for you. We can take you to her if you'd like."

"Yes, of course, if it is fine with Aerl," he looked at Sceptre who nodded his affirmation. "Thank you, Aerl," he nodded his head courteously.

"Tomorrow then," Bastian said.

"But won't we need Alpha Rion here?" asked Urana, still rattled over the news about her brother's actions.

"Not for now, but we can have him back as soon as possible. Besides Alpha Rion has not seen the modern world as you have, so this is his chance, yes?" There was a mood of agreement, which Bastian liked. "On another matter, Alpha Rion, you and Tera met Gordell as well. You have no idea where he could have gone?" He looked concerned.

Alpha Rion could only sorrowfully shake his head. "No, he was gone before I reached the portal for me to see anything, I'm sorry. Did you know him?"

"Yes, in a way, but I never met him. He was my grandfather."

"Universe!" Alpha Rion was saddened by this. "I am sorry Bastian. But I will tell you that even from the start, I liked and trusted Gordell. He was a great and honourable man." He grinned at a memory, "He even taught me how to ride a horse! And I'm sure wherever he is, he is fighting to get back."

"Thank you, Alpha Rion. My father Charles is very old and ill in Europe. He spent centuries searching and waiting for Gordell's return. You are the closest he will have come and I'm sure a visit from you and Tera will cheer him up no end."

There was sadness in his voice that even Simon had not heard before. He clasped his father's shoulder.

"Thank you, Alpha Rion, for all you've done for our family," Bastian said.

Alpha Rion returned his smile, "It is I who am honoured." Then his thoughts turned to his sister, "So no Astara?" he glumly stated, disappointed at the thought of not being reunited with his twin.

Bastian shook his head. "Lightstream stated that Cirrius, Decion, yourself and Astara were supposed to stay in the Magna Aura system."

"But of course you and Decion were stolen, so who knows what's happening there now," Urana lamented. "I hope Astara's safe!"

That didn't reassure Alpha Rion. "So, we can't get back?" he asked anxiously.

"We don't know now," Sceptre said.

Altair sounded more exasperated, "And Urana suffers from sporadic temporal flu, kind of what they call jet lag on this world."

"I'm fine!" Urana waved him off, embarrassed her state of health was being discussed openly. "I'm feeling better, time travel affects people in different ways."

Alpha Rion shrugged. "I know how that feels, believe me." He shook his head, thinking he could still hear a buzzing in his head.

Then he saw Zane standing on the periphery of the group.

"And who are you?" he asked, wondering what sort of uniform she was wearing.

"Another stinking Astral," Altair smirked, "But she's defective. Can't go anywhere in time."

"Cheers, Altair, as if you don't have a defective personality. Grow up!" she bristled at the insult.

"Zane?" Bastian admonished her. This girl had no respect for her elders.

"What is with you?" Simon asked.

Zane pulled a face. "Look at us, and think what's happening here," Zane blurted, still feeling rather uncomfortable in the presence of the Starguards and the Exmoors. "Remember, I'm supposed to be dead. I don't know how I got here or for what purpose. The Starguards show up around the same time, and now Alpha Rion! Coincidence?" she looked at everyone in the room.

"Someone very powerful is either manipulating or protecting me, or us, or both or neither, I don't know. If Lightstream was supposed to come here and see me then she would have. If she knew I was alive, when I should be dead, then it would somehow change the future or the past. I'm needed here, but what I have to do has to be done without the other Astrals knowing about it . . . hmm . . ." she thought about how the Starguards were fated to die. "But if the future reports were right, then the Starguards will die here on Earth. Maybe I'm here to stop that, because the other Astrals can't . . ."

"Or maybe you cause it," Altair spoke in a dark tone.

"Maybe. I don't know," was all Zane could honestly say. "But I have no reason to."

She stood alone and surrounded by the group, a little lost girl among near Gods and immortals, who were questioning her morality. All she could do was look to Bastian for guidance.

A lightness filled his face. "How about we discuss this after lunch," he said. "Even I'm famished now!"

And with that he turned and walked out of the room. Even though Urana and Altair wanted to continue the conversation, they followed the rest out, except Azure, who gave Zane a reassuring squeeze of the arm and a warm smile.

"The universe works in mysterious ways, Zane," she said. "I was you once and I believe you're here to save us, so thank you."

Zane smiled and nodded appreciably as Azure left. She fought back tears.

I will save them, save them all, even if I die trying, again.

It was late.

Nothing new had been discussed after lunch with Urana and Altair railing against the Astrals and wanting to return to Magna Aura. The Exmoors and Sceptre tried to thrash out a plan of action against the

Devouts. Most of the day was about agreeing to disagree but agreeing to discuss everything again the next day.

After duties had been attended to, arrangements for Alpha Rion's reunion with Tera made, and Sword Industries inductions prepared for her, Zane's thoughts harkened back to when Kellis had taken her and Aristedes through their paces at Zero Star.

Compared to that, this would be a piece of cake, she hoped.

Supper had been a sombre affair with the Starguards sharing memories of Magna Aura with the Exmoors and the Exmoors telling tall tales of their adventures throughout Earth's history. Zane couldn't say much as much of her life had been spent searching for her father and living in the future she couldn't talk much about. Then it had been time to bade Alpha Rion farewell for a while, as he was taken to see Tera. Zane had returned to her room.

The necessary repairs to man and machine from Zane's invasive visit had been completed. And though Zane was tentatively part of the group she was still on probation, thus another precautionary guard was stationed outside her room. Not that they could have stopped her from escaping, she hoped.

Her room was comfortable and airy with the latest techno gadgets and a spectacular view over the city. Just as Zane thought about getting some sleep there was a knock on the door.

She let out a low growl, "Oh, now what?" she said under her breath before loudly saying, "Come in." She put on a cheery smile.

The door opened and Simon came in, a small data pad in his hand.

Zane knew what was coming: an interrogation about the future.

There were times during the war with the Axalans when Simon had seemed so prescient, like his escape from Consention's bridge during the Christmas Day Massacre, that it had seemed he may have had some psychic ability, but now Zane knew better. It had been her all along who had told him. But that also meant Simon had known all the time what had happened in the past, yet kept it secret even from her—

The bastard!

But Zane knew she had to tell him about the future and of the Axalan War, her brother Aristedes, Lynn Kellis and her secret base

Zero Star, the alien Bions, the Superions; those turn-coat-humans-disguised-as-Axalans led by Mode, Marrathanor the Exmoor-like Axalan, and most importantly Xaul Relentus—the future Emperor-General.

Simon's eyes had widened in surprise at some of the details, as her words were automatically transcribed onto his pad, but other details he had seemed to know, like the Bions. But still he was giving nothing away.

At the end of her recollections of future history, Simon stored all the data, encrypting it only for his use.

"That was between you and me, Zane. You know I cannot even reveal to you what I know in the future, when I meet you again," he confided in her.

His pad was still whirring away, extra activity going on.

"Hmm," Simon looked at the screen, "Looks like a name search." The whirring stopped and he looked at the data. "You did say this was in the future?"

"Yes, why?" Zane nodded solemnly.

"Then who's this?" he showed her the screen.

Zane's mouth dropped open as she saw the very familiar face, the brown pony-tail and cynical smile. A file scrolled beside the picture.

"That's Lynn Kellis," Zane gasped. "But how?"

"Are you sure? It could be a distant relative?"

But Zane was sure it was Lynn Kellis. "No, it's her. Oh my God. I have to see her."

Simon was reading the data scrolling by. He frowned.

"Well, according to this, you can't. Lynn Kellis, born 1984, was some government op," he hesitated, "Um, disappeared . . . two years ago."

"Disappeared?" Zane leaned forward to see for herself, but unbelievably it was there in black and white on the tablet's screen.

Lynn Kellis was nowhere to be found. She might as well be dead.

INTERLUDE

The Chronopolis

"Father, I found Alpha Rion and portalled him to the other Starguards on Earth. What was so urgent as to call—" Lightstream stopped dead as she exited her portal and entered the Chronopolis' columned main hall.

Her father, Helexius, brother to the currently-missing Astral leader, Lord Aeon, and her best friend Sola, the daughter of the late Spheron stood transfixed in the middle of the room which resembled a Grecian temple-like chamber. However, this temple was a technological Parthenon equipped with crystalators and the so-called Oracle crystal off the left in its own small hall.

At first, Lightstream thought the shimmering light was from the Oracle, a meter-wide, spherical dimension crystal, which hovered over a waist-high anti-grav pedestal. With it they could view the universe. But Lightstream knew it was still clouded over since the Lore had attacked.

No, the light was coming from a small very shiny silver ball, the size of a fist, which rotated and pulsed at such an accelerated rate above the other two Astrals that even Lightstream felt mesmerised.

"Father? Sola?" she called out to them. "What is that?"

They were quiet for so long, Lightstream wondered if they were okay, then. . .

"Don't move, Lexa," Helexius whispered to his daughter. "It just showed up and it seems to be searching or waiting for something." He kept his eyes firmly on the orb.

"I think it's from the Lore!" Sola grimaced. "Some form of energy probe. We tried blasting it, trapping it in temporal fields, everything, but it's too fast, anticipating our moves. It stops when we stop. Thought you might have something up your sleeve." Though she was standing still she shifted her eyes pleadingly to Lightstream. She was scared.

But Lightstream hadn't heard her.

There was something about the glowing sphere. The vibration of it was. . .

"Look out!"

"Noooo!"

Helexius' and Sola' warnings were too late.

The silver sphere had shot straight across the hall and hit

Lightstream square in the forehead. And disappeared within.

Lightstream felt the fantastic orb plunge into her mind.

She was flat on her back, gray eyes staring fixedly at the domed hall's ceiling. It was an odd cold sensation. But strangely calm.

Helexius and Sola rushed over by her side. Still prone, Lightstream held up her hands to say she was okay. She gingerly felt her forehead, but there was no sign of penetration by the energy ball. She smiled and tried to get up.

"Raaargh! she screamed in agony.

The visions, the pain, the depths of nothingness wracked her. Lightstream arched and writhed wildly on the floor, screaming incomprehensible words. She couldn't breathe. Her eyes turned silver and her body turned in on itself, arms clamping her torso, knees raised to chest. She shook, convulsing, shuddering as if time itself would crack and only she could hold it together. It lasted for an eternity, every millisecond as important as the next. Then. . .

Frrriiish!

The silver ball suddenly emerged from her head, hovered high in the hall and then vanished.

Panting for breath, Lightstream lay on her side, dull eyes staring straight ahead.

"Lexa, Lexa, are you okay?" her father demanded, frantically shaking her for an answer.

"Get off me," Lightstream brusquely push him away, wiping drool from her mouth as she got groggily to her feet.

I have to remember everything.

"You were attacked!" Sola said, still alarmed, approaching Lexa cautiously. "We need to check you out in the med bay."

"No," Lightstream declined, holding her hands up again. "I wasn't attacked. I was chosen!"

"Chosen?" Helexius and Sola shouted together.

A portal flash caught their attention and their defences were raised again.

But it wasn't the sphere. It was Aristedes.

Oblivious to the traumatic events in the hall, he shouted:

"Zane's alive! Did you know?" He was frantic, angry, desperate. "Did you know?" he shouted again, breathing heavily.

Helexius, Sola, and Lightstream were paralysed with emotions.

114

"What's happening, Helexius?" Sola asked, fear creeping across her features. She turned to Aristedes. "Aristedes, we were just attacked, or Lightstream was. . ."

"I said I wasn't attacked. I was chosen!" repeated an annoyed Lightstream, breathlessly.

"Attacked," Aristedes worded. "By a red crystalline alien?" His anger was returning.

"What? No, a silver glowing ball of energy!" Sola sounded confused.

There were a babble of voices as Sola and Aristedes tried to tell their stories at the same time.

"Stop!" Helexius ordered. "Just stop, both of you! Aristedes, you first. What's happened?"

Aristedes told his story. "My friend, Lynn Kellis, in the twenty-third century just told us that Zane is alive in the twenty-first century with the Starguards we placed there!"

"What?" Lightstream had recovered sufficiently. "But I sent Alpha Rion there, too! Let's go. . . " She was intent on returning to Earth, but Aristedes stopped her.

"No, you can't! After Kellis told me this, I tried to rescue Zane myself, but I was actually prevented from doing so mid-temporal stream by a red crystalline being with a third eye in his hand! He then told me to return to the Chronopolis and transported me here itself. He knew of the Chronopolis *and* its location!" he emphasised the last part.

He saw their shocked reactions and knew they had not encountered this being.

"Another time-travelling race? A powerful one!" Helexius pondered.

"And that was my warning," Lightstream said, gaining everyone's attention. "I was chosen by that silver sphere. It was a messenger."

"From who? Where? When?" her father could only ask.

"I don't know, but it showed me things. A war far greater than we can imagine. Greater than this war Netherlord wanted. It spills through universes and eternity. We have to leave!"

"What? Leave here, but. . ." Sola choked.

Lightstream held her friend's hands softly. "We're not abandoning your father, Sola, but we're not safe here. I've been told where and when to go. And we have to go now!"

She looked earnestly at them all.

"I mean now!" she repeated more harshly.

"You believe this messenger?" Helexius was anxious.

"Yes, father, we're in grave danger. We have to leave!" She was ready to portal out.

"Give me a minute," Aristedes said, suddenly. "I have to get someone."

"Now?" Helexius gasped. "Who?"

"Yes, now. I'm not leaving her behind. Her name is Starshina." He portalled out.

They looked at the empty space, before Helexius sprung into action. "Grab the core crystalators, disable the Oracle, destroy anything else, shut the Hades thing down, and erect the temporal shields. No one enters but us four!"

Lightstream and Sola obeyed, dismantling crystalators and pocketing the critical crystals. Then the three of them began weaving temporal fields: overlapping fields of reverse, null, chaotic, fractal, asymmetric, dense, and shredded time, interlaced with an impenetrable barrier of energy, plasma strands. They also back-timed the field so no one could trace them once they had left—the paradox field would prevent a temporal incursion into their immediate past but still allow events that had occurred, to happen, ensuring their escape.

Aristedes portalled back in with a snow-white-skinned woman.

"Starshina, meet my uncle Helexius, my cousin, Lightstream, and Sola. Now we can leave!"

There wasn't much time for Starshina to react, except with a brief smile and wave.

The Astrals took one last look around the Chronopolis.

"Follow me, closely," a resolute Lightstream commanded.

Four flashes of light disappeared into the timestream; their portals sealing off the Chronopolis.

Almost at the same time, instantaneously, would have been a misnomer as the temporal field had displaced their arrival, six tall shadows appeared from portals on the outskirts of the Chronopolis.

They surveyed the enshrouded Chronopolis, empty and protected by its myriad of energy fields.

Dark coldness radiated from the beings in ethereal wisps.

"They were warned!" one of the black creatures stated tersely.

"So it seems!" another said, its whispery voice seeping dread.

Another promised, "They will not escape, they cannot hide, they will die!"

CHAPTER SEVEN

The history of criminality is one of evolution and adaptation to law enforcement, escalation of force and technology, and of out-gunning and out-running the police. Only the best—or the worst—of criminals survived the never-ending war against law and order. And it was the same in the twenty-first century when the first superheroes appeared.

Within months of the Starguards appearing, black-market manoeuvre suits began appearing, apparently manufactured to meet specific demands for warlords, militias, solo and grouped adventurers, criminal gangs like the infamous Hostile, a ruthless group of eclectic gangs bent on anarchy, and their nemesis the supra-vigilantes, the so-called protectors of the night who thought of themselves as real-life superheroes on the side of the people, but who in reality often worked either side of the law. Within a year, there was an estimated three thousand manoeuvre suits on the market, their anonymous owners causing havoc around the world.

The only name associated with these sales was a mysterious character known as the Terror Engineer. But everyone automatically blamed Sword Industries and the Starguards for exploiting their own technology for financial gain. Sword Industries vehemently denied the allegations. Even now, the U.S. and U.N. were drafting legislation against the Starguards to appropriate all of Sword Industries' assets and portion them out to U.S./U.N. control. In other words, the U.S. would declare war on the Starguards.

While this story rumbled on in the media for most of the second year on Earth, the Starguards dutifully played superheroes, saving countless lives from various disasters and engaging in numerous media and public relations events.

Sceptre had become a spokesman for the Boy Scouts of America, environmental groups, the postal service, and a clean-cut role model for sportswear companies. His billboards stretched across America, looking leisurely and approachable even while wearing his visor.

Despite not having family on Earth or being able to be identified, the Exmoors contended it would be necessary for the Starguards to hide their identities so they could have private lives and not be hounded by the press and fans.

Urana, with her looks and wild blue hair, was automatically targeted by the modelling industry, hounded everywhere she went by paparazzi and admirers. She also assisted with construction projects, especially global volcanic engineering and energy capture systems.

Azure, as the Sky Warrior, often helped with flight tactics with the USAF, posing with their newest fighter the Hypersonic Multiforce Platform—or as it was later officially known the F-56 Lancefire—the first aircraft with laser cannons. She also performed at many air shows around the world. Her role with NASA and NOAA also aided in gathering data for extreme weather events.

As for Altair, it had been hard to place him, but his bad boy image made him number one in multiple most-sexy and most-eligible magazine lists. He was never happy with his action figures and poster images. And on multiple occasions he had to be restrained by Urana from assaulting the media who constantly followed them around.

Urana and Altair were often seen out together, the media referring to them as the golden Superhero couple, to the amusement of the rest of the Starguards. And none of the Starguards understood why they were offered vast sums of money to advertise themselves, money which they didn't need. In the end, the Exmoors donated the money to charities.

For her part, Zane was consigned mostly to office work or kept in reserve, as Bastian called it. Zane was the ace in the hole—Windburst (she had kept her Multiforce name), the second-stringer for now. But she did envy the Starguards getting all the limelight for safeguarding her own world.

However, she was training. Bastian had analysed her effect on machinery and discovered Zane had a latent temporal field around her different to other Astrals. Zane's field disrupted any mechanical or electrical object when she sped around.

"If you can direct it you can target specific areas or machines rather than blitzing the whole area," Bastian had told her. So Zane was practicing, not just in running, but also vibrating her arms or hands at objects so they burnt out or shut down. "Comes in handy around surveillance devices," Bastian said approvingly.

Away from the distractions of media, the Starguards tracked down errant supra-vigilantes and Hostile members, but the more they captured the more came out of the woodwork; whole gangs controlling vast areas of inner cities, the police and Starguards working hand-in-hand to combat them.

And while the Lore may not have turned up, the new super-suited criminals were giving them cause for concern, and in the Starguards' third year on Earth, it came to a head on a hot July afternoon.

It was the hunting of the Goth that led to the end of the Starguards on Earth. A rebellious Devout and self-styled vigilante, Goth had in her possession one of the myriad black-market manoeuvre suits. The one-piece, tight-fitting, all-black suit mimicked PVC, but was more resilient than diamond-stranded materials, and was bullet and fireproof. It was completed by a red domino mask covering her pale skin and a fake black ponytail, just because. For defence against machines and other non-humans, she carried an EMP stick and an automatic pistol, mostly for show. Her own killing methods were well-known to the authorities who not knowing about the Devouts' existence ascribed her victims' gruesome deaths to the effects of some fast-working and undetectable viral drug.

There were twenty-two of them. Assassinated. Another gang off the streets of Manhattan. The Goth wasn't being altruistic. She hated guns, one reason for her one-woman vendetta against gangs. And they were in her territory. It was easy for her to use her self-termed telegothic powers to engender within people dark-horror nightmares urging them to carry out acts of graphic violence upon each other. She just had to stand back and watch as they tore, chopped, stabbed, and shot each other to death.

Her escape route from the gang's tower block den down the fire escape into an alleyway was blocked by the first police officers on the scene.

"Stop, police!" the officer aimed his gun at her.

It only took a second for the Goth to look at the officers, concentrate and they had turned on each other, seeing whatever horrors they conjured for themselves. The shots rang out even as she escaped, only to run into the next police unit who did not hesitate to fire, her armour protecting her from their bullets.

She dodged further rounds by jumping into another apartment block, ascending three steps at a time through a neighbouring building, escaping over the rooftops of the city, her suit pushing her body beyond its limits She paused for breath on top of a department store, safe. Ducking behind a generator housing, she made to change into street clothes and escape unnoticed through the front door fifteen floors below.

Beep, deep, beep, her suit pinged, detecting something—a presence in the air; not an aircraft, nor police helicopter, nothing civilian.

"Hmm, unidentified," she noted to herself. Goth ignored the suit's sensors and peeked around the generator housing, her pale-white skin growing even paler. "Shit!"

The air was already crackling as Urana sent a raging charge of energy upon Goth, who was hard-pressed to dive out of the way in time. The generator exploded, sending her flying across the roof.

Where the hell did she come from? thought Goth, panicking as another blitz of energy flashed by her.

Shit! Shit! Shit! The suit could take some hits, but not many from Urana.

Urana, for her part, had been instructed by Sceptre to bring the Goth in alive for the authorities. She had to obey, and would obey, but Sceptre hadn't specified in what condition of alive, and she intended to have some fun. Urana blasted Goth again, as she ran between rooftop generators, vents, and other structural barriers.

Meanwhile, the press had recovered from the initial shock of the Goth's slaughter of the gang, and on hearing police reports of a rooftop battle between Urana and the Goth, had scrambled to get network helicopters into the air.

On TV, news presenters relayed live reports back to the millions of viewers now glued to their screens. At least three helicopters were in the air covering the fight.

". . . And now they're working their way down to West 56th street," intoned a traffic reporter, his voice barely heard above the whirring rotor noise.

Then in a voice hysterical beyond belief, "My God! Urana just blew away that grocery store. Unbelievable! The Goth was inside; surely she must be dead . . . no, no . . . look! She's scrambled out and is running to another shop, those poor people in the shop! Are they dead? The devastation is unreal. Surely she knows what she's done!"

Inside Sword HQ's Ops control, Sceptre, Altair, Azure and Zane watched with the Exmoors as Urana again and again rained plasma energy down on the Goth to no avail, as she twisted and squirmed her way past every onslaught. Bastian shook his head in sorrow.

". . . For God's sake, she's out of control, Urana must be stopped, somebody stop her!" raged another reporter from a TV news chopper.

Off camera he could be heard to say, "Get in closer, Robby!"

The camera man in the helicopter zoomed in on Urana, clearly angered, her blue hair whipping around in the wind as she zipped between the buildings.

With a frustrated yell, Urana let loose another pinpoint staccato of energy bolts which ripped through buildings. Something stored in one exploded, sending debris into the sky.

Hovering too close, the chopper was caught in the blast veering away too late. The camera swung around dizzily. The screams from inside were sickening. The TV news helicopter collided into overhead power lines, spun out of control, and hit the ground on its side, blades smashing and fragmenting into shrapnel, cutting through the air, people, cars, and buildings. The helicopter exploded. Fire spread. Twelve people were dead.

The traffic reporter in the helicopter was silent as his pilot circled the carnage below, so quiet that sirens could be heard on the ground as emergency services began to arrive.

The reporter sobbed. "What's become of this place?"

Sceptre bowed his head in contemplation, brow furrowed and lips pursed in restrained anger.

"Altair!" he said through gritted teeth. "Bring back Urana. Take her down and return!" Altair smiled and turned to leave. "And, Altair," Sceptre continued, "no games! I'm not in the mood!" he warned.

Altair nodded in acknowledgement and started off down the corridor, making his way to the roof and flying off. He raced up into the air, stopped, sighted Urana, lined himself up, and dived.

Impact in ten seconds, he grinned to himself.

A weather-watch helicopter hovering over Broadway saw him first, the cameraman's sweaty palms fumbling to focus on the incoming figure. He could hardly believe his own eyes, let alone the camera, when he saw who it was.

On the TV screens, the cameraman had caught the blue and blond streak that was Altair smashing into Urana, sending them both hurtling to the street below. They disappeared amongst the skyscrapers, where a sudden plume of dark smoke billowed from their point of impact.

Urana didn't know what had hit her, but as the haze cleared from the crater they had created, she saw her cousin Altair pinning her down. She tried to get up, but he gripped her arms back, so she couldn't fire at him. He squeezed down on her.

"Listen, Rain, Aerl wants me to bring you back in, but we can do things my way . . ."

Urana squirmed. "Get off me, Altair, or I'll swear I'll . . ."

"Now, now," Altair said firmly. "Listen. You'll escape from me, hunt the Goth down, she'll retaliate and I'll be forced to help you before taking you in and we can both go back heroes, okay?"

Urana stopped struggling. She nodded, a sly smile on her face.

"Rain." Altair could see the look in her eyes. "Be calm." He gently began to release her.

He could feel her anger rising, knew she wouldn't control it.

"Rain!" his tone urging restraint.

She was being challenged. She couldn't let this go without any counter-action.

Altair let her go, only to be blasted as fire leapt from Urana's hands, the volley of plasma striking Altair in the chest, sending him flying across the street.

"Catch me if you can, cousin!" was her cry as she flew off in pursuit of Goth, now at large in Central Park.

Altair got to his feet slowly. That had hurt a bit more than he figured, his chest was still smarting from the blast. Now all he had to do was play his part and everything would be okay.

"There's some smoke, I think a crater or damage to the street, and Altair trying to hold Urana down. . ."

The traffic reporter had regained some composure, describing the scenes around the impact area.

"She's escaped, Urana has escaped! Altair couldn't hold her down! My god!" he gasped in horror as Urana had shot from the area and bolted past the helicopter.

Urana sped for the Goth, sensors telling her that she had crossed Central Park and was headed for uptown Manhattan. She pursued and found the Goth running through some trees almost out of the park.

"You've gotta be kidding me!" The Goth shouted to herself, picking up her pace.

Urana blasted away at a retaining wall hoping to catch Goth up ahead, but she somersaulted unscathed through the debris, escaping again.

"Urana's a fury!" the reporter cried. "She's done it again, demolished part of a building. This is a dark day for New York . . ."

"Altair did that on purpose. He let her go," Azure said quietly. She didn't want to antagonise Sceptre, whose shoulders had suddenly tensed.

Zane stood still, not daring to breathe as she considered the implications of Altair's actions. There was a long silence, until Sceptre turned and walked out of the room. He exited the emergency roof airlock and blasted off toward Central Park.

Seconds later he was on the TV screen in front of Azure and Zane. They glanced sideways at each other, allowing slight smiles to cross their lips.

There'd be hell to pay and Sceptre was collecting.

A police helicopter registered Sceptre's presence first as he flashed by in golden light, sending the chopper reeling in his wake, but the pilot, an experienced hand, regained control. He followed the action.

"Another Starguard has just entered the fray, yes, I think, yes, it's Sceptre. I think things are under control now," the traffic reporter assured himself, more than his audience.

Sceptre hadn't stopped when he passed the helicopter. He carried straight on, straight toward Altair and Urana, who hovered around a small shop where Goth had holed up. They were blasting it to pieces. They then realised someone airborne was on the way and as they turned to face him, Sceptre had unleashed a twin blast of livid energy from his hands at them.

Urana crumpled and fell from the sky, while Altair had been blasted half a block away. And still Sceptre didn't stop.

The Goth had skipped out and into an apartment block, her suit pinging with anticipation, unable to compensate for the sheer thumping of her heart, as Sceptre had crashed through the wall in a burst of light, careening into her. A screaming Goth flew out the other side and down five floors to the pavement. She lay there, still, smouldering, broken and studded with glass.

Sceptre flew out and blasted Goth again on the ground. He hovered above her, god-like.

Goth opened her eyes, her mask half-burnt away, her suit already trying to heal her. She tried to get up and run, her legs wobbly. Sirens screamed toward them. The Goth, more eager to face the police than Sceptre, crawled over to them. Sceptre remained hovering behind her.

The Goth fell to the ground again. She ripped off her mask peeling more burned skin away, blood streaks on her face and matted blonde hair as her black wig fell off. She screamed almost unintelligibly at Sceptre.

"When my Gods come Starguard, they'll eat your heart and suck your soul . . ." she coughed and cackled.

She pushed herself up defiantly, readying for one last attack upon Sceptre. He could feel her trying to scratch at his mind, make him turn violent. He could see the terrible images in his mind—Lore everywhere, devouring the universe drenched in blood.

But Sceptre had had enough. He knew now that the Devouts would stop at nothing to cause havoc and bring the Lore upon this world. He raised his hand. Burning light issued forth enveloping the Goth, vaporising her, her mouth shaped to form a soundless scream.

He hovered in front of the police, who just stared at Sceptre, half wondering if to shoot him or to cheer him. Not caring, Sceptre glided away to where Altair and Urana fallen. Altair had recovered and collected Urana, who was half-standing.

Sceptre stared at them through his visor, his eyes like pulsars burning their souls.

"If I ever have to come for you two like that again, I will not nearly be as merciful to you as I was with Goth!"

With that he simply took off, vanishing in a streak of light that arced away through the afternoon sky.

Altair and Urana walked over to the blackened spot that had been the Goth then glanced at each other, before glaring at the police, who physically stepped back, lowering their guns. The two Starguards then took to the air following Sceptre back to base at full speed.

"I. . . I think it's all over folks!" breathed the ragged reporter, wiping his brow, "Whatever that means. The Goth has been murdered, executed, publicly by Sceptre, of all people. The damage must be in the millions and there have been so many deaths, and yet the Starguards just fly off without an excuse me or an apology. Who will foot the bill? Me! You! That's who! The government should do something about the Starguards. Who will bring them to justice?"

He carried on until he was interrupted by a commercial break.

The Pentagon

General Abe Westonheimer received the call in his office.

"Yes, Mr. President. Yes sir, will do! I understand." He hung up.

All in Washington had watched the unfolding scenes in New York and been horrified at the actions by the Starguards. The debate was raging even now on TV and the internet about who had the right to kill the Goth, even though she would have gone to the electric chair anyway for her crimes. But the Starguards—weren't they the good guys? Who gave them the right to kill?

Westonheimer turned down the volume on the internet radio talk show. He opened up a locked draw, picked up a burner cell phone, dialled, waited for the pickup. Someone answered.

"The president says go!" he said, then hung up.

Thane Universal

Van Tager put her cell down with a smile of utter satisfaction. She gazed confidently across the boardroom table at Penthor Thane, his body guards, Spree and Charm, and the weasely Sagerhawk, who had all witnessed the events on TV.

Their conversations had stopped and all eyes were on her.

"The President says we're a go!" she grinned. "Who would have put money on Sceptre and not Altair being the hothead?"

Thane smiled widely, a gleam in his eye, while Sagerhawk looked a mite distressed.

"Who indeed, Elisabeth," Thane laughed. "Prep the teams. How soon can you be ready for operations, Doctor?" he asked Sagerhawk.

"We're ready now, Mr. Thane," replied Sagerhawk. "This had been anticipated. The team has been in the city since last night." He swallowed nervously.

"Excellent work!" Thane praised him.

Sagerhawk had been on edge ever since the visit to the White House. He felt as if there was more going on to his project than what he had imagined. Certainly, Van Tager was not what he had imagined and he wondered how much Thane knew about her. He'd even Googled her. A renowned scientist with her skills should have been published or have been nominated for or won awards, but there was nothing about her. She had come from nowhere. He would have to tell Mr. Thane, but not now. Not before his moment of glory.

The meeting broke up and the two scientists headed out of Thane's office and down to the labs.

"Contact the team commander and let him know they'll be required here today," Van Tager said once they were in the elevator.

Sagerhawk looked at her oddly thinking he should have been the one giving the orders. But he didn't care anymore. His work, hard work over decades, was being put into action.

"You're not coming with me?" he asked as Van Tager pressed an elevator button for another floor.

"I'll be there in a few minutes," she answered with no further explanation. The elevator doors opened and Van Tager stepped out on the sixty-sixth floor. She left Sagerhawk looking rather glum as the doors closed and the elevator descended.

Straight away, Van Tager headed for her own office. She opened her vault, excited. Taking out the Lore stone and admiring its gleam.

"Almost there," she said to it.

To her, something ghostly, imaginably ancient, and coiled up with power pulsed within the stone.

"I will have this world, yet!" she snarled to herself, seeing her reflection in the stone.

Also in the vault were her own files on the E-Corps. The teams had been finalised picked according to their genetic makeup, personalities, and abilities when they had emerged. For now, only one team would be active, the other in reserve. The first team had already been testing their powers in a Thane facility in Nevada. They had been flown back the previous night ready for their first live mission.

Van Tager read her individual files, peppered with handwritten notes, each candidate's name having a designated letter:

Jay Jupiter Lundy (X) – 'J.J.' Natural field leader. Total dedication to the project. Ex-U.S. Airforce Colonel and almost-astronaut. No wife, no kids, just like the rest of them.

Asset: Weathered good looks, twinkle in the eye for his friends, and plenty of wise-cracks, she had written.

Lynn Kellis (B) – *Normal, thank God!* Former British soldier , failed SAS selection. Resigned, joined MI6, got bored became freelancer. After Lundy, Kellis natural leader, down to earth, but ruthless when required.

Assets - Good looking, well-built, all-rounder. She and Lundy good public faces.

Starshina Tetriov (C) – Russian. Another ex-military brat. Remote in manner, grudging team worker, gorgeous without hang-ups.

Asset - deals with everything thrown at her with typical Russian robustness.

Warren Raphael (Y) – African American. No military experience, seasoned pilot/engineer in oil industry. *Assets – financial, marketing potential.*

Van Tager liked the first team and their synergy. Of the other candidates for Team Two; American Marine, Malcolm Dereign (Z), was a little too patriotic and unpredictable; Australian biotech expert Teddi Meadows (D) seemed shy and self-aware, uneasy with her powers; Japanese Army Lieutenant Hiko Nomora (V) wanted desperately to be a hero and bring honour to his family and country; and Peruvian mountain climber Jhonny Perez (W) would bring wisdom and spirituality to the team. They would be kept in reserve if Team One needed additional help or were killed. Van Tager didn't see that as an option.

There had been ten candidates all together, but only eight had passed the process, two eliminated due to unforeseen circumstances. Van Tager regarded the last two, so different, yet alike.

Jayne Ambrose (A) – the all-American girl had quit, no reason given. The other washout, Pandra Wake (E) seemed to have been the cause. Pandra was the quintessential mad, bad and dangerous to know type.

'Father never loved her' - which was a laugh as Van Tager had known Pandra for a very long time, even if Pandra didn't always remember. She was exotic, powerful, and bisexual. She claimed to hail from Texas, but that was a lie, Van Tager also knew. It was rumoured Pandra and Ambrose had a relationship, but it didn't go well, so Ambrose had left, disappeared, maybe back into the murky world of espionage.

Pity, Van Tager thought, *she would have been a perfect field leader.*

Pandra on the other hand was another matter. She had stolen her manoeuvre suit and weapon, had somehow copied the technology, and was selling herself as a mercenary with suit designs for vigilantes, like the now deceased Goth.

But Pandra was being tracked and would be caught soon, Spree and Charm assured Van Tager.

A shame, Van Tager thought since it was her who had let Pandra steal them in the first place: Nothing like a bit of anarchy in the mix and dirty money on the side. Someone had to pay for her other secret projects.

Van Tager packed up the files, left her office, and descended to the basement labs, entering a huge white room. Human-sized metal cylindrical tanks with full-length glass panels were hooked to pipes, tubing, and banks of computers monitoring the tanks arranged around the room. They had been transferred from the de-commissioned prison ship, the Tranquility Star, where the superhuman-transfer procedures had actually been carried out; international waters being a more benign space to conduct illicit experiments, create superhumans, and shield the Lore stone from Exmoor detection upon its activation.

Sagerhawk greeted her with a team of techs in tow. He actually smiled at Van Tager, for this was his arena. Here, he was literally god.

"Is the team ready?" he asked. She gave him the files with Teams One and Two selected. "Yes," he conceded, nodding approvingly. "That's the way I would have gone, too."

That seemed to irk him somewhat, agreeing with Van Tager, but he returned to his upbeat mood.

"The procedures have been above nominal. The subjects' testing has concluded they are ready for action, and their individual neural programming they received will help them control their powers. Their mutated DNA data will automatically hardwire their brain in the use of their powers."

Smart little man, Van Tager thought, all software and techware with him.

"Fantastic," Van Tager beamed. "Can't wait to see them in action!"

Sagerhawk was grinning ear to ear.

"We've done it, Dr. Van Tager, we've created superhumans!"

"Yes, yes, we have. Congratulations. And please . . . call me

Elisabeth," Van Tager begrudgingly invited Sagerhawk almost through gritted teeth, her feigned smile and taut-lined eyes teasing the man into a fake cordial corner.

His words seemed to stick in his throat, as he tried a polite smile.

"Why, thank you . . . Elisabeth," sounding her name as if it were a foreign language. "Call . . . call me Frans," he managed.

"Frans, it is."

"Yes, well, we seem to make a good team," he lied. "Maybe after we share the Nobel Prize, we will continue to work together," he practically forced himself to say, teeth bared in a rough smile.

He was nervous, lying was not his forte, but neither was reading people and he wondered why Van Tager was being so nice to him.

"Of course, look forward to it," she replied.

Startled techs looked around at each other, amazed at the fake bonhomie between their bosses. They twiddled pens, checked clipboards, and milled around imaginary water coolers, just to listen in to this priceless conversation.

"It's time. The White House wants a show, so let's give them one!" Van Tager said.

As the chief scientists got to work, a tech stole out of the room making her excuses to use the facilities. She slipped into a cubicle taking a moment to send a short coded message.

Sword Industries

Sceptre landed on the roof of Sword Industries. He stalked over to a secure airlock, which identified him, allowed him entry, and checked for any contaminants; natural and man-made. After a few seconds of scanning the airlock descended a few floors down to a guarded chamber off the operation rooms. Impatiently, he stomped through the thick steel door as it revolved away.

Simon stood in his way.

"Sceptre, you just executed someone on National TV!" He was nervous and though Aerl gave him a scowl, he continued. "There'll be repercussions, Aerl, for us and our whole kind!"

Sceptre continued to walk on without a word.

Simon grabbed his arm. Sceptre gave him a menacing glare, but Simon held on.

"Aerl, how do you know that this isn't how things start, what Zane said, the end of . . ."

The airlock door rotated again. Altair and Urana stepped through.

"You!" Simon started on Altair, angrily. "What were you thinking?" He rounded on all three of them. "This could get us all killed, bring the Lore down upon us all!"

"Simon!" Bastian had entered the chamber from the corridor. "Keep your voice down. Let's take this down to the debrief room." He motioned for the others to follow him out of the door.

With a brief hesitancy, the Starguards followed. Simon shook his head, but was slightly comforted by a pat on the back from his father.

As they went through the operations room, the dozen or so guards and comms officers turned to look over to them; sad faces, shocked faces, angry faces, accusing faces. Altair stared back and they lowered their eyes, going back to work. But as soon as the Exmoors and Starguards left the room, a low chattering started.

Qane, Azure, and Zane were already in the briefing room, the Chinese Exmoor glowering as usual.

Zane was scared. She felt she had put something into motion that could have been avoided.

It's all my fault, she thought, feeling glumly guilty.

The newly arrived sat down and they waited for Bastian to speak. "Aerl . . ."

"I know, Bastian, I know I've made things worse. I'm sorry," Sceptre spoke for the first time. "But if we're meant to die, then maybe we should be making this world a better place, getting rid of all the evil . . ."

Qane laughed; it was an unexpected, but curiously pleasant sound from him. Though Sceptre, Altair, and even Bastian gave him dark looks.

"Sorry, Aerl, I do not mean to mock you," Qane held up his hands in a defensive posture, trying to stop laughing as Sceptre made to retort. "Humans thrive on evil, the horrors around them, and their inner demons. We Exmoors have been on this world for thousands of years, we've tried to shepherd the humans, tweak their DNA, teach them other ways, but they will never change, cannot. Evil is ingrained in them, they are soaked with blood in it, when we got rid of one evil, another arose. Without evil, this world would not know what being good really means. All we can do is keep the balance and stop evil, like the Lore, from ever triumphing."

He sat back as silence hung in the air. Even Altair held his tongue.

"You sound like a verse from the Tomes of War," Sceptre said to Qane, about to explain what they were.

"You forget our ancestors were Celestian," Bastian reminded the Starguards. "I take your disparagement as an insult!" he said hotly.

With consideration, Sceptre replied, "I only meant the ancient Knights Destina were always on about the balance between good and evil, which is valid, but dangerous as well. This world needs a storm. This world reeks of evil, Qane, and maybe we were sent here to cleanse it before we die."

"You are joking," an incredulous Simon countered, "This isn't your world to cleanse, it's ours .."

"Then why haven't you done more?" joined in Altair. "You've tweaked here, you've shepherded there, the Devouts run wild, and humans die at random from things you can stop. Don't bring us down to your humans standards! Maybe you're too lenient and the Astrals, cursed as they are, sent us to do the job," he ranted.

Qane stared back, his hands clenched in fury. "Bringing you down! We're trying to enlighten you, you uncouth whelp!" spittle landing on the table.

"Ha, enlightened hypocrisy coming from men trying to exterminate women," Altair spat out, Urana hiding a smile in support.

The two were set to square off.

"Stop it. All of you," Zane shouted. "This is all my fault for saying anything and you all know it. So blame me!"

"No one's blaming you Zane," Azure said, looking around uncertainly for non-forthcoming support. "Are we . . . ?" she stressed to Sceptre.

Sceptre took a breath, "No, Zane, no one blames you," he conceded, "but we have to think we were brought to Earth for a reason other than to die. The Astrals must know the future and have seen what comes to pass. Can't you talk to them, Zane, you must be here for some reason too, maybe they sent you to guide us."

"Me, a guide?" she thought about it, but was interrupted by Qane.

A discreet message had come to him, his pad beeping softly. One glance and his facial expression grew graver, if that was possible.

"Sorry to interrupt, Bastian, the government has gone ahead with Thane's plans." He glared again at Sceptre. "This is a direct response to your actions." He glanced reprovingly at Altair and Urana who seemed unfazed.

Bastian sunk back into his chair, "We didn't think he had the capability to launch so quickly, but our spies within Penthor Thane's companies have informed us they have a new scientist, one of whom we are still trying to properly identify, and who has apparently cracked the problem. Their next phase will be to gain support from U.S. Politicians." He looked at Aerl. "They will now see us as a threat and sanctioned their own group to deal with us."

If this affected Sceptre, he didn't show it.

"As if any human group could defeat us," huffed Altair.

"If they have powers derived from a Lore stone then yes, Altair, you should worry!" Qane said gruffly.

That did seem to get the attention of the Starguards.

"Who are these people?" Azure asked.

"We don't have their identities yet," Qane answered. "That has been kept secret to the chief scientists. We do know that there are at least two teams and they will be called The E-Corps."

"E-Corps?" Zane whispered to herself. Why did that sound

familiar?

"E for Elite, apparently," Bastian explained.

"Or Esprit?" Zane said, half aloud.

"Does that mean anything to you?" he asked Zane.

Zane shrugged. "I don't know . . . maybe," she dismissed it.

Qane's pad beeped again. He frowned at the message.

"Bastian, there's a selected delegation in the reception lobby from what seems to be every authority there is in this country, along with half the world's media. I'll go deal with it."

Bastian nodded. "Take it easy with them."

"Heh!" Qane rose with his cane, made his excuses and left.

Simon picked out another detail, "There's also the issue of who is supplying the illegal manoeuvre suits. The Goth's was pretty sophisticated, it took some punishment from Urana. Imagine a whole Devout army with those. Too bad we couldn't study it for its provenance . . ." he took a dig at Sceptre.

"It doesn't matter, as long as we can destroy them—who cares?" Altair said.

"You'll turn the people against us then," replied Simon. "You're supposed to be superheroes; people like superheroes, not the villains!"

Altair open his mouth to retaliate about not having wanted to be a superhero anyway.

But Sceptre said, "I destroyed evil and that turned people against us? Why?"

"Why?" Simon gasped. "There's the law. We must be seen to be acting justly, even with evil or we're as bad as they are. Don't you have that in Magna Aura!"

"Of course, destroying evil is justice. Don't get me wrong, we do have Celestians who try to break the law, but the types of criminals you have on Earth are very rare in Celestian Society. Murderers are very rare and. . . " Sceptre looked deeply embarrassed, "well most killers or evil beings in our society have been former Celestian Knights, beings with power. You cannot incarcerate them, maybe you can negate their powers, but destruction is the only sure way, as with the Traitor Synther!"

He looked sincerely at Simon and Bastian.

"With the Goth, I truly thought I was doing both her and the world a justice, merciful and right."

"Oh," Bastian uttered as if he had just realised something. "We Exmoors aren't so different. We've all done things we regret or what our ancestors did in the name of justice. I could tell you some stories," he smiled without adding details.

Sceptre recalled Celestian violent behaviour in the distant past, the genocide of the Amethystians by the Elerae. Almost forgotten now, but which still hung over parts of the Magna Auran society.

He was interrupted as the board room doors slid open and Qane re-entered with a thin document folder in his hands.

"We're past telling stories, Bastain." He threw the document on the table in disgust. It slid along polished mahogany, stopping before Bastian. Qane remained standing, his back toward the group, seemingly staring into infinity through the wall.

Bastian picked up the file, had a quick read, sighed, and then slid it across to Aerl.

Sceptre looked at Bastian, who nodded toward the files. He picked it up and read the first page, then stopped.

". . . Cease and Desist Orders? What is this?"

"Read the rest," Bastian said, resignation in his voice.

Sceptre flicked through the pages reading some of the lines aloud, ". . . Constitute a potential threat to humanity . . . public executions . . . uncontrollable actions . . ." Sceptre looked at Altair. Then he read the last part in full. "In light of current events, Sword Industries and the Starguards have shown themselves to be capable of over-stepping the law of rule. In the case of the Goth, a mass-murdering superpowered human, we have decided to take no action against the aforementioned Parties as the Goth was at that time beyond the capabilities of the local authorities in being dealt with in a timely fashion with no further loss of innocent life. But no longer, the U.S. Government has enacted its own programme of superhumans and therefore no longer requires the services (voluntary or contractual) of Sword Industries and the Starguards. Thus in lieu of any criminal actions taken against the said

Parties against the Goth, we urge both aforementioned Parties to stand down for the immediate future."

Sceptre looked around the room at grim faces before finishing. "In the event of non-compliance, the U.S. would be obliged to report such action to the United Nations, seek Resolutions against said Parties, with further non-compliance resulting in serious consequences."

He let the dossier drop to the table. This wouldn't have happened back in Halcyon or the City States. What was wrong with this world?

Altair banged his fist on the table, a slight burn mark starting to smoke from his imprint.

"They think we are humans to do with as they please. We could lay waste to this world, rule it, and never have to worry about humans again!"

"I agree with Altair," Urana spoke for the first time. "We've been sent here for a purpose and now these humans . . ." She stopped mid-sentence, losing her train of thought.

"Rain? You okay?" Altair asked, a bit of compassion in his voice.

"Yeah, just feeling drained," Urana's head hung down, her blue hair hiding her features.

"Drained?" Altair remarked alarmed.

"This world is making me sick," came her reply. "So energy sapping . . ." She seemed exhausted, even her voice was dead.

A concerned Simon thought about it. "We thought you were getting better. Is there anything on Earth that can be doing this?" he asked his father.

"I don't know," Bastian replied.

"You did thump her pretty hard, you two," Simon accused Altair and Sceptre.

"Are you kidding?" Altair almost laughed. "Our manoeuvre suits can take that and more; even when we were children."

Sceptre nodded confirmation.

"Maybe Goth's powers affected you," Azure surmised, hoping that would have explained her behavior.

Urana shrugged.

"Either way," Qane decided. "It might be best to get down to the medical centre and get checked out. If the rest of you caught anything and the government or even the Lore decided to attack, then things could get dire."

"Agreed," said Bastian. "I'll get some meds up here . . ."

"I'll take her down," volunteered Altair, mild shock sweeping the room.

He guided Urana from her chair and walked her to the door, which slid open then closed as they left.

"He seems genuinely concerned for her," Bastian commented, a little surprised.

"Maybe he feels guilty at how he attacked her, before letting her escape to catch Goth," said Zane.

"So cynical, Zane," Azure said. "He can care for people you know."

"They grew up together," Sceptre added, "More so than with myself or her brother Cirrius. Cirrius and I were trained how to lead; Altair and Urana how to fight. They belong together, so yes, Altair is concerned. As am I," he frowned. But he couldn't dwell on it for too long. "Bastian, this file and any actions against us will jeopardise this world. We cannot stand down. We need a way to stop Thane now. How much do the governments know about the Lore or anything hostile beyond the Earth?"

Bastian shrugged. "Nothing about the Lore, but some agencies know a little about alien civilisations." He thought about the Cepheusian and Bion fiascoes.

"What? You want to tell the humans about the Lore, the Astrals, even us Exmoors?" Qane asked incredulously.

"Why not?" Sceptre replied earnestly. "Then they would understand the severity of the threat they face and that if we can't deal with it, then no one on Earth can."

"Yes, but then we'd be exposed and any enemy from the Lore, the Devouts, and other beings who would know where we were. These humans transmit every sensitive thing into space. They're a stupid lot, advertising their location and primitiveness so brazenly," Qane sneered.

Zane suddenly realised that the Axalans could be listening in on Earthly TV and radio now, though it would be a couple of centuries before they encountered humans.

"I agree with Qane," she said cautiously. "There are civilisations out there who could be listening in, and drawing up our strengths and weaknesses . . ."

"Is this referring to the future war?" Bastian asked.

Zane nodded.

"But that's your future," Sceptre said. "We Starguards could even prevent the war from occurring."

Zane shrugged at Simon.

"Maybe," Simon said, not entirely convinced.

The Exmoors had been told long ago by the Astrals that time could be as fluid as water and could be changed, but was that their choice to make? And on whose behalf?

Zane thought for a while before answering.

"You know, Simon, despite our heritages, we Astrals are half-human, too, born of human mothers or fathers, so I'm sure we wouldn't want anything to happen to Earth either, hence bringing the Starguards here. Would we sacrifice them for that? I don't think so, one because I'm here, maybe to see that it doesn't happen, and two, maybe they transport the Starguards back home and everyone thinks they're dead. Again, I can't really say what happened, but no Starguard bodies were ever found. Also, no one in the future knew about the Lore, so my guess is whatever we did didn't become public. That's my theory, anyhow."

"An interesting one, too. Did we at least win the war?" Qane asked. Everyone else was now interested.

Again, Zane thought about the answer. What harm would it be to tell the truth? Though she smiled as she gave the answer:

"We win, by a streak of good luck." She gave Simon a sly wink.

"Ah, at least that is good news," Qane sighed happily.

Sceptre brought them back to the situation at hand.

"So what shall we do then?"

"Trust the Astrals," Zane said.

"I would go with Zane on this one," Azure said. "For all we know, Magna Aura probably think we're dead."

"You mean Lightstream didn't tell the Magna Aurans where you are or what you're doing?" Zane asked, confused.

Azure shrugged. "We don't think so."

"And not by the way Cirrius has reacted," Sceptre said.

It was Zane's turn to be shocked now. She was beginning to think there was something else going on.

"Actually, I think we need to pay Thane a visit," Bastian said. "Our spies can only do so much, maybe we should do our bit." There were murmurs in favour. "Zane, how fast can you run so as not to be seen?" Bastian stroked his beard.

"I can flicker in and out of existence within a temporal field, which gives the appearance of super speed, so no one should see me. What do you want me to do?" She was excited at the prospect of a mission, but she tried to downplay it.

"Well the world does not know about you as a Starguard, so that gives us the advantage. We need to scout out his offices and labs, see what he is up to and what kind of deals he has with the government. Can you do that?"

"Of course," Zane answered gleefully, her first mission as a Starguard. Wow, she thought, If only Lynn could see me now.

"Okay, we'll get a mission plan together for you. We have some specs for the offices, fewer from the labs and nothing so far about the E-corps. We need you to try and complete the picture as much as you can. Yes?" Zane nodded. "Good, we'll . . ."

The boardroom doors burst open, Altair barging in.

"It's Rain, she's getting worse!"

"Worse? What do you mean?" Bastian said, incredulous. "There's nothing here that can harm you!"

Altair responded, "The doctors seem to think that the transition here by the Astrals interferes intermittently with Urana's own energy feedback. The more she uses her powers the worse she will get, they say. We have to get her back to Magna Aura, soon!"

"But why Urana?" Azure asked. "Why haven't the rest of us been affected?"

"It might take longer, who knows, or time travel affects us in different ways," Sceptre said. "Where is she now?" he asked Altair.

"They're keeping her down in the medical centre for observation." Altair didn't seem to happy at this prospect.

There were murmurs all round. They were a warrior down.

Qane had been sitting, half-listening to the conversation with a grave look on his face, but he wasn't concerned with Urana's plight. Something had just happened, something that would change the world, again.

"Sorry to interrupt, everyone, but I think we need to watch this . . ." He pressed a button on his pad and a hatch slid open on the table permitting a three-sided plasma screen to rise up from its middle.

The screen turned on. A news conference was about to begin.

". . . Proudly introducing the E-Corps, the Elite Corps, heroes for the twenty-first century and beyond," announced a booming voice over the TV. A studio commentator noted it was like introducing the Mercury Astronauts for the first time, the superhumans in their costumes seated behind a long desk, much like the astronauts an era before them.

"And here they are: Fusioneer . . .!"

There were loud claps and cheers for the red-and-brown clad leader of the E-Corps. His short brown hair was parted on one side above his half-mask covering his upper face.

"Venture . . .!"

The African American of the future as he was touted bowed his head and raised his arms jubilantly in the air, wearing a blue and gold costume and cowl.

"Flaunt . . .!"

A curt nod and a grin from an athletic looking woman in green and black with a black mask, and brown hair in a pony-tail.

"And . . . Angelfire . . .!"

The announcer sounded like he had introduced a prized boxer into the ring, but Angelfire, all in shades of flickering golden yellow, even behind the regulation E-Corps mask looked a prized beauty.

The announcer continued, "And now, may I present the team who made this possible, led by Dr. Sagerhawk and funded through Thane Industries . . ."

Bastian turned the sound down on the TV. The announcement of a new superhuman team had flashed around the world and it was the most watched event on TV since, well, since the Starguards came to town.

"It's obvious this Dr. Sagerhawk didn't do this, at least not by himself and now we definitely know Thane is involved."

"The Devouts must be his allies," Qane surmised, nodding agreement. "But what I don't get is that Thane's a billionaire businessman. His background is murky and the government hates him, so why they should let him do this and take the credit for it is beyond me," Qane said, his white brow furrowed.

"Look there," Simon pointed at the screen to a slender blonde, bespectacled woman in a white lab coat in the crowded background of scientists. "There's Tinker, one of our spies. Maybe she'll have some answers for us."

"She's brave," Azure said. "Where did you find her?"

"Tinker's one of the Hunters' Association's undercover agents."

They continued to watch the TV, Bastain turning the sound back up. Now the E-Corp members spoke for themselves, describing their powers. The two men were American, but the brown-haired woman was British, while the golden girl was Russian, which surprised a few TV commentators.

"That's a bit of a mix," said Simon. "I doubt that will work for too long."

Zane smiled, thinking of the exotic superbeing mix Simon would get to know in the future.

But Zane's blood ran cold when she heard Flaunt speak. She knew that voice. She leaned over to Simon and whispered, "That's Lynn Kellis!"

Simon's head flicked back and forth between her and the screen. "Oh, crap!" he mouthed.

They listened as the conference went on for an hour, much like the Starguards three years ago with most of the same questions and comments repeated by the same media hacks. When it came to discussing the recent Starguard actions. All Fusioneer would say was:

"We hope the Starguards and the E-Corps can cooperate with each other to bring about world peace. They should be keen to assist us in this worthy endeavour," he smiled, as hundreds of reporter's arms flew into the air to ask more questions.

"Assist!" Altair almost jumped out of chair, hands glowing red.

"Calm down, he's trying to goad us. It will just make things worse. We need to learn about them," Qane muttered, clearly angry himself.

Once the conference was over, Qane went over his notes, even though the Starguards' crystalators had recorded everything.

"I like to think out loud," he confessed. "So, Fusioneer can manipulate matter, Venture is the flying strongman, Flaunt has some kind of impervious force field around her, and Angelfire can turn into plasma energy and fry anything and fly anywhere," Qane summed up. "A lot of energy went into that, but we detected nothing. No conventional technology made them."

"I agree. The Lore stone was definitely involved," Bastian murmured.

Just as he was mulling things over, the E-Corps conference scene was replaced by a backdrop of the American flag and a caption 'Live from the Pentagon' appeared just as General Abraham Westonheimer marched into the room with his aides. There was little preamble.

"Thank you for joining me here today. As you have just seen, the E-Corps have become the world's premier superhuman team. While they and the others who will follow represent the world, they will be based in New York. Deliberations will begin in U.N. To have the E-Corps sanctioned as a global team. As such any other superhuman team will either have to join the E-Corps project if they are eligible or cease and desist in their actions or face serious consequences . . ."

Qane's fury got the better of him and he threw a glass of water at the large screen facing him, though it bounced off harmlessly, both glass and screen made from a break-resistant material developed by the Exmoors. But it was a shocking display of temper, nonetheless.

"Qane, calm yourself," smirked Altair, clearly in sarcastic mood.

"Calm myself?" He pointed to the screen in disgust. "They have no idea who we are and the power we have and what we can do to this world . . ."

Bastian cut him off before he could continue. "What we can do for our world is to help them; save them from the hells that reside in the universe until they learn to do it for themselves. That is our destiny, Qane!" He stared patiently at the elder Exmoor.

"They make it hard for us, Bastian!"

"I agree. But isn't that the challenge?"

"So what are we going to do?" Qane asked, not even listening to Westonheimer anymore.

"We're Starguards," Altair interrupted. "We're going to do what we do best."

"And what's that?" Simon asked, dreading the worst.

"Anything we want and whatever it takes!" Altair glanced around the room with a wide grin on his face, which grew infectious as everyone caught the meaning. "Oh, and save the world of course!"

Even Sceptre was in the mood. "Altair's right, Bastian, we were sent here for a higher purpose than to be caught up in a nation's politics. We need to act, whether behind the scenes or in full view, because the Lore won't care about laws and protocol."

"Maybe Sceptre's right, father," Simon begrudgingly agreed, surprising everyone.

Bastian thought about it for a second. "The Exmoor Council will have to decide. Defying U.N. resolutions can still be tricky and Sword Industries will have to go underground . . ."

Bastian suddenly put a hand to his ear, as he listened to news relayed through his ear comms unit.

"Thank you, Ops." He smiled as something was confirmed. "We've got more visitors," he simply said.

"Oh, who now?" a dismayed Simon shook his head.

Just as he did, the conference room door slid open and an Ops controller escorted in three men and a woman.

Alpha Rion was back, along with some guests.

Qane, Simon and Bastian headed for the newcomers.

"Good to see you again, Hunter, Jack . . ."

Sceptre greeted Alpha Rion again, glad a calm head was back in the fold.

"Welcome back. What adventures did you get up to? I see you found what you wanted."

Alpha Rion smiled and introduced the woman beside him, "Aerl, this is Tera ZaVoir, the woman I told you about before. I've been travelling with her around the world as you did with the others."

The Starguards gathered around and greeted Tera with pleasure. That she had clearly captured Alpha Rion's heart instantly made her a welcomed friend.

"It's a pleasure to finally meet you all, though these days, I go by the name Chalant, now. Long story," she laughed.

As she mingled with Azure, Urana, and Zane, Sceptre and Altair spoke to Alpha Rion.

Altair asked, "So what did you like most about this world?"

"The main thing I like about these humans is their language. They curse at anything, to anything, for any reason. They've got one for everything. That and horses, even Decion liked the horses. And when we get back, I'm going to take some for Placia."

"How?" Zane asked, walking over and laughing at the idea of the

Astrals transporting whole herds of horses and other animals to Magna Aura.

"Oh, I have stored DNA samples, images, and designs for many things we can use on Magna Aura. We can birth, clone, or replicate them," Alpha Rion stated.

The other Starguards liked this idea. Zane was suitably impressed. There was much on Earth that could be transplanted to Magna Aura.

"Go on, Altair, admit it, you'll miss Earth," Zane nudged him.

But if Altair was in the mood he didn't show it. His smile abruptly faded. And Zane felt the urgent need to be somewhere else.

The Astral wandered cautiously over to Bastian and another rugged looking man with an English accent, called Hunter, catching bits of conversation.

". . . Have the heli-jet stealthed on the roof it that's okay?"

"So this is just a social visit then?"

"Yes and no," Hunter said, "We're returning Alpha Rion and Chalant, but thought we'd have a look in at what's happening and see if you needed a hand with these E-Corps wankers!"

"Well, it's good timing," suggested Qane, "but I think the Hunters should stay back, just in case this goes wrong. You'll be Earth's only hope against the Devouts."

Hunter nodded, slightly disappointed at missing out on the action.

Bastian changed the subject. "Are the Mesolithians being kept in check?"

"As well as can be expected." The Englishman assured, his tone was serious.

Zane wondered who the Mesolithians were, but before she could ask, Hunter had spotted Simon.

"Good to see you again, Simon. Can we talk?"

They wandered off for a private conversation.

Zane was about to turn away, when the other male visitor approached her.

"Hi, I'm Jack." His dark features held a smile, but his eyes were alert.

"Hi, Jack, I'm Zane. You one of the Hunters?"

"Yep." He was proud of it. "So what do you do then?"

"Mostly stay out of the way, but I'm what you might call a speedster."

Chalant came over. "She's also an Astral," she said with a twinkle in her eye."

Jack ruefully shook his head, smiling. "Don't worry, I won't hold that against you."

Zane laughed and turned to Chalant, "How'd you know I was an Astral?" Zane was intrigued.

"By the way I can't read your mind," Chalant said without reproval. "Not that I'm trying, of course."

"Ha-ha, I had a friend who told me that many years from now. He was a good friend."

"Well maybe you'll see him again, just like Alpha Rion and myself."

"I hope so," Zane agreed. She liked Tera or Chalant, or whatever she wanted to be called. She reminded her of Aaron.

Bastian arrived and held her hands affectionately.

"Good to see you again Chalant, you should stop by more often."

Chalant laughed, as Alpha Rion joined her side.

"I wish Bastian, but these past eight hundred years or so have been busy mostly working with the Hunters' Association, as you know. (Zane felt there was a lot more unspoken in those few words). And all the while waiting for Alpha Rion to appear, and eventually he showed up and we're together again." She linked her arm with Alpha Rions.

The elder Starguards looked at each other. Was Alpha Rion in love? One of the oh-so-aloof twins was actually emotionally involved with someone other than his sister. It was a priceless moment. And Alpha Rion suddenly looked embarrassed, but proud.

"So, did you find out more about Valtare?" Bastian asked. "Where could he have gone?"

"No, we lost all trace of him back then. Valtare, his men, and

Decion have completely vanished. And there's been nothing since. Or any trace my brothers! Very strange," she sounded strained.

"I'm sorry to hear that, Chalant," Bastian said. "I know how long you have search for them. But today we have confirmed that the Lore stone is here, in this city. And after today's events with the E-Corps we're going to retrieve it, sooner rather than later!"

Chalant let out a puff of air through pursed lips. "That would make my century!"

Bastian turned to Sceptre. "Do you agree?"

Reluctantly, Sceptre nodded seeing he had the unanimous verdict from the rest of the Starguards. They were in up to their necks now.

"Yes, Bastian, we'll retrieve the Lore stone, defeat the Devouts, then we Starguards will get off this world. Agreed?"

Bastian walked over and shook Sceptre's hand.

"Agreed."

He looked at Altair, who let out a theatrical sigh.

"Agreed. Here's to sacking the quarterback!" The others laughed at his odd euphemism, Altair just glad to be getting off this world.

Little did he know he would forever become entwined with Earth's destiny.

CHAPTER EIGHT

"Get outta here, you crazy bitch!"

Urana had to be restrained by Deb and Zane, dragging the Starguard away from the night club entrance.

Four doormen were still sprawled on the ground.

"Just get outta here!" one gasped, still clutching his throat, wiping blood from his mouth. The other men staggered to their feet, dazed, while onlookers whooped and shouted in surprise, or wilted away from the altercation. Most had their cells out recording the action.

"Come on," Zane whispered, keeping her head down and surreptitiously vibrating her hand as fast as she could. "Let's go before they get suspicious. We can't afford more attention!"

"Zane's right," Deb said, as more club goers spilled out to see what had happened.

Clamping an arm each, they pulled Urana away who was resisting less, but still sporting a wild grin.

Could this week get any worse? thought Zane. *The night had started so well*, she sighed.

"Two weeks. That's what we have people," stated Bastian. "The newly-established U.S./U.N. Joint Committee on Superhuman Affairs has set a deadline for the Starguards to stand down. There are credible reports that the U.S. Treasury, ATF and FBI are planning various raids on Sword Industries and investigations into the Exmoor family assets ranging from improper registration of Starguard programmes, manoeuvre suit black market sales, and tax evasion; anything they can do to bring us down!" he almost growled, banging his fist on the table.

"We know these moves were instigated by Thane," Qane added, knowing that such intense investigations could reveal more about the Exmoors than they wanted. "But we have contingency plans," he said to the boardroom with Bastian, Simon, the Starguards, and Chalant in attendance. "Sword is now virtually a shell of an organisation, with all classified files transferred, computers wiped or destroyed, and affiliate offices quietly closed down. Bastian and I will continue to exercise authority from our secondary underground bunker not far from here. With escape tunnels into the subway, other shell companies, or Exmoor residences, we'll be ready for anything.

"Also, staff and Exmoor confidants, have been stealthily transferred to other Exmoor companies unknown to public authorities or placed back into a sleeper's life. We have hidden fortunes built up over thousands of years," Bastian grinned. "We Exmoors are the wealthiest family ever, and can afford to reward and compensate our friends and employees very handsomely—it's not worth betraying us," he added darkly.

Qane had been pleased, Sceptre saw. Clandestine operations were his pastime.

"So with the Exmoors publicly off the world stage, the Hunters Association in the UK will take over and guard against any Devout activity. The Hunters are autonomous units and not connected to Sword or the Exmoor business entities. They are on constant search-and-destroy missions against Devouts and supra-vigilantes."

Black-market manoeuvre suits were still proving deadly to police and security services and more were flooding the market each day.

"Getting the blame for this illegal activity in manoeuvre suits is killing us," Simon complained. "I hate it. I hate the Terror Engineer, whoever they are! We must end this by any means possible!" he vowed.

"And what will happen to you all?" Sceptre asked

Bastian shrugged. "In time as history was forgotten, we will be able to re-surface and build another business empire and network and protect the Earth once more. Our public time in the twentieth and twenty-first centuries is over for now," a thoughtful Bastian lamented.

That's sad, thought Zane. By the twenty-third century, only Simon was known, at least publicly. She wondered what had happened to the rest of the Exmoors.

While the Exmoors suffered, the Starguards' popularity waxed and waned as the days went by. There was still some support and sympathy for Sceptre, but it was the manner in which the Starguards operated that rankled people. They wanted the Starguards under official U.S. or U.N. control, which supported their government's stance.

The Starguards were bemused that human politics were affecting their mission. Still they had two weeks left until the deadline, so any stand-off would wait until then. Even Sceptre was resigned to the fact that they would have to defy this world in order to return to theirs.

Who will blink first, he wondered.

"Let's go out and celebrate," a happy Chalant tempted the Starguards.

The boardroom meeting had left them feeling restless and gloomy.

"Celebrate?" Deb half-laughed, "We may be on the brink of death and you want to celebrate?"

"Yeah, why not? I've been on the brink of death many times and before and after are the best times to celebrate. After all, you can't do it when you're dead!"

Chalant, Urana, and Zane were in Deb's room. Chalant had already convinced Alpha Rion and the other women to go out, Sceptre and Altair having declined. Now it was Deb's turn.

"Where are you going?"

"Clubbing. Get some boogieing going on," Chalant shook her hips.

"Are you doing this, Rain?" Deb had to ask.

Urana nodded, her blue hair bouncing, already dancing. "I'm feeling better. I may not prefer all the Fifth's music, but a night out would be good."

"What about Bastian, what did he say?" Deb seemed to be trying to talk her way out of it.

"Not that we need his permission, but Bastian said it would be fine, let our hair down and relax, be normal. He'll still have a few minders tailing us just to make sure there's no trouble, but we wouldn't even see them. So c'mon, let's have some fun," Chalant almost pleaded.

"Oh, come on, Deb, please," Zane bobbed up and down. She just wanted to go out and have some fun, like a normal girl.

"Oh, alright," Deb demurred, thinking how much like Classia, her best friend and fellow Sky Warrior back on Halcyon, Zane could be at times, "Why not?"

"Fantastic!" Chalant clapped and smiled. Zane cheered. "Meet you all in tunnel six in an hour, we're going through Rui's." The Exmoor-fronted Portuguese restaurant was earning rave reviews.

They left Deb's room to get ready. Deb stared at herself in the mirror wondering how she would cope with the festivities without the ever-cheery Classia getting her into trouble. She missed Classia tremendously and often dreamed that she, Classia and Novan were together, celebrating their successful missions and return to Magna Aura. Deb snapped out of her daydream, finding a tear in her eye.

"Oh, get over it. I'm coming home soon and tonight we celebrate." She wiped the tears away, smiled, and in her best Classia voice chided, "Oh, Deb, you're such the universe."

Having lived as a non-Starguard for most of her life, Deb chose to leave the manoeuvre suit behind and put on some real clothing even though her suit could have imitated anything she wore. But as Chalant had said, they were going out as normal. The only concession Deb made was to wear a lens crystalator to record everything she saw. She had recorded everything up to this moment, especially the Lancefire dog-fight training—which she had always won—and which would come in handy to train Sky Warriors. If only Gal Agar, the late Sky Commander and father-figure, could see her now. He had sacrificed so much for her. She could sense his spirit all around her, keeping her safe, whispering sage advice; the effects from another personal crystalator implant with enhanced visual and aural memories, though Deb liked to feel that Gal Agar was actually with her.

She sashayed in front of the mirror checking her clothing, a short light-blue dress with black heels while performing a twirl, inadvertently rising in midair, before touching down lightly at the other end of the room.

"Okay, let's go be normal."

***

After traipsing through Rui's, the eponymous chef refusing to let them leave without some sumptuous cuisine, Chalant led Alpha Rion, Deb, Urana, and Zane to a club she knew well, the Outbounder. But just before they were about to enter the club after a short queue, with Chalant convincing the bouncer they were VIPs, she seemed distracted, as if sensing something, tilting her head around as if tuning in to a signal.

After a couple of minutes, she changed her mind. "Hmm, no, we'll head to another club. It's giving me good vibes!"

The others looked at each other bemused, but followed Chalant as she traced her way through the streets four blocks away until they arrived at a club called Caresses. They filed into the club as Chalant performed the same mind trick on the bouncers, much to the chagrin of minor celebrities waiting ahead of them.

"Oh wow, men, brilliant," shouted Zane as she perused the interior.

Deb could see the delight in her face, almost a mirror of Classia's after a few glasses of nectar, but Classia knew how to play the floor, men lying at her feet as she trampled on their hearts.

I'll have to keep an eye on the young Astral, Deb mused.

The five milled around and tried to mingle, Zane leading the way onto the dance floor, blue jeans and white crop top drawing the immediate attention of male admirers. Deb was amazed at how much alcohol Zane could drink and not get drunk. Urana followed, getting into the mood, her full-bodied frame in a tight yellow dress, wild flowing hair (coloured blonde for the night) and uninhibited dancing also attracting the attention of many men, who Urana simply rebuffed, almost petulantly. No mere Fifth was going to win her.

The girls were getting on fine, Chalant decided and she sent a short-burst psi-text to Deb to say she and Alpha Rion were heading to the upper level bars for some alone time. Deb waved back, while Zane gave the thumbs up.

155

Chalant took Alpha Rion by the hand, leading him up the spiral stairs. His armour had been transformed into black trousers and a smart white shirt, which Chalant unbuttoned a bit more showing his muscled torso. His handsome looks with dark blue eyes under flowing black hair gaining admirers from women, which Chalant non-jealously appreciated. After a few drinks, too, they were dancing away on the floor, their eyes only on each other—the rest of the world and even time meaningless to them. Alpha Rion could only admire Chalant's energy and very short black dress emphasising her lithe ebony legs.

"Nice legs," Alpha Rion said

"Really, I think they've been getting fat over the centuries."

"No, more athletic, I think," Alpha Rion admired them, while they spun around the floor

"Athletic, eh? The only athletic thing they'll be doing tonight is getting wrapped around your neck."

"Sorry?"

"How about it?"

"About what?"

"You know . . ." she said, flashing her eyes.

Before Alpha Rion could answer, a woman passed them on the floor half-dancing toward the bar.

There was something about her which drew Chalant's attention—the reason she was drawn here. It wasn't her looks: above average, late-twenty-something, brown pony-tail, and world weary smile, there was something to this woman, a mystery. Chalant had to find out.

"I'll be back," she indicated to Alpha Rion leaving him a bit perplexed, dancing by himself.

Standing at the bar by the woman, Chalant caught her attention.

"Hey," she shouted over the music, while the woman waited to be served, "How's it going? I'm Tera."

The woman was a bit hesitant to answer, but she replied, "I'm Maggie. Nice to meet you."

She shook Chalant's hand, a brief inkling of her life sifting into

Chalant's mind. She prodded Maggie's mind and kept a straight face as she saw the images float through . . .

. . . Her real name is Lynn . . .

"So what do you do Maggie?" Chalant asked as innocently as she could.

The question caught her by surprise. "Oh, I'm an international IT consultant-slash-troubleshooter. Boring really, but I get to travel." She smiled in an end-of-conversation way, turning to the bar.

Ah, interesting, Chalant smiled back, *E-Corps member charged with monitoring and eliminating supra-vigilantes. Lynn loved it. She was serving a purpose.*

Maggie looked for the barman to serve her, but Chalant furtively pushed the man away to serves others before them.

"Man, what is wrong with this guy?" a frustrated Maggie threw her hands up.

"I know, guys, right?" Chalant sympathised. "Hey, where you from?" At Maggie's suspicious look at her from her continued questions, Chalant said, "I can hear the accent."

More guarded, Maggie answered, "Well, I'm from London, that's in England. Across the pond," she joked.

Almost, Chalant pierced her memories . . . born in France and moved to southern England when her parents split up when she was two years old. She was always in trouble, tomboy, with an interest in the military to escape a humdrum life. Her interest in science came earlier when her professor taught her chemistry, biology, and then the physics of sex. She managed to pull her intelligence and misspent youth together and graduate university, later completing a Masters in science at Oxford, majoring in physical biology and genetics.

"You having fun here?" Chalant leaned in closer.

"Yeah. You?"

"Absolutely. You with anyone?"

"What? Boyfriend?" Maggie waved Chalant off. "No, just out with a friend."

Lynn was a loner; the job was her life. No room for love or settling down. After Oxford, she had fulfilled her ambition and joined the British Army for some adventure, but three years in the Intelligence Corps and her failure at SAS selection, left her bored, so she opted for the civilian Intelligence Service instead. It was here Lynn found the clandestine workings of the world fascinating. It was also here she crossed paths with Stephanie Mikovitch, an ex-American spy with a grudge who had been recently recruited by Mr. Penthor Thane as his bodyguard. Steph had offered Kellis a job with a scientist that she knew who was going to change the world. It was an offer Kellis couldn't refuse. And months later, Lynn Kellis had 'died' in a fiery car crash, her remains identified by dental records—supplied by Thane.

Chalant got hazy bits of memory: a ship in the ocean, vast metal tanks, a glowing blue light, and Lynn's body infused with some energy. The scientist in Lynn's head had said it was impossible, but here she was, a superhuman.

Processing that, Chalant asked, "So you're here to party then?"

"Oh, this and that. Bit of work and pleasure, the usual. Actually, I'm just passing through on my way down to Florida."

She was awaiting orders from the boss, laying low.

"And you?"

Chalant turned, indicating Alpha Rion on the dance floor, now surrounded by gyrating women. Chalant laughed at his uncomfortable situation as he looked over at her to be rescued.

"I'm out with my partner!"

"Looks like he needs rescuing," 'Maggie' said also noting Alpha Rion's awkwardness on the floor.

Another young woman sidled over beside Lynn.

"Maggie we have to go, forget the drinks." The blonde pulled at Lynn.

"Okay, hold your horses, er, Kate—actually Starshina, the fiery one—I'm coming," she said. She waved goodbye to Chalant. "Catcha laters."

"Nice to meet you too, Maggie, and hope we see each other soon." Chalant smiled, leaving Lynn with a strange look on her face.

"What was that all about?" Alpha Rion arrived, shouting over the music.

Chalant shook her head, "Nothing." What could she say: that the nice woman was the enemy and they might have to kill her someday? She hoped it wouldn't come to that.

"Let's go home," she said, pulling Alpha Rion through the crowd, sending Deb a psi-text to say they were leaving.

"Who were they?" Starshina asked Lynn, once they had left the club. They waited as a Thane-owned limousine pulled up, upon Starshina's signal.

"Oh, no one, just a woman asking me questions. I think she wanted a threesome or something," Lynn frowned.

"Hey, kinky, more Pandra's thing!"

"Tell me about it."

They got into the limo, the driver confirming their identities as Thane employees with a simple thumb-print device he held out: Maggie Denholm and Kate Shashova.

If only the driver knew who we really were, Lynn mused.

"Where we going anyway?" Lynn lay back in the plush leather seat.

"Zero base," Starshina whispered.

Lynn sat up, startled at the news. "You're kidding, right?"

"Nope. Got a call from J.J. to meet him there. I think the mission's on soon."

"Sweet! Can't wait, I was going stir crazy. At least we got to sneak out and have fun."

"Ha-ha," Starshina agreed. "Actually, I think the fun is about to begin."

The limo sped on toward Thane Universal, parked in the underground car park and the two E-Corps women headed up to their quarters.

Chalant and Alpha Rion ended up at Chalant's apartment in Harlem, a permanent suite courtesy of the Exmoors, one of several worldwide.

They were kissing before she locked the door behind her, undressed in a frenzy by the time they reached the bedroom and she jumped into his arms.

"I just realised how much I've missed you over the centuries."

"First time I saw you I knew I loved you," Alpha Rion replied.

"I love you too, Alpha Rion," smothering him with kisses. She pushed Alpha Rion onto his back. He tried to roll over onto Chalant, but she resisted. "Uh, uh," she purred. "I've waited centuries for this!"

Deb, Urana, and Zane were left alone. After dancing, constantly pestered by men, they had retired to a side bar with their cocktails away from the cattle market of the dance floor and male-dominated surroundings.

"Back off or I'll melt you!" Urana had threatened a persistent admirer if he touched her behind again, Deb having to drag her away to avoid a carbonised puddle in the middle of the club.

Deb couldn't help but laugh at the situation as she stirred her mojito.

"What?" Zane reacted.

"Us three, practical cripples—a Lore maiden, a grounded Astral, and a sick Starguard. What a group we are!"

"I dunno, I think we're okay," Zane said chirpily.

"Speak for yourself," Urana said, her alert eyes still glued for any encroaching men, though they seemed intent on strutting their stuff from a more respectful distance. "Why would anyone want to mate with one of those Fifths?"

"Excuse me, Rain, but I am half-Fifth you know," Zane retorted, half-affronted.

Urana shrugged, a smile on her face.

Deb had to ask, "Have you already done so, Zane?"

That caught Urana's attention.

Zane blushed. "Done what?" she asked innocently.

Deb gave her a 'you know' look.

Urana was more direct. "Have you started having sex, yet?" Her face was serious, but her tone was playful.

Zane thoughts turned to Paolo, a wistful smile lighting her face. It didn't go unmissed.

"So there was someone!" Deb gasped in surprise.

But Zane shook her head. She told them about Paolo. "Could have been true love, who knows, maybe could be if I weren't dead. It's not so bad is it, being a virgin?"

Deb shrugged, a strange look on her face.

"Have you, Deb?" Urana asked the Sky warrior, catching the look.

Deb hesitated, not sure if she should say anything. "I had a dream about Novan once, just after I found out who I really was. Strange dream—almost real. We were on Cirrius' island . . ." She waved the thoughts away. "Anyway, no."

"Not even Gal Agar?" Urana teased.

"Universe, no! He was like a father to me, Rain, Universe count his soul." Deb grinned, then she remembered another half dream about Tol Valar. "There was another Sky Warrior who I dreamed tried to force me once . . ." she said, but then her grin returned, lost in half memories and thoughts.

Guiltily, Zane realised those events had probably occurred in the previous time-line before the Astrals had reversed time, saving the Starguards. She almost felt sorry for Deb, but that was such another lifetime ago. Deb was living a new life now.

Urana laughed, "If Tol Valar had done that he would have paid for it. I'd have melted his branchless tree, ripped out the stumpy roots and seeds . . ."

"Ew, Rain, that's drastic!" Zane pulled a face. Then she thought about it, "What kind of trees do you guys have? Gross." She changed the subject. "And what about you and Altair, Rain? There seems to be some . . ." she gestured for the right words, but couldn't find any.

"Yeah, Rain, what's going on there then?" Deb echoed.

Urana shook her head, "Nothing." The Starguard seemed surprised at the question, quietly sipping her drink. "Altair and I grew up together, we're half cousins, though he's more than a brother to me. If I did mate with anyone, it could be him. Who else is there?"

Zane hesitated to ask Urana, but curiosity got the better of her, "Have you actually . . ." she shyly gestured something lewd.

Urana pursed her lips. She took up her glass to sip her cranberry cocktail and just before it touch her lips: "No," she whispered.

The three looked at each other then burst out laughing.

"Great, three crippled virgins," Zane laughed.

"Well Zane," Urana explained. "We're different to normal Fifths, sorry humans, and Celestians. I guess when Millennius arrived on Earth, he, and later your father had no choice in their mating situation. Though maybe they knowingly or unknowingly found women with Celestian ancestry, not tainted by the Devouts, hence the inherited abilities of the Astrals.

"On Magna Aura, there are only the Starguards. The so-called elite families, in our supposed egalitarian society, are few and far between and mating with normal Magna Aurans does not appeal to me. I am the Protectress of State on Placia; no mere ordinary man would be my consort. Celestians can expect to live between a hundred and fifty to two hundred years and we Starguards can expect to live maybe five or six times as long. So we have time to decide who we want to be with."

"Cool," Zane was impressed. "What's it like there?" she asked intrigued. She hadn't seen too much of the civilisation beyond what the Chronopolis' Oracle had shown her.

Urana carried on, "The Celestian home worlds were paradises of orderliness, but things changed when we arrived at Magna Aura. There is still order, but too much uncertainty and fear, even with the Sky Warriors who are akin to your police, defense, exploration, and community forces in one. They maintain peace, but apart from the Lore War deal with nothing as drastic as what you have on Earth.

"We were lucky. Magna Aura was the fourth system we came across which was closest in type to the Celestian home worlds. Halcyon and Placia; the twin worlds, Magna Prime with its many moons, the City-States in space. Placia was perfect with thirty-five hour days, four hundred and twenty-eight days a year; Halcyon with just a little less of both. They are peaceful worlds. We tamed the land, oceans, and weather where required, and lived contentedly, no poverty or incessant chaos like on Earth."

"Sounds amazing. I'd really like to visit one day!" Zane was thoughtful. But still thinking of procreation, she asked, "What about Astrals or Exmoors? They live long. My uncle Helexius would love you, and you know Lightstream, his daughter," she said, knowing it was a lost cause.

Urana twisted her mouth. "No offense, Zane, they may be nice as you're family, but they treat others like . . ."

"Crap," Zane filled in for her. "Yeah, I know, but we are all family, so it will change I'm sure, once this is all over," she hoped.

"Hope so," Urana said.

"What about Simon?" Deb asked mischievously.

"No," intoned Zane and Urana together with the same expression of disgust.

"Exmoors as consorts could be interesting though," Deb conceded.

"Except for Simon, he's not very likeable in the future," Zane countered. "Come to think of it, he's the only Exmoor I met or heard of in the future, so maybe he is, compared to the others."

"Plus their main mission seems to be to exterminate women," Urana added.

"Okay, I'll give you that," Deb's mouth screwed ruefully. She leaned closer to Urana, "Why not Aerl, he seems nice enough, very handsome?" she asked.

Urana shook her head, "No, not my type, too stiff and regulated. I like wildness."

"That's definitely Altair," Zane laughed. "A real Captain

Caveman!"

She didn't explain it to Urana, though Deb seemed to get it. Zane sipped her white wine, a bit too sweet for her liking, but harmless to her, though she felt she was getting a bit tipsy. Which is why she said: "Well, maybe you and Altair can get it on tonight? Time's running out, you know. You can do what you want on Earth."

There was a sly smile on Deb's lips as she looked across at her fellow Starguard. Urana's face didn't show anything either way, as if she didn't hear.

"Don't worry, Rain, we won't say a thing . . ." Zane flashed her eyes, making a zipping motion across her lips.

"I think, young Astral, you've had too much to drink."

"No, no, drinks, drugs and such don't harm me, Astral constitution and all that," she patted her stomach. "Just think about it though, you have freedom here and now, and you know . . ." She stopped herself from saying too much.

"We might die here, thanks for the reminder, Zane. . ." Deb put in, non-too-sternly.

"I think we should stop talking about it," Urana said, putting an end to that particular discussion.

"Well at least Alpha Rion seems to have done alright. I really like Chalant, but what is she, like a million years old or something?" Deb quipped. "Alpha Rion is way out of his league, but they're in love."

"Ha, no she's only a few thousand years old . . ." Zane stopped suddenly as a clear thought struck her: Wasn't Aaron around the same age? she thought. How much of a coincidence would it be if they knew each other, too much if they were actually long lost brother and sister, surely? She would definitely have to ask Chalant next time.

The three had a couple more drinks as the night wore on, chatting about their time on Earth.

But they were interrupted by a particularly couple of brave men who waltzed over, drinks in hand. Zane knew from their previous attempts they weren't going to take no for an answer. A blond male, muscles bulging from his loose-collared red shirt, leaned over to Urana, lunging for her hand for a dance.

"That's it!" snarled Urana, "I'm going to zap this guy into sterility!"

She angrily raised her hand, just as Deb grabbed it, pitching the table up spilling their drinks on the man's crotch.

Urana laughed. The man's face grew red, as surrounding dancers laughed, too.

Whether he meant to strike Urana would never be known, but as his drunk mate blundered into him ostensibly to pull him away, the blond man's raised fist connected hard with Urana's cheek as he and his friend toppled onto the table, drinks flying everywhere.

The club seemed to enter a state of slow motion. The blond man was on top of Urana. He swore her eyes were glowing fire. He could feel a heat rising around him; his fear raking the back of his neck, sweat trickling over his eyes. There was a noise, growing, vibrating through him.

Urana stared at the man on her. His ragged breath on her cheek, his wide eyes empty of vacuous bravado, his hands still on her chest frozen in fear. His presence offending her, defiling her. An inner surge of burning rage built up in her.

"Raaaargh!" Urana scream in fury.

She punched the reclining man hard, sending him flying into the group of newly-arrived security guards. They all looked at Urana, then at the man, limbs splayed on the floor. He wasn't getting up. The security guards' first mistake was to assume Urana was finished.

One bouncer tried to help up the unconscious man. His friend then turned on Urana.

"What the hell, it's her fault!" he pointed at Urana, who obligingly punched him over the table.

Security then turned to Urana. "Hey, let's go, lady!" one of yelled. "We don't want any trouble or we'll have to call the cops. Come on!" He tried to grab Urana's arm.

Second mistake.

Zane and Deb had been standing aside. They were too late in trying to drag Urana out.

Twenty seconds later and the guards were on the floor in pain, bloodied noses. Even as more security poured in, Urana's blurred fists made short work of them.

Zane waggled her hand furiously, disrupting any electronic instruments. Hopefully that had taken care of anyone recording them, she thought. Her powers also seemed to have stunned people who moved in a stupefied fashion, dizzy and disorientated—mild temporal dislocation, Bastian had called it.

Sure comes in handy, thought Zane as she and Deb forcibly dragged Urana from the club, leaving injured bouncers shouting at them from the doorway.

"Hah, that was fun!" Urana laughed, caressing her fists and ignoring the insults hurled their way. "I hate Fifth men!"

"Seriously, you had to start a fight tonight?" Zane chastised her "What's wrong with you? You could have killed that guy!" She tried to walk ahead, angry at Urana who made a face at her.

"Let's just head back," Deb said, hearing sirens behind them.

As they walked, two men nonchalantly joined them, quickly identifying themselves as Exmoor employees, before Urana had the chance to spear them with plasma rain. Their minders directed them to a black SUV then drove them back to another Exmoor company, masquerading as a law firm, whereupon they walked through another tunnel into Sword HQ itself.

After a particularly frosty elevator ride, Zane left the two without saying anything. Deb felt guilty at Zane's silent treatment. They had had some fun at least. She promised she would make it up to the young Astral in the morning.

"Goodnight, Urana," she said, wearily pushing a compliant Urana into her own room.

Pausing at the door, Urana sighed. "I know I ruined Zane's night. I'll apologise in the morning," she swayed inside. She hugged Deb, sharing a smile. "Good night."

Deb retired to her room.

But Urana could not sleep. She stared at the ceiling or tossed and turned. The bedside clock showed two thirty AM. Her thoughts harkened back to earlier conversations with Deb and Zane and actions. Perhaps she had been angry at something else. Her fitful dreams had been full of images she hadn't contemplated before.

What if Zane was right about Altair? What if there was no better time than now? What if. . . . ? Urana tossed and turned.

"Oh, I hate you, Zane!"

Urana got out of bed, put on some plain jeans and a t-shirt and left the room. Down the corridor and to the left she paused outside the door, before knocking twice. There was no answer. She shook her head.

"Stupid me." She started back to her door.

There was a noise behind her as the lock clicked and Altair opened the door.

"Rain?" he said, his eyes still full of sleep, "Is anything wrong?"

Urana turned around, regarding Altair as he stood there, his naked, muscled torso peeking invitingly out the door. Urana cleared her throat and walked toward Altair, who looked confused. She brushed by him and stood in the middle of the room, waiting.

"What's wrong?" He took her hand, concerned for her.

They stood face to face, searching each others face for answers.

Urana cupped his face, his blond stubble sending sensual shocks through her fingertips, and shivers down her body. She kissed him, his lips forming around hers in a gentle caress.

He broke off, shaking his head, puzzled.

Urana held him still. "This is our time, Altair," she whispered.

She kissed him hard and he responded. Their hands slowly explored their new surroundings, hard and soft; her breasts pressed against his chest as they entangled in passion, fumbling for useless zips and buttons on the Fifths' clothing, which perversely heightened their anticipation.

They dragged each other to the bed and dropped on top of it, Urana straddling Altair, whose uncertainty gave way to a shy grin, as Urana pulled off her t-shirt and brought his hands to her firm breasts. Starguard blood was directed to the only place that mattered.

"Urana, I . . . uhh!" he sighed with pleasure as Urana directed him inside her.

"Shh," Urana put a finger to her lips, as she began rocking back and forth.

For once, Altair was speechless.

Zane woke up.

She knew she wasn't alone in her room. Her head darted around seeking the intruder. And in the corner shadow stood a darker shadow: tall, unmoving, silent darkness.

She stared at it defiantly, sitting up, her heart beating so fast it ached to breathe.

"Who's there? Come out," she hissed.

The shadow moved toward her slowly, the dark clinging to it like a shroud.

"Lights," Zane called, but nothing happened. She screamed, but there was no response from outside. She panicked and clambered out the other side of the bed.

"Zane Astral," the shadow spoke with a deep echoing voice, the shroud of darkness lifting away from it, "Do not be afraid. I am here to give you the answers you seek."

Zane stood in the far corner of the room opposite the shadow. Her chest ached from the deep breaths she was drawing. She couldn't run, couldn't hide.

"Okay, that's nice of you . . .!" she gasped, trying to sound calm. "Tell me now or I'll call for help."

"Zane Astral," said the calm, smooth voice. "We are not in your room, go see." An arm pointed toward the bedroom door on her side of the wall.

Zane looked at the door. It occurred to her to run as soon as she reached it, but as she pulled it open, there was nothing. The open door led to nothing but nothingness. She stood on the edge of infinity.

She looked back at the being, astonished at what she saw. It, he, the thing, was at least seven feet tall, and entirely made of what looked like crystal, blood-red crystal, with two golden eyes shining from its face and another on the palm of his left hand, which he held face-up toward her. Zane realised that though its crystal head had features which resembled facial features, it had no mouth to speak from, only the eyes. Its head was crowned with jagged crystals that seemed afire, glowing slightly when he spoke.

"Oh, I see," Zane guessed. "You're in here!" she tapped the side of her head. "What is it with you telepaths?" She closed the door, but remained by it.

"Yes, Zane Ast—"

"Stop calling me that. Zane will do just fine."

"Zane, I have travelled far in time, space, and mind to meet you. I am honoured. But there is not much time. You must save the Starguards. History must happen as is. The future must run its true course."

"Who are you? Did you save me from Netherlord and bring me here then?" Zane was desperate to be get answers.

"I am not important. You are. The Time Empress has sent me. She saved you."

"Time Empress? An Astral? We have no Empress!" She wanted to ask more, but he continued.

"Zane, dark forces work against the Astrals and the Starguards. They fear what you will become. They have destroyed you both once before, but you have been resurrected. There is a war coming and you and the Starguards must save the only hope for the future."

"If it's the Lore you're talking about then it's not up to me to fight. There are others that can."

"It is not the Lore, Zane."

"What?" a staggered Zane was shocked: something worse than the Lore? "Then who? And why me? Why not the other Astrals, or my brother. He's stronger than me. I can't even travel time."

"It is you, Zane. You must."

"No! Choose Aristedes."

"He cannot!"

"Why not, they are all better Astrals then me. Why not you?" she changed tact.

"They cannot! I cannot!"

"I don't know what to do. How will I know?"

"You will know when the time is right. Your time approaches, Zane. You will act!"

"And you know this how? From this supposed Time Empress?"

"Yes, it has been foreseen."

"And I'm supposed to save the saviour of the future?" Zane asked, almost flippantly. "Who is it then?"

There was an ominous pause: "Your father, Zane. Lord Aeon."

Zane woke with a start.

Was that a dream? she thought. She found herself alone in her room. She didn't know whether to laugh, cry, dance around the room, or even believe what had just happened. She lay back on the bed ready to dare to dream again. . .

Just as the security alarms went off.

CHAPTER NINE

Pre-emptive strike.

It had such a ring of ominous melodrama and provocation about it that Van Tager could not resist when it was suggested. As the Archwitch, Van Tager had an affinity with Lore energy. She was the closest thing to being a Loremaiden without actually being born one. She could manipulate the raw living energy through the Lore stone, minutely affect time around her, help to create superbeings by fusing snippets of enhanced viral Lore stone energy to their DNA, and she also possessed a longer than average human lifespan. It was why she had been chosen out of all the Devouts for this mission, by her mother and their lord.

Obitumary was the brain-box of the Devouts. It had been her plan.

"So you're telling me that the Lore stone has as much energy stored within it as several hydrogen bombs if bombarded with the right—or wrong—energy?" Van Tager was fascinated by this information.

"Yes," replied the trained physicist. Obitumary had been the one to train Van Tager in modern twenty-first century science when she had arrived. "But there could also be repercussions felt through time, like temporal shock waves."

Van Tager folded her arms in thought. "Do it," she ordered calmly.

Five milligrams of the Lore stone was all that was needed, Obitumary had calculated, to cause a minor explosion, nothing too deadly, but enough to warn the Starguards or provoke them. They knew it would be the latter.

Only Van Tager could safely touch the Lore stone. In her lab with the cautious assistance of Obitumary, she had carefully shaved off the required amount with a charge of her own energy which also contained it within a small generated temporal field. The chip hovered in the round blue field.

Van Tager laughed when Obitumary had theorised, "And the best thing of all is that the Exmoors won't be able to detect the Lore stone chip, unless it is activated. Once the shard is sent over it will phase in and out of reality. And a five-milligram piece floating through phase space wouldn't be detected at all." Obitumary made an explosive gesture with her hands and face. "Then all hell will break loose!"

"Sylphia," Van Tager called out. "Follow me!"

The willowy Devout attached to that name shambled forth. Her plain pale face framed by lank blonde hair lit up as she attended to Van Tager. Her light blue manoeuvre suit was dirty, a patch of tomato sauce on her sleeve a result of a hastily eaten burger for lunch. She was always hungry and even now was chewing on some candy.

As they trooped up to the roof, Van Tager lamented the choice of Devouts around her. Kids mostly. Young Clair, Kinecity and Cin a couple of rebellious teenagers, Sylphia a little older, and pensioner Peril. Only Obitumary was a responsible adult, older than Van Tager even. She didn't envy the job Obitumary had taken in discovering and forging them into a team before her arrival. But now they had to be ready. Van Tager studied the faces of the Devouts, young and fierce. Now the kids had to grow up.

She looked at Sylphia and held out her hand with the blue shard of Lore stone balanced upon her palm.

Sylphia held up her own hands, generated a breath of wind, and lifted the alien chip. The speck of energised material was sent aloft on a raft of air. The gathered Devouts watched as it phased in and out of real timespace toward its intended target.

"This is revenge for the Goth!" Van Tager swore loudly, "Retribution for all the other dead Devouts throughout time; a strike at the ones who have persecuted and committed genocide against the Devouts and against my husband's people!"

They stood on the roof, holding hands. They cheered. This was the beginning of a new Devout era.

Deb slept. She dreamed of home, of towering spires, and deep blue skies lovingly layered to fly in. The Halcyon firmament was endless. Her body breathed in the air, catalysing the atmosphere within her into kinetic energy as she throttled up into the heavens; the horizons around her darkening, the air thinning, and breaking apart, and Deb found herself choking . . .

She sat bolt upright in bed, her eyes aglow with a fierce blue light.

The Lore!

Azure leaped from her bed and coasted out the room, flying down the corridor in an upright position barely aware, as if in a trance.

A couple of night duty security officers patrolling the corridors called out in greeting to the Starguard clad in a scanty nightgown. But Azure continued on her sleep-journey, oblivious to the world. She stepped into the airlock rising to the roof. And then she was gone, flying off to destination unknown.

The officers looked at each other. The senior of the two contacted Ops. "Er, are their any scheduled Starguard missions tonight? Azure just took off in her nightgown and her eyes were glowing blue!"

They waited for a reply. Seconds ticked by.

Suddenly the alarms blared around them.

"Take your stations, boys," the Ops supervisor ordered, the two officers already running on their way to secure the perimeter.

Roused, the Starguards and Exmoors convened in the Ops.

"What's happened?" A manoeuvre-suited Sceptre was ready for action.

"Where's Azure?" Urana asked, anxiously looking around.

"That's the problem. Azure just took off. Security reported that her eyes were glowing blue," Bastian explained, checking screens and reports.

"Universe! The Lore are here!" Urana gasped. "How could they get here without being detected? Why didn't Azure warn us?"

"I'll find out," Altair was gone before anyone could stop him, even Sceptre.

"Let him go," Sceptre conceded. "He'll make sure Azure is protected. But we need to know where she's going."

"She isn't going anywhere," Qane said as he entered Ops, open tablet in hand. "She's just hovering above the building, as if waiting." He showed them the shining blip on a map above the building.

"Huh, weird," Simon muttered.

They looked at the tablet and each other in confusion, before racing to the roof.

"What's happening Obitumary? I can't sense anything," Van Tager complained, straining her eyes across the city.

Obitumary was confused as well, "I don't know," she almost growled as she checked her sensor readouts on her laptop. "The Lore stone chip should have exploded by now, even allowing for its unpredictable temporal nature."

They all pressed tightly around her screen looking for any signs of the stone.

Sylphia then shouted, "Hey, look! There's a bright blue light hovering over the Sword building!"

"A what?" chorused Van Tager and Obitumary.

They looked up in disbelief and sure enough, across Manhattan, there was a bright blue light hanging over Sword Industries like a protective star.

"What the hell is that, a forcefield? They've got no defences against the Lore stone, do they?" Kinecity said, her echo-like voice increased by her agitation, her rapid pacing sending small sparks from her body.

"Mary, you're the tech. I need eyes on that, now!" Van Tager ordered. "Clair, what do you have?" she glanced back at the diminutive psychic.

Clair Voyant looked up at Van Tager, an utter look of bewilderment in her big brown eyes, her voice unusually hesitant, "I . . . don't know. I can't see. I can't see," she said, almost in tears. "There's nothing there."

"Clair?" Van Tager took her by the shoulders and shook her. "Clair,

I need to know," her voice a terse order.

Shivering visibly Clair shook her head, her voice cracked, "There's nothing there. The future's all . . . muddled up." She stared at the blue star above Sword. "It's that! It's . . ." she struggled as if straining her senses, "It's her, she's coming for us!"

"Who is she? That's impossible," laughed Obitumary.

"I think we've screwed up big time," a frantic Sylphia fretted, wringing her hands.

"Shut up, will you," Obitumary admonished her.

"No!" she gave Obitumary a dark look; a mixture of fear for her life and anger at herself for being seen as weaker than the others. "I think they have something we don't know about and they're going to use it against us. We need to leave, now." Sylphia made to leave.

"No, dammit!" Van Tager said, gritting her teeth, "No, there is no leaving. It ends now. We'll never have a better time, no matter what that is out there," she pointed in the general direction of Sword Industries. "Besides, I have an idea."

She ushered them all back inside down to her suite, the atmosphere inside like a bomb shelter waiting for the raining down of shells.

Van Tager took out the Lore stone from the vault. "Come on, Mary, let's do another one." She held up the stone from its velvet pouch, ready to take another chip off the temporal block.

"Um, with all due respect, Elisabeth, are you crazy?" Obitumary asked, incredulous, shying away from any potential backlash from the Archwitch.

"No, Mary. Our attacks won't be seen, the humans have nothing to detect it with, but the Exmoors have a great big blue beacon above them shining away for the whole city to see and if they use it against us, then we'll be the victims and the world will rally with us against the Starguards. And we've got the E-Corps on our side, Thane will see to that."

Dubious, Obitumary looked around at the others. She had been the Devouts' nominal leader before Van Tager had appeared and they still looked to her as a matter of course. But Obitumary still believed in Van Tager's mission and if this was the time to stand and fight then so be it.

"Okay," she smiled, with renewed determination. "Let's light this Lore candle!"

Van Tager was relieved, but hid it behind a commanding smile, "We shall. Bigger bit this time!" Her eyes flashed wildly.

Altair stormed up to the roof ready to blast off into the night sky in pursuit of Azure, but he didn't get far.

The roof was bathed in blue light emanating from Azure who floated vertically, fifty feet above Sword Tower. The night was absolutely still and silent, the eerie light casting flickering shadows.

Altair looked around. *Where are the Lore? Isn't Azure's power to detect and destroy Lore?* he thought.

His visor was picking up nothing. He tried to report to Sceptre, but is comms were jammed. *Azure's energy?* he wondered. Altair looked up again, not sure if to approach Azure.

Azure moved. She held out her hand and something small, delicate and blue appeared in it. It lasted for a second then flashed away into nothingness. Azure slumped in the sky, though still aloft. The blue emanation disappeared. Almost immediately, she looked around, dazed and more than confused.

Altair shot up to her. "Azure, what happened? What was that?"

Azure looked at Altair, shaking her head, "I was in bed. What am I doing out here?" Then she recalled. "I had a dream about the Lore, but it was dying. I searched for it and it came to me and died, right in my hand." She looked down at her empty hand. "Then I was here." She shrugged, not knowing what to make of her own dream.

Gathering herself, she realised what she was wearing. She blushed as Altair comprehended belatedly and looked away from the virtually see-through gown.

"Armour," Azure commanded and her two-toned blue manoeuvre

suit covered her. She thought about what had just happened before grasping the reality of the situation. "The Lore stone," she thought aloud. "The Devouts must have somehow taken a piece of it and transported it over here. The power in it would have been immense. But I absorbed it." She looked at her hand, devoid of any injury from the explosion. It set her mind wondering on her powers.

Altair laughed, "They didn't reckon on you, Azure. For the second time, you've saved us. You are a Starguard after all," he grinned.

His comms crackled into life, just as there were shouts from below. The rest of the Starguards and Exmoors arrived on the roof. Altair waved down to say everything was okay. He turned to assure Azure—
"Aaahhhh!"

—Intense light, searingly blue flash blinded Altair so much so that he couldn't face Azure. He could barely make out the ground where the others also shielded their eyes from the glare.

Altair dared to turn back, his visor hardly coping to shield his eyes. He cried out in pain as light burned into him, and he was horrified by what he saw.

Azure shimmered. She screamed. Her body fluttered, expanded, and transformed between the physical and energy—fluid blue energy. Like her father.

Altair shrunk away from the raw energy pouring into him. He cowed from the haunting image before him, wanting to escape. He dared himself to back off. But couldn't. Azure needed his help. She was a Starguard. Not her father.

He had to reach her. But not before a blue bolt of energy reached out and slapped him across the body.

Azure convulsed violently. Energy ripped through her. She could feel the grip of the Lore clawing at her, stronger than last time as her body tried to absorb the energy of a one-ton yield bomb. She'd almost lost it, her temporalmorphic nature wanting to take over and fully transform into a raging Lore. But she fought it, bringing the energy under control. There was a final pulse of searing blue, which shattered the air around her with a sharp clap of thunder. She felt cooler; the energy dissipating, her rage assuaging, until the black night sky of Earth swam around her. She sagged against the sky, catching her breath.

She laughed aloud for no reason other than being alive and being right.

"It was the Lore stone," she said to herself. Bits and pieces were being thrown their way. The Devouts were trying to destroy them, using the Lore stone. "Idiots, they have no idea what power the Lore stone held. No idea at all!"

Azure had to stop them before they released her full Lore. The Lore could not win. Before anyone could react after the attack, Azure soared off accelerating through the moonless night toward Thane Universal.

Altair found himself flat on his back on the roof. The blue energy tendril had whipped him to the rooftop. He coughed a couple of times, drawing in breath. The others crowded around him, but he pushed them away.

"Did you see that?" They stared at him blankly. He shook his head to clear it. "She changed into a Lore for a few seconds. She absorbed more Lore energy again. If she finds that Lore stone . . ." he let his thoughts go unfinished as they all imagined the horror that would release.

"Hell," Simon exclaimed, suppressing a grim smile at the thought that Azure could be the Lore the Starguards were meant to stop.

No need to stir that pot, he thought.

Sceptre was the first to react, "Zane, I need to know what's happening there, go! We're on our way." He switched comm signals placing a separate call.

"Alpha Rion, emergency at Sword. Meet us at Thane's building!" He ended the call before getting a reply.

Zane grinned wildly, her first mission. She sped off down the stairs, first to get changed into her newly-issued manoeuvre suit—she wasn't fortunate enough to have a neuro-crystalator-controlled suit—

and then she raced down the stairs, popping in and out of time. It took her five point two seconds to reach Thane's building across town, guards already building up outside on the orders of Thane who had been alerted to an attack by Van Tager. The E-Corps were already on standby in the building.

She easily snuck past them and into the building, flitting around and making her way to find Azure who had to be in the building already.

This was going to be fun, she laughed to herself.

Rather than observe from the roof, Van Tager trained one of Obitumary's roof-top telescopes on Sword Industries as they launched their second attack. Their eyes were still smarting from Azure's pulse as the computer monitor the telescope was hooked into almost blew apart just from the glare.

"Oh, hell!" screamed Sylphia.

"How can she being doing that?" Obitumary asked herself angrily. The Lore stones was beyond the limits of normal physics. "Impossible!" she muttered again.

Van Tager was already calling Thane.

"It's me, the E-Corps are needed. We're under imminent attack from the Starguards! Thank you." She hung up, stressed.

They watched the monitor in shock as the blue-clad Starguard came streaking toward them.

"She'll land on the roof. Go get her," she told the Devouts, some of whom baulked at the suggested. Van Tager glared at them. "Bring her down to the labs, alive." Her tone brooked no argument.

"What makes you think we can do that and she doesn't vapourise us like the Lore stone?" an anxious Kinecity asked, pacing up a fuzzy blur.

"Stop whining," Van Tager said. "She's never shown she can do that before. I think it was the Lore stone. She'll make a great test subject and a hostage against the Starguards. Now go," she forcefully ordered.

Obitumary led Kinecity, Cin, Peril, and Sylphia out.

"Clair, a word," Van Tager called back the young Devout.

Van Tager whispered into Clair's ear, the girl's eyes widening in shock.

"But . . ." she began to protest.

But Van Tager cut her off, "Just go."

Clair stood in defiance for a while, tears forming in her eyes, "Goodbye, Elisabeth," she murmured discontentedly. She turned and walked out the door.

Van Tager held the tears back. It was like watching the daughter she never had leave home. But she knew Clair needed to be away from the fight and survive, whatever happened here tonight.

Alone, Van Tager grabbed the Lore stone, she risked the journey in an elevator, and descended to the labs.

"Where are you, Windburst?" Zane heard Sceptre's voice over her suit's comms.

"Reaching the top now. Whoa!"

"What?" came his concerned reply.

"Azure's not here, but a bunch of Devouts are, they've seen me, one's giving chase, she's fast, but not fast enough . . . oww! She shoots bloody sparks as she moves. Hold on Scept'!"

Zane altered her path and popped through several walls and floors, effectively shaking off Kinecity. She then popped into a cleaner's cupboard and called back Sceptre.

"Okay, I'm here."

"Did you just call me Scept?"

"Well, yeah, I was in a hurry being chased by an electricity-churning speedster and all. Cool in a way," she laughed. "Anyway, Azure's not on the roof so I'm going down."

"Take it easy there, Windburst, Bastian thinks the labs are in the basement. Rain and I are on the roof now, but there are no Devouts.

Think they're heading your way. Any sign of Altair?"

"No, haven't seen him either, thanks for the heads up, Windburst out!" She ran off again, popping her way down.

Like bloody hide and seek around here!

"Okay, we're near site," Alpha Rion checked in with Sceptre, but comms seemed to be jammed.

"I'm tracking them, don't worry," Chalant reassured him.

Rather than engage all the armed security posted intimidatingly around Thane Universal they had opted to enter through the roof from an insurance company building across from Thane's building. Chalant steadily drew back her psi-bow and fired it across the windy distance.

"What are you doing?" Alpha Rion asked, a little amused she was shooting psi-arrows across the way.

"I'm shooting a line across attached to my psi-bridge then we can walk across!"

Alpha Rion did a double-take, "Psi-bridge!" He wondered if she was joking, but then she let loose from her imaginary bow and an imaginary line soared across night sky.

"Perfect," Chalant purred, satisfied that an apparent bridge had been secured fifty meters away. "Let's go."

Alpha Rion adjusted his visor's sensors. "Chalant, I can't see it," he protested, a little more than apprehensive. His manoeuvre suit may be able to take a fall sixty stories down, but he didn't want to chance it. The Alphatronius clan, apart from the eldest and youngest brothers, Novan and Solandus, respectively, weren't natural fliers. And his armour had no propulsion provisions. He looked down, looked at Chalant, cursed the Earth, and followed her lead.

They stepped off from the edge, the bridge surprisingly sturdy for something that wasn't there. A gust of wind caught Alpha Rion and he swayed uncertainly in his steps.

"Use the handrails," Chalant said matter-of-fact. She was enjoying his discomfort. He was in her world now.

"Handrails? Of course there are. Handrails," he sarcastically commented. He shook his head in resignation and reached out feeling tenuous lines in his hands. "How are you doing this, Chalant?"

"It's all in the mind. It's the way my power manifested. I have a psi-bow with which I can do many things. I guess it's just an aspect of the original Chryrian's nature. And there we go, we're across."

Alpha Rion smiled. He hadn't even noticed the rest of the walk. "Thanks, Chalant, and you still owe me the story of why you changed your name!"

"All in due course, m'love!"

The roof was empty.

"Well, Sceptre said to meet him here," Alpha Rion said. He keyed his comms, but nothing happened, "Still jammed!"

Chalant saw the door leading downstairs, "Let's go find them."

Azure had shunned the roof, knowing she would be targeted there, so she had circled the building up close to confuse any attackers and crashed through windows about midway down the building, her manoeuvre suit's forcefield shoving aside the glass debris. She was in a meeting room, tables, chairs and equipment knocked over by her entry.

Producing her Sky Warrior meta-staff from her hip clasp, she ventured into the corridor in search for the Lore stone. It wasn't energised like the two previous shrapnel-sized bombs, but it had given Azure a faint scent to follow—the stench of the Lore was too hard to resist.

There was a loud crash behind her in the room. She spun sharply, staff raised ready to fight.

Altair landed beside her. "You ready?" he asked; a mischievous grin on his face, his hands already glowing red.

She smiled at him relieved for the company. "I think the Lore stone is in the basement." Ready to leave the room and let her senses lead them, Altair held her back.

His lips twisted in a wicked smile. "Let's surprise them," he said, as he started to burn a hole into the floor.

182

***

In the labs Van Tager sought out Sagerhawk, who nervously scurried around the room like a mad weasel grabbing every file, disk and flashdrive he could to save.

"What's going on up there?" his high-pitched demanded, looking like a scared schoolboy caught stealing his own prized possessions. He clutched them to his chest.

Van Tager gave him a pitying stare. She didn't have time for him anymore, now or ever again.

Van Tager had a lot to thank Dr. Frans Marius Sagerhawk for. After being sent to the future, Van Tager, with Clair Voyant's help, had sought out the foremost biologist to aid in the Devouts' quest. Under the guise of wanting to create superhumans, Van Tager had sacrificed Devouts and normal humans for Sagerhawk to study and to pour his research and knowledge into until he had inadvertently found the combination of genes, energy, and technology in order for Van Tager to use the Lore stone on males who possessed the ancient genes from the stars, passed down by their maternal Devout lineage.

Van Tager had been elated and now on the cusp of his greatest moment, Van Tager decided to share with Sagerhawk her most precious possession: the Lore stone.

She cupped the stone from the box, slipping it lovingly from its velvet wrap.

Transfixed, it took a while for Sagerhawk to find his voice. "Wha . . . what's that?" Sagerhawk backed away, despite his curiosity. "Is it a new element?" He shifted his glasses for a better view, peering closely at the stone, his face now of wide-eyed fascination.

"Frans, I want to thank you from the bottom of my heart for all you've done for me and my girls. You've made the world a much better place." Van Tager leaned forward and kissed Sagerhawk's sweating forehead.

"I . . . I don't understand . . . are you leaving?" His voice betrayed elation, his mouth quavering between a smile and frown.

Van Tager smile. "No, you are!" Her smile grew wider and crueller.

Recoiling, Sagerhawk found a modicum of courage. "Who are you? You're no scientist, not really. I did this all by myself," he hysterically exclaimed, all the time backing away.

"Sagerhawk, you stupid man. You truly do not understand. Did you really believe human technology could create those superhumans?" she laughed, advancing upon Sagerhawk slowly.

"Human?" Sagerhawk's mouth quivered, soundless words stammering out.

Disregarding his ignorance, Van Tager shouted, "It was me! All of it!" She pushed him back. He almost stumbled, kept his balance until he was backed against the wall.

"Me . . . and this!" She held out the Lore stone. It shone in her hand like a brain-sized star.

Sagerhawk swore he could see something dark and menacing swirling around inside it. He was mesmerised and horrified, wanting both to study it, yet run away, but he couldn't. And never would.

"Say hello to the Lore, Sagerhawk!"

Van Tager's eyes flashed as she pressed the Lore stone to his forehead. It burned. Sagerhawk screamed. And Van Tager laughed while he cried and smouldered and was no more; disappearing in an acrid pall of smoke.

Van Tager put the stone back into its wrap and box. Dusting off her hands, which still basked in the warmth of the stone, Van Tager recited:

"Memo to Thane: Dr Sagerhawk, due to unforeseen circumstances and stress, has decided to take a sabbatical. Forever," Van Tager laughed to herself. "Little stupid man."

She could hear the rest of the Devouts running down the corridor. They didn't have Azure.

At her vexed expression, Obitumary explained, "She smashed into the building somewhere! Not out fault!"

Nor did Van Tager feel better when Sylphia said, "No doubt on her way here." The weather witch shivered in fear.

"That will make our job easier then, won't it?" Van Tager sneered with sarcastic enthusiasm. "Get—"

At that moment, they looked at each other in alarm as the building started to shake.

Zane sped around searching for E-Corps and Devouts alike, sending sporadic reports to Sceptre, though comms seemed to be jammed. As she entered a corridor she thought she could hear voices and almost spun out of control when she heard one in particular.

It can't be, she thought. How?

But that's when Zane saw her: Lynn Kellis.

At her speed everything else was so slow she could check to see if it was true. But Zane recognised her instantly from the set in her body, her bearing, though somewhat younger, and the pony-tail. She was in her green and black uniform, just like her future Multiforce one, but with a green mask, the E-Corps member called Flaunt.

Kellis was with someone Zane didn't recognise. They were about to split up and search for the Starguards. As soon as they did, Zane slid around the corner, rushing over to Kellis, almost knocking her over.

"Lynn, Lynn, it's me, Zane." She hugged Lynn, but found she couldn't actually touch her. Zane stood back astonished. She could see a faint glimmer of light hugging Lynn's body; a forcefield. "Oh my God, you do have powers," she beamed. "That's so cool. I've got so many questions, so much to tell you." Zane's words gushed out.

But Zane's words were cut off as she was violently brushed off by Kellis. She stepped back looking shocked, quick-drawing a gun from her hip holster.

"Stay where you are, or I'll shoot! And don't think your speed will save you." Kellis tagged her comms system on her collar. "Fuse', I've got one, girl, young, name unknown. Copy?"

There was only static on the line. Something was still jamming the lines.

Zane was confused. "Lynn? What are you doing? It's me, Zane. All

I've done is dye my hair, you must recognise me?"

"I don't know you, kid. Now, shut up!"

Zane's eyes widened as the truth dawned on her. "Oh, my God. Oh my God. This is your real past. That's why you hid your past from me and Aristedes." She stood in silence, looking at Kellis as if for the first time. She had to tell her, to let her know. "Lynn, you have to listen to me. It won't make sense now, but it will soon."

Kellis shifted uncomfortably, gun still pointed squarely at Zane's chest. "Stop calling me Lynn," she hissed, "How do you know me anyway?" she glared through her mask.

"That's what I'm trying to tell you. We don't have much time, either. Lynn, pretty soon something's going to happen and you're going to end up two hundred years in the future. There's a war on and you're going to help fight it. You, me, and my brother Aristedes are friends and you'll discover us in the Zero Star computer room looking for our father. I always wondered why you befriended us and that's because of now. I'll be younger then, black hair, and all shy, but you're like my older sister, Lynn, and I love you. And Lynn," Zane rushed as she heard footsteps running toward them. "Don't tell anyone I'm not dead. You'll know what I mean . . ." She looked behind her as the leader of the E-Corps, Fusioneer, came running toward them. "Trust me, Lynn. Gotta go . . ." she said.

Before Kellis or Fusioneer could do anything, Zane sped off, "Say 'hi' to Starshina . . ." Zane's voice trailed off.

Fusioneer caught up to Kellis. "What happened Flaunt, you had her?" He stopped short of an accusation.

Kellis just shook her head. "I don't know. She was too fast." She stared after Zane's trail, not knowing what to think, "Let's just go!"

The two took off in a jog through the corridor and headed up the stairs.

All Kellis could think was: What the hell am I doing? I don't even know this girl and I'm trusting her?

She was about to tell Fusioneer, but then they heard a huge

explosion from below.

"The labs," yelled Fusioneer. The two E-Corps members changed direction and raced downstairs. "Hope Angelfire and Venture heard that!"

Zane stopped three floors up. She held back tears as she caught up to her thoughts. *Something is happening to me and whatever it is, it wasn't random,* she reasoned.

First meeting Kellis in the future, then her own supposed death by Netherlord, her encounter with the Starguards, and now Kellis again in the past. Zane realised for the first time with certainty that someone was manipulating her timeline, someone powerful, and probably an Astral, if not this Time Empress that the weird crystal being had mentioned. And that scared Zane. Someone was controlling her life. But she had to forget all that, for now she had to warn the others that the E-Corps were on the way and keep Kellis from being killed. History had to repeat itself come what may.

"An Astral's work is never done," she sighed.

Zane was almost knocked off her feet when an explosion from below shook the building. She sped off again down to the labs.

And ran straight into hell.

Altair savagely blasted holes down through twenty-five floors as he and Azure crashed down to the basement. Alarms blared everywhere as machinery, flooring, and furniture caught fire, sprinklers activated in their wake.

Upon rampaging downwards into the main basement labs he and Azure had been met with a barrage of fire and energy from Devouts Cin, Kinecity, and Van Tager, the latter wielding a metal staff which channelled her powers.

The two Starguards could see a carved wooden box on a lab bench behind Van Tager, which they guessed housed the Lore stone. Altair closed in, standing in the centre of the room blasting anything that moved. Trying to outflank him, Cin and Peril charged. They died instantly in his counter-attack, red energy piercing their bodies.

"No!" a horrified Van Tager screamed. She fell back with the rest of the Devouts to well-guarded positions behind metal counters just as a veritable army of well-armed soldiers burst in, weapons trained on the two Starguards until the two were surrounded. Van Tager, Obitumary, Sylphia, and Kinecity stayed hidden. They knew what was coming.

"Don't move," a serious-sounding but anxious sergeant yelled. He was tall, his dark skin glistened with nerves, and his thick moustache almost hid a small scar over his lip. His men formed a tight circle, ears pinned back for orders, tense eyes glued to their targets.

Thane, cautiously slipped into the room, shadowed by the armed Spree and Charm.

"Shouldn't we wait for the E-Corps?" Ms Charm whispered to Thane, but annoyingly he shook his head. Charm looked over at Spree and they decided it was best to get Thane out. But Thane shrugged them off as he wanted to listen and watch the spectacle before him.

The sergeant stowed his gun to his holster, reached up and revealed an envelope from his top pocket. Removing the contents, to Altair and Azure, he announced: "By the authority of the United States government and the United Nations, the Starguards are under arrest for breach of U.N. Security Council Resolutions, acting without authorised permission upon U.S. sovereign soil. Surrender quietly and no harm will come to you," the soldier finished, his uniform feeling distinctly clamming on his back. He resumed brandishing his weapon at Altair's head.

Altair and Azure looked at each other. They couldn't believe this was happening—Fifths trying to arrest them and thinking that projectile weapons could penetrate their forcefields, let alone their armour.

Having studied Altair for so long, Charm and Spree recognised the look on Altair's face and without care took hold of Thane's arms and pulled him down, toward a table. And just in time.

Altair decided to demonstrate his bubble pulse. Releasing energy from all over his body simultaneously, the manoeuvre suit's crystalators controlled the energy output as it burst outward in one big, circular red kill zone.

The sergeant and sixteen soldiers died in an instant as the pulse flared out to four meters before retreating back into Altair, Azure's armour letting the energy flow around her.

Thane, Charm and Spree lay flat on their stomachs behind a bank of computers and counters just out of range.

"Uhnn!" Thane had a splitting headache. He held his head, which felt as if it was about to explode like something was trying to get out.

Altair was almost at the Lore stone. But a loud noise from the direction of the lab doors heralded the arrival of the E-Corps.

Stopping short of the dead soldiers' bodies. Angelfire blasted Altair with plasma energy, which had its desired effect in driving him back.

Covered by Angelfire, Fusioneer rapidly touched the floor, transforming it into liquid concrete, sinking Altair and Azure. He quick-dried the quagmire into a smooth slab, leaving the Starguards buried in a stony tomb.

"Quick, get Thane out," Fusioneer turned and commanded Flaunt and Venture. Then he spied Van Tager. "Doctor Van Tager, where's Doctor Sagerhawk and his team? Get out now!"

Van Tager stood up, "They killed Sagerhawk, we're all that's left." She tried to sound panicked. She ushered the Devouts out. Kinecity, out of sight, sped off without looking back.

Coward, Van Tager thought after her.

She tried to retrieve her box with the Lore stone.

"No time for souvenirs, doc!" Fusioneer shouted. "Get out, we've got incoming!"

No sooner had he warned them, when the far wall behind Van Tager disintegrated and Sceptre and Urana stormed through, with Zane, a black and purple blur, in their wake.

The sight of so many dead bodies shook Zane as she looked around. She was thrown off balance as the ground shook and a red

189

burst of energy broke from the floor as Altair and Azure stormed out.

The E-Corps protecting Thane and the separated Devouts all ducked as Altair again blasted anything that moved. Obitumary had made it to Thane's position, covered by Angelfire and Flaunt, but was stuck with them and the E-Corps, while Van Tager and Sylphia remained trapped together on the other side.

Sceptre wasted no time and blasted Fusioneer, who wasn't fast enough to deflect the energy. He crumpled and lay on the ground in pain, slow to get up. Angelfire responded in kind, but Sceptre's armour simply absorbed the plasma, bathing him in a warm glow.

The battle continued back and forth, energy slung around the labs, charring walls and destroying equipment, no one closer to getting the Lore stone.

Energy swords carved through the reinforced wall, Alpha Rion piercing an entry into the rear wet room labs, after descending the stairs, intending to out-flank the fighting. The white room's large glass window separated them from the main lab, pockets of Starguards, Devouts, and E-Corps squared off throughout the workspace.

"The Archwitch!" Chalant immediately recognised Van Tager. She pointed her out to Alpha Rion. "Valtare's wife! But how?"

"Damned Astrals, of course!" snarled Alpha Rion.

Before he could plan anything, Chalant had already raised her psi-bow with Van Tager in her sights.

Out of the corner of her eye, Sylphia caught the motion and saw Chalant, panicked, and directed a blast of hard air toward Chalant.

Everything between Sylphia and Chalant, equipment, benches, and instruments went flying through the air. The Lore stone box was buffeted. It tipped and opened on the edge of the table. The lab glass shattered over Chalant. Thrown off-balance, her shot went wild hitting the Lore Stone.

Time stood still. Everyone watched as the gleaming Lore stone slipped from its wrap, tottered, spun clockwise, and then fell from its perch on a bench.

The closest person to it was Altair. He reached out to catch it.

"Altair, no! Don't touch it!" screamed Azure who rushed forward, but he couldn't hear her.

His fingertip brushed the stone, before it hit the ground and fractured open.

Time bubbled, jerked, stretched and throbbed. A lurid aura coupled with a vertiginous sensation punctured the air. An almighty rush of blue nebulous light burst out within the lab. It exploded into a searing sinuous kaleidoscope of colours ripping through everyone, except Altair. He stood, trapped, motionless at the epicentre of the maelstrom, as if frozen in time.

Azure felt the power rush though her. Instinctively, she quelled her lower nature trying to repulse the energy back into the stone. But the damage had been done, the Lore stone was waking up, the being feeling its way into life. The blue light vomited out again and an ear-piercing ethereal scream retched forth from the stone as the energy metamorphosed into its natural state: a Lorelet—a Lore virus come to life. Like a phoenix, it uncoiled from the stone, an alien avian of energy, all wings and teeth, hungry for more energy.

It swirled voraciously around the room, Azure and Zane its prime targets for more Lore energy and temporal release.

Elisabeth Van Tager watched, enthralled.

So this is what the Lore stone was, a creature of energy turned to stone? Then she reasoned, if the stone was hers to control, so should the beast be hers to tame.

She struggled to stand up in the ravaging whirlstorm of energy whirling around the labs. The Starguards fired ineffectually at the impervious Lorelet. Standing unscathed, Van Tager wielded her Archwitch's staff which protected her from the Lorelet's energy.

The Lorelet screeched around Altair who was still caught as if stuck in time. Everyone else was battered in the storm-like eddies of temporal energy, while the Lorelet sucked at their energies.

Sceptre, Urana, Zane and Azure shrunk back to protect themselves, weakening every minute as the ravaged Lorelet drained them. The E-Corps, less adept at the protection of their energy lay writhing in pain on the ground while the Lorelet fed from them.

From the wrecked rear labs Alpha Rion and Chalant could only watch as Van Tager approached the Lorelet, her arms outstretched with her staff. The sinewy beast squawked at her in an alien shrill. Chalant peered around a counter and through the door which was now off its hinges, trying to see who was still alive, until she caught sight of someone. Her breath caught in her throat as she stared at Penthor Thane. A lost ghost from her long past.

>P'ntar?< she psyed into the psychic-air.

His eyes flashed open, bewilderment, pain, fear, then recognition on his face. He search for and found her, confusion reigning his thoughts.

"Sister?"

He tried to reach out, but it was too late.

Goaded by and in a heightened state of self-preservation from Van Tager's advances the Lorelet charged the Devout leader. The Archwitch's staff failed to absorb or to contain it. She wrestled against the energy's heaving and pitching, her arms vibrating wildly in the Lorelet's too-close presence. Van Tager prised her staff away, but it struck the Lorelet hard.

Van Tager screamed in fury, just as the Lorelet opened its mouth of a million energy teeth. It surged forth and devoured her. A shuddering jolt to time resonated through them all. Unfettered energy from Van Tager and her staff was too much for the Lorelet to control.

Zane could see what was about to happen. She opened up herself to the universe. There was a tiny, rippling surge of heat in the pit of her stomach. Zane closed her eyes.

"Universe help me!" she prayed.

The Lorelet shattered and exploded.

The explosion was heard clear across New York city as a giant blue flare shot up through Thane Universal and into the night sky illuminating the city under an eerie glow of blue lightning that flickered menacingly within the clouds. The following storm lasted two hours; the city in the throes of punishment. And people swore they had experienced moments of deja vu over and over. It was a few more hours before emergency services could even get near the building as the light lingered around Thane Universal like a protective shroud.

In daylight, the devastation was clear to see. The building had collapsed upon itself, fires still burned and smoke and dust filled the air around the melted concrete, glass, and metal bones of the building. There was no sign of life; at least not anywhere inside, but around the building, thousands gathered as the emergency services and the media swarmed around the site.

"What was that explosion?"

"What was that blue light?"

"Where was Thane?"

"Where were the Starguards? The E-Corps?"

"Was there a fight? Did they die?"

The questions mounted well into the twilight hours almost twenty-four hours after the blast. The building was being picked apart piece by piece in an effort to find any bodies. Nothing had been found and it was looking grim even after specialist equipment was on hand to scan beneath the rubble.

Fireman Mac Glassman was on double duty. Tired, he wiped more grime from his face as he scrabbled over some rubble to work his designated search area. He sighed, looking at the devastation surrounding him. The sky was a deepening purple and empty, a no-fly zone imposed. So busy was he looking up that when the sky wobbled, it took him a moment to realise it had been the ground which had trembled. At that instant a sudden blip on his hand-held scanner made him jump. Sweat ran dirt into his eyes, blurring the reading, but it was there.

"Chief! Chief! I've got something . . ."

He waved his supervisor over, followed by other searchers and firemen. The collective gasp from the distant onlookers heightened the expectation as they saw some kind of action unfolding. Media crews braced themselves for some breaking news . . .

Crack! The ground shook again, rubble shifting. The firemen ran for cover.

Craaaack! A louder roar from the ground saw the ground ripped open. Deep pits and fissures gulped in surface debris.

Boom! The rest of the rubble disintegrated. A ruby red heat swirled in the craters of the ruins.

A bright red light lanced into the new night. It almost blinded those nearby and knocked Mac and the chief to the floor. The light was closely followed by a blurred figure who flew off at speed over the fallen building. There was no stopping as the red light arced out over the Atlantic and then was gone. The night sky returned to normal.

But there was no doubting who it was: Altair.

Mac and his supervisor stood up and dusted themselves down. Mac wandered over to the hole which Altair had created on his exit; a hole that Altair's energy had melted into an almost perfect tunnel which could be used to enter the lower levels of the building and find any possible survivors.

Even looking into a pit from hell, Mac didn't hesitate. "Well what are you waiting for, an invitation?" he called behind him. "Get the equipment, we're going in now!"

But there were no survivors, just dozen of bodies; soldiers and security, office workers and lab techs. Dead on the scene. No trace of the Starguards, E-Corps, or Penthor Thane was found.

No one could explain it. Newspapers, TV commentators, bloggers, social media and magazines exploded with theories each more outlandish than the other. They were all disintegrated by Altair. Sword Industries' planned coup had failed. They had faked their deaths. They had been abducted by aliens. A military experiment had gone wrong.

The rumours went viral; Altair doing to stop them. If he had not been responsible then at least he knew what had happened to them. But in his absence and without any word from Altair himself, his silence and arrogant disregard for any discussion on the event fuelled the rumours leading to an inevitable conclusion: Altair was guilty.

The World Court was pressed into issuing international decrees for Altair to be brought to justice to answer for any crime that may have been committed at Thane Universal, to answer for the presumed deaths of the Starguards, Thane and the E-corps, and even the death of Goth. The poster boy for the Starguards' misdemeanours was to be tried.

But Altair steadfastfully remained tight-lipped, refusing to heed any warnings or answer any questions. He had disappeared. His association with Sword Industries tainted their already beleaguered brand and image. But the Exmoors had finally move underground, isolated from scrutiny.

Months passed. Fake sightings of Altair abounded. Mysterious deaths of women around the world were attributed to him. He was causing earthquakes, volcanoes to erupt, and tsunamis. Even weather changes were the fault of Altair.

And just as suddenly he arrived out of seclusion. He deigned to accede to a U.N. proposition for an informal discussion. However, on the day it came to a head even before the press conference. The teeming reporters had turned on Altair accusing him of everything under the sun. Altair's anger had boiled over and in a fit of anger he lit his hands up with angry red energy. Two reporters had been killed in the resultant stampede away from the Starguard; red energy caught on camera for the whole world to see.

Altair had flown away uncaring about the dead and injured. The media could now brand Altair as a callous superbeing; a murderer; one who held himself above the law and who was unstoppable by conventional means.

Altair was the world's most wanted man.

Four months ago

Darkness had surrounded him. He couldn't breathe, move, or barely think.

Had it been a dream?

But he had remembered touching the Lore stone.

No that had been real!

The shrill screams of the Lorelet had vibrated through his mind, piercingly hour after hour after the event. Temporal rivulets rolled over him, coursing around him, pinning him down. When the building had collapsed it had pressed heavily down upon him, dust threatening to encrust him. His own energy blocked as a consequence of the Lorelet partially draining him. Either he got his powers back or he'd be trapped forever in a temporal tomb or crushed to death if the temporal field shut down. He was defenceless.

Altair couldn't see or hear anything from the other Starguards. His comms relayed nothing, fried by the Lorelet, his crystalators silent.

This cursed world has killed me, thought Altair, depressingly. *Dead at the hands of the Fifths. You cruel universe!* he cursed. He snuffed the urge to acknowledge the wetness in his eyes.

He lay entombed for more hours than he knew, maybe even sleeping. All of a sudden he opened his eyes barely able to breathe. A huge steel girder was pressed vertically dead centre of his chest. Its intense presence was keenly felt. Altair realised the temporal field had shut down. He was caked in dust, choking on building remnants settling down his throat, the girder eager to skew him. He shifted his head to look at his arm, raising through the debris. He concentrated. He prayed to the universe. His hand lit up red.

He laughed to himself, relieved.

The rest was easy. Producing his red energy bubble, he made crawl room space for himself careful not to cause more collapses, his girder friend was placed to his side. Searching for any other survivors, all he found were dead Devouts or Fifths. The Starguards were gone.

An icy fist grabbed Altair's heart.

Are they dead? Did the Astrals take them? He had to know. *I really am all alone. Abandoned on a world I never wanted to come to.*

Altair's anger rose. He needed answers. Now.

He blasted straight up out of the living hell he was in, ignoring the Fifths below, who receded behind him. He fought down his fear of being alone. He wanted his brother back, Aerl, his constant pain in his backside; his cousin Urana, her love and presence; Azure, only just beginning her journey; and even Zane, as annoying as the young Astral could be, but innocent. He also wondered about Alpha Rion and Chalant. Had they been in the building? Did they escape? His anger was at boiling point as he flew, angry at this world.

Before long, he found himself flying over the Himalayas. He needed time to think and blow off some steam. Small mountains found themselves the victims of some angry target practice.

He repaired his comms. His first call was to the Exmoors. It was brief.

"Any sign of them Bastian?"

"None, I'm afraid. I'm sorry!" Bastian lamented. "They think we're all guilty. We Exmoors are underground now."

Altair knew the implications. "I'm on my own now." He kept the mixture of fear and joy out of his voice.

"We all are!"

"Farewell, Bastian. Universe save you."

"And you."

With nothing else to do, Altair built himself a shelter. He needed rest, a plan of action, a way off Earth. No Starguards. No Astrals. No Exmoors to help him. The only answers he would get were from the surviving Devouts. Over the next few days, the crystalators had revived themselves purging errant Lorelet viruses from its matrix. He listened to news from around the world, heard himself being vilified, listened to the memorial services for the Starguards, Thane, soldiers and scientists who had died. There was currently a massive global manhunt for him.

He shook his head. *This world is ignorant of the dangers around it*, he knew. It was time for a change. His brother-cousin wasn't around to stop him. He had grinned at the prospects.

Utilising Exmoor data on his crystalators, Altair had made it his mission to avenge his fellow Starguards. Criss-crossing the globe he had hunted down several Devout enclaves leaving a trail of dead bodies in his wake.

ALTAIR ON A RAMPAGE
SUPERHERO TURNS SUPER ZERO

ALTAIR – GOD OR DEVIL?
STARGUARD ON A MISSION OF DEATH
ALTAIR WATCH – victim or witness? Contact us!

the headlines had shouted, the Starguard not caring about his story for once. His next targets had been the supra-vigilantes, whether they knew the Devouts or not.

While various governments were glad to be rid of these criminal and superhuman elements previously unknown to them, they nonetheless detested the fact that it was Altair who was indiscriminately entering foreign territories without permission and committing murder at will.

After the death of the two reporters months before, sixteen Peace International members protesting outside a company accused of being owned by the Devouts, which Altair had publicly announced he would destroy, were caught in the crossfire and killed. Altair duly destroyed the building. The blame was placed squarely upon Altair, who blithely ignored pleas for his surrender and cessation of action.

The U.N. amassed an international army designed to stop Altair. The world was geared for war. The U.S. authorised E-Corps Team 2 into action, who had been kept in stasis in Thane's California facility.

Bastian contacted Altair secretly pleading with him, if not to surrender, then to leave Earth.

"Where would I go?" Altair replied.

But he had a difficult decision to make. And to make it before it was made for him. The next day he declared he would attend the U.N. and make a public announcement.

On a dark Monday morning Altair flew to the U.N. building, landing in front of it by a podium hastily set up for his announcement. There were no press present, for their safety, but cameras had been set up to record the event. The army had set up perimeters around the site, tanks and personnel carriers blocking streets and snipers on rooftops. Several brave authorities were present to arrest him immediately after and the World Court in the Hague prepared for their unprecedented court case.

But before that, Altair issued a statement:

"In my tenure as a Starguard, I have acted in ways that I have seen necessary to rid this world of its evil, but my methods have apparently not met with your approval. You see me as evil as the evil I fight. So why am I here, in front of your media? I am here to tell you a few truths, now that the pedestal you placed me upon has crumbled.

"You saw me as a hero once. But I was never a hero, none of us were. We did what we had to do. It's called survival, a basic instinct that everyone has every day. Since the untimely . . . disappearance of my fellow Starguards, almost six months ago, for which I do not have to atone for, because I was not at fault, I have been the sole super-being on this world and I had sought to keep my own counsel, to hunt down those responsible for the disappearance of your heroes. But your governments have pursued me for their own global agendas, while I tried to bury my grief and to better my perception and understanding of this world. But everything I did and said to save you, help you, understand you; you turned your backs to me. So be it. I regret that I ever came here or helped you.

"I was never yours to order around. As for your so-called politicians and entrepreneurs, rubbing their hands together, hoping to make money and political gain from me: no more! I am not your gravy train. With all my powers I could have bent you all to my will, subdued you, but that is not my way. I thought that you needed protection, not from the outside, but from yourselves. I thought that you needed guidance; you were losing your way. But I realised that you needed none of these things. You need controlling. But I won't be the one to do that.

"You may as well know, now, that I am not from this world. Where I am from, all are superior. But you, you Humans, Terrans, Earthlings, Man or whatever you call yourselves, are a diluted strain, inferior, forgotten, and alone. Your entertainment devices depict real and imaginary tales of war, destruction and invasion. You spread violence, live to spread violence, breed violence. You dream of such things, waiting for visitors from afar; welcoming them in peace, only to turn against them in war. Well, we came. And you turned against us.

"Duplicity rules the human heart, hand in hand with ignorance. You want a utopia that will never come! You will always destroy it. I could have brought myself to control you, even destroy you, you and your dark, ugly ways—I still can. But I care no longer. For I am leaving this world.

"Humans, you are walking down a path of destruction in which this world shall surely burn. And none, least of me, shall shed a tear. As far as I'm concerned, you humans can go to hell!"

And with that, Altair swept up into the cloudy sky in a streak of livid red, straight up like a warning flare to Earth, disappearing into the twilight.

"This is Martin Patchak, reporting live from the U.N. . . ."

". . . Did he just say 'you humans'?"

". . . And the BBC has learned that the Pope just condemned Altair as a blaspheming alien . . ."

". . . in suspected anticipation of an alien invasion, the Cult has stockpiled enough supplies and weapons for two years. The ATF have surrounded their compound . . ."

". . . Expecting some form of official announcement from the FBI about their investigations in Sword Industries . . ."

"CNN hope to bring you live comments from the White House on developments . . ."

". . . This reporter has been reliably informed that the World Court has indicted Altair in his absence for the death of Penthor Thane, the Starguards . . ."

". . . So there is the situation as it stands: the Airforce has just scrambled two Lancefires, ostensibly to escort Altair to wherever . . .

possibly the boundaries of outer space."

"We just turfed out Superman . . .!"

". . . he's flying into space?"

"Ladies and Gentlemen, Altair has left the building!"

". . . Will keep our viewers informed. But now this commercial break!"

It took days to find and smuggle out, detected accidentally as it was by Exmoor operatives working as construction workers. It took a further two years to study; the blue material unlike anything ever seen.

The Exmoors of Sword Industries were no more. After the demise of the Starguards, the U.S. authorities raided Sword with charges of fraud, corporate manslaughter, alien invasion, and other charges. But the Exmoors had already disappeared from public view. Underground, safe from any arrests, they waited and planned, ready to emerge once again when needed.

So it was that after three years, a new company proudly presented the new element to the world. They called it thanium—a tribute to the humanitarian Penthor Thane. Qane had almost choked when he heard the naming suggestion from Simon, but it made the new company seem more benevolent in light of Thane's and the Starguards' deaths.

Thanium was hailed as a cleaner and more efficient fuel than any fusion process and fissionable materials.

Publicly, Sword Industries holdings had nominally been bought out by Telhome Engineering, a British company and secret Exmoor subsidiary. Within a century, the heiress of Telhome would marry one Abel Tantillion, the heir to the Martian Terraforming conglomerate.

But the Exmoors had also discovered other related Lore stone secrets from the shards they had recovered. Other phase states existed: lorite and lorium. They kept these secret. Lorite was a hard metal crystal separated from thanium and was time-sensitive. They could produce temporal ammunition and magnets. The gaseous lorium, also possessing extra-temporal properties, had a potential greater than natural gas and methane. The Exmoors may have been no more publicly, but they could still ensure that the Starguards' deaths weren't for nought and that the Lore stone, something that had caused so many deaths, could ensure a new energy age for the Earth.

The power of thanium was untapped by Earth scientists. But derivatives and hard-won synthesised thanium slowly replaced many of the fossil and chemical fuels used for transportation, energy and space travel, not knowing that within three years, thanium would be needed more than ever.

AFTERMATHS

PRELUDE TO THE END

THE REVISITED

The Far Regions

Mindscream stood on the edge of oblivion. Space surrounded him and though he wore a standard thin, pressurised suit with an oxygen supply, the sheen of his psi-shield masked his presence from the Superions, he hoped.

Before him stretched the long, narrow lattice-worked gantries leading off into the distance toward the habitat dome where he knew Mode awaited. Behind Mindscream rose the massive metal dome of the spaceport, wherein Kellis and her assault force battled Invadress. The cold and forbidding vacuum cloyed around his protective psi-shield. He was all alone.

It had been a long couple of weeks since Lynn Kellis had gathered Xaul Relentus, Simon Exmoor, Aaron Danor, Starshina Tetriov, and Aristedes the Astral together and revealed her secret past, her version of the events; revelations which had rocked the Multiforce.

Zero Star

"And the rest you know!" Kellis finished. "Altair flew into space, bivouacked on Mars for a couple of weeks stealing equipment from orbiters and landers, then disappeared from the Solar System. I don't know what happened to the others. But Starshina and I ended up in the twenty-third century for our sins!" she tried to smile some feeling back into the room.

The conference room was quiet, Xaul, Simon, Aaron, and Starshina all awake and not just from the copious amounts of cold coffee drank during the night.

"Is all that true?" Aristedes asked, glaring furiously at Simon. "Did you, the Exmoors, know this all the time?" His eyes were narrow slits of grief. "The Exmoors are supposed to be our allies!" Starshina stroked his arm to comfort him without much success.

Simon Exmoor nodded. "Yes, I knew all about Kellis, Zane, and more." He looked shamefully at Xaul Relentus, Emperor-General of Earth and Axala.

His meaning dawned on Relentus. "All this time you knew!"

Relentus accused Simon, never having felt as betrayed as he did now.

Simon argued, "Zane and I had sworn each other to secrecy! What else could I do?"

Relentus shouted, "All those people dead, you could have saved them: my crew, General Hawkhurst—you knew didn't you? You let that man die for me!" He felt sick at being a pawn in history.

"There was nothing I could do. It was history! History!" Simon defended himself. He hoped Xaul wouldn't actually go further and accuse him rightfully of having caused Hawkhurst's death.

Both of them were quiet, staring defiantly at each other.

However, even Simon knew his usefulness was over. He couldn't 'foresee' what was to occur anymore. And a trust had been irrevocably broken.

Xaul confirmed his feelings. "Well, Simon, I feel it would be best if you transferred back to Earth and coordinate Home activities from there." He didn't look at Simon. But it was an order, an effective demotion and dismissal from his service.

Simon's jaw clenched. He had no argument. He turned stony-faced to the others around the room. Some sympathy from Aaron and Starshina comforted him, but both Aristedes and Kellis shared the same look of anger and disappointment on their faces.

Clearing his throat, Simon stood up. "Yes, sir." Without ceremony, he walked out of the room. Walking down the corridor to clear out his cabin then on to the docking bay, he was glad his father and Qane weren't alive to see him shame the Exmoor's name again. But that was the past. Now he had a future to rebuild, both for Earth and the Exmoors. He was free. Simon smiled at the opportunity. He knew just where to begin.

Back in the conference room, Aristedes still fumed. "I'm sorry, Xaul. The Exmoors are supposed to be our sentries on Earth, be the guardians in our absence. I hope I never see him again." He gazed down sadly at the floor. "Where did they go wrong?"

"What did happen to them?" Kellis asked, recalling how powerful Sword Industries had been. "The Exmoors all but disappeared."

Time shook his head. "It doesn't matter," was all he said. He stared hard at Kellis. "You know I have to look for her," he stated, galvanised into action. "Zane could still be out there or I could rescue her just before the explosion!" He stood up to leave.

"No, you don't!" Kellis warned, leaning forward across the table. "I'm sure she's safe!"

"Safe! From an explosion? Come on!" Aristedes anger grew. "She's my sister! You could have told us as well. You're as bad as Simon! So you don't get to tell me what to do anymore!"

He glanced at Starshina, who looked at Kellis, torn. But she nodded to Aristedes. The Astral walked to the corner of the room and opened a portal. With one last look, he vanished away.

"So that's how they do that!" Relentus gaped at the disappearing portal. "I wouldn't get tired of watching that!"

Kellis smiled at him, but there was some reproach in Xaul's eyes toward her, too.

"I'm sorry," she said softly. "You didn't know the whole truth about me. . ."

Relentus waved her off. "You were protecting the past, but Simon. . ." he shook his head, "he let people die, good people." He sat silently, Kellis knew he was thinking of everyone on Consention Base.

None of them mentioned the fact that Kellis had stopped Aristedes from changing time in order to save Consention Base from being destroyed by the Superions. Aristedes hadn't quite forgiven her for that.

Seems the time traveller had got a raw deal from her and Exmoor. That didn't comfort Kellis. But her attention was now drawn to Aaron. He had remained quiet during the whole recounting of her past.

"Aaron?" She seemed to have broken some spell he was in, as he looked blankly at her. "Are you alright?" she peered into his eyes.

He smiled back weakly at her. He opened his mouth to speak—

The room brightened again. A portal. Aristedes shot through. He was clearly shaken.

"What the hell, Aristedes? What happened?" Kellis feared the worst. "Is Zane. . ."

Aristedes held up his hand. He took deep breaths, his face full of dread and determination.

"I was stopped from finding Zane!" He shook his head in disbelief.

"What do you mean?" Kellis rose from her chair walking to Aristedes.

Still upset, he replied, "I mean on my way to the twenty-first century, I was stopped mid-temporal stream by some alien made of red crystal!" He looked at his own hand. "It had a third eye in its hand."

"More aliens!" Relentus asked, incredulous. He wondered how many challenges there would be for Earth.

"Did it attack you?" Kellis asked.

"Are you okay?" Starshina rallied to his side concerned.

"I'm fine." A terse smile crossed Aristedes' face. "No, it didn't attack. It warned me."

"A warning? A threat to Earth?" Relentus asked just before Kellis. They looked at each other. Earth wasn't ready for a new war.

"Look, let me just tell you. Then I'm going. There isn't time!" He saw their shocked faces. "So, I was stopped by this alien. I challenged it. And it told me 'Aristedes, your search for Zane ends here. You and the Astrals have a bigger war to endure. Go to them. Go home, Aristedes.' Then I suddenly found myself in the Chronopolis. I told them about Zane and this being, expecting help. But they had dire news of their own. Lightstream was warned by another apparent alien that the Astrals are under imminent attack. There's a war coming for us. We don't know the nature of the attack or from whom, but these unknown aliens seem to be helping us." Aristedes seemed calmer from having told his tale.

"Jesus, so now what!" Kellis said, her mind racing from the terrible news.

"That's what I'm here to tell you," Aristedes said. "My uncle, Helexius has made a decision." He looked into the eyes of Aaron, Kellis and Relentus. "I'm sorry, but I have to leave. The crystal being was right: there is a far bigger war than the one Netherlord wanted to start, so we Astrals are retreating into the temporal plane to plan our strategy. I can do no more on this plane and without my father or Zane, there is no need for me to be here."

"But Aristedes, we need you against the Superions, not for revenge, but for justice and your abilities," Kellis argued.

But Aristedes could not stay and he had another shock for them: "Kellis, I'm taking Starshina with me. She's a wreck and not fit for battle. I love her and want to take care of her. She'll be safer with me."

He was adamant, his shoulders set in his usual haughty way.

Kellis knew he was exercising his right as the future Astral leader and as Starshina's lover. She didn't want to lose another team member, but she had no choice. He was right of course, but Starshina also had a say.

She turned to her snow-skinned friend for an answer. Starshina gazed into Aristedes' eyes. She knew where her future lay as she walked over and stood at Aristedes' side.

"I'm with you," Starshina held his hand.

Kellis inclined her head in sadness, trying not to feel betrayed and fighting back the tears. She and Starshina hugged.

"Maybe one day we'll sneak out again and go clubbing," Starshina added, with a sad smile on her face.

"You remembered that?" Kellis had to laugh.

"Yeah, strange. Things are coming back all the time," Starshina smiled. "Thanks to you."

"Well, I'm sorry I got you into all this mess, Star," Kellis said. "But I'm sure we'll cross paths again."

"I will return!" Starshina promised, a wide but sad smile on her face. "Count on it."

"I am sorry, Kellis," Aristedes offered. He clasped hands with Aaron. "Goodbye my friend, I have learned a lot from you. I will miss you."

Aaron could only reply, "Thank you for my life, Lord Aristedes." He smiled at the young Astral. "Our lives take mysterious paths and I know we'll see each other again someday."

The two men regarded each other, remembering a fateful day in the desert a long time ago. The universe had seen fit to bring them together and now their journey's bond was over. The understanding between them deepened as they realised that their destinies were only just beginning.

"Emperor-General," Aristedes bowed. Xaul saluted him, adding, "I hope you find your father one day. Thank you for all your help to the war cause." He unclipped one of his own medals from his uniform and pinned it upon Aristedes' tunic, "For the valour you have shown. Godspeed."

Aristedes smiled his thanks to Xaul and gave the group one last acknowledgement. And then Aristedes and Starshina were gone in a flash of light.

As the room darkened, a sense of loss permeated the others. Kellis found herself shoulder to shoulder with Aaron. Their hands touched. Fingers interlaced. Looking into Aaron's eyes, Kellis realised he had been as depressed as the others, more so as a telepath with all the raw emotion soaking into his mind. But there was a glimpse of something else still nagging Aaron. Kellis' heart went out to him. Whatever it was would have too wait.

It was almost mid-morning when the three of them decided to decamp from the room. After freshening up and a quick breakfast, Kellis and Aaron escorted Relentus to Zero Star's launch bay for Relentus' departure for the Bion homeworld. Muted acknowledgments were exchanged, seeing as there wasn't much more between them to say after all they had been through.

"I'll make sure Zero Star remains active as a secret base behind its starry disguise," Relentus promised, looking around at the bay and assorted Bions who had come to wish him well.

"There's still much to do," Kellis replied.

They all shook hands before Emperor-General Xaul Relentus and a small Bion retinue boarded an unassuming ship. The small, sleek craft sighed out of Zero Star.

Kellis felt more alone than ever. Her past seemed to be catching up to her, but everyone else was moving on. However, she still had an ace up her sleeve.

The forcefield warped around her hand as Kellis handed the prisoner a mug of coffee. He was whistling some tune, Kellis thought she should recognise, but couldn't place.

"Thanks." He grabbed the plastic container taking a grateful sip.

"Ah, proper coffee!"

The Superion, Warper, had almost died during the battle in the future of the world called Home. A stray energy beam from Netherlord had struck him, Warper last seen reeling out of the sky. He had been found half-alive in a canyon, his forcefield powers having protected him, dissipating the kinetic energy away from him.

Captured by Tantillion Post Forces, Kellis had intervened using Relentus' authority to have him released into her custody, before Warper could be hauled back to Earth and a lengthy prison stay. Now on Zero Star, he was undergoing psychiatric analysis by the Bions and debriefing by Kellis.

Warper, or rather Warren Raphael, had been a good friend in the E-Corps. He was no traitor, Kellis knew. His memories, like Starshina's, were slowly returning; his after years of manipulation by Psyren. The blue disguise had come off and Kellis welcomed the recognised handsome features of Warren, though he had now shaven his head.

Kellis sat outside his cell, a floor to ceiling forcefield separating them as he lounged on his bed savouring his coffee.

"God, I missed coffee," he said. "The Axalans had nothing like it. And the closest they did have had spikes in it!" He pulled a face at some old memory. He started to whistle again, but broke off. "Ha, did you also know Axalans can't whistle. They can make a weird noise in the back of their throat, which grated my teeth." He smiled mirthlessly.

Kellis listened patiently waiting for Warren to finish.

Regarding Kellis seriously for a moment, he said, almost like a confession. "I remember everything, Lynn: you, J.J., Starshina and then the explosion. You know, I think I have your powers," he chuckled, Kellis seeing a faint haze around him. "Must have transferred during the mix."

"My powers?" Kellis laughed. "You do at that, Warper," she let the name escape, instantly regretting it.

"Don't call me that. I hate that name," he bristled. He swallowed the rest of his coffee, placing the cup on the floor.

"Sorry, Warren. Bad habit."

"Yeah. Well, I'm not Venture anymore either, he's dead," he

211

sighed. He changed the subject. "So what became of Starshina and J.J., anyway? They here too?" He folded his arms under his neck trying to relax as he stretched out on the bed.

"God that's a long story!" Kellis looked up at the ceiling. She had to go through it all again. She told him as much as she could remember from that fateful night at Thane's.

"I felt myself burning like millions of needles pulling me apart when that creature exploded." Kellis could still hear herself screaming as if going mad. "Then I found myself in a futuristic space lab. We had ended up in the same location, but another building in the future. We were transferred under guard to a secure facility until the powers-that-be decided we weren't enemies or an invasion force. From then on we were studied and that's when I learned I had lost my powers."

"And the Starguards?"

"We think they're dead. There's been no sign of them. Only Altair escaped and he exiled himself from Earth!"

"Seriously? Space!"

"Yep, flew off never to be seen again."

"Amazing!"

"Yeah, we live in a crazy world of superbeings and aliens. Who knew. Even weirder, I was then befriended by Simon Exmoor. . ."

"Exmoor? Of Sword Industries? They still around?"

Kellis smiled. "Yes, the same Simon Exmoor. He's lived a long life," she said without irony, "but Sword Industries is no longer around. Simon introduced me to Xaul Relentus, a base commander." She omitted her brief relationship with Xaul. "On Simon's advice he had me transferred to Zero Star and admitted me to ExA, the Extra Solar Agency," she explained to Warren before he asked. "They've been around for centuries protecting Earth from Aliens and also liaise with the Bions who run Zero Star!"

"Geez, there's so much!" a fascinated Warren gasped.

Kellis nodded, continuing. "Starshina was comatose, so I had her brought here. Her powers had also transformed, inherited or mutated from Sylphia's weather abilities. Unfortunately, the other time-displaced escaped, taking you as hostage, so we couldn't stop them at the time. I don't know their identities. But Earth Forces Command tasked me with tracking you down. Only later did I learn that you were masquerading as the Superions and fighting against Earth."

"As for J.J., I don't know, Warren. He could be dead. You sure he's not one of the Superions?"

Warren shook his head, "No, I'm sure I would have recognised him. Things were blurry in the early days though. Somehow Mode brought us together and we survived our first encounter with the Axalans and impressed the Emperor into working for him. Mode was quite the charismatic leader. Though saying that, I never even got to see Mode's face and he did have Fusioneer's transmuting powers. I can't believe J.J.'s dead if we're not. And if he's still alive, I can't believe he would turn on earth like that."

Kellis mulled that over. Was it possible that Fusioneer as Mode had turned against Earth?

Warren lay back on the bed. "You know, with all this fancy tech in your little hidey-hole, I bet they could transfer your powers back."

"Not on your life, Warren. I'm glad to be normal again."

"Normal?" he cackled, "Lynn Kellis, you're anything but!" They laughed like in the old days, before his face grew serious. "Anyway, Lynn. I know why you're really here, though it's nice to talk about old times." He looked at Kellis through the forcefield. "So let me tell you all I know about the Superions, what they can do, and where they are. And let's go kick their butts!" He face lightened up at the prospect.

Kellis got all the information she wanted, though she had bad news for Warren. He was going nowhere

"The E-G is adamant about not letting you out. Not just yet. You've been through a lot. . ."

"He doesn't trust me."

"He doesn't trust the Superions. They know all about you as well. And you could be a liability." She didn't sugarcoat it.

"I understand. Thanks." He slumped back onto his bed.

"One day you'll be a great addition to the Multiforce, Warren. Just get better."

But for now, it was just her and Mindscream. Leaving the cells, Kellis reflected on that grim thought.

The Far Regions

Mindscream marshalled his defences, his skin wearing a thin film of perspiration like a tertiary protective shield. He couldn't afford to use his powers on dampening peripheral functions such as sweating. All that was needed for defence.

Mindscream stepped onto the long support gantry, his magnetised boots forming a decent enough contact with the struts and girders. Surrounded by the utter blackness of the void, the quarter-mile long bridge seemed to stretch forever. Mindscream couldn't help but admire the framework structure, the metals and fabrics blending together to form the Superions' base of operations in the backwater Far Regions of Axalan Space.

Only Mode could have performed such a feat. Mode: Universal Enemy Number One, transforming broken matter of the void, old space ships, and shattered moons to construct their formidable base, could have been a great force for good.

But Mindscream had to kill him.

Mindscream was infiltrating along the outside of the station between connecting gantries and modules which linked the docking port, command, and habitation sections, large domed structures. He was sans tether and jet pack to avoid alerting the Superions.

Almost halfway across, Mindscream found his thoughts drifting. Far below he could see the lattice work of more bridgespans and smaller domes. Again, Mindscream admired Mode's simplicity of complexity. It almost reminded him of his brother's penchant for building little clay or wooden figures and totems when they were younger on the millennia-old deserts and plains of Africa.

He cursed himself for not concentrating on the moment at hand, his defences slipping.

He suddenly stopped.

Cocking his head, he listened with his mind. A whisper of a presence had just flitted around briefly, then out of existence. Then again. Mindscream whirled around, careful not to drift off the bridge. Nothing was there. But he had definitely felt someone or something was there. There, again, over to the left. No, behind him, all around him. Mindscream whirled and whirled, but still nothing was there.

A phantom in the void, Mindscream mused. Or one in a zone! He scanned for Zone telepathically, but found no trace of the teleporter.

>Show yourself< Mindscream commanded, but only silence crept through the darkness. Mindscream started on his way again.

No sooner had he clunked ten paces when he was struck from behind and flattened to the metal grilling. He rolled onto his back keeping himself psychically tethered to the gantry. He found himself still alone, but he distinctly heard the remnant of laughter as it faded into the cosmic background.

"Zone!" Mindscream snarled to himself. Catch me if you can, eh?

Though his psi-shield and suit were still intact, he instinctively raised his arm across his helmet's screen, trying to wipe away the tangy taste of sweat from his mouth. Channelling his temper, he focused it within his mind, formed it, and waited for the right moment.

Now!

He unleashed a spread burst of mental anger, radiating ten meters out around him saturating real and psi-space.

He waited.

In real space, nothing seemed to happen. But in psi-space, the mind's eye, the sky became aglow with a myriad of colours and sensations unknown to the naked eye. The faint outline of a figure could be discerned in the fuzzy psionic background, his hands gripping his head as if in pain. The colours faded, psi-space fading away into real space. And there was Zone.

He collapsed to his knees, as best he could, feet hooked under a boom of a solar panel twenty meters from Mindscream. Still clutching his head, his nose, ears, and eyes bleeding beneath his shielded uniform, he was vulnerable.

He's still alive! Mindscream was surprised Zone had survived.

Mindscream pushed himself up and approached the Axalan impersonator. He was breathing heavily, lung damage no doubt. Mindscream looked into the eyes of the man heaving in pain. The hatred behind the mask was evident as they tried to burn their way through Mindscream's psi-shield. Mindscream looked down upon the man with disdain. This man had helped Mode kill people and cause untold misery on Earth. His DNA must have been susceptible enough to have somehow gained his teleporting powers from the explosion on Earth centuries ago. But he had used those powers for Mode's bidding to prolong a war that was not theirs. Zone deserved to die, Mindscream thought, but not suffer like this . . .

"Oof . . ."

It was a desperate manoeuvre. With his last ounce of strength, Zone drove at Mindscream forcing them both off the gantry.

Armandes Graff wasn't dead yet. He knew his own weaknesses and strengths, and if he was going to die, he wasn't going alone. That was his rule; Mr Spree's rule.

Even as Mindscream found himself toppling back off the bridge Zone's hands clenched around Mindscream's protected throat.

Zone's life flashed before his eyes: A young Armandes Graff always getting into trouble, the first time he killed a man for disrespecting his deceased mother, his flight from Cuba and various jobs as a hired killer, the mentoring under Thane, and total friendship with Ms. Charm. Then had come the future; the allegiance to Axala against Earth, and now this, the end of his days. He just wanted to teleport home.

So he had tried.

Before Mindscream could telekinetically clamp onto the gantry, Zone had teleported them away from the base and into deep space.

They reappeared so far away that Mindscream could just make out a speck of rotating light that was the Superion's base.

Zone maintained his death-grip; a true enough reflection seeing as Zone had given his life for his last act of defiance. His open eyes stared out into the cosmos.

Rotating away, the two drifted in space. Mindscream minutely flexed his psi-shield around his neck, releasing Zone's lifeless hands.

Searching for the base again, Mindscream reached out mentally and pushed against Zone's body sending him floating away before he disappeared into the void. Mindscream extended his mental push. He had lost a lot of time and energy. He concentrated on his energy while nearing the base.

Thankfully, he finally made it, and clambered onto the bridge by a docking port, having a short rest. Mindscream knew subtlety was out of the question now. He knew Zone's death would not go unnoticed. The rest of the Superions would be waiting for him.

Two massive doors of the port barred his way. Mindscream wrenched them open with his mind. He had expected any air locked inside would depressurise violently. But it didn't. The air inside was calm, a seemingly invisible barrier separating the two conflicting states of being. Mindscream thought he could detect a faint presence within the station. He moved in.

As he opened the inner doors, he saw the dark corridor before him. Eerily quiet, only dust motes accompanied him. He stepped through cautiously. The doors slid shut behind him. He looked around at them, then back again. To his horror, an overwhelming sight greeted him. The corridor had changed. Physical reality wasn't functioning correctly here.

Before him, the former corridor had shifted into a cavernous hall, with metal stairways leading in every direction, ascending and descending into darkness. And in that darkness, a voice called out to him, imploring, irresistible:

>*This way*<

He ditched his spacesuit and helmet to be less encumbered. In a twisted upward path he couldn't have navigated naturally, Mindscream found himself at the top of a stairway. It led into another large cavernous square of a room. He was dazed from the maze-like climb. His ears drummed with the rhythm of blood pushed through his body. There was no other sound or sin of life, only darkness.

Then, looking across the room, he saw the figure standing before him on a floating square slab, in the middle of hundreds of floating metal squares among the stairs; the temptress herself, Psyren.

The slabs moved and she descended each floating square to the ground, inviting Mindscream to follow. Mindscream chose a more prudent method stepping off the edge and telekinetically floating down to the floor with Psyren.

Instantly, the room, more like a small empty hanger, shifted again and was now stairless, the squares having attached themselves flat to the walls or created a continuous high-level balcony. Psyren stood like a statue, an impostor in Axalan blue. Only her dark blue hair and glinting eyes showed any sign of life. Mode had once boasted that her psychokinetic powers were stronger than Mindscream's.

And if Mindscream had doubted that before, he was convinced of that fact when Psyren had lashed out with a staggering melee of psychokinetic energy, like raging lightning.

Floored, Mindscream found himself lanced with stabbing pain, inflicted from Psyren with venom, each throw of psi-force a double-edged slash of agony. Psyren reached out and Mindscream found himself thrown up into the air, bounced bone-crushingly against walls and smashed furiously back to the ground below, as if invisible hands had reached out and grabbed him.

Mindscream looked up through the pain, crumbled on the ground. He witnessed Psyren's psi-force change. A fire encircled her head and arced out across the room to envelope him. Mindscream writhed on the ground in renewed agony.

He was going to die.

***

There wasn't much time left, Kellis knew. Her forces outnumbered Invadress twenty to one, but the tall, steely, assassin was stronger than them all with her electromagnetic powers, which Kellis suspected were being recharged.

Even before she and her force had landed at the Superion's docking port, they had all known that they were the diversion, the sacrificial lambs, while Mindscream hunted for Mode. It had more than troubled Kellis that Mindscream had become more than distracted the closer this mission had approached, but she could not figure out why and what was wrong. Even if the Superions didn't know Warren was still alive, they would still expect to be found and attacked at some point. It was a trap, either way. But they knew that they had to try or lose their chance to take out the Superions once and for all. The Earth-Axalan war may have been over, but the Multiforce's was really just beginning.

Kellis looked around at her Multiforce stand-ins, a veteran bunch of Earth Forces volunteers and Axalan Warriory under her command. She realised a lot of them, maybe all, including her, could die.

But not for nothing, never for nothing, she thought. This would be revenge, revenge for the death of Solitude, for old friends missing or dead, for the Multiforce, and nothing was going to stand in her way. Not even the Superions.

Kellis gazed over the storage bins she had nestled behind for the past half hour. The dock was huge, airy, and devoid of spacecraft, save for the broken *Dragon Charger.* Kellis and her team had seen fit to destroy that first as they blasted their way in. No escape for the Superions that way.

The *Esprit* was parked outside, as Kellis liked to imagine. The gaping hole in the side of the dock, their forced point of entry was a ragged maw that had now ceased to suck the dome's air out. They were all in their space suits, jet packs ready in case the gravity ceased as well within the spinning station.

Kellis was glad she was backed by these soldiers. They could fight in any environment, kill anything, though she still wished her whole team was here, including Zane and Solitude.

In the dead air, nothing moved, except for tumbling bits of machinery and parts. Invadress was playing cat and mouse with them. Kellis' troops were scattered around, laser rifles ready. To Kellis' reckoning, they had Invadress surrounded, but something kept her from closing in too soon. With Invadress' powers, she and her men would be easily within her strike range and slaughtered. Last time they had cornered Invadress she had injured three of the warriory with her electrical charges, scattering the rest. Invadress had then shorted out the power to the port, plunging it into a colder darkness. And now Invadress was evading their scans for her. Kellis didn't want that to happen again, so the search for Invadress was proceeding much more cautiously.

She's hurt for sure though, Kellis guessed, *maybe seriously.* Kellis had clocked the Superion a few times before she had disappeared. But she wouldn't be able to withstand another heavy attack. In her state of mind, Kellis wasn't sure what Invadress would do to survive.

Kellis thought about where she would hide if she was hurt. The dock was sealed off and in utter darkness. Even the spacesuit's helmet visor's images were blurry.

Interference from Invadress, no doubt, thought Kellis. She looked at her scanner, the small unit strapped to her forearm. There was still no movement or sign of Invadress.

Casting a commander's eye over the battlefield again, Kellis surveyed the area. The exits and entry hole were covered, the *Dragon Charger's* engines were mangled; chaotic debris and stores flung around from blasts and decompression with wires trailing and flailing around as electric sparks continued to rain down occasionally. Above, catwalks, gantries, and piping crisscrossed the murky darkness, eerie creaky noises permeating the dock as metal swayed about.

Her troops were closing in on the center of the port, where a dim overhead light seemed to hold the *Dragon Charger*'s caved-in crew cabin in its feeble beams—their target. Kellis wished if only she could get up higher for a bird's eye view.

The thought struck her squarely, suddenly, as her eye caught the swooping movement from above on the creaking catwalks. It all seemed to happen in slow motion as Kellis automatically raised her rifle and fired into the dark shadow that descended like death. Short, rapid pulses of light caught the figure barely ten feet away from Kellis, who in response almost took a blast of energy to her chest.

They both fell to the ground in a heap, Kellis' head smacking the deck hard and crumpling on her side feeling a rib crack, even as Invadress hit the ground heavily, the sound resonating through the dock and Kellis' body.

The fallen Superion stirred first. Invadress wasn't done for yet. Teeth barred, red blood clashing with her faux-blue skin through her personal self-generated forcefield around her, she pushed herself to her feet, only to be caught by more than a dozen beams of concentrated laser fire from Kellis' troops. Invadress' armour started to melt, but still she stood, the sparkle of the forcefield surrounding her. Step by step Invadress lurched toward Kellis, though her skin pealed, her eyes flashing such fury that Kellis thought she was looking into the eye of a laser beam.

Kellis realised Invadress was absorbing the laser energy even at risk of injury to herself and recharging her powers. That wasn't known about Invadress. Kellis tried to warn her troops, but discovered her comms were down; damaged in her fall. They were all dead if the troops kept firing, but she couldn't relay that message in her state.

The troops' lasers suddenly ceased, drained from the sustained high-energy volley, by Invadress who wandered inexorably toward the injured Kellis. She tried to scramble back away from Invadress' gleaming eyes. Blasting nearby soldiers with shots of her own, Invadress now stood toe to toe with Kellis, who was panting for breath after painful breath.

Several of the soldiers powered up their jet packs charging

Invadress, but a few more blasts from her hands downed them, blood trailing in their tumbling wake. The others took cover again. Kellis was on her own.

The two women, for their part, didn't made a move. Invadress towered over Kellis as they stared into each others eyes.

A knife suddenly appeared in Invadress' hand, its long, sharp serrated edge glinting in the dim light, but she made no movement to draw back and stab. Kellis' troops tried to rush in again, but Kellis stopped them with a raised hand.

Kellis understood Invadress' intentions. It was the same as her own when she had first 'arrived' in this century, out of time, out of place. One just felt utterly disconnected, overwhelmed, like dying. Kellis shook her head at Invadress. She wasn't going to do it.

"I'm not giving you the easy way out!" Kellis said through gritted teeth, not caring if Invadress could hear her.

It was either being a prisoner in this time or death.

But that is what Invadress didn't want. She had nothing to go back to and everything to die for here.

"Who are you?" Kellis interrogated Invadress. "Surrender now and live. Just live!"

Obitumary cursed herself. It was over for the Devouts. Van Tager had promised them everything and now she was dead; eaten by some alien monster. Mode had led them down the wrong path. She was too injured and had no way of escaping. And she realised in a terrible split second she had forgotten her real name. What was life worth living for in a twenty-third century prison? They had lost in the past and now in the future. As Invadress she had power again, but time was slipping away and she wasn't about to be anyone's prisoner, let alone be sent back to Earth. But she just didn't have the guts to kill herself.

"I'm not going back!" she spat at Kellis.

Kellis watched as Invadress sank to her knees in despair. She felt Invadress' pain and stood uneasily to give Invadress a hand back up. A chance to surrender.

Invadress lashed out, slashing Kellis' arm through the suit, which began to hiss air. Kellis fell back clutching her arm in an effort to stem the loss of air. Invadress grinned and dragged herself over to Kellis. She raised the long knife high again.

Kellis could do nothing. Raise her good arm to defend herself and the air would escape; lay there and she was going to die.

Kellis' eyes widened in fear as the knife slashed down.

Lieutenant Commander Paolo was a good soldier, a loyal one and usually obedient of orders. After Zane's death and the still-unexplained events surrounding it, Paolo had transferred from Home and Tantillion Post looking for new opportunities. And he had duly been handed an opportunity by Xaul Relentus.

In the aftermath of the war, the Emperor-General had established the Dare Units: an elite rapid space corps under his direct command to quell any remaining human or Axalan insurgencies and to guard Earth's forward bases. Their HQ, the Dare Unit Command, or the Dukedom as it was affectionately known, was set up on the newly constructed Consention Base II, close to the centre of all Earth forward bases, the Dare Unit Commander, or the Duke, sending his Daremen out where required. The Duke had a wide latitude in his remit and allowed his men certain liberties in their actions.

Paolo's eight-person Dare Unit consisted of himself, Lothar Bliss —a pilot who has recently transferred from his classified space-courier duties, commsman Tyndale, engineer JB Toyer, specialist Kathy Atherton, and gunners Francisco Nemerset, Ash Pennyhill, and Leyton Turttle. They were a good seasoned bunch with the latest weapons at their disposal and a fast assault ship, too. Paolo had christened her the *Zane*.

Paolo had started to sequester files on Kellis, whom he was finding more mysterious by the minute. She had come from nowhere and been ushered into Xaul Relentus' circle, along with Aristedes and Zane, by Simon Exmoor, whose own history was also suspect. Then had come her equally mysterious team with Aaron and the white-skinned woman. Their identities had escaped him. Kellis' team had been through something on Home, ostensibly defeating a being with super powers, but who weren't the Superions. It killed Paolo, gnawed at his conscience that he had received no straight answers from either Kellis or the Emperor-General. It was like Zane's death didn't matter.

Well it matters to me! he savagely thought. And he was going to get answers.

He had continuously sought Kellis' whereabouts through sightings of the *Esprit*, because more often than not Kellis was often off the grid —in some secret base—Paolo now knew, appearing in strange places in impossible times. Even for a supposed Xeno-specialist, Paolo knew Kellis was involved in Above Ultra Classified missions, even above the Duke's level, but he was desperate for answers concerning Zane's death.

Then he had his chance. He knew at some point Kellis would want to get revenge on the Superions, whether killing them or bringing them to justice. His tracking algorithms for the *Esprit* now showed her entering Axalan space. He submitted a training mission with his unit to the Duke. But his men knew better, the glint in Paolo's eyes foretelling their mission. They trailed the *Esprit* at a discreet distance.

Five hours later, in the Far Regions, Paolo had held station behind a lop-sided potato-shaped asteroid. The unit watched as Kellis and her forces had assaulted the docking bay. They watched until Paolo thought he had given Kellis enough time to cause enough trouble and sufficient time to probably need help, or at the very least she was winning and they would join in the party. Either way, they wouldn't let Kellis die there. Paolo wasn't going to let anyone else die under his watch again. And he would get his answers. Paolo decided that it was time to enter the fray. The *Zane*'s engines fired up and in they went, Paolo piloting himself.

"Ready or not, here we come," he muttered to himself.

***

Mindscream lay on the ground, paralysed with pain. His body burned as Psyren poured down molten psi-fire upon him. She had cut through his defences like a scythe carving him up. He had managed to shut off his mind to her, protecting it. He could heal his body later, but it was his mind which held the core of him, his vital being and that was what Psyren was trying to destroy.

That was her mistake.

Psyren stood several feet away. Mindscream switched from the blurry pain-filled vision of real-space to the swirling mindscape of psi-space and sure enough his suspicions were confirmed. Psyren's head was aflame with telekinetic energy, but her body was left virtually unprotected. She'd expected to easily slice through his mental defences then eat away at his body. She'd thought he was already beaten.

So nearly was that the truth, he thought in the depths of his protected mind. Soaking up her barrages, Mindscream chose his spot and time.

Now!

He opened up his mind, the swiftness of the deluge overwhelming Psyren like a glacial tsunami, her psi-force flickering like a candle in a hurricane. Opponent stunned, Mindscream followed up with his own torturous assault, wave after wave of psi-energy crashing down on her.

Psyren shrieked and writhed in torment sinking to her knees, unable to cope with Mindscream's retaliation. In the mind's eye, Mindscream had Psyren trapped in a void, trapped forever, falling into a black hole, falling forever, never to escape, dying in seconds which lasted forever, dying forever. He bombarded her senses, sending her into the utter depths of the black hole, the black hole that would be her final resting place, her mind—never to return. Any second now . . .

BOOM!!

The resonant sound of the explosion rocked the room. Mindscream was thrown to the ground, his grip upon Psyren's mind momentarily lost, but in that heartbeat of a moment, Psyren broke free. Mindscream recovered but was hurled about the room with the sheer brute telekinetic force the desperate Psyren could muster. She swatted him around the room throwing loose stair and wall debris at him.

She's desperate! No power to assault my mind, Mindscream thought, which was good. Though he wondered what had caused the explosion.

No sooner had he thought that when his mind was assailed with stinging nettles, stabbing at his brain. Psyren was in his mind again, back in control.

He felt his own psi-force smack clearly into Psyren's mind, the two now standing across the room from each other, leaning into the fierce psi-storms they were generating, squaring up like two cowboys out-drawing each other.

They launched simultaneously into a full psi-battle, a duel which ripped the room apart like gigantic invisible hands clawing through the air at each others psi-shields. Psi-space lit up with jagged bolts of energy filling the void with livid rage. The storm of energy thundered around them, lightning crackling between them, their shields glowing in response. Mindscream's head was a halo of golden sparks, showering the mindscape in a crescendo of psionic arrows. Psyren simmered in dark red spikes, reaching out like talons to tear Mindscream's head off.

Neither gave in. The first to falter would be the first to die. Stalemate.

Invadress stabbed downwards with all her force.

Kellis instinctively formed a rough inverted 'y' shape with her arms to catch the death blow in the crook of her forearm and wrist which covered her torn suit. She twisted over onto her side rolling Invadress with her and kicking her away into a heavy pack of equipment crates. Kellis quickly scrabbled to her feet, breathing heavily and clutching her arm to stop more air escaping, but she knew it was only a matter of time before too much air escaped and she would fall unconscious.

Invadress still had life in her, fuelled by anger. She had been someone back on Earth once. Invadress could feel her energy recharging even with the broken equipment around her feeble with energy. She had ample reserves, feeling it tingling in her body, coursing through her veins. Invadress squirmed free of the crates, struggled to her feet and charged the injured Kellis, her energy coalescing and directed into the knife.

All Kellis could do was to raise her arms in defence. She closed her eyes as the death blow came.

By the time Kellis heard a scream, Invadress was spinning and tumbling into her. She clung hard to Kellis' shoulders, dropping her knife. Kellis looked down at the Superion, Invadress seemingly smiling in gratitude at the death she wanted. The fury in her eyes went out. Kellis let Invadress' limp body slide down her to the ground, blood glistening as it flowed down her spacesuit and into droplets around her. Her own breathing was laboured, pain and lack of oxygen clouding her vision, but she had the strength to look over to her rescuers by the open docking bay hole.

Paolo slung his compression rifle across his back as he and his team jet-packed over. Tyndale, also the med officer, caught Kellis before she fell. She administered an Ox-boost shot then a gen-stim to give Kellis energy, before wrapping an emergency patch around Kellis' pierced suit arm.

Kellis took her time to recover then looked appreciably at Paolo. "I bet you've disobeyed orders, Paolo," she said, somewhat breathlessly. She knew Xaul wouldn't have wanted Paolo on this mission.

Paolo sighed and nodded.

"Thanks," Kellis mustered. "I wasn't sure you would this time, but good to see I wasn't wrong." She smiled to herself, still catching her breath while her side ached.

"Who is she?" Paolo pointed to Invadress.

Kellis shrugged. "A Superion, a human disguised as an Axalan, but I don't know her identity." She had an idea. "Can your med officer get a DNA sample for me?"

227

"Sure," replied Paolo, calling over Tyndale and relaying instructions. "What's next?" he asked.

"Now, let's go find Mindscream—" she let slip.

"Mindscream?" he asked.

Kellis grimaced from the pain as she rose to her feet unaided . "I'll tell you everything after, Paolo, even about Zane, but first we have to get to Mindscream, Aaron," she said by way of explanation.

Grateful, Paolo nodded. "Anything you need, commander."

"Good," Kellis felt better limbering up. As she did, she spotted Invadress' knife on the deck. "We'll split up. I'll go across the exterior of the connecting bridge to the command module, while you and your men go through the station."

"Yes, commander," Paolo acknowledged, compartmentalising his curiousity for now.

The troops split up, Paolo and his Dare Unit picking their way through the wrecked port and corridors.

Now that they were out of the way, Kellis picked up and stowed Invadress' knife in her belt. She had made up her mind about what she had to do. She searched her own force's eyes in turn, each returning a look of understanding of what they each had to do.

"It's almost certain death," she told them.

She would never have ordered them to follow her into certain death, but none of them budged or said a word.

Kellis nodded in appreciation. "Let's go!"

They trudged over the trashed dock back to the blown exit. She took a laser rifle and jet-pack from one of her dead men and donned it before they jetted out and along the trellised support strut toward the command station where Mindscream had entered.

Kellis knew they would let her go alone. *It was her right*, she thought as they made it uneventfully across the bridge. She stepped into the blown airlock, the inner airlock doors not opening. Without having asked, her men handed her the last of their charges.

They jetted out of the airlock just as the explosion ripped the inner doors apart.

There, Kellis thought, *that should cause enough of a diversion for Mindscream.*

Oddly, the air had stayed cooped up within the dome, though Kellis knew that the blast must have been felt some distance away. No surprise attack from her, just a frontal assault.

She quickly jetted through the wrecked airlock into the corridor, laser rifle on the prowl, followed by her unit. And was unceremoniously uprooted as the corridor swivelled a full circle dumping her on the ground. She looked back in shock. The Airlock was gone, replaced by a solid wall. She was alone.

Behind her was another matter. She was confronted by a crisscross network of metal stairs in a cavernous room.

"Oh, hell," she muttered to herself.

Taking the closest stairs at random, Kellis climbed up the smooth steps, each step taken as gingerly as she could with her suit and jet pack still on, unsure if to remove them in this hostile environment. Her back was against the spiralling wall, laser rifle pointed up the ornately-carved hand rail. She also pulled out Invadress' knife from her belt, clutching it in the other hand, feeling its power as if it was her very lifeline.

She had been climbing for what seemed like forever, doubling back over branching stairs which she swore had moved, when she finally reached a large doorway that led out onto a gantry. A glowing light issued forth from below. Sliding cat-like onto the gantry, Kellis edged forward to the waist-high barrier and peered over. The hairs on the back of her neck stood up.

Below her, in a spacious square room of dark metal panels, stood Mindscream, facing off against Psyren, both in perfect stillness. The room was hot and an unseen force charged menacingly about the room. Though she could see nothing, Kellis knew enough from Mindscream's mock battles with Solitude that this was a psi-battle, each one rapt in complete concentration. She could see the scars and burns on their physical bodies, but there was no telling how much mental damage had been done.

Time to end this détente, Kellis thought, as she raised her laser rifle and took aim at Psyren. Die, bitch!

She fired.

A stray, unshielded thought infiltrated psi-space, commanding both Mindscream's and Psyren's attention: Intrusion.

Psyren was fastest to react.

The laser bolt exploded from Kellis' rifle in a blaze of particles.

Alerted to the threat, Psyren deflected the energy with a burst of telekinesis in a speed unimaginable, redirecting it at Mindscream.

"Uhh!" Mindscream fell, hit square in the chest. He was flung through the air crashing against a wall.

"No!" Kellis roared, her adrenaline pumping. Impulsively, she vaulted the balcony edge, falling twenty feet to the ground below. Her suit did not cushion her fall as expected, her ankle giving out beneath her as she landed awkwardly. "Ahh, shit!"

Her laser rifle skittled away from her. Clasping the knife, wary of Psyren, who stood triumphantly a few feet away, Kellis managed to limp to Mindscream's side.

Mindscream lay on his back, his chest smouldering from the impact. Kellis finally unsealed and removed her helmet staring down at him, her eyes welling up with tears, mind wracked in guilt and pain. She didn't know how to help, her hands flittering from head to chest, unhelpfully.

Mindscream's eyes opened slowly and stared into hers. They seemed distant and strange, Kellis could see into the depths of them, all of his life from four thousand years ago in a few seconds. Yet his eyes were the same all-comforting, all-encompassing.

Kellis found herself in his mind, the mind's eye, absorbing his core. She found herself completely renewed, an added strength to her life's essences.

She was him. He was her. They were one.

And the being needed to act as one. They looked at the knife in

Kellis' hand.

Psyren's mind was still in disarray. She could see Mindscream had fallen. Now Lynn Kellis had literally jumped to his rescue.

Stephanie Mikovitch felt weak. Ms. Charm, one-time contender for the E-Corps, now had the powers she had craved back on Earth. Until Thane had come along, she had no purpose, but to kill for money. Now all that had been taken away, the moment they had been blasted into the future. Obitumary had once surmised that Steph, like Armandes Graff, also had DNA susceptible to the Lore stone, endowing her with powers. Obitumary saw that eventuality as too great a coincidence to have happened randomly and suspected that someone must have manipulated them in joining with Thane for just such an outcome. But they had never discovered if that was true.

It had been an overwhelming experience for Steph. Earth was no longer her home. She would have to make a new life for herself in the here and now. Even though she and Mindscream had helped save the universe from Netherlord, she knew she still had to kill Mindscream, if she wanted to survive. They would never stop hunting her down. And Lynn Kellis was trying to bring her down again. Times would never change. Charm had almost lost, but Kellis had saved her life unknowingly. Now it was time to end hers and Mindscream's.

Suddenly, Psyren felt Mindscream's psi-force fade then die.

She rejoiced. Mindscream was dead.

Kellis was hunched over him, crying. Psyren almost jumped for joy; this was better than sex. She had won. She marched unsteadily over to kill Kellis with her bare hands, but within a few steps, she felt a sudden shift in the psi-force. By the time she realised what it was, it was much too late.

Sensing Psyren's approach, Kellis whirled and launched herself in the same motion. The Mindscream/Kellis entity swung the knife at Psyren, burying it into her chest, while a psychic blade plunged into Psyren's mind.

Psyren staggered back, her hands on the knife lodged firmly to the hilt within her heart. Her hands slipped on the blood unable to grip the knife to pull it out. Even before she hit the ground, the dagger of psychic shock exploded within her mind. Her eyes exploded out in gouts of blood. The mindscape faded and blinked out of existence. But her last sight in the mindscape had been of Mindscream, alive. Still alive.

Kellis watched Psyren die through eyes which were not completely her own. Then as suddenly as the thought crossed her mind, she felt herself again. Her inner strength abandoned her, a familiar presence had left her. She sagged onto the ground, her ankle collapsing again.

She turned to see Mindscream struggling to his feet, dazed. Kellis ignored her pain and leaned over to help him, embracing him, not wanting to let go. She realised what he had done; hiding his psyche within hers, waiting for Psyren to attack, before unleashing a double-edged attack of their own. Mindscream had saved them both. At this moment, she had never loved anyone more than she did Aaron.

Mindscream felt at peace with himself. After merging his mind with Kellis' he had felt the love she had for him and in that moment, for the first time in his life, Mindscream realised how much he really loved Kellis. He couldn't let Kellis lose him forever.

They gazed into each others eyes. Embracing, they kissed passionately, knowing it would be their last time; a kiss which seemed to enlighten the room. The light grew too bright to be just their imagination. They separated hurriedly to stare at a section of the far wall that melted away.

A five-metre-diameter, opaque crystal globe hovered within the darkness. A stairway of metal rippled into existence from the room up to the globe. And within that globe, becoming more transparent every second, controlling the air, space, and all the matter around them, from a throne of crystal, sat Universal Enemy Number One: Mode.

Slumped against the wall, attempting to heal his damaged chest, Mindscream could only stare in stunned silence as Mode's mask melted away to reveal the face of the man all too familiar to him.

"Hello, brother," Mode said, with mock sincerity. "Fancy seeing you here after all this time." His grin was razor sharp.

"Penthor Thane!" Kellis called out.

"Ah, Miss Kellis, I told you we had met before." His eyes lit up in greeting. "Here I am, the man who helped give you your powers, which you seem to have lost. Oh, what a magnificent creature that was! Pity it ate Van Tager!" he laughed. "But it has given me a glorious opportunity in the future!" he gloated.

He stared down at Psyren's body. "Of course, you will pay for the deaths of the other Superions. I felt them all die." His voice was genuinely distressed, bitter even. Turning back to Mindscream and Kellis, he said, "I had hope it wouldn't come to this, but I can see you still want to destroy me." He sighed deeply, shaking his head. "I can't let you!" he shouted. "Shall we continue where we left off, brother?"

Kellis tried to dive for her laser rifle.

Mode threw his arms out, a rush of psychic energy like a tornado in Mindscream's and Kellis' minds, throwing them across the room. "Didn't think I still had it in me, did you?" he sneered. "What a surprise it was even to me when that explosion two centuries ago restored my abilities. I believe I also acquired a few from Fusioneer as well. Let me show you what I can do," he grinned. "Just like I destroyed Consention Base!"

Kellis stared at Penthor in disgust, but she and Mindscream had barely caught their breath when the wall behind them began to melt. Then the next one beyond that, until the outer bulkhead had been reached. They could only look at Mode and glance sideways at each other as the outer wall curved away. Everything in the room, except Mode, rushed toward the hole as the vacuum sucked everything towards its dark maw.

Kellis screamed as her ears rebelled against the loss of air, her lungs gasping for air. Mindscream hung onto her by the tips of his fingers, telekinetically grabbing on for dear life to the edge of the wall.

Mode, unaffected by his own deed, glided toward them, his face one of triumph. He gripped Mindscream's hand which held on precariously to the wall, ready to pull.

Mindscream looked back at Kellis, pain etched in his eyes.

In her head, she heard >trust me!<

And he let go.

Kellis went flying toward the open hole toward space, her screams stolen by the vacuum.

The action caught Mode by surprise, giving Mindscream a heartbeat of time to launch himself at Mode, grabbing his head, getting inside, communicating Chryrian to Chryrian.

He psyed >If this is what the Chryrians stand for then we will both die!<

Mindscream then wrenched at a portion of Mode's mind and reformed the outer bulkhead wall, just as Kellis smashed into it, knocking the wind out of her. She lay on the station floor while the air recycled into the broken corridors.

Mode and Mindscream were still locked together head to head in psychic battle, their Chryrian sides having taken over.

>P'ntar, you have caused untold evil over the millennia. This should not be. It is not what the Chryrians wanted<

>Aranu, you are still weak and deluded. These humans need controlling. They destroyed our people. I saw it. The Astrals and Exmoors are not our allies, but our enemies< His voice was a vicious torrent in the mindscape. >*Look!*< he hissed.

Terrible images followed, almost real to Mindscream. Astrals and Exmoors sweeping through the land, scouring the Earth, capturing and killing Chryrian/humans.

The angry wind returned. >I was one of the last left. I repressed my Chryrian nature for centuries to escape detection, made new lives for myself. Even I did not know who I really was after some time, until T'ra had appeared with the Starguards just as my building exploded. I do not know what happened to her, but it was the doing of the Astrals and their Starguard mercenaries. Join me, Aranu. We will avenge our sister and our people<

Mindscream wasn't sure about what he had seen and how true it was, not with knowing the true natures of Aristedes and Zane. But he knew the feelings behind the images were real. But he also knew he couldn't trust Mode, his own brother, not even after four thousand years. It had to end now.

>*I cannot join you, brother!*<

>*So be it!*<

Kellis started to come to, air getting back into her lungs and she gratefully sucked it in heavily. As she sat up, she saw Mindscream's and Mode's heads touching in some communal conference, but the light shining around their heads suggested a psychic battle. Until she saw Mode's hands start to issue forth a black substance.

Mindscream felt the blackness envelop him, suffocating his cells, as they were transformed into an oily mass. Mindscream screamed, but did not let go. Instead he increased his grip on Mode's head and mentally wrenched once more. This time, the target was the Chryrian mind itself.

"Nooo!" Mode screamed, aloud. His hands let go of Mindscream as he realised what he was doing.

Mindscream pulled more, siphoning out the Chryrian from Mode's human mind. The life force was sucked out of the four-thousand year old body, which started to crumble into a husk as age caught up to it. The body of Mode was dead.

But the psychic battle had only just begun within Mindscream's mind as the two Chryrians fought for control. Mindscream cried out in pain and rage as the psi-beings warred throughout eternity within the psi-scape. Mindscream's brain a battlefield of psi-lightning striking, surging, and crackling in every neuron mustering allies, destroying rebels. In real time, ten seconds passed, before there was a cataclysmic burst of electricity from Mindscream's head. He staggered and fell back onto the deck, his head and body jerking in spasms of shock.

Kellis crawled over to him. He looked at her with blank eyes, feeling for her face, which was wet with tears.

"Had to kill Mode and his Chryrian, but . . . " he whispered.

"Shh, shh," Kellis hushed him, "Aaron, no don't . . . we're meant to be together. And we will be together."

He touched her brow and Kellis felt the same psi-force enter her. Kellis could see Aaron's life from his early days on the plains of Africa, his family, his sister . . .

A flood of Kellis' own memories came back. "Aaron, look, your sister. I met her on Earth. She's happy, can you see her?" Kellis showed the image to him: a night out in a club so long ago.

Aaron smiled. Then his head slumped.

Kellis stared at his lifeless body, unable to believe Aaron was dead. She tried, but couldn't hold back the tears; her grief filling the psi-scape even as Paolo, his unit, and her own force arrived, already knowing that death awaited them.

There was nothing to be said.

Paolo and the soldiers carried Mindscream back, their boots kicking through the dust that had been Mode. Kellis remoted the Esprit De Corps to pick them up at the closest airlock. The Daremen had set their own charges throughout the base, leaving the Superions behind.

As the Esprit and the Zane rocketed away in silence, the Superions' base blew up. The cabin in the Esprit lit up, shining its light across Aaron's face, as Zero Star had done almost two years ago.

Seated by Mindscream on a cabin couch, Kellis stroked his head and gave him a kiss on the lips. It would be a long five-hour trip back to the nearest Axalan base and then a further three days back to the Earth-Axalan frontier.

She and Mindscream had all the time in the world.

Three weeks later

There had been a well-attended service on Zero Star for Aaron, Starfighter Machine, Zane, and the other fallen soldiers. Kellis had then placed Aaron into a cryo tube, ready to be fired into space for burial when she was ready. But for now she wasn't ready to let go. Her love hadn't died enough. She wasn't sure it ever would.

She had intended to speak to Paolo. He needed to know about Zane. But first, Kellis found herself up for a medical on Zero Star. Her injuries had already healed, but that was due to her surprise new-found ability left by Aaron. Her head was still adjusting to having an extra passenger in it. She wondered how the Chryrian felt about having a new host.

"We have some good news for you, Kellis, and some unexpected news. Which do you want first?" Jo-Fean asked. The Bion's multicoloured eyes were unusually expressive today.

"Um, good, I suppose."

"Well, from all our tests, your psi-abilities from Aaron seem to have settled in well. The Chryrian mind likes you. You're psychokinetic now, Kellis. Isn't that great?" Jo-Fean beamed.

Kellis sat in stunned silence. "Yeah, great. Still can't believe the cheeky bugger did that to me!" She sighed. "Okay, what's the unexpected news?"

Jo-Fean gave a suitable pause before announcing:

"You're pregnant!"

To say that Kellis was floored was an understatement.

"Pregnant? That can't be right! I haven't had sex in five years, Jo. What the hell kind of medical unit do they have on Zero Star? I know you Bions can't have babies like us humans, but you've still gotta know about the birds 'n' the bees!" Kellis paced the room totally exasperated.

Jo-Fean could only look at her charts again. "It says so right here," she said in a meek voice, handing the chart to Kellis.

Kellis stared at it hard and long. Only when she saw the scan of her womb did she realise what had happened.

"It's not a normal baby is it?"

"Well, we can only guess it's a normal human/Chryrian baby. But we've never seen one before."

"So, when Aaron transferred his powers to me, he also somehow impregnated me?"

"Yes," Jo-Faen seemed unsure. "We assume that's how Chryrians reproduce being non-corporeal. It seems either Aaron or the Chryrian part of him wished you to be pregnant and seeded you with a part of Aaron. We assume all this of course." Jo-Fean looked suitably embarrassed for her lack of knowledge and as confused as Kellis about the whole situation.

"Can it be removed?"

Jo-Fean looked at her, slightly surprised. "Removed, as in terminated?"

"Yes," Kellis then hastily added, "No. Just in case it's dangerous or doesn't go well."

"Are you serious? Really?"

"Well, crikey, I've just immaculately conceived! I'm no virgin mother. I'm no kind of mother!"

"Lynn, this is another piece of Aaron, besides his powers. His gift to you. Think about it."

Kellis put a hand to her belly then smiled at some distant memory.

She sighed. "Thinking's what got me into this mess!"

INTERLUDE 2

IN TRANSIT

Dreaming

During the infinitesimal moment between the explosion in the lab and somewhere else, Zane blinked and dreamed a dream. It was a recurring dream she had again and again while on Earth, but it was much more vivid now.

The spectral darkness, the galaxy within her mind, had suddenly fissioned like a nova and her mind was awash in brilliant light, turning quickly into hot, swirling dust and gas that streaked and blossomed into a spectra of colours ribboning across the cosmic sky. She gazed above her, entranced, until she was aware, as she always was, of another presence.

She smiled and found herself sitting in a desert at the foot of a large throne-like boulder, upon which was seated Mindscream. He was always in the chair; thinking, opening his mind to the universe, expanding his consciousness. Maybe she always dreamed him in his chair, because it gave him a sort of parental quality, an aloof, authoritative persona. A silence hung in the void, which chilled her so she had to hug her knees to her chest, before being interrupted by a question.

Mindscream always started the dream with the same question, and this is how the dream always went:

"Do you remember the old times, Little Bird?"

"Yes," replied Zane, remembering his pet name for her, the first time they had met. "Yes, I remember those times with you, Kellis, Aristedes, Starshina and even Solitude."

"Why?"

"Why?" As if he didn't know. "Because I loved you all, we were a family, a family I never really had before and could never forget."

She always looked up at this point in her dream, seeing Mindscream set against a hot blue sky and grainy yellow sand, looking compassionately down on her.

"Oh, Mindscream . . ." her eyes glazed over in wistful memories and she smiled into the nothingness, "I remember meeting you for the

241

first time after Aristedes had brought you to Zero Star, half-dead from your brother's attack; how you and Kellis fell in love; and Aristedes and Starshina in love. And then . . ."

"Yes, go on . . ."

". . . then the Superions came, and then Netherlord, the hand of death." Her face clouded over. "Netherlord killed me," she said with venom.

"Except he didn't."

"No. I was almost dead; the look he gave me before he fired terrified me. His power pulsed around me and then I was gone. I wanted to escape. And I somehow found myself on Earth, alive, and I never knew why."

"You know why." Mindscream began to walk away, as he always did, looking and pointing at the sky.

Zane looked up but saw nothing. She was almost in tears. "Why Mindscream, why am I still alive? Why won't you tell me? Mindscream? Mindscream?"

"Goodbye, Zane . . ." Mindscream walked off into the desert, his image fading, his voice sounding far away as he disappeared like a ghostly mirage.

Zane ran after him, but he was not there. He was gone, forever. Zane knew that now. And she cried.

The sky closed in. Blackness returned. And a turbulent nightmare began.

Imagining

Azure woke up.

Her first reflex was to strike out to defend herself against the creature which had exploded from the Lore stone in the lab. But it wasn't there. In fact, neither was she. She was in a bed; a comfortable one, almost like the one she slept in back home on Sky Command, except white veils hung around her giving the bed an ethereal quality like it was floating in space.

She was still groggy, but she could hear muffled noises beyond the whiteness.

"Hallo?" she croaked, tentatively.

The noises stopped and the veils to her left wafted with movement.

A face, a friendly face, pushed through the veils. Azure stared at her. There was something different about the face, a woman's face which now stared back at her.

"Oh, you're awake," the woman said in a Halcyon accent.

Azure was shocked. Where was she? But she couldn't speak. She was too weak. She lay back down.

The woman scanned her with a device like they had on Halcyon, smiling at the indication of improving health. "I will get the Sky Commander for you. She will explain everything." She left and then a few minutes later, Azure heard more voices, one of which seemed very familiar.

Another head poked through the veil. She smiled wildly at Azure.

Azure's heart almost skipped a beat: Classia! Older and wiser, yet the same Classia all over. Her curly brown locks were slightly shorter, brown eyes sterner, and pouting lips held a cynical lilt. Her youthful puffy cheeks and girlish figure were replaced by a well-honed warrior's frame.

Azure couldn't say her name, couldn't speak, but the flood of tears said everything. She was with Classia again, her oldest and best friend in the universe.

But how?

"Medtech, please," Classia ordered (even her voice was sturdier) and Azure had a shot of something to her arm from the first woman she saw.

It was an instant boost to her system and Azure found she had more movement. And she could speak.

"Classia? Universe, I don't understand. Where am I?"

Classia looked at the medtechs gathered around, a little puzzled. "I was hoping you could tell me that. We found you in the middle of the city, well ship, I should say. You're in Celectral City, here on Meccus. Weren't you sent by the Starguards or Gal Agar?"

Azure shook her head. "Meccus!"

She knew she had a lot to learn, but also there was so much to tell, but she managed to tell Classia all that had happened, about the final Lore attack on Magna Aura, her being a Loremaiden elevated to a Starguard, the Astral intervention, and their enforced voyage to Earth and then . . .

"Then I can't remember, Classia. The creature came forth from the stone and I guess my powers must have somehow re-activated, I thought I was going to die and I thought of you. And after that . . . I was here!" she shrugged, looking plaintively into Classia's questioning eyes. "Am I the only one here?" she asked, hoping even Altair was with her.

Classia shook her head. "You were alone. No Starguards, no Lore." Her tone was almost on the edge of accusation.

"Well I have no idea how I got here," Azure said. "Guess I'm destined to be different everywhere I am," she tried to smile.

There was quietness, while Classia pondered Azure's revelations. She grinned saying, "I always knew you were special. I wish I had known how much so." Then she turned her head toward the veils at the foot of the bed. "Is that all, my Lord?"

"Yes, Sky Commander. I am satisfied."

Before Azure could respond, the veils lifted from the bed and Deb found herself in a medroom and face to face with Novan.

"Novan!" Azure almost jumped from the bed, but decorum prevented any embarrassing scenes. She found her emotions racing through dozens of states, love over-riding all.

Azure could only stare into his blue eyes, fairer than hers, which were accentuated within his golden skin and feathery white hair, much like his mother, the Goddess Elysius. But the biggest change was his uniform. Where once he wore white armour, the eldest son of Alphatronius now wore the black and red of his father's clan.

Gaining her breath, Azure said, "I don't understand, Novan. What is happening?" She looked at Classia again. "Sky Commander?"

"There's a lot to explain on our side, too," Classia stated calmly. "Sword Celectral made it out of the Magna Aura system, but we still battled Lore along the way, losing many brave warriors. Only Swords Celectral, Confiance, and Temprocity survived from our fleet. *Venturon* was lost half way through our journey. No one knows for sure what happened, but . . ." She didn't elaborate. She stared blankly away.

Azure could hardly think the worst of the crew. *It must have been an accident,* she told herself, looking at Classia's haunted eyes.

"Five years into the journey following the Goddess Elysius' directions we found her. *Relentance* gave their lives for us to run to the Ribbon system, under Lore attacks. By then I was the highest-ranking surviving Sky Warrior and awarded the Sky Commander position." She looked lovingly at Novan, leaving no doubt to Azure. "And over time, Novan and I had fallen in love. We are now joined." Her voice was triumphant as Novan fondly returned Classia's gaze.

Azure's smile almost dropped from her face. Part of her was glad for Classia, it was her dream come true, but the dominant part of her wanted Novan all to herself, like it could have been.

Damn time! Damn those Astrals! She felt her face blush, even more so when she found Novan looking at her curiously. Had he read her mind?

Classia, pretended to be oblivious to Deb's pain, continuing on with her tale.

"So here we were, in a remote region of twisted space dominated by dead, bloated bodies of giant stars which had gone nova millions of years ago. The expanse of space was scarred with intense ribbon nebulae of stretching for light years. It was hard to find, but finally, in this throng of dead stars hung one sole planet. Novan had flown down to search it and found the Goddess Elysius, clinging to life. She had fashioned a psi-bubble around her city-ship for survival."

Novan joined in. "After escaping the Lore on Galatia through Alphatronius' portal, my mother happened upon this world where they crash-landed. She named this world Meccus after her father, and the floating nebulous lights—the Ribbon System. From there she had fought on alone, protecting the fifty-thousand who had followed her!

"But the Lore had not been trapped in our dying universe as envisioned. They escaped and followed. They were inexorably drawn by the vast feeding ground that was the Ribbon System. Each time they were gorged and energised by the nebulae they would attack Meccus, my mother repelling them time after time. She also spent all those years reaching out to find fellow Celestian Knights. Eventually she discovered our civilisation on Magna Aura. She had called me to her. And together, we have been fending off the Lore." Novan seemed mildly distressed, Azure guessing what he was about to say.

"The Lore are returning, aren't they?" Azure stated.

Novan nodded gravely. "Yes, they're almost finished on their latest feeding frenzy and by my calculations they will be back in a matter of days and in greater numbers."

Azure sensed a finality in his words.

"Your arrival cannot be a coincidence, Azure," he said. "We need your help."

"Daughter of the Traitor Synther or not," added Classia unhelpfully, with a thin smile.

Azure made a face at her. "Of course, I'll help. Whatever I can do," she assured Classia and Novan. For now she could feel nothing, her powers remained inert. And she wanted time to figure out how she ended up on Meccus.

"We'll leave you to rest, but tomorrow, I'll be back to rescue you from the medtechs," Classia said, Azure reminded of a similar scenario years ago on Sky Command after being poked and prodded by medtechs following the first hitherto unknown blossoming of her Loremaiden powers.

Azure's visitors left and as the veils surrounded her bed again, Azure lay back and drifted off to sleep, strange dreams of creatures with a million teeth floating in her head. It was strangely comforting.

"Come, let me take you on a tour of the capital city of Meccus," a happier Classia invited Azure. They had breakfasted in Azure's room talking of old Sky Warrior times and of Gal Agar. Now they walked along the corridors of Celectral City.

Sword Celectral was more than just a spaceship. Like Alphatron and Millennius City-States, swordships could serve as a space-borne city or land on a planet and act as an enclosed city, until planetary environmental conditions were suitable. Needless to say, the Lore constituted an unfriendly atmosphere.

"But Novan has plans for more cities under transparent domes," Classia explained. "And the launch bays are where our Sky Warriors train and are unleashed to fight the Lore!" she further stated walking Azure through the bays. Azure wished she could join in the training. Classia appreciated her desire. "Maybe one day we can train with them." Then her age-old mischievous smile returned. "I am looking for a good Deputy Sky Commander, though!" she playfully shoulder-barged Azure, laughing freely for the first time.

Azure laughed with her. *Same old Classia.* She was glad her friend was back.

As they walked through the city, citizens greeting Classia with friendly waves and smiles, the Sky Commander explained more.

"Of course, Elysius could not go on protecting all the swords. She was getting weaker even with the extra forcefields provided by the swords and crystalator generators. We still barely hold off the Lore. But Elysius had foreseen that in the fortieth year after escaping from Galatia, there would come a miraculous saviour from out of the nebulae to vanquish the Lore forever. We all thought it was Novan, but it seems we arrived a few years too soon." Classia looked deeply at Azure.

"We waited and fought on with the hope that the ribbons of light would produce the prophesied saviour; the other Starguards, other surviving Celestian Knights, anyone. . ."

Now her look at Azure was distant and if Azure didn't know any better, slightly resentful. *Jealousy?* Her friend was slipping away again.

"Here we are," Classia's voice became sombre.

Azure saw that Novan was waiting for them outside a sealed room, formerly an aft cargo bay converted into a temple devoted to the Goddess Elysius.

Without a word or ceremony, Novan closed his eyes, as if in prayer, and the doors opened.

Azure was impressed. Novan was working on his psionic abilities. The three stepped into the room. Cold metal walls glowed dully from a circular artefact in the middle of the room.

While Classia hung back, Novan led Azure toward the person-sized spherical, crystaline chamber, floating in the air as if by magic. The Goddess was in constant vigilance against the Lore and her physical shell had almost given way to her psi-self. Sealed in the chamber, her pale-skin, still-long golden hair hung limply, and her white ethereal gown shadowed her thin delicate body. But she was still as beautiful and radiant as the day she had stepped into the chamber.

Azure knew she was in the presence of Divineness, but she herself was a Starguard and daughter of a Celestian Knight, even if it was the Traitor Synther. Nevertheless, Deb felt awed in Elysius' presence. Others in the Celectral crew said they could feel her presence, blessing them on their mission, though she only spoke with Novan.

Until today.

"Come forward, Loremaiden," whispered a voice so weak, Azure wasn't sure if it was inside her head. "Last daughter of the Traitor Synther, Azure of Halcyon, step forth!"

Azure did as she was commanded. "I am here, Goddess." Her body and mind tingled as she stood inches from the sphere.

Within, Elysius managed a smile. Her closed eyes slowly slid open and she turned her head to look at Deb.

"Azure," her voice was weakening even more. "She told me you would come."

"Who?"

"The Time Empress. You will deliver peace."

"Time Empress? The Astrals? They have no . . ."

"Sky."

"Sky?" Deb shook her head. What did she mean?

Elysius convulsed, staring straight up, "Sky . . ."

Alarms suddenly pierced the city air. The energy gorging had finished once again.

"The Lore. They return," confirmed Novan, without emotion.

Azure could feel them. Millions upon millions of the energy creatures, wave after wave of the soulless beings crashing down to engulf Meccus. Even now, the world around her was turning blue like a descending mist before her eyes, as energy coursed through her.

"Goddess, I can feel them," Azure gasped with clammy fear. But she didn't fight it.

Novan looked into the sphere with concern, "Brace yourself, mother. You and Azure can protect us!"

But Elysius was looking beyond them and smiling radiantly.

"I hear you, Alphatronius. I forgive you. I am coming." She tried to reach out, froze, and fell limp.

More alarms clamoured for attention.

"The forcefields have failed," Classia called out, forearm crystalator abuzz with commands and data.

Novan rushed to the sphere in an instant. He knew. Felt it.

"The Goddess is dead," he said in shock as he felt for her presence in his mind. "She is with my father now," Novan calmly said, despite the Lore hell descending upon them. The room was steadily growing blue.

Classia had to rely on her crystalator scans, but it too confirmed her husband's call. The Goddess Elysius was dead. Classia cried out in grief, but cut off mid-cry. She stared behind Novan in disbelief.

Novan turned to see what his wife was looking at, but the room was now a blue sun about to explode.

Azure stood still, entranced, a blue cloak of fierce energy fissioning around her, radiating, swirling, coalescing into something livid, naked. . .

She was alive. The energy was burning, raw, delicious—

Oh, sublime ecstasy!

Azure, youngest of the Starguards, exploded in a raging blue nova.

A glorious eruption tore through Celectral enveloping Meccus like a flame of vengeance, flaring out into the ribbons of stardust above, disintegrating the Lore into constituent energy forms.

It had lasted mere seconds.

The Lore were dead. Meccus was saved.

And then the blue slowly faded . . .

Remembering

Alpha Rion and Chalant had barely escaped as Thane Universal had exploded and collapsed around them.

Instinctively, anticipating the Lorelet's cataclysmic explosion, Alpha Rion roughly grabbed Chalant close to him. She surprisingly resisted, but Alpha Rion held on tightly and prayed to the universe uncertain his gambit would work. Unsheathing a meta-sword he forced open a large enough dimensional portal with the sword, he forged forward.

"No!" Alpha Rion heard Chalant vehemently scream as he pulled Chalant through the portal and disappeared.

The portal vanished behind them landing the two with a bump on a hard, stone-cold floor.

"No, no, no!" Chalant still fumed, thumping the stone floor. "What did you do?" she shouted at Alpha Rion, her breath frosting the air between them.

A confused Alpha Rion stared back at her. "What? I saved our lives!" he gestured angrily at her. "That creature would have killed us when it exploded!" He couldn't think why Chalant would act this way.

"I know, I know," Chalant cooled down, her face one of bewilderment. "What of the others?" She thought of her brother mostly. Or had she been mistaken about Penthor Thane?

Alpha Rion shook his head. "I hope they made it." His tone didn't convince Chalant. They were both thinking of Zane's 'history' of the Starguards on Earth.

"We need to get back!" Chalant said. She needed to know. She then noticed her surroundings. "Uh, where are we anyway?" she asked looking around in amazement at high foreboding enclosed walls and dark corridors receding into the shadows.

Alpha Rion recovered himself from the stone floor pulling Chalant up, too.

He grinned with some relief and pride. "Somewhere Decion believed I could never be!" He remembered his training with Decion and Astara on Alphatronius City-State. Decion had almost cleaved him in half for Alpha Rion's impudence of trying to use his portals in battle other than for his swords.

If only Decion could see me now! he laughed to himself.

Aloud he said, "Technically, we're nowhere. Just in transit." Alpha Rion seemed hesitant at first, as if he was not sure himself, "But this," he waved his arms around, "is my fortress, well the fortress of my kin and ancestors where all our weapons are held." He regaled the walls with fondness. "I haven't been here for a very long time."

"Why not?" asked Chalant, dusting herself off while noting the sadness in his voice.

"Short history? The fortress was built back in the hallowed dawn of the Celestri, an older branch of the Celestian Knights. Their ancient line ended with the disappearance of an entire generation and the Celestian Knights were born to take their place. The fortress was hidden in another dimension so that the warriors could have their weapons sheathed away. Only certain Celestian Knights and their kin could enter the fortress dimension, let alone command a weapon from the fortress. At an early age, each eligible warrior is taken to the fortress and they choose their personal weapons, which are bonded only to them. Our thoughts open a portal to our weapon and it is transported to their hand, obviating the need to carry heavy weapons around and, needless to say, causes an element of surprise in battle. What I've done is to reverse the procedure and follow my swords as they returned to the fortress, a difficult and very rare maneuver."

"Well, you're smart of course, so you did it," Chalant chirped and kissed Alpha Rion as he finished his story. "This really is a magnificent fortress." Her eyes were full of awe, not only at the fortress, but also at Alpha Rion.

Chalant had always admired the way in which he summoned his swords and to see their source was quite astounding. She suddenly realised Alpha Rion had pushed his portals to the limit to save their lives; his gleaming swords still in his hands and providing light in the otherwise dark hall. Nevertheless, she had the urge to explore, if only to keep warm in the chilly passage.

"So, which way? How do we get back?"

Alpha Rion looked up, uncertainly in his eyes. "I'm not sure, not having been here in years. Even if we did leave, I'm not sure where we would end up. But I do know of a room which could help. This way," he indicated, walking off into the gloom.

The brown stone walls of the many-roomed and corridored fortress were covered with weapons, emblems, and symbols, grouped to particular families and individuals, their names transcribed by each weapon. There were hundreds of weapons and Chalant wanted to know all of their histories, but Alpha Rion just kept walking, their footsteps echoing off the ancient walls.

Alpha Rion explained. "There is a throne room up ahead built by the ancient reigning leader of my kin, Atrion. Beside it is an annex, a map room of the weapons and their traced locations. If I can read the map, I may be able to take us anywhere we want to go. Getting into the fortress is easy, since we have a portal to my weapons to follow, but getting out is complicated since both weapon and user are in the fortress with no portal or signal to follow out to a correct location. We could wind up in a completely unknown dimension with no escape."

"Life's never easy, is it?" Chalant said.

"No," he agreed. However, as they travelled, Alpha Rion thought about Chalant's words more. Supposedly he was home in the fortress of his ancestors. Chalant was alone in the universe.

He wondered if she ever felt that way.

"You never told me what ever happened to your civilization,

Chalant? Did you find your brothers or any others like you over the centuries?"

Chalant seemed saddened by the thought. She didn't want to tell him about Thane.

"Well, as I said before, I travelled for a while and had some great adventures, but on finally returning home, I found it was absolutely gone. No trace of it anywhere—no huts, animal corrals, nor my friends, family; my brothers were missing. As far as I know I'm the only one alive. Though I suppose others like Valtare exist. I've just never met any others. My home was my place of solace, of inspiration, a hideaway and comfort. Now it's gone. I can only hope that they're some place safe." She looked expectantly at him.

Alpha Rion almost blushed. She did have an intense glare. "Don't worry, I'll get you home," Alpha Rion assured her.

"I hope so," she smiled back. "Anyway, I later came across the Exmoors and worked with them for a time until I met you and my life really began. Then Lightstream took you away. I worked with the Exmoors again after that." Her demeanour darkened, but she gave nothing away.

"So is it the Exmoors who re-named you Chalant?"

"Oh, no." She gave him a mischievous look. "That's a story I'll save for later."

Alpha Rion sucked his teeth. "Fine, but I'm holding you to that promise, just as soon as I get you home. Then we can live." They sealed his vow with a kiss.

After a few wrong turns and sauntering down endless cold passages, it was not much longer before Alpha Rion found the throne room. However, something eerie flickered ahead in the dark. A faint glow illuminated the throne, which stood regally raised on a platform. It took a while for Alpha Rion to realise there was someone sitting within the dim light. Chalant saw it too and instantly drew back her arms, her psi-bow shining into existence. Its own glow penetrated beyond and lit the room up.

Alpha Rion's eyes widened in disbelief, a gasp of frosted air bursting from his lips. There, on the throne, with a bright golden sword across his lap, the source of the glow, was someone he had never expected to see again. Older, yet kingly, despite the wrinkled features and long grey hair, but imposing as ever: his father, Alphatronius.

Alpha Rion signalled to Chalant to lower her bow.

"That's my father," he spoke in a quiet voice. He walked slowly over to the figure on the stone throne.

Chalant stared back. "But I thought you told me he was dead!"

Alpha Rion did not answer. He was too confused, yet elated. And scared.

"Father?" he called. "Father, it's me, Alpha Rion. Father?"

The old man looked up as if waking up. He was old, like his cold blue eyes had seen all of time pass by and were now ready to close in endless sleep. For a long silent while, he studied the face of the young man in front of him. Then his eyes started to move and light up like he was remembering times past. He curiously surveyed the room as if seeing it for the first time and then back at Alpha Rion. He jolted from his seat, but could not stand up as if he had turned to stone over the countless unmoving years. The living statue glared down at Alpha Rion.

"Be gone!" he spat venomously. He clutched his sword with weak hands. "I need no spirits to keep me company. I'll die alone with my sword as my only witness!" When the apparition did not disappear, he shouted again. "I said: Be gone! Or I'll cleave you from head to foot, spirit or not!" His very being shook with rage. His raised sword swayed uncertainly, but ready to strike.

"Be careful," warned Chalant, whether to Alpha Rion or his father, re-animating her bow, Alpha Rion did not know.

But Alpha Rion was undeterred. He cautiously approached closer. "Father, it is me, Alpha Rion, your son. I am here, I'm real. Touch my arm." He stretched his arm out for his father to touch.

There was hesitation, the older Celestian's eyes, heart and very

254

soul battling amongst themselves for control, for trust, for sanity. A muffled groan, like the lifting off of the weight of ages, issued forth from Alphatronius as he hefted himself from the throne. He maintained his balance, one step at a time, as he descended the four steps of the platform to Alpha Rion. Sword in right hand, he feebly reached out with his left and gently touched the solid flesh of his son.

The old Celestian almost staggered back and fell from the shock, but Alpha Rion reacted faster and held him fast. There was a shifting of emotions in his father's eyes and he grasped his son around the shoulders and held him close. Alpha Rion's arms found themselves around his father. It was a strange feeling for Alpha Rion. He had never held his father before nor had his father shown tenderness. None of his brothers or sister had. Emotions like these were not for warriors.

Eventually, Alphatronius released his son and still holding him by the shoulders took a good look at him and tugged at his armour in inspection.

"Alpha Rion, you truly are my son." But his praise turned to sorrow as he said, "You have come to witness my death!"

"Your death? No father!" exclaimed Alpha Rion, "I can take you from here, back to where we all escaped to and now live. Beautiful worlds, father, you would love them. We are all there ... your children ..." he hesitated, "... and our mother, if Novan is right ..."

Alphatronius pushed him away with frightful force. "No! I must not see . . . will not see her again. All the shame I have caused, the pain, anguish, and the deaths," he started to sob.

"Father, what do you mean? What shame?"

Alphatronius gathered himself. He was quiet for a while before he spoke.

"The prophecy!" he spat with disdain. "The prophecy foretold that our generation would be the last Celestian Knight generation. We accepted that . . . at first, which is why we Celestian Knights created the vortex for you all to escape. Then the Lore attacked and we were winning. And I thought how could we be the last generation if we won?

Our deaths would be for nothing if we stayed on Galatia. So in my vainness I told the others that there was no reason for us to stay if we won. We could join you all, our children and our people, and live in peace. Some agreed, Elysius did not. She saw a trap. The Lore could escape with us and spread their evil to other dimensions. But Millennius," he sorrowfully shook his head, "Millennius was as arrogant and as vain as I. He commanded me to prepare to re-open the vortex to the universe you had all escaped into. But as I did so, the Universe bless her, Elysius had been right. The Traitor Synther and his Lore attacked at our weakest moment, shattering my portal into multiple fragments escaping through them. We Celestian Knights were caught up in the portal maelstroms and scattered. I escaped to the Fortress. I do not know who else survived or where they are!

"The Lore can be everywhere now; uncontained, rampaging, festering evil. And it is my entire fault. My vainness, arrogance, my mistake allowed this. And I am being punished. I could not allow Elysius to see me in my great shame. But my son, thank you, for giving me hope, for letting an old man know that he continues on through his children. I have been here in this fortress, lost from home, for untold centuries, trapped, weary and alone, awaiting the time of a visitation from my kin or death from the Lore . . ." He crashed back down in his throne, tired. "And now is the time."

He reached out for his son. "Alpha Rion, when you return home, tell them all, my dear wife Elysius, and my dear children, and all the Celestians that I am sorry. I have continued to cause them sorrow and pain. Our greatest moment ruined by my weakness." His voice grew weaker. "Tell them . . ." His eyes glazed over. "Oh, Elysius," he whispered, "Forgive me."

He smiled faintly at some faraway, fond memory of his wife. And then his breath dropped away.

"Father?" Alpha Rion stood there numbly. The fortress was eerily silent, too, in mourning for the passing of its master.

"I don't sense him anymore, Alpha Rion," Chalant solemnly

reported as she appeared at his side. "He's gone."

"I know, Chalant. He's already been dead for a very long time. Now he's more alive than ever. And with my mother." He lightly touched his father's armour, still as bottomless black and searing red as ever. One last touch, one last look. There was no reason to grieve really.

Alpha Rion carefully hefted his father into his arms. He was light even in his full armour. There was a place they needed to go. Chalant followed silently, not wanting to disturb Alpha Rion's ritual. She was surprised when he spoke a short distance down a dark and noticeably colder corridor which sloped deeper into the fortress.

"The Tombs of the Elders," he said by way of explanation to Chalant's unasked question, "For those who choose to be buried here."

There were lit firebrands here on the large-bricked wall and old stone tombs further back in the shadows. Alpha Rion stopped and looked around the cavernous hall. While Chalant stuck to the shadows, Alpha Rion went forward into the tomb.

"I, Alpha Rion, son of Alphatronius, son of Novan by Theronius, lay my father here with his forefathers to rest forever!" he bellowed into the chamber, his echoing voice seemingly greeted with sympathy from the walls.

Further to his right, he placed his father into an empty sarcophagus, positioning his sword across his chest. He then picked up the heavy stone lid and sealed his father's body in eternal peaceful darkness. He then held aloft his own sword, carved his father's name onto the sarcophagus and prayed to the Great Universal Father.

It was some time before Alpha Rion emerged from the shadowy tomb chamber. Chalant was waiting for him.

"Are you okay?"

"Fine," he answered, absently rubbing his forehead.

"Tired, hungry, cold?" She caressed his cheek. "It's been a long day."

Alpha Rion glanced appreciably at her. Chalant had been through it all with him. She had not complained nor overcrowded him with emotion. He had not thought to think that this may have taken a toll on her as well, after all, she had lost everything herself. And staring into Chalant's eyes, he could see it had affected her as well.

Regret in his voice, he said, "I am sorry Chalant, I wasn't thinking. This must be such a strain on you too. I can't offer you much here; it's pretty much a fortress of cold walls, dark places and weapons. But we'll see what we can do."

That put a smile on her face, but she shook her head. "Don't worry about me, Alpha Rion; I'm more concerned for you. But I could do with a nibble."

"A nibble?"

"Food!"

They laughed together, a sound of life these walls had not heard in millennia.

With one last look behind him, Alpha Rion took Chalant by the hand and they went in search of food. He had to admit he was hungry as well and had not eaten since before the night at the club.

But the fortress was not meant for habitation. There was no kitchen. No one had been there for centuries. There was no food.

They were tired too, the events having been a greater burden than expected. They agreed to get some rest and then when awake check the map room for ways to escape. A few corridors from the throne room they found quarters comfortable enough to sleep in, making up a rough bed. Alpha Rion dreamed of his father, his strength, courage and. . .

Something woke Alpha Rion up. He wasn't sure what it was, a sound or feeling, but a strange sensation emanated through him from not far away. Chalant stirred beside him and awoke. She was about to ask what was happening when Alpha Rion suddenly bolted out of bed and with a great heave, tugged Chalant behind him. He raced through the corridor, faster than she imaged he could, down unfamiliar corridors.

It had taken him a while to remember what the sensation was. And as they rounded a corner, he was rewarded with a familiar sight.

There was a portal opening. Someone from his family was about to use a weapon.

The weapon was already vanishing and there was no name to indicate who was using it, but the portal was closing fast. Alpha Rion drew his own sword and swiftly jammed it into the portal to keep it open.

Alpha Rion looked at Chalant. "This is our chance to escape."

Chalant looked worried. "Do you know where we're going?" she asked.

"No! Ready for another adventure?" He looked back at her and winked.

Chalant nodded with a wide grin.

And with that he worked the sword in a wide circle widening the portal and jumped in, pulling Chalant behind him.

The portal flared shut, leaving the fortress once more in the care of its dead warriors.

CHAPTER TEN

Overwhelming heat. That's what Gordell felt. That and more than a modicum of desperate despair. As far as he could see barren red wasteland stretched in all directions, a hell-red glow cast by a bloated yellow sun stranded in the sky. And boy it was hot.

"Cette chaleur est un meurte," he cursed at the sun.

It had been two weeks since Gordell had been spat out of a portal, he now knew the transport method to be, and transported lord knew where. He had landed on his ass just behind Decion, whose great black sword had arched a menacing path over his head and would have lopped it off had he been standing up. Gordell had barely escaped with his life as he had brandished his own sword to parry Decion's downward blow that followed. By rights, the lancesword should have snapped Gordell's sword cleaving the Exmoor in two as well, but it did not. His sword had held, Decion's eyes wide in astonishment. Gordell had taken his chance before another attempted death blow and before more soldiers had arrived, running—or strategically retreating—to the nearby hills. Decion set for pursuit.

"Leave him be!" Valtare ordered, having watched from a distance. "He'll die before the week is out! There's nothing out there except death! *Allez,*" he recalled his men to the silver fortress.

Decion reluctantly watched as his prey got away.

Gordell was grateful to escape, but then again, his freedom hinged on hiding in an imposing and imprisoning desert world with little sustenance or hope of survival.

But I'm alive, he told himself. *There was hope.*

Over the following days, he had survived by catching and eating small rodents and squeezing morning dew moisture from scattered fern-like plants in the lee of the foothills behind him. They led into the jagged brown mountains which had been his refuge since his abrupt arrival, hiding away from the small furry creatures that hunted him.

261

Well, some creatures, Gordell thought, reflecting on the strange metallic beings he had seen.

Scouting parties were either led by Valtare or Decion with human soldiers, but the others were metal men. Gordell didn't know if people were inside the metal armour or if they were truly metal people. As an Exmoor, having already lived five hundred and fifty years, worked with Astrals, Chryrian hybrids—like Tera—and other beings, Gordell supposed that metal men would also exist. But whose world was this and where was he?

Gordell raised a crystalator to his eye with his thumb and forefinger. The five-centimetre wide by two-millimetre thick octagon-shaped crystal reacted to his motion, reconfiguring itself into the magnifier mode he wanted. Gordell focused by blinking twice. A small readout scrolled across the top of the crystal.

"Save," he said, the readout and picture he had taken disappearing into an invisible memory. "Okay," he said to himself. "That's that. Back to camp."

He skillfully scrambled back through the foothills, always watching his back, keeping low and to the shadows, where they existed. Twenty minutes later he was in the mountains proper, where he scaled a hundred-foot cliff-face, shimmied along a ledge and then through a narrow crevice set back between two jutting curtains of rock leading into a cave. He shoved a few medium sized boulders into the entrance.

In the darkness he set a rectangular crystal on the ground and tapped its centre. Light shone from within dimly illuminating the cave's interior, roughly five metres in diameter. He then sat on another medium sized rock.

Retrieving the octagonal crystalator, he set about studying its data. It had been a long couple of days, but he had completed the task he had set out to do once he realised he was stuck here. If Alpha Rion and Tera were going to rescue him, they would have done it already if they could get through the portal. He had realised that the portal must have been a trap set for them. Only he had come through alone and escaped from Decion and the soldiers awaiting him.

No, he was all by himself, and he would have to use all of his five hundred years of training and expertise to get himself out of this mess. And the only way to do that he reasoned was by getting into the only thing that existed in this place not made of rock. He brought the crystal to his eye.

"Retrieve images."

The crystal clouded and then cleared showing the unmistakable outline of walls; silver walls, big metal, crenelated, shining battlements. Gordell dubbed it the Silver Fortress.

"Rotate."

The image rotated, showing the almost exact image on each of its four sides. There were no gates, the metal just seemed to pull apart whenever soldiers came in or out and then melt together again. There was no obvious way in for him. But there was a way out, back to Earth within the fortress. Gordell was sure of it.

"Off."

The image disappeared, the crystal turning black. Gordell tucked it away in his pouch with the others. He had already placed seven in and around the cave walls and even strapped one to his head when left the cave, to protect him from Valtare's roaming mind. This crystal he now removed from his scruffy white hair, which he gave a good scratch before smoothing it down. It smelled.

Gordell next turned his attention to the second mystery, his sword. He knew there was no way an ordinary Earth sword, even enhanced by the Exmoors, could have survived Decion's lancesword's blow. He visually inspected the sword, running hands and eyes along its blade, but apart from its distinctive H-shaped cross-guard, he could see no visible sign of a superior forging technique. He chalked it up to sublime luck, until he decided to examine it with the crystalator. He drew along the blade. Within seconds, the crystalator began to reveal markings, strange runes, on the sword's blade as if they were beneath the metal's outer surface.

"So, you're no ordinary sword after all," he remarked, repeatedly passing the crystal over the sword's surface. He recorded all the images hoping the crystalator would be able to translate the runes. He let the programme run while he prepared to get some rest.

Laying the sword beside him, Gordell slipped off his rocky perch and lay on the ground, which fortunately was a little more earthy than rocky. He removed his armour, using his leather tunic as a pillow. It would be night in a few hours and he wanted to get the remainder of the night images of the fortress to see if any nocturnal changes occurred. He also wanted to get out of the cave. On several occasions he had heard weird sounds in the rock and had strange and shifting dreams, more like nightmares. He wondered if it was the cave or just him. Another mystery to investigate. It wasn't like he was going anywhere soon.

Gordell closed his eyes and was soon fast asleep.

They watched him. He came and went from their cave, a strange man; like the old ones, solid, ancient clothing and technology. They whispered to him sometimes when he slept. They tried to watch his mind, but the crystals he held prevented them from doing so. Nevertheless, they liked him. He was not like the other solids and the metal ones. He was not hostile. He hunted them and they him. His enemies were now their enemies.

They had been so alone for a long time, and now these solids had come. Why? They wanted answers and this solid could answer that, their leader decided.

They slipped forth, phasing through the cave's rock, and drifted to the recumbent solid. They touched Gordell's mind.

There was a scream.

Valtare looked out over the battlements. Behind him were low silver metal barracks for his men, the Devouts, and various other buildings for meals, elimination, corrals, recreation, and training. The metal creatures needed no shelter. Decion was putting the soldiers through their paces. Even L'Coyle was impressed by the big man's swordsmanship, if not a little jealous. But there was no rancour between them, only growing impatience. If Valtare had to hear Decion ask him when the war would begin, he would. . . would do nothing. He was just as impatient. And his Lord had seen fit to go silent.

Valtare sighed. Ahead of him, the red desert surrounding the fortress shimmered in heat even as the sun went down. He tried focusing his mind on finding Gordell, but nothing. He knew Gordell to be an Exmoor who no doubt had some form of technology blocking his mind. Or maybe he was even dead, somewhere in the mountains from lack of food and water. But Valtare didn't believe that. He knew Gordell was capable of surviving in the desert almost indefinitely. It was in an Exmoor's genetic heritage. Valtare had fought and escaped them long enough to know they were survivors and that the longer Gordell survived, the sooner the Astrals and Exmoors would find out where he was, even here, in this desolate wasteland.

Valtare's memories floated back two weeks ago. He had been toasting his wife's portrait with a glass of wine:

"My dear Elisabeth, where are you now?" He drained the glass and threw it into the flames of the fireplace. "L'Coyle!" he shouted for the hawk-faced man who turned up almost immediately.

"Yes, my lord?"

"Round up the villagers. It's time!"

L'Coyle bowed and rushed off to deliver the orders.

There was a noise behind him. Surprised, Valtare turned, as Decion had entered the hall from the stone steps.

"Something wrong, Valtare?" his gruff voice seemingly concerned.

Valtare was about to reply in the negative, but opportunity offered him a chance to sow the seeds of doubt and destiny.

He hesitated, trying to figure out how Decion would react. "I'm sorry, my friend, but I have some bad news for you." He paused as Decion drew himself up for the news. "I have had word that your brother and Guillaume De Roth have decided not to join us, and even now are plotting against us!" He braced himself, in case Decion attacked him.

But Decion remained calm enough, at least in action. "You lie!" he snarled. "Where is he that I may ask him myself?" Turning to stomp back up the stairs, Valtare called him back.

"He's not here, Decion. They have gone to fetch De Roth's army and they will return to fight."

Decion laughed, amused at the very thought. "Fight? Fight me! My brother would be very foolish to do such a thing!"

"Be that as it may, De Roth is not who he claims to be. And you already suspect Alpha Rion does not share our desire for the war ahead. But he is too late. My Lord is preparing for us now, even as we speak. This castle and the surrounding village are to be destroyed so no one can reveal our secrets. All my knights will come with us, to serve and to fight. We have no time to wait Decion. Will you join us?"

Decion pondered his situation. Though he reviled the Astrals for taking him away from Magna Aura, he was now free to do what he pleased, without Novan or Aerl ordering him around. As for Alpha Rion, if he didn't want to fight in the ultimate war then he wasn't much of a warrior . . . and less so without his sister. He sighed, worried for the fate of his brother. "What will become of Alpha Rion?" he asked.

"I do not know," Valtare answered truthfully, "but dare I say that the Astrals will find him and return him home or he may be stranded on this world," he stated, not really caring about the younger Starguard's fate.

However, Decion seemed convinced. "Then what are we waiting for? The war awaits!" His rough smile was half hidden within his black beard.

"Follow me," Valtare said, his plan working better than he thought.

He turned and made his way to the courtyard. L'Coyle had already gathered the knights together. They stood, about three hundred of them, in ranks in the paved courtyard, which had dried out somewhat after the rain.

"My Liege," L'Coyle started, standing in front of the ranged soldiers, "the villagers have been rounded up and wait in the chapel, as ordered." His brown hair hung down to his shoulders and Decion now noted the thin scars on his face. But the man's eyes told a tragic story deep within his dark orbs. This man knew pain, Decion saw.

"Thank you, L'Coyle," Valtare responded. With Decion beside him, Valtare announced: "My noble knights, the time has come. A great destiny awaits us, more beyond this mere crusade beholden to a weak king, more beyond this world; a great war awaits and a new beginning for us all. And while you may think we are too few, there is a magnificent castle and army awaiting us on the other side. I have been shown this. But first, we must leave our old lives and attachments behind. We must destroy the village and castle, burn them to the ground, so that none may follow us. On to victory," he shouted.

His army cheered for him and victory. The gates opened, the drawbridge lowered and the soldiers marched out to the village to destroy it. Valtare, Decion, and L'Coyle remained.

Valtare commanded, "L'Coyle, burn the chapel down."

L'Coyle turned to stare at Valtare, slight hesitation on his scarred face. With a wordless curt nod of his head, he obeyed and trotted toward the chapel.

Decion was appalled. "Valtare, what are you doing?"

He had turned to the little chapel, hearing people inside, the little faces of children peering out from the stained glass windows. Wood and straw were piled liberally around the chapel. L'Coyle held a lit torch and started walking around the building lighting the wood and straw.

Decion stared in disbelief but had not moved even as he could hear the dying screams from within the chapel.

With no sympathy in his voice, Valtare said, "Decion, I have been manipulating their minds for years, especially those who worked within the castle. They have seen and heard much. When we leave, their memories will return and the Exmoors will wring every last bit of information from them. We cannot spare them."

Decion was silent. As a Starguard, he could not bear to see innocent life ended in this way. He could have acted and slaughtered Valtare and all his knights to save the villagers. But then what? He would still be stranded on Earth. These villagers weren't his people. He would have accomplished nothing and the Great War would have eluded him.

No, Valtare was right, he convinced himself, quelling his heart's pounding. *They had to succeed and leave undetected.* He heaved his shoulders in acceptance knowing such a decision would cost him some morality, but all the same he walked away from the fire-engulfed and collapsing chapel.

Watching closely, Valtare smiled behind him.

Half an hour later, the knights had returned to the castle from sacking the village. They barely paid attention to the charred chapel. Decion realised Valtare had taken care of that.

"Your men are not like you?" Decion asked.

Valtare shook his head. "You're perceptive. No, I am one of the last of my kind left. The Astrals and Exmoors decimated our numbers centuries ago fearing we were too powerful. If I am to die, then I'll die in the greatest of battles." He looked at Decion with a smile. "Our plans may have changed here, Decion, but in my master's realm, the war will truly be fought."

Valtare could see from Decion's dark smile that he understood and grudgingly approved. A bond born in impending war was drawing them together in not-quite-friendship, but in loyalty. Valtare had to make sure. . . maybe with a test of some kind. But first. . .

"Now we must destroy the castle!"

An uproar erupted; a mixture of incredulity, joy, fear and trepidation. But they obeyed their liege systematically destroying the guardhouse, stables, shelters and walls. In a couple of unfortunate incidences knights fought each other, Valtare sighing world-wearily at their undisciplined nature.

Even Decion took part, his lancesword scything through stone battlements. He tried not to notice soldiers picking through the remains of the smouldering chapel for meager trinkets the former villagers had possessed.

Universe, save us! he prayed.

After about an hour, the castle, too, had been sacked and sat burning forlornly on its hill.

Precisely at that time, Valtare suddenly sensed that Alpha Rion and De Roth were returning, though their presence was somewhat masked.

He called over to Decion, "Your brother and De Roth are returning with an army. They will not be joining us, unless . . ." Decion nodded. Valtare continued, "A trap will be set on the other side of the portal our lord will open for us! If they enter, they would either join us or die, even Alpha Rion."

Decion could not bear the thought of his brother's death, but the war ahead, the glory, the stories he had learned from the Knights Destina made it worth it, even over his brother's life.

Valtare had his hand out.

Decion clasped his forearm. "This is how we seal our agreements!"

Valtare shook his arm. "Then we agree." Decion had proved his loyalty to him. He called his men together. "We go now! On to glory!"

Valtare psychically called to his master and in a flash of light, they were gone. All that was left was a tantalising slice of portal, which unfortunately only De Roth had entered, only to escape them. Valtare had not been best pleased by that outcome, not with his master watching, but at least he knew he could not be stopped now.

Valtare and his entourage had been deposited just outside a large silver fortress. They stood and marvelled at the city's silver walls, even under the awful heat of the sun. Valtare held his hand up high and a section of the wall shifted to one side. He marched his men in through the gap and was greeted by the most bizarre of sights.

There was an array of soldiers to meet Valtare, Decion, and their army. There were some women, too, Devouts, as Valtare had called them, subjects of his wife. But the most enthralling scene was the sight of ten thousand metal beings, the Surge, Valtare introducing them to their leader, Spearhead, a red nine-foot being with a head shaped like, well, a spearhead, Decion saw. The mass army saluted the newcomers.

"And this is only one quarter of my army," boomed a new voice above them. "Welcome to Destinia!"

Decion looked up and recognised the figure flying overhead.

"Ah, funk!" Decion cursed.

"Close enough," said Valtare. "You recognise my master?" he smiled in anticipation of the reunion.

"Yes, I do," Decion growled, swiftly drawing his formidable lancesword from its portalled-sheath. "And if I had known beforehand, I would have killed you."

For the first time, Valtare was scared of Decion. "Why?" his voice barely above a tremble.

"Because . . . your master is the Astral, Archron."

Revulsion filled Valtare's face. "Oh, fuck!"

"That's the one!"

Gordell awoke from his nightmare. He was aware, acutely aware of everything around him as if his senses had been sprung from his mind and wandering by themselves, feeling, tasting, smelling, and hearing everything at once. But then he sensed another presence. Something was in his head, sharing his mind; an internal tingle that he couldn't scratch away or shake off.

And then the tingle spoke to him.

>Do not be afraid<

He dived off the make-shift bed, spinning on all fours frantically looking around the cave for intruders. It was empty. In horror, he realised the voice was in his head.

Gordell yelled, clutching his head. "Get out of me," he screamed, beating his head and rolling on the ground. "Get out! Get out. I know what you are!" He squeezed his eyes shut trying to imagine how insane he would become with a Chryrian in his head.

But the being said, >Gordell, you are not an ordinary human. You are an Exmoor. You will not go insane. You will need us to survive and to defeat your enemies, especially the one you call Valtare<

Gordell thought carefully about this, his breathing still ragged began to calm down. "*Merde*! I guess I have no choice, but you could have asked first. Is this how you take over people, by forcibly invading their minds? This is what you did to the humans on Earth!" he grumbled, half-believing he was actually talking to himself.

The voice was calm, soothingly so. >No, the mergers long ago were mutual. And we can see what you and the Astrals did all those years ago to our kin. But we forgive you. Some humans could not adjust to ways of peace as we had hoped. As for now, we tried to talk to you while you slept, but your mind was protected by the crystals. We needed direct communication. We have been waiting for one like you for so long. We had thought that all the humans were dead!<

"Dead? How long have you been waiting?" Gordell still spoke aloud. "And where am I, which planet?"

There was a pause as if the Chryrian was reluctant to speak. >Gordell, we are the last survivors from the humans we had merged with. They are now all dead. That was millions of years ago. And where else do you think you are—this is Earth!<

There was mad laughter in his head, Gordell not knowing if it was him or the Chryrians. And it didn't stop. The laughter got louder and louder. He was going insane.

Epilogue

"Where are we?" Sola asked, quietly.

"Hera's buggerhole!" Helexius cursed into the pitch blackness. Even their portals had not pierced the depths as they flashed in.

"Hush!" Lightstream hissed.

There was an echoing quality to their mystery surroundings.

Lightstream stepped forward. "I came as your messenger requested," she shouted into the void with a little trepidation. "Show yourselves."

A slight change in the air to their right caught their attention.

"You're safe!" said a voice emanating from that direction.

"Who are you?" demanded Helexius, prepared to battle for this life, as figures advanced toward them.

There was humour in the voice when it said:

"We are you!

APPENDIX A

FAMILY LINES

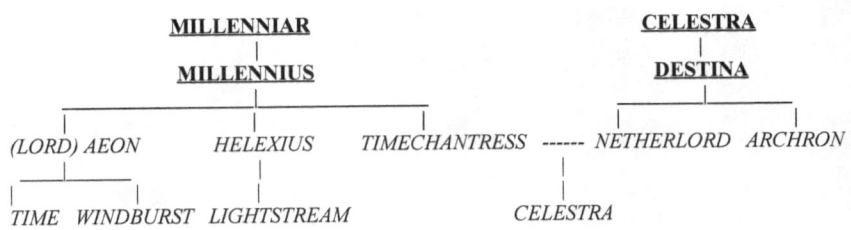

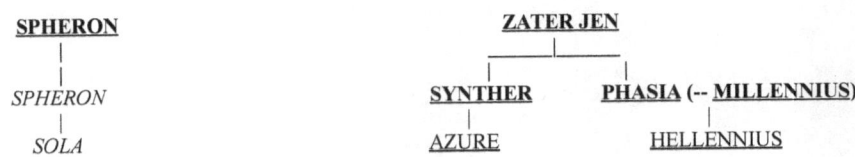

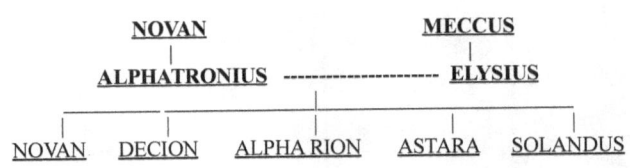

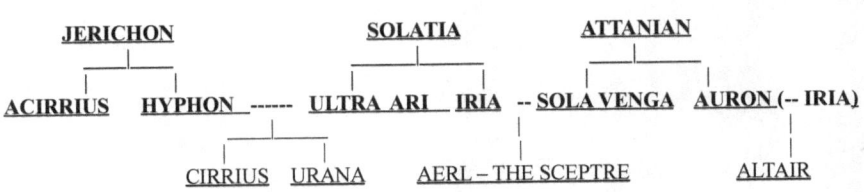

APPENDIX B

Xaul Relentus, the Emperor-General of Earth and Axala, died at the age of one hundred and nineteen in the year 2291. The whole of the Constitutionate of Earth, Axalan, and Bion celebrated with week-long remembrances, holidays, and renewed pledges never to war amongst themselves again.

Relentus had never married retired Admiral Della Steelchapel, but she had been his constant companion, until she had died ten years before him. They had no children. Relentus had always insisted he did not want to found a dynasty nor have his children compared to a living God. As per his wishes, there would never be another Emperor-General again. He had never ruled Home, though its capital, Relenta City, had been named in his honour.

APPENDIX C

There shouldn't have been a knocking sound coming from there. But there it was, the hollow knock, knock, knock coming from the region of the airlock. It reverberated hauntingly throughout the station.

In the Unity galley, Cosmonaut Anatoly Ravonov stop dead from slurping on his plastic re-hydrated drink pack. He looked 'up' in mild alarm at the rotating Jose Carey, the American swiftly grabbing hold of the wall strapping to steady himself. He listened too.

Knock, knock, knock.

"Vhat vas dat?" Anatoly asked, letting go of his pack.

"Don't know. Where are Christine and Nate?" he asked of the other two astronauts, worried about space debris penetrating the station.

Anatoly grabbed a stowed laptop and looked at the schedule. "Columbus," he stated. "Ostermann is still in the Cupola and Tomas. . ."

"Here!" Tomas Angusavic had just floated into Unity, questions written across his face.

Knock, knock, knock.

The three looked in the direction of the noise. It had moved.

"That's definitely closer!" Jose said a little rattled.

"Hey, what's that—?"

KNOCK, KNOCK, KNOCK

. . . the ringing noise cut off Italian astronaut Christine Denegreni's question, followed by Nate Vanse. Denereni's puffed face mirrored the others' floating around in the station.

Stu Ostermann dived in from the other direction.

"Should we suit up?" Tomas asked anxiously.

KNOCK, KNOCK, KNOCK

Above them now.

"The Cupola!" Anatoly led the way, swimming and guiding his way to the viewing ports. Even before they were all there, he shouted, "There's a man outside!" Then his voice rose in panic. "Bòzhe mòi! It's that superman. Look, look!"

The six crew huddled around the seven-window observatory. Sure enough there was a man floating outside.

"Holy shit, that's Altair!" Carey shouted.

They had all been told of Altair's infamous actions on Earth and heard his speech at the U.N. not ten minutes ago. And now here he was outside the ISS.

The crew stared dumbfounded as Altair grinned and waved at them, the thinnest of sheens around him indicating his forcefield.

He made a gesture like a shrug, arms up at his side.

"Vhat does he vant?" Anatoly asked the others, the answer slowly dawning on them.

"Nothing good," spoke the other U.S. Astronaut, Nate Vanse. "Nothing good at all!"

Altair now floated upside down in his slow spin, a faint red tinge at his hands and feet directing his motion. He raised his hand to his mouth and spoke into his forearm comms.

"Hello in there. Let me in or I'll huff and puff," Altair said, with dark humour.

"Is he serious?" Denegreni asked, wide green eyes staring out at Altair who grinned back with relish.

"Are you going to argue with him?" Carey responded, his voice a little shaky.

The six looked at each other. The silent vote was unanimous.

"You're the commander, Anatoly," Carey stated, the others hovering away, disowning any responsibility.

The Russian blinked slowly and gulped. He pulled himself to the view port and gestured in a back-and-over motion behind him. The Quest airlock lay opposite them.

Altair nodded and flew off, above and past them.

The crew waited. Then came the mechanical sounds of the outer airlock hatch opening, depressurising then repressurising after it had closed. The anticipation made each crew member feel like they were the loneliest human being alive, wrapped in a multi-purpose tin can which was about to burst.

Knock, knock, knock.

They all jumped, sending themselves spinning. They looked expectantly at Anatoly.

He resignedly shook his head, held his Russian pride up high and opened the inner airlock door. He floated backward as Altair entered.

The Starguard regarded them all, their shocked faces trying to absorb the fact that he had just flown through space to the International Space Station and boarded it like it was some kind of space hotel.

"I need to stay here for a night then I'm gone," he informed them breezily. He floated to the galley grabbing a meal pack. "Thanks," he grinned. "You can tell Houston you have a problem, later."

Have you enjoyed this book?
If so, why not write a review on your favourite website?

THE STARGUARDS
OF HUMANS, HEROES, AND DEMIGODS

continues in

BOOK 4 – THE DESTINIA APOCALYPSE